THE
MINDERS

JOHN MARRS

DEL
REY

1 3 5 7 9 10 8 6 4 2

Del Rey
20 Vauxhall Bridge Road,
London SW1V 2SA

Penguin
Random House
UK

Del Rey is part of the Penguin Random House group of companies
whose addresses can be found at global.penguinrandomhouse.com

www.penguin.co.uk

A CIP catalogue record for this book is available from
the British Library

Paperback ISBN 9781529100655

Typeset in 9.93/12.25 pt Palatino LT Pro
by Integra Software Services Pvt. Ltd, Pondicherry

Printed and bound in Great Britain by Clays Ltd, Elcograf S.p.A.

Penguin Random House is committed to a sustainable future for
our business, our readers and our planet. This book is made from
Forest Stewardship Council® certified paper.

MIX
Paper from
responsible sources
FSC® C018179

'If you have something really important, write it out and have it delivered by courier, the old-fashioned way . . . because I'll tell you what: no computer is safe.'
Donald Trump

'If you want to keep a secret, you must also hide it from yourself.'
George Orwell

PROLOGUE

He grimaced and pinched his nostrils as he made his way up the dimly lit staircase towards a set of double doors.

The stale-smelling offices Lee Dalgleish was about to enter were located close to the banks of London's river Thames and a stone's throw away from the former Battersea Power Station. The heatwave was making the odour of stagnant water and damp crawling up the walls particularly putrid.

Two empty desks and a chair with a broken spine were the only pieces of furniture to be housed in this section of the building, alongside a bank of empty telephone sockets stretching the length of the floor and two broken television screens hanging lopsided from a wall. There was no indication to the untrained eye what else might be hidden under this roof.

'Much of the government's most important work isn't carried out within the walls of Westminster or Downing Street,' he had been informed the morning of his orientation, months earlier. 'It's in places like this. It's all about hiding in plain sight.'

Dalgleish handed his canvas shoulder bag, mobile phone, wallet, tablet and coat to one of three security operatives before stepping through the full-body scanner. He had passed four other guards earlier, located at the entrance. And like the ones before him now, they too were armed.

Being scanned always gave him the jitters. It made no sense as he went through the same routine for every shift and he had done nothing that contravened the many rules governing him. He behaved in the same manner each time he approached the airport ticket desk or NOTHING TO DECLARE lane at Heathrow – like a man burdened by guilt. He opened his mouth as an electronic saliva reader glided across his tongue before a green light flashed.

'You're all clear,' said the guard without a smile. She was a new face he didn't recognise. Her delicate features, large, blue eyes and long lashes contradicted the muscular frame that rippled under her white shirt and body armour.

'Thank you,' he muttered, and quickly looked away, realising he had held her gaze for too long. Strong women, either physically or mentally, scared and aroused him in equal measure.

He held his hands shoulder height and pressed his fingerprints against a screen, then spoke as both biometric devices scoured his eyes and his voice patterns. Then a final set of metal doors ahead slid open.

The recently rebranded global heating was to blame for another hot, sticky March morning which left Dalgleish feeling irritable. He had kept the windows of his second-floor flat wide open but the adjacent nightclub must have overhauled its sound system because the thump, thump, thump of electronic beats was all he could hear for much of the evening. He had eventually managed to fall asleep with balls of toilet paper stuffed into his ears but slept through the alarm on his phone. Each time he missed a gym session – which was rare – it made him recall the bullied, overweight teenager he once had been and a mild anxiety spread through him. One workout wasn't going to bring back the Dalgleish of old, he reminded himself. But he still vowed to go to a spin class no matter how late he finished work to make up for his morning absence.

He pushed his shoulders back and forth to release the building tension as he made his way to the unisex changing rooms. Under the watchful eye of another security operative, he stripped off all his clothing and placed the garments inside a metal container. Only then was he presented with his daily uniform: a fresh set, never been worn before. It was made of an undisclosed fabric with no pockets or hems to smuggle anything in or out. Underwear and socks were not permitted under this standard-issue T-shirt, trousers and sandals.

Once dressed, he made for his workstation inside a windowless, open-plan room. He counted forty or so people, each holding or operating tablets, wearing earpieces or VR headsets. Dozens of television screens were projected onto walls, each featuring separate locations but none of which included buildings or people – only roads, motorway bridges, the sky and stretches of water.

He tapped the shoulder of a man on a seat. He was fixated by a screen in front of him. 'Oh hey, Lee,' he responded and yawned. 'Is it that time already?'

Dalgleish nodded. 'Sure is. What have I missed?'

'Same old,' replied Irvine. 'Nothing. No traffic route deviation, the power levels are still running about eighty per cent and tyre pressure is constant.'

'Where are we heading today then?'

'We should reach the M90 and Queensferry Crossing Bridge in a little over an hour, then up to Perth and Dundee before turning around and heading back through Scotland. By the time your shift comes to an end, we'll be somewhere in the region of Newcastle.'

Irvine rose to his feet, removed his earpiece and smart glasses and dropped them both into an electronics shredder under his desk. 'See you tomorrow,' he said and tipped an imaginary hat.

Dalgleish took his seat and typed a seven-digit code into an aluminium security box he'd picked up on his entry.

When the lid opened, he retrieved and slipped on a fresh pair of smart glasses and inserted a new earpiece. Then he removed a protein bar from his drawer and made himself comfortable.

The image he would be watching for the rest of the day was the same one he had watched each day of his employment. It was the empty cab of an autonomous articulated lorry. The corner of the screen revealed that the vehicle had been travelling for seventy-six consecutive days with no stops. It recharged its batteries using wireless energy from coils under roads and its tyres shed their skin like reptiles to reveal another set underneath. Travelling at a steady 55 mph, the lorry calculated and chose for itself the routes it would take. Dalgleish's job was to ensure there was no threat to its security.

As he chewed on his bar, he checked the status reports sent to his computer from the cab's central console to confirm Irvine's update. Then he monitored the outside of the vehicle and its surroundings from a multitude of cameras attached to the sides, rear and undercarriage. The only section his security clearance made it impossible to oversee was inside the trailer.

To other road users, this articulated lorry was indistinguishable from any other on British roads. It was an unbranded, mass-manufactured driverless vehicle. The only difference was the cargo it carried. That was more important than anyone could ever imagine. Only a restricted number had a vague idea of what was hidden inside, including Dalgleish. Even fewer knew the precise details. He had signed countless Non-Disclosure Agreements and Official Secrets Act papers forbidding him from telling anyone what his job entailed.

He glanced in the direction of his other colleagues' workstations. Most were doing the same as him, focusing on their own lorries. Two also kept their eyes on a solar-powered plane and a small team was dedicated to observing the deck of a cargo ship. It was loaded with containers and travelling on an infinite loop across the North Sea, alternating its direction to avoid storm tides and changes in barometric pressure.

With Dalgleish's right eye returning to his own lorry, his left was getting up to speed with the day's news as it appeared on the lens of his smart glasses. It had taken a couple of weeks for him to quietly perfect this type of multitasking but even now his eyes ached by the end of a working day. Viewing the same image day after day was, as he once told Irvine, 'as boring as hell'. And quietly, he wondered how much more he could take before he begged to be removed from this surveillance detail and put on to something more challenging.

An hour passed and Dalgleish had moved on to his third Sudoku grid when an image on screen caught his attention. Something had flown past the lorry. It was fleeting and likely a large bird of prey, so he almost didn't bother to rewind the footage. But he was duty bound to investigate everything.

He slipped off his glasses: playing it in slow motion made the image clearer. It wasn't a bird, it was a drone. They were a regular occurrence in British skies and he had seen them fly past his lorry before. But after viewing this one from a dozen different camera angles, he realised it seemed more persistent than the others. It was as if it was following the lorry, keeping it within its sights. His stomach tightened. Something about this scenario was making him uncomfortable.

Dalgleish turned his head to look for his supervisor, Dominique, who sat at a desk in her office in the corner of the room. Nervously he approached and tapped on her door.

'Dom,' he said. 'Sorry to bother you, but I think I might have a potential amber alert.'

She shut the lid of her laptop. 'Why, what's happening?'

By the time she reached his desk and they both focused on the screen, two more drones could be seen from the windscreen cameras. Rear and side cameras revealed it was surrounded by even more.

Dominique tapped her earpiece and spoke into it and within moments, they were joined by her three superiors. Dalgleish had caught glimpses of the two men and a woman entering other offices in the same building but had never conversed with them. He felt self-conscious as they huddled around his desk behind him.

'Are everyone else's vehicles safe?' Dominique asked across the room and received a series of yeses.

'Holy shit, what's that?' Dalgleish asked, his surprise making him forget the company he was in.

From the cab camera, a dark shadow was beginning to block the outside light. He switched to another device attached to the roof and rotated the lens so that it viewed above. What they saw was the underside of a helicopter, its rotating blades sweeping above it.

'We're under attack,' one of Dominique's superiors said, watching closely as three figures using ropes landed on the lorry's roof. The shadow lifted as the helicopter moved up and out of sight. 'They know what we're transporting.'

'How?' asked Dalgleish but his question was ignored. 'What should I do?' he said instead.

'You wait until I instruct you.'

The room fell silent as they watched the trespassers remove a cylindrical device from a backpack and clamp it to the trailer's roof. They moved as if walking on the moon and Dalgleish assumed magnetic footwear was preventing them from losing their balance.

'They're not trying to hijack it, they're going to steal from it while it's still moving,' Dominique exclaimed. Suddenly there was a cloud of smoke and a gap the size of a manhole cover appeared in the roof.

'What's the road's status?' a second nameless superior asked.

'The lorry is on the M90 and about to join the Queensferry Crossing Bridge, approaching the first of the three towers that supports it,' said Dalgleish.

'And traffic?'

He scanned the motorway APR cameras. 'Moderate, no delays.'

'Collateral damage?'

Dominique scanned her tablet. 'Low if we act now.'

Dalgleish could smell sweat beneath the aftershave of the man as he leaned across the desk and tapped furiously into the keyboard. A box appeared on a separate screen where he then inputted a long code before placing his fingerprint against it. A projection of a button appeared on the desk below. He turned to Dominique.

'Are we in agreement?' he asked. She looked to the screen just as the first assailant disappeared inside the hole in the roof.

'Yes. Red alert,' she replied.

They waited until the third figure entered before he pressed the button.

Flames and smoke shot out of the hole and the lorry began to veer left. It remained on the road and continued past the first bridge tower, gradually picking up pace until, at 78 mph, they watched in silence as it ploughed through the metal safety railings and plunged over the side of the bridge. More than 200 metres later, it was engulfed by the depths of the river Forth below.

PART ONE

** CONFIDENTIAL **

TOP SECRET: UK EYES ONLY, CLASSIFIED 'A'

THIS DOCUMENT IS THE PROPERTY OF HIS MAJESTY'S GOVERNMENT

MINUTES OF JOINT CYBER-ESPIONAGE / INTELLIGENCE COMMITTEE ASSESSMENT MEETING 11.6

'THE ALTERNATIVE APPROACH TO STORAGE OF CLASSIFIED DOCUMENTS'

** Please note this is an account of the minutes taken from the above meeting. Portions of text and certain participants have been redacted to prevent threats to security. **

LOCATION:
███████████, ████████

MEMBERS PRESENT:
Edward Karczewski, Operations Director, ████████ ████████
Dr Sadie Mann, Director of Psychiatric Evaluations
Dr M.J. Porter, Head of Neuroscience
████████ ████████ ████████, Ministry of Defence (MoD), Porton Down
████████ ████████, MI5

William Harris, HM Government's Minister for Central Intelligence

NON-MEMBERS PRESENT:
Prime Minister Diane Cline

EDWARD KARCZEWSKI: For the benefit of the Prime Minister, who has not been privy to our meetings to date, I'd like to begin by summarising how we have arrived at where we are today.

PRIME MINISTER: But first, Edward, I would like it noted in the minutes of my displeasure at having only been made aware of the existence of this programme in the last twenty-four hours. Prior to this, I have been deliberately kept in the dark. I will therefore be launching an internal investigation as to how this came to be.

EDWARD KARCZEWSKI: And you will have our full cooperation. But I hope that by the end of this meeting, you'll have gained a greater understanding as to why it's been kept under wraps. So, to summarise, two and a half years ago, an organisation made up of cyber criminals and widely referred to as the Hacking Collective infiltrated our burgeoning driverless vehicles network and reprogrammed hundreds to collide with one another. This malicious act of terrorism caused 5,120 deaths and injuries and was the single biggest loss of life on British soil since the Coronavirus pandemic of 2020. The Collective claimed the attack was an act of 'ethical hacktivism' and they claimed they had a moral responsibility to bring to the world's attention our former Government's unlawful interference in how autonomous vehicles made life-or-death decisions in the event of an accident. These actions were not, as we were led to believe, based on preserving the highest number of lives, but on social and economic factors. The more value a person was pre-judged to have in our society, the higher their chance of survival.

WILLIAM HARRIS: May I take this opportunity to clarify this was not the fault of the Government in its entirety, only certain participants. ███████████████████████████ ██████████ have all been dealt with, the exception being the late Member of Parliament, Jack Larson.

PRIME MINISTER: His murder by the Hacking Collective was regrettable but not entirely unexpected given the leading role he played in organising that interference. But nobody deserves to be executed in a car bomb and have it live-streamed.

EDWARD KARCZEWSKI: Indeed. Now it appears vehicular hacking was only the tip of the iceberg. Recently the Collective has taken a new approach – hacking countries in ransomware attacks. Turkey and Albania were first. By breaking into their 5G phone networks, they disabled government hardware and shut down everything from data control centres to traffic lights, emergency services and pay networks for shops and businesses. They also overloaded their smart grids leading to nationwide blackouts and sent their satellites spinning off course to burn up in the earth's atmosphere. Both countries paid a ransom of tens of millions of bitcoins to return to operational status and restore damaged data. But that was loose change compared to what the Collective had planned next for Estonia and Romania. The latter have had all their sensitive information held to ransom, from weapons locations to federal reserves. And the collective threatened to make this and their state secrets public if they weren't financially recompensed.

PRIME MINISTER: How did they gain access to this information?

███████████ ███████████, MI5: The countries concerned stored their sensitive information in data centres and bunkers like ours, which have extreme physical security. But these are static, immovable locations and were identified by their enemies. The collective managed to break encryption keys, and infiltrate the centres' biometrics, interlocks and CCTV through both sites' online cooling systems which had a lower level of protection. And once they had access, they located all the sensitive information they needed.

PRIME MINISTER: What is the current status of both countries?

███████ ████████ ████████, MoD: Satellite footage taken this morning reveals Estonia's northern states have already been picked off by Russia and ground-source intelligence suggests the southern states appear ready to surrender. With no weapon codes to prevent invasions, Romania has paid in full. Its security and borders are intact, but it's now bankrupt. This morning, Saudi Arabia came under attack. This is likely to become a global epidemic.

PRIME MINISTER: What is the threat level to the United Kingdom?

███████ ████████, MI5: Severe, which is one point below imminent.

WILLIAM HARRIS: We have invested billions in protecting ourselves both on the ground and online. Are you saying this was wasted money?

███████ ████████, MI5: No, but the risk is escalating. We have every available programmer, both in-house and outsourced, battling to ensure our servers remain impenetrable. But we are fighting a losing battle, Prime Minister. Quantum technology means that the enemy's computers are tens of thousands of millions of times faster than many of our own, which makes breaking our encryption codes easier. The tech to defend ourselves isn't moving as quickly as that built to attack us. It's like running away from a machine gun that has a never-ending supply of bullets. Eventually, we are going to be hit.

PRIME MINISTER: So you're telling me that the one and a half million men and women who lost their lives fighting for our freedom in two world wars died for nothing? Because it sounds to me like a hundred years later, an invisible, faceless enemy is about to rob us of everything that made us great.

EDWARD KARCZEWSKI: They can't if there's no information to steal.

PRIME MINISTER: What are you suggesting?

EDWARD KARCZEWSKI: Six months ago a decision was made to take our National Archives, both historical and current, offline.

PRIME MINISTER: By whom?

EDWARD KARCZEWSKI: It has been part of an ongoing top-secret project that began before you came to power. It culminated in all our sensitive information being taken offline and put on the road. Seven articulated lorries, a plane and a cargo ship were used to take hard copies of everything we didn't want made public on continuous journeys across the country, the air and sea. And for months, it was a success. Until yesterday, when a lorry was compromised and we were forced to abandon the programme.

PRIME MINISTER: What kind of information was being transported?

EDWARD KARCZEWSKI: Everything that wasn't needed on a daily basis or that wasn't fluid. Before computers, they were filed in secret locations throughout London. Then they became stored electronically in datacentres hidden around the country, crammed with hard drives and processors. And that's where they are again since the lorries were taken off the roads. But even though these locations are protected by military-standard physical security and Californian earthquake-resistance standards, these hackers will eventually find a way in. So, I'm suggesting a fresh approach into keeping our data offline.

PRIME MINISTER: More lorries? I can't believe such a ludicrous idea was ever green-lit in the first place!

EDWARD KARCZEWSKI: No, no more lorries. That was only a temporary measure while we were developing an alternative approach to keeping our classified information secure and impossible for outside sources to locate. All I ask is that when you learn of our idea, you try to keep an open mind. If I can direct your attention to the video screen ahead.

** EDWARD KARCZEWSKI has used an electronic keypad to turn on a screen **

PRIME MINISTER: Why are there dozens of random shapes, numbers and letters speeding around the screen?

EDWARD KARCZEWSKI: It's how we are going to find the people we need to protect our country.

Chapter 1

FLICK, LONDON

'Oh, come on!' Flick protested. 'You're living in cloud cuckoo land if you think you're going to get that much for it.'

She shook her head as an estimated asking price of £445,000 appeared on the television screen. The sum delighted the young couple who'd renovated the formerly dilapidated bungalow. But not Flick. As a regular viewer of daytime television shows, she had become an armchair expert in anything property related.

Flick removed a cigarette from a packet lying on the coffee table and lit it with a disposable lighter. She flinched ever so slightly at the sound of the flame and the cigarette crackling to life. Then she took a long, deep drag until the smoke and heat blazed the back of her throat. The astronomical price of cigarettes meant she had promised to limit herself to a handful a day. However, it was only mid-morning and this was already her fourth.

The TV screen suddenly split into two, catching her off-guard, and an image appeared of someone outside her front door. Even with his head tilted downwards, facial recognition software recognised him as Theo, one of her brothers. She took another long drag and chose to ignore him. Twice he pressed the bell before shouting through the letter box.

'I know you're in. I can smell the smoke coming from under the door.'

Flick rolled her eyes. She didn't want to be troubled by Theo or any other member of her family today. Or any day, in fact. But there was no point in pretending she wasn't there. She was *always* there. She rolled the tip of her cigarette against the side of the ashtray to preserve the rest until later and picked up a can of air freshener to spray it around the room. She unlocked three bolts and two latches before typing a code into a pad. As the door opened, the youngest of her four brothers eyed her up and down.

'You look like shit,' he scoffed.

'You've grown a beard,' she replied. 'You look like Grandad.'

'It's the same one I had the last time you saw me.'

Flick shrugged.

'That's how long it's been since you've got off your lazy arse and bothered to come and see us.'

'If this is a tough-love routine, then don't waste your breath ...'

'No, this is a friendly dose of reality.'

Daylight was creeping in through a gap between the closed curtains. It highlighted a fine, smoky mist. Theo entered the flat and drew the curtains wide open and dragged his fingers across a coffee table. They left three clear lines between a layer of dust and the woodgrain. Even without the gesture, Flick knew he was judging her on the unwashed dishes, piles of dirty clothes spread across the kitchen floor, two bulging bin bags, a box of empty wine bottles and a full ashtray. She couldn't criticise Theo for his negative assessment.

Like many of her failings, she blamed the mess on someone else. *That Man.* Only afterwards, when she had seen for the first time inside his flat courtesy of photographs uploaded online, did she question how she'd have coped with such fastidious tidiness. She figured the obsession with an organised home was likely born from the chaos of the rest of his life. A part of her recognised she'd had a lucky escape from who he really was. The other, smaller, part still retained belief that she might have been the one to have changed him.

'I tried calling you at the restaurant because you never answer your mobile or respond to voicemails,' Theo continued. Flick didn't reply. She had an inkling of what was coming next. 'So imagine my surprise when they told me you'd employed a manager to do your job because you'd taken time off for personal reasons. *A year ago.*'

Flick shrugged. 'I'm on indefinite leave. So what?'

'What personal reasons?'

'The clue is in the word *personal*. People take work sabbaticals all the time.'

'But you've taken a sabbatical from your whole life. You're still pining over him, aren't you?'

'Who?' she replied but they were both aware of who he meant.

'You know this can't continue, Felicity. Just because it didn't work out doesn't mean it won't work out with somebody else.'

'He was my Match,' Flick replied.

'You could've been one of those couples whose results were tampered with. That happened to thousands, didn't it?'

'We Matched after that happened,' she said again, her tone firmer. Theo had no recourse.

Flick recalled with clarity the day an email informed her of her successful Match Your DNA pairing. Years earlier, scientists had discovered a gene that all humans possessed and was shared with just one other person. They could be of any sex, religion, age or location, but they were the one your DNA was genetically programmed to be with. Your soulmate. In the space of a few short years, it had become the most popular means by which couples came together, with 1.7 billion people registering their DNA through a simple mouth swab.

Flick's email confirmation had arrived months after a malicious security breach in which thousands of couples had been falsely Matched, but it was already too late for Flick to meet him. He had been murdered.

She had only just started coming to terms with his death when she learned who he really was and it had left her hollow.

Theo flitted around the lounge, tidying up papers, throwing away empty crisp packets and sweet wrappers and collecting castaway clothes. 'I'm trying to help you, sis,' he continued. 'It's not just me who's worried about you, it's Mum and Dad and the rest of the family. You didn't even come to Gran and Grandad's sixtieth anniversary party.'

Flick spat out a laugh. 'Yes, that's just what I need, isn't it? To be surrounded by people reminding me that no one is ever going to love me enough to be by my side sixty years from now.'

Theo muttered something under his breath and began throwing clothes into the washing machine. 'Hey,' Flick protested, 'leave them. They need to be colour separated.'

'Right, because separating colours is a priority for you in this pigsty, isn't it?'

'I said leave them,' she snapped, but Theo ignored her and opened up the machine's drawer, pulling out an empty washing cartridge.

'Where do you keep the spares?'

'Theo, I'm telling you, leave my stuff alone.'

When he began rifling through her kitchen cupboards, Flick stopped holding back. She marched over to him, grabbing his arm. Despite being slighter and smaller than her brother, she twisted it behind his back and frogmarched him towards the door.

'For fuck's sake!' Theo yelled. 'I want to help you.'

'I didn't ask for it, and I don't want it,' she barked and opened the door, only releasing her grip once he was across the threshold.

'I'm telling you this as your brother and as your friend,' he continued, shaking the ache from his limb. 'Match or no Match, he's not worth throwing it all away for.'

Flick wiped her brimming eyes with the cuffs of her jumper. And with the saddest smile she had ever mustered, she closed the door on him.

She threw herself back onto the sofa, aware that everything Theo had said was correct, with the exception of her finding love again. That much she assumed to be impossible; her opportunity had been torn from her. She would have done anything to return to the days when she'd wake up each morning wondering if the email would arrive announcing her Match had been found. Because back then, there was hope. Now there was none.

Flick tapped away the burned strands of tobacco and relit her cigarette, then turned over the TV station to a rolling news channel. *'An exhibition by an anonymous artist is already causing controversy ahead of its premiere tonight,'* the newsreader began. *'The installation has been inspired by the murder of twenty-nine women by a serial killer in London three years ago and which led to one of the biggest manhunts the country has ever seen.'*

'Pause TV,' she shouted, her heartbeat amplified. She needed a moment to steel herself. There had been no avoiding the story of the killer who had plagued the capital, murdering random women before his campaign of terror came to a sudden halt.

'Play TV,' she said and the news channel cut from the studio to an art gallery containing painted portraits of every corpse, some gruesomely bloodied. The detail turned her stomach.

'The artist, who has not been named, claims the portraits are a tribute to the victims and that they are not exploiting the

murders. However, victims' relatives disagree and have hit out at the exhibition, claiming it is in "poor taste" and calling for it to be banned.'

'TV off,' Flick said and the room fell silent. She made her way to the Juliet balcony and opened the double doors. It had been days since she had last set foot outside and the rush of air against her skin almost took her breath away.

All she wanted was to forget about that whole dreadful period of her life. But it was easier said than done. Only last night, it had been victim number thirteen who'd revisited her: Kelly, a young waitress with a nose piercing who she'd employed at the restaurant a month before her death.

It was only weeks later that Flick Kennedy learned that the man responsible for the killings was Christopher Bailey, the man who her DNA dictated was the love of her life.

Chapter 2

CHARLIE, PORTSMOUTH

Charlie made his way through the pub's beer garden, one hand clutching his pint glass and the other carrying bags of kale crisps and nuts. He eased his way through the expanding crowd, careful not to spill his drink until he reached the wooden table with benches and a 'reserved' sign in the centre of it.

England's World Cup qualifying football match against arch-rivals Germany meant the outdoor space was much busier than usual for a regular weeknight. A loss for England would result in failure to qualify for next year's tournament, so the game was make-or-break. His surroundings were familiar. Since reaching the legal drinking age Charlie and his friends had chosen the Wig & Pen as their haunt for all important fixtures and the custom was to continue tonight.

He took a seat and the first sip of his lager, then glanced at his watch. There were fifteen minutes left before kick-off. His eyes switched to the giant wall projection. Celebrity football pundits were offering their predictions but it was hard to hear them against the chatter of the pub crowd.

'Are these seats taken?' a voice asked sharply. The clearly irritated man was standing with a group of friends. Charlie's face reddened at their attention.

'Yes, sorry,' he muttered apologetically. The man looked as if he was ready to argue but changed his mind, turned his back on Charlie and mumbled something incomprehensible.

Charlie conceded he too would've been irritated had he been on his feet while somebody else hogged seven empty seats. That he had paid to reserve them weeks ago did little to prevent him from feeling awkward.

Tonight meant more to Charlie than anyone in the pub could know. It had been two and a half years since the seven friends had last been in one place together. He thought back to Terry Stelfox's wedding and how it had marked the beginning of the end of friendships formed at infants' school. Charlie had naively assumed that when attending different universities hadn't come between them, nothing would. But he hadn't considered Match Your DNA. One by one, his friends found the women – and for one, the man – who they were biologically designed for. However, Charlie was the exception. His Match had yet to make themselves known. And he had never envisaged feeling so alone by his mid-twenties.

He glanced towards the wall projection again. It was now four minutes until kick-off. He had finished off his snacks and begun chewing his fingernails, biting too deeply and causing an intermittent throb. He removed an anti-anxiety transdermal patch from his pocket, no larger than a pea, and attached the adhesive side to his forearm.

Charlie took his mind off waiting for the chemicals to absorb and make their way towards his brain by inserting an ear bud and listening to the recorded messages on his phone.

The first was from Travis. 'Sorry, mate, not going to be able to make it. The twins were being little buggers today and Lisa's frazzled so she's gone to bed. See you soon, yeah?'

The next was from Stelfox. 'Is that tonight? Shit, sorry, Charlie, I've got dinner with the in-laws.' The excuses from the others followed a similar path.

Charlie remained in his seat as a cheer rang out around the garden when the England squad appeared onscreen and a chorus of 'God Save the King' rang out across the pub. The teams assumed their positions and the referee's whistle signalled the start of play. But after only a few minutes, Charlie knew he wouldn't enjoy the game on his own. He downed his pint and made his way to the exit.

'Those seats free now, Billy no-mates?' sneered the man who'd confronted him earlier. A humiliated Charlie wanted to retaliate but the empty seats didn't lie. The stranger had summed him up with brutal accuracy.

Outside in the street, Charlie used an app to choose the delivery of a random dish from his favourite Chinese take-away. Then he removed his bike lock and cycled the fifteen-minute journey home. The drone that had delivered the meal-for-one to his doorstep was already returning to the restaurant by the time he arrived.

Inside, he removed the lids from the foil cartons and placed the food on a table without plating it up first. Then he loosened his belt by a couple of notches. His weight gain had been slow and steady since they'd all stopped playing Sunday-morning league football. He missed the camaraderie, of heading out into town the night before, waking up with a hangover from hell early the next morning, before playing a match and then sharing a Sunday roast at a pub afterwards. It made him feel as if he belonged.

As Charlie tucked into his meal, he recalled a conversation in which he'd learned of a shift in their relationships. Stelfox had let slip that some of the group came together with their wives and girlfriends for dinner parties and for kids' play dates. Charlie hadn't been invited because they assumed "family stuff isn't your cup of tea". He nodded his agreement but quietly; "family stuff" was everything he craved.

Tonight, those feelings of rejection were returning in earnest. He wondered what might have happened had he taken the lead and removed himself from their group and simply stopped contacting them. When would they have noticed they hadn't seen him around for a while? Would it have taken days, weeks or months? Or would he have simply faded into their backgrounds until they'd forgotten about him completely?

More than anything else in the world, Charlie wished he had done just that and not desperately clung on to old times like he had with the two-year-old recorded messages he'd listened to in the pub. His friends were never going to join him because his behaviour had destroyed everything. He stuck another anxiety patch to his arm, and then a third.

He picked up his tablet and directed his attention towards conspiracy-theory websites and message boards that he'd grown obsessed with. Previously, he'd never given credence to wild theories about anything to do with UFOs, assassinated leaders or missing weapons of mass destruction. He'd assumed they were the madcap notions of crackpots with little better to do than formulate outlandish theories using flimsy evidence to support their arguments.

But because once he'd immersed himself amongst them searching for an explanation for the day that changed his life, he understood he shared a common goal with those 'crackpots'. They were all searching for the truth in a world where authenticity lay buried under a constant stream of misinformation and deception. Soon, Charlie was visiting the websites multiple times daily, continuing the narrative with opinions of his own.

He refused to accept the government's official version of events and the hushed-up investigation that followed. Meanwhile, his own guilt for the role he played continued to wrap itself around him like wild ivy, its roots constantly threatening to choke him. It was responsible for his constant anxiety, his estrangement from his family and the dark cloud forever hovering above him.

Before he clicked on a link to another familiar forum, an advertisement caught his eye.

Click **here** to start your life again. Less than one per cent of the British population can solve this puzzle. Can you?

Almost immediately, he recognised a shape and words hidden amongst the random letters, shadows and silhouettes. Perhaps it was his basic knowledge of computer coding or his number-form synaesthesia that allowed digits to appear in his mind like mental maps. 'It can't be as easy as that,' he muttered, but set to work anyway, using his finger to move shapes and objects around the screen until it all made sense.

It was a brief distraction from dwelling upon the faces of the people he had helped to kill.

Chapter 3

SINÉAD, BRISTOL

'Is that what you're wearing tonight?' asked Daniel. His voice startled her; Sinéad was lost in thought as she attached a second band of false eyelashes onto the first. She hadn't noticed him in the reflection of the bedroom mirror.

'Yes,' she replied, and patted out a minor crease in the sleeve of her yellow dress. 'Why?'

Her husband was standing by the doorway in his fitted dinner jacket, white shirt and black bow tie. Light bounced from the tips of his polished Oxford shoes. He was every bit as handsome as the day she first saw him in his online profile. Yet the sight of him made her skin prickle.

'I thought we agreed you were going to wear the purple one?' he continued. There was disappointment in his tone.

'Did we?'

Sinéad had spent days trying to settle on the best outfit for Daniel's company party and thought she had chosen something they both liked. Back when she purchased clothes without first seeking his approval, this dress wouldn't have reached her online shopping basket. The hem was within touching distance of her ankles and the sleeves covered her wrists making her feel shapeless and frumpy. But Daniel was so enthusiastic about his gift when he'd given it to her that she didn't want to upset him by admitting she didn't like it.

'Don't you think this yellow one's more suitable for an Easter party?' Sinéad asked.

'Perhaps when you first bought it, but not so much now.'

She turned to face him. 'Why?'

'Well, it's a bit, you know ...'

'You know?'

'Babe, don't back me into a corner. It's unfair.'

'Go on.'

Daniel sighed. '*Clingy*. It's a bit *clingy* in the wrong places.'

'Do you think I've put on weight?'

'No, no, no, of course not. But I know what you're like, you'll start comparing yourself to the other wives and girlfriends tonight.'

'You think I've let myself go,' she said flatly.

Daniel rolled his eyes. 'No, now you're putting words in my mouth. I'm just saying ... I don't know ... well, how many times have you been to the gym recently? I bought you a twelve-month membership and personal training sessions but you've only been twice.'

'Have you been checking up on me?'

'I ran into Miguel in the changing rooms and he said he hadn't heard from you after the second session.'

'I've been busy.'

'So why did you ask me to hire him then?'

'I ... I didn't,' Sinéad stuttered. 'You suggested I needed toning.'

'No, you asked if you could do with firming up. Think about it, why would you ask me a question about your appearance if you didn't want me to help with your weight problem? You know that I'm a fixer, I'll do anything for you. When you tell me you're feeling unattractive, of course I'm going to read between the lines and help.' He shook his head. 'Sometimes it worries me how much you misremember our conversations.'

Sinéad didn't recall telling him that she'd felt unattractive. But Daniel was correct when he said he was a fixer. He solved her problems, even ones she didn't know that she had.

'Now why don't you slip out of that dress and put on something that fits you better, like the purple one? Do you want me to pick your accessories too?'

'Okay,' Sinéad replied, defeated. She turned to look at her reflection again in the mirror. Perhaps Daniel was right. As he'd told her many times before, she was a work in progress and he always had her best interests at heart.

He kissed the back of her neck as she checked that her false eyelashes were attached properly. *I'm lucky to have him*, she reminded herself. *Plenty of men would have left me after what happened.*

But something snagged in the back of Sinéad's throat. She barely felt it, but it was there.

Strings of white fairy lights hung from exposed wooden beams inside the converted barn. Cascades of white roses covered a wall, mirrored by flowers inside metre-tall vases on circular tables.

An army of coordinated waiters and waitresses carried desserts on trays to each of the two dozen tables surrounding the dancefloor. Sinéad glanced at the brightly coloured dish about to be placed in front of her, then at Daniel, and politely declined. The four courses preceding it had been delicious and had he been absent, she'd have happily devoured every morsel. Tonight, she made sure to leave a third of each plateful untouched, in case Daniel was calorie counting on her behalf.

She'd been subdued for much of the car journey from their apartment to the country hotel. It wasn't until Daniel suggested it that she'd worried just how glamorous the partners of his digital media colleagues were going to look. After a previous function Daniel had casually suggested she might benefit from facial fillers, pointing out that the only thing her once expressive face was now conveying was tiredness. He even made the clinic appointments on her behalf.

Each table contained an electronic device that enabled guests to pick songs from an expansive list to play through the automated DJ system. Joanna, the wife of one of Daniel's team, who she'd met several times before, was sitting next to Sinéad and passed her the gadget.

'Do you want my help?' asked Daniel.

'Why?' Sinéad replied. She interpreted his look to mean *You know why*. 'I was going to choose something by Ed Sheeran,' she continued. 'I loved his songs when I was at college.'

'Really?' Daniel chuckled. 'I don't think anyone else wants to hear *him*—'

'He was quite popular in his day,' interrupted Joanna.

'You'll have to excuse my wife,' Daniel said apologetically. 'She's not very good when it comes to judging the mood of a room.' Sinéad's eyes sank to the table like a scolded dog. 'She only listens to songs past their sell-by date. And nobody wants to keep something that's past its sell-by date, do they?'

He draped his arm around her shoulder and pulled her closer for a hug. Sinéad rarely enjoyed the guitar-heavy songs Daniel favoured but he had an encyclopaedic knowledge of music and therefore, he assured her, a better taste. But his music brought with it dark colours and she'd been surrounded by enough of those to last a lifetime.

She'd attempted to explain to him several times what she saw when she heard music, how notes unintentionally evoked colours in her mind's eye. She told him it was no different to him listening to a familiar song and it reminding him of a special moment in time. 'Back in the day, you'd have been put in an institution for admitting things like that,' he sniffed. She hadn't mentioned it again.

'How's your apartment coming along?' asked Joanna. 'You were renovating it when I last saw you.'

'Just cosmetic things like painting and wallpapering,' said Sinéad. Her mind flashed to one room in particular. One that she couldn't bring herself to enter no matter what the decor.

'I love moving house and starting afresh,' Joanna continued. 'It drives Tim mad but I'm never happier than when I'm in the middle of a redesign.'

'Daniel makes our decorating decisions. He's quite specific with his taste.'

'You surprise me.' Joanna curled her top lip as if a sour taste had crept up her throat and into her mouth. That and the tone in which she said it took Sinéad by surprise. Everyone who knew Daniel seemed to adore him. They were drawn to his enthusiasm and determination. He possessed an ability to talk people around to his way of thinking. It had been part of his appeal in their early days together. It was rare to find someone who didn't like him.

A waiter appeared and Daniel signalled for his attention. 'I'll have a rum and coke. Joanna?'

'A red wine, please.'

'I'll have a gin and tonic,' said Sinéad.

'Perhaps it's best if you stick with the soft drinks, now?'

'It's my song,' said Joanna as the opening bars of an Amy Winehouse track played. 'Do you remember her?' Sinéad nodded – Amy was a favourite of her late mum's. 'Come on then,' continued Joanna. 'Let's relive our youth.' She grabbed at Sinéad's arm and as they stood up, Sinéad caught a glimpse of her husband. His disapproving expression marred her enjoyment of the moment. She felt self-conscious with each twist of her arm or move of her foot. She couldn't wait for the song to finish but as she hurried back to Daniel, he blanked her and walked towards the bathroom. Sinéad felt Joanna's hand on her arm again as she reached the table.

'You don't have to put up with this shit,' she hissed.

'With what?'

'You know what. You are not the idiot he wants everyone to think you are. I'm sorry if I'm stepping over the mark but I can't hold my tongue any longer. Every time I see you together at one of these functions, he behaves in the same patronising manner and it really pisses me off. Daniel belittles you in front of everyone at every given opportunity. Over the years I've watched you transform from this warm, confident woman into someone who processes everything she thinks before she says it in case her husband doesn't approve. He is a bully and you are not yourself when he is around. You yearn for something more; I can see it in your face. You just don't know how to find it. There is more to you than what he allows you to have.'

Sinéad opened her mouth, ready to defend herself and her husband; to explain how Joanna didn't know the real Daniel; how he'd remained by her side through the single worst moment of her life. And for that she owed him everything. Yes, sometimes his words were cruel but that was just his way. He didn't mean it. He wanted the best for her. But for the first time in their relationship, she couldn't bring herself to defend him.

'There is a life to be had away from your husband,' Joanna continued. 'And you need to find it because mark my words, if you don't, he will grind you down to nothing. It's not too late to start again.'

Chapter 4

EMILIA

Emilia's body convulsed as if someone had plunged something sharp and electrified into the crown of her head. Her eye sockets pulsed as she arched her back, threw her head to one side and tried to emit a scream. But her throat was too hoarse to make a sound.

She attempted to lift her arms to protect herself from whoever was hurting her but they were too weak to move and flopped by her side. It felt to her fingertips like she was lying between the sheets of a bed. She unpeeled her eyelids; they were bone dry and the bright lights made everything surrounding her dazzle and blur. Only when she opened and closed them in rapid succession did they moisten.

When the room started coming into focus, Emilia realised she was alone. Nobody was attacking her despite the excruciating pain she'd felt. Her arms were weak so it took several attempts for her hands to reach the top of her head where she'd felt the initial throb. There was nothing attached to it, no wires or electrical current. Had she imagined the electrocution? Because it had felt so real.

Overcome by an urgency to pull herself around, Emilia began pushing her body up the bed, centimetre by centimetre, her feeble wrists tingling with pins and needles.

When she reached close to a ninety-degree angle, she clenched and unclenched her fists, trying to encourage the blood to circulate and help her regain feeling. Her fingers trembled as she reached for a clear bottle on a bedside table. She drew it to her nose, sniffed it then sipped the water until her thirst was quenched and her voice progressed from a croak into something audible.

Her mind raced as she cast her gaze across the unfamiliar surroundings. *Where the hell am I? How have I ended up in here? What is this place? Do I even know my own name?* 'Emilia,' she said in a husky voice.

A new, all-consuming fear spread through her when she realised this was the only thing she knew for certain about herself.

Emilia moved to feel the gap under the bed: there was enough space for her to slide beneath it and hide if necessary. She caught herself as she felt the urge to search for something to use as a weapon to defend herself. *Why do I feel threatened?* She had no answer, it was just her intuition warning her she was in trouble and that's all she could rely on.

Her accommodation resembled a private hospital room yet there was none of the equipment she might expect to find in one. There were no seats for visitors. A single monitor sat on a table in the corner of the room, the screen facing in the opposite direction. Translucent patches were stuck to various sections of her arms, legs and torso under her grey hoodie and jogging bottoms. She felt around for wounds, bandages or laparoscopic incisions but there were none to be found, indicating she had not been operated upon.

Have I been in a coma? Her mind raced with possibilities. She remained convinced about just one thing: something about that place was a threat to her safety and she must leave immediately. But when she tried to recall where home was, she drew a blank. Likewise, when she tried recalling what it looked like, who she might share it with, or her career, her family, her friends and her interests, there was nothing. It frightened her more than the room itself.

She calculated that it would take twelve footsteps to reach the door. Slowly, she swung her legs over the side of the bed and placed her bare feet onto a tiled floor. The sound of whispers took her by surprise and she turned her head but she was definitely alone in the room. She must have imagined it.

A heel brushed against an object and she picked up a pair of black trainers. The soles were discoloured, indicating they'd been worn. *Why would a coma patient need footwear?* She slipped them on – they were her size – and discovered she could walk, albeit shakily. She made her way across the room and to the monitor to see if it might shed any light on her circumstances.

There was no keyboard attached, so she touched a couple of the screen's icons to make it operable. It contained live footage of her empty bed. Instinctively, she knew how to operate it, pressing more onscreen controls until a timeline appeared. She rewound it, stopping moments before she awoke. Then she watched herself, lying on her bed, eyes and mouth wide open, motionless and zombie-like. The footage chilled her. *What happened to me and who's been watching?*

Emilia rewound a further twelve hours before she saw two men in white porters' uniforms helping her to her feet. She watched herself shuffle towards the door as if sleep-walking, both men propping her up. Her attention was drawn to her own face: her emotionless expression, her deadened eyes. Then upon her return later, they sat her on the bed, one spoonfeeding her from a plastic bowl while the other flattened her crumpled bedcover. They helped her back under the sheets and left her alone, her expression as blank as when they arrived.

She jabbed at other icons until the screen split into four sections. Each one contained a different person – two men and two women – sitting in a chair by a desk in a sparse room, seemingly unaware they were being filmed.

Emilia's urge to escape intensified and she made her way to a frosted glass door with no handle. She hesitated when she spotted a touchpad attached to the wall. She went to place her hand upon it, then hesitated. Again, fuelled by instinct, she unclipped the front and found an emergency keypad hidden beneath it. She typed in a series of letters and numbers, timing the gaps as she input them. She held her breath until a green light flashed and to her relief, the door opened. Emilia clenched her fists and hurried away.

Her door led to a series of corridors illuminated by movement sensors. She silently padded from one to another, terrified of being heard and confronted. Emilia didn't question how she knew where she was going, only that something was pushing her in a certain direction. She had little choice but to trust her instincts. More whispers and muffled voices seeped out from behind closed doors, but whomever they were coming from remained out of sight.

She used the same series of letters and numbers to gain access to eight more doors leading into eight corridors until she approached a door that was slightly ajar. Inside a room were dozens of metal lockers, a handful of them open with some containing clothing. She rummaged around until she found a jacket that fitted her and a pair of dark blue jeans. From there, she returned to the corridor and made her way into another room and a metal staircase which led to the building's basement. Behind a tenth door lay a dark, cylindrical brick tunnel. Emilia was hesitant; she couldn't see much further than her own outstretched hand. But she was convinced this was her only way out.

She pushed her way forward, her heart thrumming and fingertips leading the way along the exposed brick walls, until the door behind her slammed shut, startling her. Now she was in pitch black. Footstep by footstep, she inched her way along until her feet began sloshing through cold water. Its odour was stale, but to her relief it emitted no sewer-like stench.

Finally, after what felt like an eternity, something came into view ahead of her, the size no larger than a pea. It was natural light. Emilia picked up her pace and hurried through the water; the legs of her jeans were now soaking wet, but she didn't care. Eventually, she reached a metal gate at the end of the tunnel. She pushed to open it, but it was locked. Fumbling around the surrounding walls, she located a keyboard under a clump of moss and typed one last code before it unlocked and she pushed her way through it. She was free.

Emilia paused to survey this new environment. It was a public park with mown lawns, woodland and ponds. Looming skyscrapers and historic buildings surrounded it. She hazarded a guess that she was in London. However, instead of the relief that freedom brought, she was still every bit as scared as when she'd first awoken. She remained a prisoner of all that she didn't know.

She began to walk in the direction of a built-up area. And for a moment, the assault on her senses threatened to overtake her. She held her hands over her ears to block out the noise of vehicles and machinery and squinted as she struggled to adjust to daylight, flashing billboards and neon shop signs. As she approached a busy road, she became aware of yet more voices. They began quietly as whispers, gradually becoming more strident. She couldn't make out what they were saying but they left her uneasy. Had the hospital she'd found herself in been an asylum? Was she crazy? But if so, how had she been able to escape?

A sudden thought spooked her – what if they'd followed her from the place she'd just escaped? What if she were being tracked? She turned her head but she was alone. Regardless, Emilia quickened her pace. Weaving in and out of crowded pedestrian streets, every dozen or so footsteps she turned her head to try and locate the whispers while still trying to grasp her bearings. And eventually she saw them: four figures appearing from behind a line of trees, too blurry to identify their features, but all ominous with their presence.

Their whispering grew louder and began disorientating her, making her head spin and her temples pulsate. She remained unsteady on her feet and threatened to fold like wet cardboard. She mustered up the strength to break into a slight run, but over her shoulder, they too picked up the pace.

Then without warning, it all became too much for Emilia's body. Her legs buckled and she felt herself swaying and stumbling along the pavement, unable to find anything or anyone to grab on to and prevent herself from falling into the road.

The last thing Emilia heard was the sound of a car horn before experiencing a feeling of weightlessness as her body was scooped up into the air and tossed back onto the pavement with a thud.

Chapter 5

BRUNO, EXETER

Bruno glanced around the room. He had anticipated wood-panelled walls, a table large enough to fit a dozen people around it, leather chairs and a musty smell emanating from well-thumbed legal literature. Instead, the prestigious law firm was of modern design, comprised of soundproofed glass walls, floor-to-ceiling windows, expansive sofas and low-level, spectral lighting.

He fidgeted in his seat, too packed with nervous energy to settle. The more he tried to remain static, the more he wanted to shift. He wished he had worn something light and casual and not his one and only suit. That, along with a thick cotton shirt, made his underarms sweat. He was too embarrassed to remove his jacket and have the damp patches seen by everyone.

Bruno turned to his solicitor. She was scrolling through pages on an electronic device. 'How much longer do you think they'll be?' he asked.

'No idea,' Emily Laghari replied without returning eye contact. 'They make you wait to put you on edge. Don't let them get the better of you.'

'They already have.'

'And remember, as tempting as it might be to contribute, leave the talking to me. That's what you pay me for.'

Bruno nodded and surveyed the room again, catching a glimpse of his reflection in a window. It was a stark reminder of how much he had aged in the last two and a half years. He appeared much older than a man in his mid-thirties, his once dark brown hair streaked with white lines like road markings. The tan he'd developed back-packing around South America in his early twenties that had never completely faded was finally doing just that, leaving sun-damage patches around his blue eyes that had long since lost their sparkle. The person who'd warned him that nothing ages a person more thoroughly than grief was telling the truth.

Bruno flinched when the doors finally opened. He counted six lawyers of varying ages, sexes and appearances, entering in single file. But each shared the same air of confidence.

'They've brought the cavalry,' Bruno whispered and went to rise to his feet until Emily placed her hand on his arm, instructing him to remain seated. A bead of sweat trickled from his neck along the centre of his back, only stopping when it reached the waistband of his underwear. The opposition sat two suits per sofa in a semicircular format, surrounding Bruno and Emily as if cornering the enemy in battle.

'Well, Mr Yorke,' began the youngest-looking of them. 'Our sincere apologies for keeping you waiting.'

'That's o ...' Emily touched his arm again so he stopped, mid-sentence.

'Do you have a final settlement figure, Mr O'Sullivan?' Emily asked. 'This case has been dragging on for much longer than necessary. Mr Yorke has been remarkably patient.'

'That's what we are here to discuss,' O'Sullivan replied, then fell silent. A glint in his eye unnerved Bruno.

'Well?' Emily continued. 'Do I have to ask you again?'

'We have made our final settlement offer,' he replied. Bruno's stare moved to O'Sullivan's mouth. It was itching to smirk.

'Let's not play games, shall we?' Emily disputed. 'You've said nothing.'

'Which is our offer. Our client will not be offering Mr Yorke any financial compensation for his loss.'

Bruno turned to Emily, his muscles tensing. 'What does he mean?'

She ignored him. 'Then why have you summoned us here if you've yet to make a decision?'

'You misunderstand, Ms Laghari. On our client's instruction, we will not be making you an offer, period.'

'And your reasoning behind this is …?'

'There is a morality clause in each contract that forbids sexual relations between co-workers.'

'This is old news, Mr O'Sullivan. It's why Mr Yorke resigned from his position in the same firm when they began their relationship.'

'I wasn't referring to Mr Yorke.'

Bruno looked at the lawyer, perplexed, and then to Emily. She appeared to understand the conversation's subtext. She turned to Bruno, her sober expression juxtaposing the honeyed tone that followed. 'Perhaps you might want to step outside for a few minutes,' she said. A sick feeling erupted in the pit of his stomach.

'No, I want to hear it.' Bruno looked at O'Sullivan who was by now barely able to contain himself. 'Tell me.'

O'Sullivan beckoned one of his colleagues to continue, a man with a slight build, pale skin and slicked-back, raven black hair. 'Mr Graph, would you please continue.'

'On the day the Hacking Collective took over so many cars on our country's roads, Zoe Yorke, your client's spouse, was travelling inside an autonomous car registered to her employer, Howles Technologies. She was accompanied by a colleague, Mr Mark Bancroft, who wasn't registered as a Passenger in her vehicle for that journey, but he should have been, as per company policy.'

'We know this already. Even if this is policy, at a stretch, it would have been punishable with a verbal warning.'

'The couple participated in a series of sex acts inside the moving vehicle.'

'Bullshit,' Bruno blurted out. 'Zoe wouldn't do that.'

'This is the sole basis of your refusal to pay?' asked Emily. 'Speculation and post-mortem accusations without evidence?' She began to stand up and buttoned her jacket. 'We'll see you in court.'

'Perhaps you should remain seated at least until the next part,' Graph continued. 'We have video confirmation.'

Emily shook her head. 'You know very well that under privacy laws, video footage taken from inside an autonomous vehicle has no relevance in a legal or civil insurance claim and therefore cannot be used as evidence either for or against anyone involved in a fatal accident.'

Fatal accident, Bruno repeated to himself. The words came as no surprise but still they skittered across his skin like icy cold drops of rain. When O'Sullivan leaned closer, Bruno was struck by how narrow and dark the man's eyes were; almost inhumanly so.

'We didn't say the footage had been taken from *inside* the vehicle,' O'Sullivan disputed. 'It contains actions perpetrated inside the vehicle moments before the accident.' Finally, O'Sullivan released his conspiratorial smile. 'You might want to turn your head, Mr Yorke.'

Bruno ignored him as O'Sullivan and Graph's colleague projected moving images taken from above Zoe's car.

'This footage was filmed by a passenger inside a double-decker coach,' Graph continued. 'The cameraman was a member of a rugby team travelling to an away match. As you can see, the privacy windows in Mrs Yorke's driverless car have been activated making it impossible for anyone to see inside from road-level. But she failed to darken the glass of her panoramic sunroof, making the view from above quite clear.'

Bruno barely breathed as footage gradually closed in on his wife. She was writhing on the lap of a man he didn't recognise. She wore a shirt but no skirt and his trousers were just about visible around his ankles.

'He's making her do this,' Bruno protested, but he could barely hear his own voice. 'He's forcing her.'

Now the sick feeling rose up into his throat as he desperately hoped an alternative camera angle might show Zoe resisting the actions of her colleague. When he realised that would mean the sex to be non-consensual, he was selfishly unsure of which would be the lesser of two evils. The unrelenting footage panned close in on her face. Cheers rang out from the cameraman's fellow teammates when Zoe appeared to climax, none the wiser to her audience. Then when her companion finished moments later, she pulled his face to hers and kissed him with a passion Bruno could barely remember her sharing with him.

He tore himself away from the screen and glared at the smug expressions of the defence team. When Emily made no effort to reassure him, he knew both the battle and the war were over.

'It has also come to our attention that Mrs Yorke has been involved in and attempted to initiate sexual liaisons with several members of staff managed directly by her,' Graph added. 'They have come forward to claim that they were also harassed by her into performing sex acts if they stood any hope of career progression. The fatal accident that followed was as a result of autonomous vehicles being hacked, but that does not affect the facts. Your wife was a sexual predator. And as per Mrs Yorke's contract, her employment can be terminated immediately or even retrospectively, after her passing. Our client feels this is their only option.'

Bruno allowed the sofa to swallow him, his thoughts suddenly turning to someone else. 'What about our son?' he choked. 'What will happen to him now?'

Chapter 6

FLICK, LONDON

Flick skimmed through her phone, deleting hundreds of bookmarked websites and news feeds she had visited over the last three years. Most of them were about her Match, Christopher, and his crimes. But a slip of the finger meant that instead of deleting one, she opened it instead in error.

SERIAL KILLER MURDERS PREGNANT WOMAN

The twenty-seventh murder victim of London's serial killer was pregnant, police have revealed.

Syrian-born Dominika Bosko was five months pregnant with a baby son when she was found dead in her kitchen, garrotted by cheese wire. The body was discovered yesterday by a colleague concerned by her absence from the bookmakers where they both worked.

Detective Sergeant Sean O'Brien said: 'We can confirm the body of the child was discovered by his mother's side but we won't speculate on the cause of his death until a full post-mortem has been carried out.'

Flick closed her eyes. All this time later and the impact of her Match was not lessening. She continued to erase her bookmarks until none remained. Next, she would cut out those she followed on social media who were leading more fulfilling lives than her. Flick's television and socials were her only window to the outside world. She'd long ceased following online the comings and goings of her brothers, friends, members of her Muay Thai martial arts club and employees at the restaurant she co-owned. It'd become too much for her to read about their perfect lives, perfect families and perfect homes. She'd been robbed of all those things because her DNA had been Matched to that of a psychopath.

She had not been a bitter person until post-Christopher. Her glass had mostly been half-full, and positively overflowing when she'd first learned she had a Match. Now, not only did she hate him for leaving her dreams in tatters, but she also loathed her own cursed body for their biological link. With no one else to punish for the cards she'd been dealt, she took it out on herself with harmful behaviours. Smoking, alcohol and highly saturated convenience foods were her weapons for a slow, torturous suicide.

Now, as Flick culled more former friends she envied on Instagram, an advertisement caught her attention. It was familiar, having appeared to have followed her around other sites she'd surfed that day. *Clickbait*, she thought.

Click here to start your life again.

The notion was enticing. Who hadn't dreamed of starting afresh? Flick fantasised about it regularly. But if something appeared too good to be true, then it probably was. You couldn't press a restart button by clicking on a link. Or could you? She paused and then, throwing caution to the wind, she hit the link and was immediately taken to a website that she mirrored on her TV screen for a clearer view.

Less than one per cent of the British population can solve this puzzle. Can you?

The screen was taken over by dozens and dozens of three-dimensional graphics, along with brightly coloured random floating letters, numbers and shapes, all of them moving in indiscriminate directions. Flick sat upright to gain a better view, then allowed the television's sensor to pick up her line of vision so that she could control the screen with her eye movements.

In her head, ordered sequences including letters and numbers or even months of the year had specific appearances and personalities. 'Your daughter has a type of synaesthesia called Ordinal Linguistic Personification,' a psychiatrist had told her worried parents when she was nine. He went on to assure them she wasn't suffering mental health issues when Flick admitted she saw a woman with red hair when she thought of the number nine or that March was represented by an introverted teenager in a beanie hat. 'Duke Ellington, Marilyn Monroe, Kanye West and Stevie Wonder have all lived with synaesthesia,' the psychiatrist added.

Now, in under a minute, she'd rearranged everything to form a sphere with various words and patterns across it. She waited, expecting her 'reward' to be redirected to a website where she'd be given the hard sell for a product she had no interest in buying. Instead, her screen went blank, then returned to the television channel she'd been half-watching. *Is that it?* she thought, deflated.

She made her way to the open doors of the Juliet balcony, picking up a cigarette packet from the table. As she scanned the communal gardens below, she flipped open the lid but it was empty. When she returned to the kitchen, there were no packets left in the cupboards either. It was against the law for cigarettes to be dispatched with online grocery deliveries, leaving her little choice but to leave the flat for the first time in weeks and bulk-buy them in their hundreds.

The nearest supermarket was a fifteen-minute walk from her east London apartment, and once outside, it felt like Flick's first day on earth. Everything was alien to her, from the close proximity to people who brushed past her to the brightly coloured, revolving advertising billboards adorning building walls. The world outside was moving too quickly for her and it made her anxious.

Beds of brightly coloured flowers in a pocket park caught her attention. It was like an oasis in a desert of concrete and asphalt. Once upon a time, London had felt like an exciting, boisterous, vibrant city and a perfect place in which to be young and single. But as she approached her mid-thirties, it became overpriced, overcrowded and designed for a youthful, woke generation. She desired wide open spaces now more than ever. *If only I could start my life again, I'd live it by the sea*, she thought. *A home by an endless ocean*.

Flick spied in the centre of the park a line of street-food vendors cooking on mobile pop-up stands. Clad in her typical uniform of shapeless tracksuit bottoms and a sweatshirt, she felt self-conscious next to the smartly dressed office workers on their lunch breaks. They queued to order freshly cooked, steaming cartons of exotic foods. Flick couldn't remember a time when she'd eaten a meal that hadn't required a clear film lid to be pierced first, so she joined a line for Thai food.

'Can I have the beef with sticky rice, please?' she asked. The chef poured the contents of two plastic boxes into the pan where they sizzled as they came into contact with the cooking oil. But almost immediately, the noise and smell they omitted triggered Flick's imagination. She put her hand over her nose and mouth as the crackling of raw meat and the beef's aroma conjured up the night of Christopher's death.

Someone had intercepted him at the home of his planned thirtieth victim. There, they had strangled him with cheese wire, the murder weapon he favoured, before dragging his body into the rear garden, covering him with a duvet and white spirits, and setting him alight. Once he'd been identified by his DNA, teardrops were found on the dead bodies of a baby and his mother which linked Christopher to at least two of the murders. Eventually, there was enough evidence to connect him to eleven more. But it was widely assumed he was guilty of all twenty-nine. However, the person who had turned the tables and killed Christopher remained unknown.

Months later when Flick had taken the test and been informed of her Match, his name hadn't sunk in even when she'd typed in his email address to contact him. Police had kept his account open in the hope someone they had not questioned and who was unaware of his murder might get in touch. An officer monitoring it responded with a visit to her restaurant, questioning her on the nature of their relationship. Only then did she learn she had been paired with the most prolific serial killer of the last forty years. Unwilling to accept it, Flick paid twice more to be tested but received the same results.

Over the following three years, her need to learn more about him became an obsession. She'd visit his crime scenes or track down his victims' families and engineer casual meetings with them to learn more about their lost loved one. She'd even lurked outside Christopher's boarded-up home in West London, trying to find a way of breaking through the metal shutters that blocked every entrance.

THE MINDERS

Now, as her lunch sizzled and spat, Flick imagined it being Christopher's flesh as the flames burned his corpse. She couldn't remain there a moment longer. She pushed past others in the queue and ran to the edge of the park, steadying herself against the railings. She inhaled deeply, searching for cleansing breaths to rid herself of the stench of beef clinging to her lungs.

Back home, she locked and bolted the door behind her, leaned her back against it and slid to the floor. It was only as she went to reach for the cigarettes that she remembered she had not made it as far as the supermarket. She would have to do without as she wouldn't be leaving the house again today.

Flick held her head in her hands and sobbed as long and hard as she had the day she discovered on the dark web a poster who had access to Polaroid photographs Christopher had taken of his victims and kept as mementos. She'd paid a month's wages in bitcoins to download them, partly to see how depraved the man was that biology had paired her with and partly to put paid to the doubts creeping into her mind about her own self and what she too might be capable of. Perhaps as well as their DNA, they shared the same latent desires, the same latent tendencies?

When she vomited after seeing the fourth garrotted, bloated victim, she knew for certain she and Christopher were nothing alike. Nature had played a very cruel trick on her. Time might have passed for the rest of the world since that day, but it remained frozen for her. And she was at a loss as to how it was going to get any better.

She wiped her eyes, closed the curtains and made her way into the kitchen to pour herself a rum and coke. As she took a handful of ice from the freezer, a message alert appeared on her phone.

FAO: FLICK KENNEDY

Private and Confidential

Dear Miss Kennedy, following your successful completion of our puzzle, we are offering you a unique opportunity to start your life afresh. Please find attached to this email an address, date and time, along with non-disclosure agreements and brief notes of what will be expected of you. You will be financially compensated for your time.

'Start your life afresh,' she repeated as she scanned through the attached contents. It looked too elaborate to be a scam. She pressed the accept button and hoped whatever lay ahead of her was better than what had preceded it.

Chapter 7

CHARLIE, PORTSMOUTH

There was very little left of Charlie's fingernails for him to bite by the time the coach driver steered the vehicle into an empty bay at London's Waterloo station.

Charlie used the last of his transdermal patches to combat his fluctuating anxiety levels and tapped at a copper-coloured wristband. His doctor had suggested that wearable therapy, with its electrical, vibrational, temperature- and scent-based stimulants, would also assist with his unease. But today it was having little effect.

He questioned whether he was about to become the victim of an elaborate hoax. But there was something too tempting to ignore about the offer to start his life again. The invitation to London first appeared by email minutes after he had deciphered the puzzle. He'd been informed that his speed and accuracy had taken him through to the next round of a competition, the winners of which would be offered the opportunity to enter a programme to restart their lives. Naturally, he was sceptical. But the allure of the unattainable was too tempting not to explore.

As his fellow commuters removed luggage from over-head storage areas, however, Charlie remained stationary, once again weighing up the pros and cons of whether he was doing the right thing.

Way into the early hours of last night, he had trawled the internet searching for clues as to the advert's origin and what previous participants had to say about their experiences. But it had seemingly flown under most of the conspiracy theory community's radars. Some users had spotted the puzzle but failed to solve it. Regulars on scientific forums suggested it could only be solved by people whose brains were in a particular stage of evolution or wired in an alternative way to the majority. Charlie wondered if that included his synaesthesia. Others claimed it was simply clickbait. But clickbait rarely lured you out of the virtual world and into the real one.

He was the last to disembark the coach as he threw his bag over his shoulder and stretched his legs. He considered taking a taxi to the address he'd been emailed, but chose to walk when he struggled to find a non-autonomous one. He slipped in his earbuds and left it to a map projected into the left lens of his glasses to direct him.

His mind wandered and he found himself asking his OS to play the latest news headlines about the Hacking Collective, a popular subject within his online communities this week. As Charlie crossed Westminster bridge, he mulled over what might happen if the United Kingdom was next to be held to ransom. He had still been a child when the post-Brexit riots divided the country but all these years later, divisions between leavers and remainers lingered. He could foresee history repeating itself and opinions being split as to whether we should pay up or stand our ground.

What the Collective was doing around the world was inexcusable, he reasoned, but his obsession with conspiracy theories had taught him that governments brought the threat of public exposure upon themselves. If they were more transparent there'd be no need to keep so many secrets.

His irises flicked towards the map – he was only minutes from his destination, a side street running adjacent to the Embankment. His anxiety levels were on the rise.

What if I'm not being duped, what if this offer is genuine? he asked himself. *What if they really are giving me the opportunity to start my life from scratch?* Perhaps he might make a better job of it second time around.

What would I be turning my back on if I accepted? I have very little family, even Mum and Dad split up and moved away to be with their DNA Matches. Who would miss me?

A Match was never far from his mind and he removed his phone from his pocket and asked his OS to log on to his Match Your DNA account. Charlie had registered his details five years earlier but his counterpart had yet to do the same. At this point, he no longer cared if they were decades older than him, located on the other side of the world or if *she* was in fact a *he*. He was desperate to know what it felt like to be wanted. *'No messages,'* the website's inbox read. The hollowness inside him was to remain but it helped to make his mind up for him. Whatever was going to happen today, he had little to lose.

'You have reached your destination.' An automated voice spoke through his earbuds. Adjacent to the Embankment's dual carriageway was a narrow side street accessed only by concrete steps and a passageway under a building. There, he found himself in an oblong courtyard surrounded by six-storey offices.

Charlie glanced at them all, searching for a building number. There were none above any doors, no keypads, handles, locks or intercoms and each window was tinted so it couldn't be peered into. He paced around the courtyard, double-checking the address in the email and scanning the buildings again to see if he'd missed an obvious entrance. Again, he drew a blank.

I'm an idiot, he sighed. *I knew this was too good to be true. It's a con.*

But for what purpose? Why had they gone to so much effort to get him there? They'd paid for his travel and compensated his bank account handsomely for his loss of earnings.

Charlie turned and headed back towards the staircase when a set of double doors to his right opened inwards. He paused, waiting for someone to either exit or greet him but no one came. He'd viewed enough thrillers to know that he should keep on walking in the opposite direction of a pitch black lobby. But a sudden confidence stirred inside him. Instead, he tapped a button on the arm of his glasses to zoom in ahead: whatever lay inside was too dark to focus on, with the exception of a pattern on the wall. It was barely visible but Charlie recognised it immediately. It was the solution to the puzzle that had brought him there.

He clutched the patch on his arm, subconsciously rubbing it. 'You feel too much,' an acquaintance had once advised him. He'd wanted to protest but she was right. Perhaps it was good to feel nervous about what was inside that building.

The lure of a second chance became too great for Charlie to walk away from.

Chapter 8

SINÉAD, BRISTOL

He will grind you down to nothing.

Joanna's words followed Sinéad like her own footprints in the snow. She wasn't a person Sinéad knew well, in fact they had only met on a handful of occasions over the years. But she had got the measure of Sinéad and Daniel's relationship. And she recognised something inside Sinéad that she was too reluctant to see for herself. For each day she spent with Daniel, another tiny piece of her former self was eroding.

The suggestion that she yearned for something more than the life Daniel allowed her played on her mind days later. Yet through misguided loyalty, a part of Sinéad still wanted to defend him. For a long time, she'd reasoned that his placing of her inside a gilded cage meant that he'd wanted to protect her, to shape her into a better version of herself. But Joanna's warning was encouraging Sinéad to view their relationship from someone else's perspective. And it was far less blinkered than her own.

There is a life to be had away from your husband, Joanna advised. But was there really? There had been before they met, she recalled, but it hadn't been a notable one. Daniel was supposed to be the answer to her prayers. But what if there was something better for her beyond their marriage;

something she'd been too short-sighted to have seen earlier?

She ran a fingertip along the double row of her false eyelashes to check they were still in place. Daniel hated it when she was without them, yet he had been partially responsible for her need to wear them. Then she picked at the lunch he had packed for her in a Tupperware box as she sat alone in the office staff room. Today's selection included a red apple, a plain yoghurt, a chicken sandwich and a low-calorie granola bar. On the lid, a blue Post-It note read, 'No cheating – no chocolate!' with a heart instead of a dot under the exclamation mark. It was his way of reminding her that he loved her enough to care about what she ate. Wasn't it?

A pop-up advertisement appeared on her screen.

Click here to start your life again. Less than one per cent of the British population can solve this puzzle. Can you?

Sinéad took a bite from her sandwich and absent-mindedly moved around random words, shapes and letters until the puzzle made sense. It was complete in less than half a minute.

She recalled how she'd always hoped to replicate her late parents' happy, loving marriage. Soon after she and Daniel had met, he'd convinced her that he was the one to save her from a lifetime of unhappiness following a string of bad relationship choices. She had been too willing to believe in love to realise she didn't need someone else to make her happy.

Their attraction was immediate. His eyes were the lightest brown she had ever seen and his lips were plumper than hers. He was tanned and lean and next to him even then, she felt pale and shapeless. Yet for some reason, this beautiful, intelligent man had chosen her. It didn't make sense why he hadn't been snapped up already. And despite her friends' warnings at the speed at which their relationship was developing, they were married within two months.

Sinéad glanced at their wedding photograph, the screensaver Daniel had put on her phone. She recalled the moment he saw her walking up the aisle. After choosing the dress, all she had wanted was to witness her husband-to-be's reaction as he waited at the altar. Only when he turned his head, it wasn't the grin she'd hoped for. If anything, he appeared a little disappointed. It was later in the day that he admitted he'd have picked something that suited her better.

An empty-battery symbol appeared and turned the device's screen black. Instead of immediately putting it on charge, she was too preoccupied with reflecting on their early months of marriage. What began as Daniel's suggestions of ways in which they could grow together became proposals only directed at her. They ranged from her taste in clothes and make-up to her attention to detail with housework, the books she read, the music she listened to and the friends she chose. 'This is what couples do,' Daniel assured her. 'They try to better one another.'

Joanna's voice echoed again. *You don't have to put up with this shit.*

Sinéad complied with Daniel's wishes because above all else, she wanted to make him happy. And when he was in control, he was just that. Occasionally, he might throw her off kilter with sudden praise, following a well-cooked meal or a new outfit that pleased him. But gradually she recognised that he only offered her praise if it served his needs.

Her biggest sacrifice in the name of love had been her career. As an office-based Space Environment Coordinator, her role had been to assist in locating orbiting waste from used rockets and broken satellites that was at risk of colliding with working orbital technology. She determined what debris to recycle in space foundries and what to direct to burn up in the earth's atmosphere. It was high pressured and skilled and she loved it but the three-hour round-trip commute into London had been impacting the time she spent with Daniel. Only now could she see what a mistake she'd made to have given it up on his suggestion and taken a more menial job closer to home so they could spend more time together.

There is more to you than what he allows you to have.

The only thing she had fought her corner for was their child. In her one act of persistence, she insisted they start trying for a family. She fell pregnant almost immediately but miscarried after a month. Twice more, nature dealt her cruel blows before Daniel demanded they took a break, suggesting her body was hostile and unsuited to nurturing life. 'Perhaps it's a sign that motherhood isn't something you're cut out for,' he said.

Suddenly Sinéad felt a sharp pain in her left breast and she cupped it, holding it for a minute. A series of images erupted, so she shut her eyelids tightly until they disappeared. And with her appetite now all but gone, she slipped her uneaten food into the recycling bin and returned to her desk.

'Shit, Daniel,' she muttered when she realised that she'd forgotten to call him at the time he'd designated. She placed her phone on its charging pad and looked at the clock on the wall – she was now quarter of an hour late. And when it came back to life, she panicked when she noticed his six missed calls.

Sinéad hurried back into the toilets to call him privately, her smart watch buzzing to warn her of her rising pulse. If she didn't come up with a satisfactory explanation for the delay and convince him how sorry she was, his bad mood might stretch for days.

He answered after one ring, but said nothing. Sinéad opened her mouth but just as she was about to speak, she heard Joanna's voice again.

There is a life to be had away from your husband.

There is a life to be had.

Away from your husband.

Away.

And for the first time in her marriage, Sinéad chose not to apologise to keep the peace and hung up instead. His name flashed on her screen almost immediately but she rejected it again. Then she left the bathroom, made her way back to her desk and grabbed her handbag.

'Everything okay, Sinéad?' asked Richard, her manager, from his desk in the corner of the room. Richard was an old friend of Daniel's and another of her husband's sycophants.

'Never been better,' she announced. 'And now I'm going home.' She didn't await his reply before exiting the building. It wouldn't be long before Richard called Daniel to report her unusual behaviour. But it didn't matter because Sinéad wouldn't be returning. By the time she reached their apartment ten minutes later, Daniel had called another seven times.

There is a life to be had away from your husband.

And there is, she realised. It had taken someone else to lead the way to the door, but now all she had to do was open it. Brimming with anticipation and fretfulness, Sinéad packed a suitcase with clothes and toiletries and considered where she might go. It had been too long since she'd emancipated herself from the friends who'd warned her about Daniel's controlling behaviour. She was too ashamed of her conduct to simply turn up on their doorstep with an apology and a plea for a roof for the night.

Her phone vibrated and, assuming it was Daniel, she was going to ignore it. However, it was an SMS message.

FAO: SINÉAD KELLY

Private and Confidential

Dear Mrs Kelly, following your successful completion of our puzzle, we are offering you a unique opportunity to start your life afresh. Please contact us as soon as possible to discuss.

It's a hoax, she told herself, shaking her head. Yet she found that her finger was hovering over the telephone number listed.

Chapter 9

EMILIA

For the second time in a handful of days, Emilia awoke to find herself lying in an unfamiliar bed. Only unlike before, it didn't panic her. With its off-white, yellowing walls, stiff sheets and blue plastic chairs, it was immediately clear this was a National Health Service building and not a private facility. She turned and squinted at a window looking out into the corridor. From between vertical blind slats she saw and heard nurses and patients going about their business.

Her head pounded sharp and heavy as the events of how she ended up there slotted together. She recalled escaping the last institution through corridors and a tunnel before reaching London's streets. And she remembered losing her footing and being hit by an oncoming vehicle. But in trying to push her recollections back further, she remained unable to shed any further light on anything about her past, besides her name.

Emilia ran her hands across her head and found a tiny lump no wider than a few millimetres on the crown and a raised bump the size of a large marble along the hairline. Her left side and thigh were sore to the touch, and likely bruised. To her relief, there were no debilitating plaster casts. She had escaped lightly. A drip had been inserted into a cannula in the back of her hand and a wireless heart monitor silently captured her rhythm. For a few moments, Emilia allowed herself to relax, before a chill ran through her when she recalled the cause of the accident – she had been trying to escape four blurred figures following her.

Who were they and what did they want from me? Were they following me from the first building? If so, what did I do to make them want to take me back? And who am I?

With no immediate answers, a frustrated Emilia distracted herself by taking in the rest of the room. A second external window offered a view across the hospital rooftops with sporadically scattered air-conditioning units and aerials. And on the sill was a vase of fresh pink flowers alongside a card. *Someone must know I'm here!* she thought. *They can help me piece it all together!*

But before she could read who it was from, the door to her room opened. Two casually attired female doctors, identifiable via lanyards hanging from their necks, appeared with a male uniformed nurse and somebody else typing notes into a tablet who read from a digital clipboard secured to the wall above her head.

'Good afternoon, Emilia. Is it okay if I call you that?' began the man whose name badge read, 'Dr Fazul Choudary, Senior Consultant'.

'How do you know my name?' she replied.

'You gave it to the Resus team when you were admitted three days ago.'

'And where am I?'

'King William hospital in Dulwich, south London.'

'What else did I tell you when I was brought in?'

'That you couldn't remember who you were but that you were being followed.'

Emilia nodded. For some reason, on her admission she had held back from telling them she had only just escaped from somewhere else. And she was reluctant to rectify it now. 'What's wrong with me?'

Dr Choudary consulted the notes before he continued. 'Physically, very little aside from some minor cuts and bruising. There was a risk of brain swelling which is why you were kept sedated until this morning. You were fortunate that the bodywork of an autonomous vehicle is designed to cause minimal impact in the event of an accident. However, mentally – and this is only according to your preliminary psychological evaluation and from what you told us on admission – you may be suffering from episodic memory loss. This means that while you know how to walk and talk and carry out bodily functions, your brain is struggling to encode and retrieve what you have done on a daily basis throughout your life. You can't figuratively go back in time to a specific event and remember it.'

The diagnosis was welcome; there had been moments when she thought she might be losing her mind. However, it left her none the wiser as to how she might rediscover her identity.

'Will it return?'

'In most patients, it does, given time. But we would like to perform an MRI scan of your brain to rule out any underlying cause.'

'No,' Emilia said quickly. Her immediate refusal took both Dr Choudary and his team by surprise. Something deep inside her was warning her not to allow anyone insight into the contents of her head.

'It's a non-invasive procedure that I would strongly advise you to consider ...' Dr Choudary continued, but Emilia was adamant and shook her head. 'Okay, but I wouldn't be doing my job if I didn't tell you I'd like to discuss this with you again.'

'I don't mean to be rude, but it's not up for debate. Just tell me what I need to do to get my memory back so I know who I am.'

'There's no one-fix solution as it can vary from patient to patient. But after further tests, we will have a greater idea of what might work for you, such as hypnosis, acupuncture, neurofeedback, bilateral sounds ... there's a lot we can do, but none of it is an exact science.'

Emilia became tearful after their departure. The notion that she might never know who she was again terrified her. She turned to lie on her side but a sharp pain tore through her ribcage, stealing her breath. Slowly, she slid further down the mattress and brought her knees to her chest.

The pain medication must have eased her to sleep because she awoke with a start when she sensed someone else was in the room with her. Without thinking, she clenched her fists, ready to lash out until she could see her visitor properly. He was a tall man, with dark, knotted eyebrows and thin lips. He had high cheekbones and almond-shaped eyes behind horn-rimmed glasses. He wore no lanyard around his neck and held no medical device in his hand, suggesting he was not a staff member.

He offered an audible sigh of relief as he approached her bed and leaned over her.

'Thank God,' he began. He gently manoeuvred her hair to one side and planted a gentle kiss on her cheek. Emilia pushed herself backwards.

'What are you doing?' she demanded. His muddled expression suggested it wasn't the response he had been expecting.

'I ... I'm sorry,' he said and edged away.

'Who are you?' Emilia asked.

'Do you not remember me?'

'Would I be asking if I did?'

'I'm Ted,' he said and offered Emilia a nervous smile. 'I'm your husband.'

Chapter 10

BRUNO, EXETER

The room was so silent; it was as if no world existed beyond theirs. Bruno lost all concept of time and wished they could remain in their own private universe for ever.

He couldn't lift his gaze from his son, who was sitting on the floor in the centre of the dimly lit room. He could just about make out Louie's eyes, wide-open and hypnotised by the twinkling lights as they danced across the ceiling and walls. Louie's mouth formed an 'o' shape, indicating that he was calm and relaxed. His father, however, was the opposite.

Bruno was grateful for the gloom, unwilling to display emotion even if it was in front of a boy who didn't recognise it in others. He slipped into the corridor outside, just as the family's support worker approached, flanked by a younger trainee.

'Good morning,' began Cally. 'We were just coming to check on you guys.' She instinctively picked up on his upset and asked her student to keep an eye on Louie in the sensory area as she led Bruno away. Inside a staff classroom, a whiteboard fixed to the wall read 'Coping with Autism Tantrums' and associated words like 'meltdown' and 'self-harm'. Bruno was experienced in them all.

'You think you've failed him, don't you?' she asked.

Bruno nodded.

'I promise you, every parent feels the same when they walk through our doors.'

'I told myself that no matter how hard it gets, I'd never give up on my son. I wouldn't abandon him. But that's just what I'm doing.'

'You're not, though. You are putting his needs above your own. Your circumstances mean you're unable to look after him but it doesn't mean you're abandoning him. This is Exeter's best facility for young people on the autistic spectrum. Louie will be cared for and supervised twenty-four hours a day by staff who've spent their careers training to help kids like him. He will thrive here, I promise you.'

'But what happens when the money runs out? You know I can only afford six months of care.'

'Let's worry about that further down the line when we need to. Now, shall we take him to his living quarters and settle him in properly?'

Returning to where he'd left Louie, Bruno placed an arm around his shoulder and encouraged him out of the room and into one of a dozen modules that made up the centre. Two other under-eighteens would be sharing Louie's living quarters alongside three live-in carers working round-the-clock shifts. At twelve years of age, Louie was the youngest resident but with the most needs.

They entered the bedroom, Louie first and then his father. Louie would be sleeping in here alone, but cameras and motion sensors would monitor him at night, alerting the staff to any problems. As he was non-verbal, a standard-issue monitor had also been inserted under the surface of his wrist to measure health issues that he couldn't communicate. Bruno had already laid out Louie's clothes and toys in strategic positions around the room so they were instantly recognisable to help with his transition. His favourite toy, a stuffed green Tyrannosaurus rex, was sitting upright on his pillow.

Bruno and Cally watched carefully as Louie tried to make sense of why all his possessions were now here and no longer at home. And when he began tapping the side of his head with his fingertips, his father recognised it as a sign of agitation. He removed his phone from his bag and passed it to Louie to play with. It was a useful calming tool that often stemmed outbursts of negative emotions.

'Leaving him alone for a few minutes each day over the last few weeks means he's used to spending time here,' Cally assured Bruno. 'When you feel ready, I'll see you back in the lounge.'

Bruno watched quietly as Louie worked his way around the phone with more skill than his father. He appeared to be playing some kind of complex word and shape puzzle that looked too advanced for someone who'd yet to reach his teens. But Louie had a habit of surprising his dad.

'What are you doing, mate?' he asked, peering over his son's shoulder. Bruno began recognising hidden patterns and numbers but Louie was way ahead of him, slotting them all together. Bruno's synaesthesia, known as Personification, was the most common; it enabled him to give human-like personalities to numbers, letters and days of the week. He would never know if it had been inherited by Louie. But Bruno assumed that it had and that it was much more powerful, enabling him to solve puzzles like this and others with lightning speed.

Louie looked at his father and showed him the completed puzzle, before directing his attention towards a box of Lego under the window. He frequently lost himself for hours in the world of colourful building blocks. It was Bruno's cue to leave. He only wished that his boy could say goodbye.

Bruno perched on the edge of the single bed, surveying his own room. To his left was a kitchenette, comprising only an oven, a sink and three cupboards. Ahead was a sofa-bed, a television, a wardrobe and a chest of drawers. The room's pitiful square footage could have fitted inside the lounge of his and Zoe's family home. Outside and across the corridor was a bathroom he shared with the owners of the Thai restaurant below. It was a world away from all he loved.

His home and most of its contents had been sold or auctioned to repay his mortgage arrears, for legal bills and for Louie's private care home. His wife and son were gone along with Bruno's determination and hope for a brighter future. The only plus in a world of minuses was that for now, Louie was receiving the best help money could buy.

Bruno had taken very little with him from the house he had been forced to leave. Family photographs had been stored in the Cloud, to be played on a loop and on a digital frame in Louie's room. Bruno, however, wanted no such reminders of Zoe around him. He didn't believe the accusations that made her sound like a predator prowling her office corridors, harassing colleagues and promising promotions in return for sex. But at the very least, she'd had an affair. Now when he thought about her, an image of her having sex with the man she died with obliterated fifteen years of marriage. He would never forgive her.

The alarm on his smart speaker sounded, making him aware of the time. He opened the bathroom cabinet and removed a tub of Vaseline. As a recent employee of online retailer 1-STOPSHOP, he was low down the pecking order of his warehouse depot job. And it meant that he was only permitted to wear the basic exoskeleton models used to lift heavy pallets. They were engineered to reduce joint pain and aching backs and had not been built with comfort in mind. Even covering his shoulders and wrists with Vaseline wasn't enough to stop the metal frame from leaving him chafed most days.

Suddenly his watch vibrated: it was an email alert congratulating him on solving a puzzle and urging him to respond as soon as possible. It was the third he'd received that week, along with several missed calls. He drew a blank when he tried to recall entering a competition, then remembered the game Louie had played on his phone. Louie must have completed it. Bruno wondered if there was a cash prize involved that might go towards paying for a seventh month at the care facility. It was worth a look, he decided, and opened it.

> What would you say if we offered you the opportunity to start your life again?

Once more he glanced around his bedsit. And without giving it any more thought, he pressed the 'read more' button.

** CONFIDENTIAL **

TOP SECRET: UK EYES ONLY, CLASSIFIED 'A'

THIS DOCUMENT IS THE PROPERTY OF HIS MAJESTY'S GOVERNMENT

MINUTES OF JOINT CYBER-ESPIONAGE / INTELLIGENCE COMMITTEE ASSESSMENT MEETING 11.6

'THE ALTERNATIVE APPROACH TO STORAGE OF CLASSIFIED DOCUMENTS'

** Please note this is an account of the minutes taken from the above meeting. Portions of text and certain participants have been redacted to prevent threats to security. **

LOCATION:

███████████, ███████

MEMBERS PRESENT:
Edward Karczewski, Operations Director, ███████ ███████
Dr Sadie Mann, Director of Psychiatric Evaluations
Dr M.J. Porter, Head of Neuroscience
███████ ███████ ███████, Ministry of Defence (MoD), Porton Down
███████ ███████, MI5

William Harris, HM Government's Minister for Central Intelligence

NON-MEMBERS PRESENT:
Prime Minister Diane Cline

PRIME MINISTER: Have you all lost your bloody minds?

EDWARD KARCZEWSKI: I appreciate that on face value, yes, it might appear that way. And I accept this is a very radical, revolutionary solution.

PRIME MINISTER: Might? It *might* appear that way? First you send our classified information off on its travels in the backs of lorries and boats and God knows what else and now you're trying to convince me that the fate of our country lies in the hands of people whose only qualification is solving a bloody puzzle? ████████████████ please tell me I'm misunderstanding something.

████████ ████████, MI5: My initial reaction was similar to yours, Diane. But please hear them out.

EDWARD KARCZEWSKI: It's much more complex than that, Prime Minister. I'd like to introduce Dr Porter, Head of Neuroscience at Dunston Laboratories. She is the leading scientist behind this procedure and can explain it in more detail.

DR PORTER: Prime Minister, what you're watching on the screen in front of you isn't just a puzzle. It's a complex configuration made up of three-dimensional images and letters, colours, shapes and numbers, all hurtling around at pace and in random directions. It's designed to test certain aspects of the brain's functions, such as recall, problem solving, identification and separation of information using the parts that interpret vision and hearing. To people with a condition called synaesthesia, this all makes perfect sense. What can take us hours or even days for our brains to interpret – if we can do it at all – they can locate in seconds.

PRIME MINISTER: My university flatmate had synaesthesia. It's where people see colours when they hear musical notes or time can have specific shape, isn't it? She swore blind she could taste flavours based on a photograph or a sound.

DR PORTER: That's correct. Approximately one in 280,000 people are born with a form of it. We believe it's a cross-wiring in the brain that leads to the blurring of senses. Our brains are split into four separate sections. Some synaesthetes are born with all four sections' connections uniquely overlapping. And it's that abnormality which will enable them to solve our puzzle that as yet, no computer algorithm can decipher.

PRIME MINISTER: Your use of the word *abnormality* concerns me.

DR PORTER: I assure you, the term is used in a positive way. Their abilities demonstrate how receptive their brains are to storing massive amounts of data, specifically when it's broken down into code. As you are aware, DNA is a single molecule that stores all the data that makes us who we are as individuals. But we can now turn anything into code, even voices and images. A limitless amount can be stored onto a single strand of DNA, the equivalent of seventy billion floppy disks. For four years, I've been leading a team of scientists turning everything hidden from public view in our nation's archives into binary code. It's now ready to be stored in microscopic DNA and injected into the part of the brain critical for memory and learning.

PRIME MINISTER: Can these selected people access this sensitive data?

DR PORTER: If they wish to, yes. But they will be trained not to. The DNA will be stored inside a plastic bead and injected into lesser used sections of their brains where the contents will disperse and can only be retrieved in a laboratory procedure where they are encouraged to migrate back to the bead. The bead cannot be transferred from one person to another or survive outside the body beyond our specialist laboratories. It is also biodegradable and after a period of five years, will dissolve and be absorbed into their system. All they've have learned will disappear with it.

EDWARD KARCZEWSKI: But by then, our nation's security will be permanently unhackable.

PRIME MINISTER: If this bead is so small, why not just store it somewhere else? Anywhere else? Somewhere completely off-grid. Not in a human ... perhaps an animal?

EDWARD KARCZEWSKI: It's an option that's been thoroughly investigated but only human brains have proved suitable. Besides, if it's stored anywhere else, a record of it would always exist somewhere, placing it at risk of being hacked and held to ransom.

DR PORTER: However, a person cannot be hacked. And who would think to look inside a human being?

PRIME MINISTER: But humans are fallible. They can be compromised.

EDWARD KARCZEWSKI: Not if they're of the correct mindset. We've calculated the risk potential of candidates turning rogue after we have rebuilt them and it's negligible. Each will be eager to start their lives afresh under a new identity and will have access to funds to make this happen. But first, over several intensive months of training, their consciousness will be stripped and rebuilt according to the criteria required for a successful deployment.

They will be taught to assess all risks and react accordingly, to trust no one, and to die or to kill for their country if necessary. Keeping themselves and what they know safe will be their only priority. Once their five years are complete, we will help them to relocate anywhere in the world they desire and they will be financially compensated.

PRIME MINISTER: And if they are, for example, discovered and tortured for what they know?

EDWARD KARCZEWSKI: We have developed a medical procedure to ensure the somatosensory cortex and thalamus do not recognise pain. So, our candidates could break a leg and feel nothing. Please read the attached contract of employment for further details.

PRIME MINISTER: And if they choose to sell or give our secrets away? I assume there to be consequences?

█████████ █████████, MI5: The candidates will sign the Official Secrets Act and will be reminded of the severe ramifications to any friends or families if they put the programme at any risk. We are prepared to punish not only them but anyone they have been close to by ███████ ████████ ████████ and if necessary, ████████ ████████ ████████ ████████ ████████.

They will be deemed an enemy of the state.

PRIME MINISTER: How do you propose to find these candidates?

DR SADIE MANN: Mass media and targeted online advertising. Those who complete the puzzle in the fastest time will demonstrate a defined ability to retain and process data. Under anti-terrorism laws, we have access to every recorded online click a British citizen makes. Our analysts will gather a candidate's personal data from hundreds of private and public sources, including their phones, work and home Wi-Fi to make estimates about their personalities and how they might fare in different scenarios. Entrants will be filtered until we have the most suitable candidates and they will be invited for an interview. Inside this document you will find in detail everything they will undergo in the programme.

** EDWARD KARCZEWSKI has offered printed documents to each person in the room **

PRIME MINISTER: Where will you hide them once their training is complete?

████████ ████████, MI5: They are free to travel to wherever they please within the confines of the British Isles.

PRIME MINISTER: And how do we follow them? Do we implant tracking devices in their wrists like we do with our children?

EDWARD KARCZEWSKI: There will be no way to follow them either by GPS or by satellite. If we can't find them, our enemies can't either. I am the only person who will know their identities and roughly, their whereabouts.

████████ ████████, MI5: Other members of this programme will be aware of how to communicate with them. The public message board ReadWell is the largest online book club in the world with twenty million subscribers. Our 'Minders' will regularly log on for updates and only if their mission is at risk will we send them a recall notice to pre-assigned safe houses.

PRIME MINISTER: William, if it came to it, have you calculated the cost of giving in to the Hacking Collective's demands?

WILLIAM HARRIS: As our economy has grown and we are now one of the world's fifteen wealthiest countries, we estimate the one- to two-trillion-pounds mark.

PRIME MINISTER: I need time to consider this.

EDWARD KARCZEWSKI: Unfortunately, we don't have that luxury. After the attack on the lorry, our data is once again vulnerable.

PRIME MINISTER: You must all appreciate that if this crackpot scheme of yours backfires, it's my name that will for ever be associated with bankrupting our economy. That is a legacy worse than taking us to war with no proof of weapons of mass destruction, the Brexit referendum or the response to Covid-19.

EDWARD KARCZEWSKI: I understand that, Prime Minister. But we need to give our programmers and engineers time to find a way of stopping the Hacking Collective, securing critical infra-structures, and creating deterrence tools and an infallible, unhack-able system. And we estimate it will take at least four to five years to create it from scratch. The Minders will give us the peace of mind and breathing space to do just that.

PRIME MINISTER: And when will your programme be ready to roll out?

EDWARD KARCZEWSKI: Very soon, once we iron out some teething issues.

DR PORTER: They are very minor and I am confident it can happen within the next couple of months.

EDWARD KARCZEWSKI: Are you sure of that …

THE MINDERS

DR PORTER: I stake my reputation on it.

WILLIAM HARRIS: This is about staying one step ahead of the enemy, Prime Minister. We need to protect ourselves now and make sure we are future proof. Our freedom depends upon it.

PART TWO

PART TWO

CONTRACT OF EMPLOYMENT

I [INSERT NAME], have been selected as a suitable candidate for Operation ███████ ███████. I agree to becoming a data storage device of confidential information relating to the United Kingdom and its overseas territories, allies and enemies.

I am aware my further involvement in the programme is confidential and subject to the Official Secrets Act.

By participating, I provide my explicit consent to the medical and surgical procedures outlined below to be performed by medically trained representatives of His Majesty's Government.

The proposed medical procedures involve:
- Injecting genetically enhanced, microscopic DNA containing the confidential information into the subject's pyramidal cells of the brain's limbic system.
- Invasive neurostimulation to improve learning and handling of stressful situations.
- Thalamus manipulation to provide significant reduction in feeling physical and emotional pain/consciousness.
- Ongoing psychological assessment and re-education.

The procedures have been explained to me, in terms I have understood, including information about: (1) how the procedures are to be performed; (2) associated risks to me personally which may include, but are not limited to, strokes, depression, anxiety, paranoia, schizophrenia, reduction in pain and emotional sympathy, resulting in mutilation, and harm to self and others, and infertility.

In exchange for my service to King and country, I will receive recompense to ensure I can live a fulfilled life in my chosen location within the United Kingdom for the five years I will be a Minder. I will be required to adhere to all policies and rules which include:

- Severing all ties with my former life, including family, employers, friends etc.
- Maintaining a normal existence so as not to draw attention to myself.
- Avoiding all internet/online usage which could result in a trail being left.
- Not to divulge in any way the confidential information I am retaining.

PROTECTION OF THE INFORMATION I RETAIN IS PARAMOUNT. VIOLATION OF THE FULL TERMS I HAVE BEEN PROVIDED IN TRAINING WILL RESULT IN REMOVAL FROM THE PROGRAMME, AND WHEN NECESSARY, CRIMINAL PROSECUTION, PERSECUTION OF MY FAMILY OR MY JUSTIFIABLE KILLING.

SIGNED . . . .
DATE . . . .

WITNESS . . . .
DATE . . . .

Chapter 11

FLICK, ALDEBURGH, SUFFOLK

Name: Flick Kennedy

Previous Name: ██████ ██████

Age: 36

Previous Occupation: Restaurateur

Dependents: None

Strengths: Quick to learn; adaptable; loyal

Weaknesses: A conscience; contemplative; self-critical

As the driverless robo-taxi made its way towards the coastal town, an unexpected cloud of summer rainfall hovered above it. Fine droplets gently drizzled against the windscreen as Flick absorbed the countryside passing her by.

The changing climate wasn't discouraging ramblers in waterproof jackets from following well-beaten paths through the flat fenlands. And something about the pigs taking shelter under their corrugated-iron sties made her smile. This was already a completely different world from the one she had left in London that morning. Here, there was space to breathe.

Flick was vaguely familiar with the Tudor town of Aldeburgh, located on the Suffolk coast. She had spent a long weekend there years earlier when she had tagged along on a thirtieth-birthday celebration weekend for Heidi, a friend of her brother Theo. It was a much more sedate weekend than she'd imagined. Instead of non-stop drinking, it involved beach walks, coffees in cafes and gorging on pub lunches and the seafoods the town prided itself upon.

Once equipped with a completely new identity and history, Flick had been given the choice to relocate to almost anywhere she wanted within the British Isles, her home town of London being the exception. Aldeburgh was the first place that sprang to mind. Perhaps its sedentary nature might be the perfect antidote to the constant cycle of depression she had found herself swallowed up by in London.

It had also helped that the last four months of intense physical and mental training and re-education had altered Flick's perception of herself, her past and the decisions she'd made. It had been like an internal spring-clean. Christopher Bailey was no longer going to dictate her past, present or future.

'Taxi, pull over,' she said aloud and the cab decelerated, choosing a layby adjacent to the beach to come to a halt. She withdrew a blank, black numberless credit card and held it up to the paypoint until the door opened. The card resembled every other one but was completely untraceable, and gave her almost unlimited funds with which to kick-start her new life. All her possessions were now tucked inside a blue canvas rucksack slung over her shoulder. Everything else was consigned to an anonymous lock-up unit somewhere in Wales.

Her family and friends were also consigned to her past. Flick couldn't inform anyone where she was going or what she was doing before she vanished from their lives. The team charged with rebuilding her had used her identity to inform her contacts by email that she was leaving London to travel the world for the foreseeable future and they could follow her adventures via social media. Carefully curated fake photographs of her had already started appearing on Instagram and Facebook and were updated regularly. Phony location check-ins and replies to direct messages were created by an algorithm. Her bank accounts, mortgage, birth certificate, driving licence, National Insurance number, National Identity Card and any reference to the old Flick Kennedy were frozen.

She had been trained to alter everything about herself, from her favoured brand of clothes and perfume to the supermarkets she shopped at, the colour of nail polish she wore and the beverages she picked at cafes and bars. All that remained of her past was what she chose to remember.

Flick exited the taxi and ignoring the rain, she reached inside her jacket for a packet of cigarettes that weren't there. *Old habits die hard*, she thought. She made her way on foot across the shingled beach towards the relatively calm North Sea. Above her, a rainbow arched from empty fields towards the middle of the expanse of water. Suffused with excitement and possibility, she wanted to dive in and swim until she reached its end. Instead, she dropped her rucksack to the ground, removed her socks and trainers, rolled up her jeans and paddled.

A grin crept across her face. She couldn't recall the last time anything or anyone had made that happen.

To Flick's relief, Aldeburgh high street had changed very little since she'd last walked along it. By avoiding chain stores and favouring small independent boutiques, the town hadn't suffered from the continuing boom in online retail, unlike many of its contemporaries. Clothes shops, fine art galleries and book retailers nestled amongst staples like cafes, pubs and an abundance of fish-and-chip shops, all untouched by e-commerce.

Inside a cafe, she ordered an Indian spice herbal tea, sat at a table in the corner and reached for her standard-issue mobile phone. It was the one gadget she was permitted and allowed access to a single site – ReadWell, the world's largest website for booklovers. Millions of subscribers regularly used it to discuss novels, share opinions and leave reviews. She searched the site until she found a discussion thread with the title of Shakespeare's play *The Two Noble Kinsmen*. There were no posts under its heading which was good news. A message there would indicate something had happened and her handler Karczewski was recalling her to a safe house. She had been assured the chances of that happening were negligible.

Next on her to-do list was choosing somewhere to stay. She made her way back to the far end of the high street and to the digital information board listing a commercial breakdown of the area. Instead of sending suggestions to her phone, she had to memorise the locations of all hotels and bed and breakfasts. The smallest caught her attention and after a two-minute walk, she arrived.

As far as she could tell, the two-storey property with a 'vacancies' board in its front window contained two entrance and exit points. A camera was installed above a secure modern front door. Aside from that and a cable exchange cabinet two doors away, Flick reasoned the technology inside was likely to be limited, which suited her.

Driftwood sculptures were scattered about its front garden, surrounded by yellow rose bushes and a selection of vegetable crops in raised beds. The brickwork's rendering was painted a nautical blue and there was a first-floor balcony and seats offering an unspoiled view of the sea. It was so far removed from her own contemporary London apartment that it was just what Flick was looking for.

She knocked on the door and caught her reflection in the window. She hadn't been this toned and fit since she trained in Muay Thai martial arts classes in her twenties.

The programme's self-defence courses and regular gym workouts had helped her to shed more than 2.5 kilos. The cheekbones she hadn't seen in years had reappeared, along with the sparkle in her brown eyes.

A young woman wearing baggy clothes and with hair tied loosely in a topknot answered. Her appearance was at odds with the building's quaint presentation.

'Hi, do you have any vacancies?' Flick began.

'We do, come in, come in,' she replied enthusiastically and ushered Flick inside. 'Would you like to see the rooms we have?'

Flick examined the lounge and its kitsch floral wallpaper, matching curtains and sofa fabric. 'No, I'm sure it's fine,' she replied.

'I know what you're thinking,' said the girl. 'It's like Laura Ashley and Cath Kidston came to visit and exploded, isn't it?'

'It has a charm about it.'

'It was my mum's place, she passed away last year. Alzheimer's. It got the better of her a fortnight before the meds to cure it were given a licence and became available to buy.'

'Oh, I'm sorry.'

'Thank you.' For a second, her gaze fell and Flick recognised her grief was still raw. 'I've taken it on until I either decide what to do with it or I'm swallowed up and spat out by the chintz. I'm Grace, by the way.'

The two women shook hands as Grace explained the rates and amenities. 'How long do you think you might be staying for?'

Flick shrugged. 'I have no idea.'

'Shall I put you down for a week for now?'

'That sounds perfect.'

Later and alone in her room, Flick unpacked her few possessions from her rucksack and placed them inside an old oak wardrobe. Then she cracked open the window, lay back on the candlewick bedcover and spread her body out into a star shape.

She closed her eyes and took in a handful of deep breaths through her nose and released them from her mouth. Even from inside her room, the salt in the sea air brought a warmth to her skin. *This is what happiness smells like*, she thought.

Chapter 12

CHARLIE, MANCHESTER

Name: Charlie Nicholls

Previous Name: ██████ ██████

Age: 25

Previous Occupation: Graphic designer

Dependents: None

Strengths: Determined; sociable; capricious; focused

Weaknesses: Headstrong; prone to spontaneity

Charlie opened the curtains that ran the width of his fiftieth-storey hotel room.

He turned off the lights by hand, having already deactivated the room's OS and all Wi-Fi capabilities, and gazed across Manchester's dusky landscape. He dropped the thick white towel that covered his waist and it fell into a crumpled heap on the floor. Naked, he rested his forehead against the glass, rubbed his hands across his sculpted torso and positioned them by his side. Then he closed his eyes and imagined plummeting to the ground before catching flight.

'This will be the headspace you return to if your thoughts become too intense or muddled,' his programme therapist had advised. 'And in the early days, there will be occasions when it will happen. Think of this as a form of self-hypnosis. Use this as your release.'

Charlie thought of the wind catching his body and pulling him back up into the sky. There, he circled the city below him, swooping and diving, always out of sight and aware he could fly in any path as long as it was forward.

He opened his eyes and pushed himself back into a standing position. He had once been ashamed of his nudity, but now it didn't embarrass him. In the tallest building in the city centre, there was nobody to see him, unless a drone had been deployed. And while he'd learned the response techniques should he ever find himself being tracked by one, it was improbable.

With a new appearance, a new backstory and nothing tethering him to his old life, Charlie was even more alone here than he'd been back in his home town of Portsmouth. There, he'd been waiting for someone else to give him meaning. But here, he had no such concerns.

Manchester wasn't how he'd imagined it before his arrival that afternoon. After expanding to become Britain's second-largest city, it had hidden much of its historically important architecture behind neon advertising signs, rotating billboards and giant television screens. A city couldn't afford to dwell on the past when money was a factor. Everything was now a moving image. Even the driverless trams and buses were adorned with screens that changed what they were promoting by reading online purchases from your phone. However, the algorithms struggled with Charlie's device. The standard-issue clamshell was so featureless that when he'd disembarked the train inside Piccadilly station, the screens on a passing bus repeated targeted ads for the woman in front of him, offering him sanitary towels.

La Maison du Court was the first hotel he'd spotted as he wandered through the city carrying all his worldly belongings inside a rucksack strapped to his back. The towering skyscraper housed a grand, marble entrance and floor-to-ceiling fish tanks. Fresh flowers in vases towered above him and a waterfall flowed behind the reception desk. It was far removed from the Travelodges he'd been used to. But access to the programme's funding meant he could afford the best and he vowed to begin his new adventure in style.

Charlie had been kept away from the outside world during his training. He picked a rolling news channel on a television to watch as he lay inside a warm, soapy bath. It felt quite old-fashioned to rely on the television to bring him news as for his whole adult life, digital assistants had given him access to it where and when he required it. Like other obsolete tasks such as reading a physical copy of a newspaper or using a key to unlock a door, it was going to take some getting used to.

His stomach rumbled just as his door buzzed and opened itself. He had not needed to slip on his towel when room service turned out to be an automated trolley that wheeled itself into the room. The menu had offered Farm or FabLab meats, the latter an epithet for Fabricated Meats and an inexpensive option bioengineered in laboratories from animal cells. Charlie had decided to treat himself and chose Farm – and the priciest veal steak on the menu. He glanced at the empty seat at the table next to him and briefly wondered what it might be like to have someone to share this with.

Charlie logged on to the only website his phone could access, the ReadWell message board. To his relief, a quick search revealed no response to *The Two Noble Kinsmen* thread.

He devoured the last mouthful of the tender meat and thought of his old friends Stelfox and Travis and what they might think if they could see him now, dining on expensive foods in a hotel that would cost them a week's wages for a one-night stay. He raised a glass of mineral water to silently toast them.

With his stomach fit to burst, Charlie sent the trolley back to the kitchens and examined his appearance in the bathroom mirror. He approved of what he saw. The beard he once relied on to hide his pitted, acne-scarred cheeks was now unnecessary following skin resurfacing treatment. He ran his fingers over his chest and stomach; everything was tenser and tighter since he'd lost 20 kilos. He'd worked hard with personal trainers and learned combat techniques, self-defence and weapons training from former SAS soldiers. And he'd removed all junk food from his diet to create this new, leaner version of himself.

He wondered how many other Minders there were and if, like him, they'd taken advantage of the cosmetic procedures on offer. Charlie had replaced his crooked teeth with sparkling new veneers, and straightened the wonky nose he'd twice broken playing football. Three tattoos he'd had since his teenage years had also been lasered from his chest, arm and left buttock. He rubbed his fingertips against one another and marvelled at how smooth they were since his prints had been erased. He felt like a completely new man because that's exactly what he was.

Yawning, he dimmed the lights again, returned to the window to rest his head and close his eyes. And once more, he imagined himself in flight.

Chapter 13

SINÉAD, SUNDERLAND

Name: Sinéad Kelly

Previous Name: ███████ ████████

Age: 33

Previous Occupation: Space debris coordinator/office worker

Dependents: None

Strengths: Appraises all scenarios well; methodical; organised

Weaknesses: Compassionate; prone to guilt and introspection

It took Sinéad around twenty minutes to reach the summit of Sunderland's Tunstall hills.

She had last completed the walk with college friends Imani and Cally some two decades earlier. They had accompanied her on the 288-mile journey from her home town of Bristol to offer their support as she carried the small mahogany caskets containing her parents' ashes. Today she held only a small bouquet of red and white carnations.

Sunderland had been the first place her parents relocated to after emigrating from Ireland, so it seemed fitting that following their deaths during the Mumbai tsunami that claimed 2,000 lives, their ashes were cast to the breeze atop of a high hill overlooking the north-eastern city. Sinéad was one of very few people who knew the truth of what really happened that morning in the Indian city. And of everything she'd learned, it gnawed at her the most intensely and most frequently.

The wind brushed her cheeks and caught her new shoulder-length hair extensions. It was the first alteration she had requested from the programme's image-enhancement team after years of keeping it short to please Daniel. It was also no longer a nondescript mousey colour, but a rich brown with subtle lowlights. And she couldn't stop running her fingers through it. It was one of a handful of alterations made to her appearance. Laser eye surgery meant she had no more use for her glasses, and the combat techniques and Pilates had made her physically fitter. She gently ran a fingertip against the edges of her eyelids, tugging ever so gently at the recently implanted lashes, as if challenging them to come loose. Once, she would have pulled at them until they detached in their twos and threes by the root, only ceasing when her eyes watered. But not any longer.

If only Daniel could see me now, she thought, then reminded herself that he'd still probably find fault with something.

Amongst the many techniques Sinéad had learned throughout her training was how to breathe again. Instead of the short, shallow bursts she now drew in deep breaths, pushing her stomach out as she inhaled and drawing it in as she let the air out. It was a simple exercise but one that she had come to rely upon to keep her gathered.

There had been little time to dwell on anything other than the programme during her training. But now that Sinéad was completely on her own for the first time, she wasn't sure how she should be reacting. She couldn't remember the last time she had so much control of her life; it was going to take time to acclimatise.

As would never seeing Daniel again. She had long cast him aside, but she'd yet to completely forgive herself for allowing him to gaslight her for so long.

Why did I keep giving in to him? she regularly asked herself. *If I'd stood my ground earlier might we have had a better marriage?* Her therapists had suggested not, agreeing that her relationship was doomed from the start. Without her parents, Sinéad's desperate need to be loved and taken care of and Daniel's desire for coercive control meant that together, they forged a co-dependency, not a relationship. And it would likely have remained that way indefinitely, had it not been for Joanna's intervention.

Her handler Karczewski had already informed Sinéad that Daniel reported her missing to the police five days after she abandoned her marriage. She wondered what had taken him so long, and assumed it was because he was expecting her to return with her tail between her legs. But now she was out from under his spell, hell would freeze over before Sinéad returned.

'What will happen if Daniel tries to find me?'

'He won't succeed,' said Karczewski.

'I know my husband. He won't give up without a fight.'

'We are maintaining surveillance on his activities and we will continue to thwart all his efforts. We have led a private investigator he's hired to believe you may now be living somewhere in Europe. That, of course, will be a wild-goose chase and once you are released from training, if we can't locate you, then neither can he. The only way you will see him again is if you choose to.'

Joanna had likely heard on the grapevine that the couple were no longer together. It was doubtful that Daniel would publicly admit his wife had left him. He had probably spun a lie about her disappearance. 'He can tell everyone I was a whore who slept with half of Bristol if he wants to,' she told one of the counsellors. 'I'd actually prefer them to think I have a will of my own than be remembered as the pushover I really was.'

On her departure from the facility that morning, Sinéad had purchased a non-autonomous car and filled the boot with supplies for the long journey ahead. But first she had posted a thank-you card to Joanna. She left the inside blank, hoping Joanna might guess its sender.

Like the pieces of the online puzzle she'd solved the afternoon she escaped from her marriage, everything was slotting into place. It was that same afternoon when she had plucked up the courage to dial the number contained in the message inviting her to attend an interview for the chance to start a new life. An hour later, she found herself picking up a ticket that had been reserved in her name at Bristol Temple Meads train station to London. She checked into a hotel room that had been organised for her and the following morning, she nervously awaited an interview with a panel. The timing couldn't have been better. She had nothing – and no one – to lose and after a series of scans, tests and medicals, she passed through to the next round. The rest of the day was a blur.

Sinéad placed the bouquet of carnations on Tunstall's grassy hillside, propping them up against a rock. Then she took in one last view of the city landscape. It would be a few more hours before she reached Scotland and her reinvention could begin in earnest.

She vowed not to take the past with her. There was no room for ghosts in her present. She would no longer punish herself over her failings, only learn from them. She'd forgive those like Daniel who had taken from her and put to rest those she had lost, with one exception. Sinéad would never want to forget *her*.

Chapter 14

EMILIA

'What do I know about myself?' Emilia said aloud.

She typed her name using capital letters into the tablet Ted had left her with. She couldn't even spell the surname they shared. Then her fingers hovered above the virtual keyboard as she came to an abrupt halt. A week after waking up in a south London hospital and following a barrage of tests and procedures, she was still no closer to learning the truth about who she was.

There were a handful of things she'd learned. She had next to no interest in film and television but enjoyed listening to classical music. She preferred clothes that covered her, not attire that left little to the imagination. She understood how the machines in her hospital room operated. And she was married to a man she didn't recognise.

Emilia used the tablet to see if the internet could shed a sliver of light upon her identity. But as far as she could tell, she had no social media presence. There was no Amazon account in her name, no LinkedIn profile, no subscriptions to online publications and no match when she took a selfie and tried to image-search it.

Through the open door to her hospital room, she spotted her husband and two broad-shouldered men approaching. Yesterday, Ted explained they were part of his security detail but when she'd questioned him further, he changed the subject. She'd Googled his name too but that also drew a blank.

Being married should have reassured Emilia that there was at least one person in the world who knew her as well as she had once known herself. Yet she felt as attached to him as she might a stranger. She did not find him physically appealing; his constant asking of questions irritated her especially when he offered little in the way of answers. She could only assume that at some point in her life, he had ticked her boxes. Because now, they were blank.

When Ted had returned from lunch yesterday, she had pretended to be asleep but overheard him in the corridor discussing her progress with Dr Choudary. Emilia was uncomfortable at the thought of being released into the care of a man she didn't remember, even if he was her husband. In the hospital she felt safe; much more so than the first building she'd woken up in. She glanced out of the window across the rooftops and into the hospital grounds. The unknown of the outside world scared her.

'Have you remembered anything else?' asked Ted, greeting her with an encouraging smile. She shook her head and felt unexpectedly guilty for disappointing him. 'No, sorry.'

'Don't apologise.' He rubbed her forearm as if to reassure her that it didn't matter. But it did matter to her, it was the *only* thing that mattered.

Ted returned to their table from the self-service section of the hospital cafe carrying a tray of toast, a blueberry muffin and a black coffee for Emilia – her favourites, he said – and a banana and fresh orange juice for himself. He moved his hands to hold hers. Yesterday, he'd caught her out with the same level of intimacy. This morning, she was prepared and withdrew them before contact was made. They rested on her thighs.

'What's your first memory?' he began.

'As I told you before, it's of waking up in that other place.'

'And you don't know how you got there?'

'No. I only remember feeling that I had to get away, but not why. And something's been bothering me. I must have some kind of link to it because I knew the codes to the electronic door locks.' Emilia's chest tightened when she thought about it again. 'Ted, I need your help. I need you to tell me what you know about me.'

'Darling, your consultant warned us not to bombard you with information as it might be too much to grasp immediately ... you need time to get used to being around me so that hopefully, your memories return naturally and not by being prompted.'

'Put yourself in my shoes. Imagine what it's like not having the first clue who you are; being told you're married to someone you don't recognise, and that one person who is supposed to be fighting your corner is refusing to tell you anything. How do you think that might make you feel?'

'I understand, I really do.'

'Do you? Because sometimes it doesn't seem like that.'

'It's not easy for me either, seeing my wife like this. But Dr Choudary told us ...'

'No, I only have your word that he told "us" because I was asleep when you had that conversation. He told *you*.'

'What do I have to gain by lying to you? Don't you think I want you to get better?'

Emilia let out a long, exhausted breath. Her head drooped as she cupped her coffee mug. 'Of course you do. I'm sorry, I didn't mean it. But we've been going around in circles for days and my memory isn't improving. I just don't remember anything.'

Swallowing hard didn't dislodge the lump in her throat and she started to cry. She didn't want to be this vulnerable in front of a stranger but holding back was proving impossible. This time, Emilia didn't recoil when Ted's hands went under the table. They were soft and warm and strangely reassuring. She wondered if they'd been a close couple.

'Have you considered this might be for the best?' he asked gently. 'There are some people who would kill for the opportunity to start their lives again, baggage free. At this juncture, you have a unique opportunity, to be whomever you want to be. Isn't it even a little tempting?'

It was a peculiar question as her answer could have backfired on him. If she were to hit the restart button, what was to say she'd want him as part of her new life? Emilia gave his suggestion little thought before she answered with a firm 'No.'

Ted's shoulders slumped and he withdrew his hands from hers. He appeared thoughtful, as if searching for the right words before finally continuing. 'Okay, if you are sure this is what you really want then let's start.' Emilia held her breath.

'You were born in St Neots, Cambridge, and you will be thirty-seven years old on November the fourth. Your parents were Alison and Richard, both of whom passed away within two years of one another when you were in your late twenties. Your dad died from pancreatic cancer, your mum from complications following heart surgery. You and I met through friends on a blind date twelve years ago and as corny as it sounds, it was as if we were drawn together like magnets. We married two years later at a private ceremony in City Hall, New York. Our only witness was our photographer. We don't have children as we mutually decided that parenthood wasn't for us. My work often takes me to Europe while you worked in London in banking for Barnett-Vincent Brothers. We live with our dogs Riley Blue and Peggy in a house we designed and built ourselves.'

Emilia sat upright in her seat, hanging on to his every word. But it was as if Ted was talking about a stranger because none of it resonated with her. He must have recognised it in her expression because he removed a phone from his pocket and unfolded it. His Cloud contained images of their wedding, reportage-style photographs taken against colourful murals in Brooklyn, along with other pictures and videos of them together and apart over the years. They included her university graduation celebrations, her as a child with her parents, and pictures taken on beaches around the world. It was clear she had lived an exciting, adventurous life. Only she didn't remember a single second of it.

It unexpectedly all became too much for Emilia. She pushed Ted's phone to one side and hurried towards a sign for the unisex bathrooms. Inside, she splashed cold tapwater to cool her flushed face and patted it dry with a paper towel before catching sight of herself in the mirror. Her uncombed, long blonde hair resembled a bird's nest piled upon her crown and was held in place with a pencil and a rubber band. She was wearing jogging bottoms and a loose-fitting baggy sweatshirt that Ted had brought with him from home along with underwear and toiletries. She felt uncomfortable being this scruffy but didn't know why. *Is this how I always dress?* The question was innocuous but represented all she didn't know.

'You said that you often work in Europe but you used the past tense to describe my job,' she began when she returned to Ted's table. He appeared relieved to see her, as if he'd been half-expecting her to disappear again. 'You said "worked". Why?'

She noted a hesitancy before he replied; his gaze left hers for the briefest of moments as if he were unsure how to answer. 'You decided that you wanted a change so you were on a career break.' Ted's pupils were dilated. He wasn't being honest with her.

'There's something you're not telling me,' she said and he shuffled in his seat.

'Let's leave it for today, shall we?'

As he folded up his phone and slipped it into his pocket, this time it was Emilia's turn to grasp her husband's hand.

'What happened?' she asked. Only when Ted winced did she realise the strength of her grip. She let go. 'Please, I have to know.'

'It wasn't your fault. You were working horrendous, horrendous hours, sometimes nineteen, twenty a day. It was unsustainable. You weren't sleeping, you weren't eating properly and the pressure you were putting upon yourself and your team was intolerable. It's no surprise that something had to give.'

'And that something was me?'

'Yes, you suffered a mental breakdown.'

'Was there a specific trigger that pushed me?'

Again, Ted glared at her as if begging her not to ask him to expand. But Emilia wasn't ready to back down. 'I can take it,' she said. 'Tell me.'

'One of your team members was driven to breaking point. She arrived at your offices one morning and stabbed four of your colleagues to death before she tried to kill you.'

Chapter 15

FLICK, ALDEBURGH, SUFFOLK

Flick examined her mobile phone from all angles: she vaguely recalled playing with an old clamshell like this belonging to her father back when she was a child. The case of the clunky, ugly, silver obsolete gadget was reflecting light from the sea ahead and that was the most interesting thing about it. It had no working camera, games to play, text message facility, emails, cloud access, voicemail or GPS. She couldn't download apps or maps and internet access was restricted to only the ReadWell website. It wasn't associated with any network and piggybacked other people's mobile phone hotspots or Wi-Fi to make a connection. The phone was completely incognito and left no digital footprint attributable to her.

'Every Minder will get this exact same model,' Karczewski had advised.

'I thought the idea was to blend in? This'll make us stand out.'

'You'll simply tell people you're part of that ever-expanding Neo-Luddite movement that rejects intrusive technology like the kind found on phones.'

'But won't it seem hypocritical if I then use a credit card?'

'Since the abolition of cash as a valid payment form, you don't have a choice.'

Flick soon found it liberating to be living off-grid and not beholden to any form of technology. The programme strictly forbade Minders from using anything that might lead to their identification. That meant no email address, social media accounts, online shopping, or banking. Everything was to be paid for in person via the credit card she had been issued and that was funded by dozens of untraceable foreign shell accounts. Only Karczewski had any idea of where she was.

From her bench by Aldeburgh's Crag Path boating pond, she watched a dad with two young children pushing paper sailboats. Flick hoped to make new friends while she was here but it wasn't going be an easy process. What she knew had to be protected at all costs. She had been trained to trust no one and because friendships were a two-way street, connections were going to be hard to make for someone who travelled only in one direction.

As she relaxed, her brain began casually decoding random fragments of implanted data. It was against the rules but not always possible to control. Today, she saw the face of a much-loved politician who had been caught in a hushed-up, potentially career-destroying sex scandal. Next came a once redacted but now readable report of secret military operations and coded maps of British weapons bases hidden worldwide. Then she learned the truth behind the closure of the nearby Sizewell nuclear power station and its hidden catastrophic environmental impact. The ruthlessness and power her country's leaders had over the truth was frightening.

It was days after the implant procedure when similar details began seeping into her conscious mind. It was as if she was recalling someone else's memories and it fascinated her. Karczewski advised her it was all perfectly normal and part of the healing process for knowledge to occasionally leak like it was today.

To harness them, Flick put into practice a range of mind-fulness routines. She closed her eyes and concentrated only on what she could hear in the present; the animated voices of the children in front of her, the gentle thud of boules landing with a thump on crushed stone and seagulls squawking as they circled wooden fishing shacks. Soon, the insight she was a party to migrated back into the box from which it'd escaped.

She took a leisurely walk along the sea front and in the direction of the neighbouring village of Thorpeness. Her brother Theo's dog Rupert would have loved this hike and she briefly considered if adopting a pet of her own might keep her company. *No dependents*, she reminded herself. If she needed to beat a hasty retreat, she couldn't allow anything to slow her down, not even a canine companion.

It was still the week of her arrival and it wasn't the first time she'd walked this five-mile round trip. Again, she made mental notes of the landscape, focusing on bridleways, roads that went somewhere and others that led nowhere, fields with locked gates and low hedgerows and those surrounded by streams or marshland. She knew the area off by heart and had mentally mapped out a dozen potential escape routes. She hoped she'd never have call to use one.

Later, on her return, Flick chose to walk along a decom-missioned railway track that had been converted into a public walkway. She passed ramblers and dog walkers, all making a point of either smiling at her or saying hello. She was learning to ignore her natural instinct as a Londoner to be suspicious of friendly types. There were many aspects of this new life that would take time to become accustomed to.

Yet despite all the hope that filled her, something buried inside pecked away at her like a vulture picking at a carcass. *It's all too good to be true*, it warned. *Your time here is limited. You'd better lead with your head because your heart will get you killed.*

Chapter 16

CHARLIE, MANCHESTER

Mapping out a city centre using his long-term memory was a challenge. Much of his first week had been spent holding a fold-up map, a novelty for his generation who'd grown up relying on smart glasses or phones to direct them. But anything that could track his whereabouts was strictly off limits. He'd used the map to navigate every street, cul-de-sac and dual carriageway, along with train routes, taxi ranks and trams until he knew Manchester off by heart.

It was an ever-expanding metropolis and its tentacles spread out in so many directions that it would have taken months to put to memory each area beyond the inner ring road. The city's redevelopment over the last two decades had seen an influx of workers relocating there, especially from the south of England. Demand for housing meant buildings of historic interest and high-rise offices and apartments jostled for space in the sky. It also housed its own slum area where low-income immigrants had made their homes inside a sea of tents before the country's borders went into lockdown.

Meanwhile, high-speed trains meant a commute from London to Manchester took as long as getting from one side of the capital to the other. The daytime footfall of residents, tourists, shoppers, office workers and shop staff followed by the night-time demands for bars, restaurants and entertainment centres meant it rivalled New York as a city that didn't sleep.

Charlie had become proficient in what one of his trainers had named 'dry-cleaning' – a counter-surveillance technique to ensure he wasn't being tailed. He made mental notes of anyone he saw more than once in a short timeframe and cars that slowed needlessly in his proximity. He avoided patrolling police and traffic officers wearing body-armour cameras. He ate his meals in a rotation of different cafes so as not to create a pattern and he mixed his outfits to keep his appearance varied. He checked to see who might be walking behind him using the reflections in shop and car windows or the paintwork of dark vehicles. And he also carried a spare set of jeans, a sweatshirt and trainers in his backpack for if he needed to change quickly. After each day of exploration, Charlie slept soundly knowing he and his secrets were safe.

The novelty of living in a plush hotel had yet to wear off, but he was aware that it wasn't going to be conducive to a spiritually rewarding second life. He could afford to remain there for his five-year tenure, but he needed a purpose, otherwise he would be replicating one non-existence with another. Charlie knew that he performed better when he was in a routine and around others. A job would help.

Unable to access the internet on a device of his own, he had made use of Manchester Central Library's community computers to search for employment. And there was one role in which he could utilise all he'd learned during training – a sector referred to as Monetised Mothering. For a monthly subscription, individuals and businesses hired personal mentors and coaches in just about any subject from life skills to gym instructors and educators. And clients didn't need to leave their houses or offices to make use of them. 'Virtual-reality systems bring the world to your door,' the advert read. 'If you have the skills to help clients change their lives, then we want you.'

Following a Skype interview with an AI chatbot the following day, Charlie was offered training as a 'positivity mentor' and offered a temporary contract, to begin two days from now. To celebrate, he went against medical advice and rewarded himself with a pint of cider at La Maison du Court's bar.

Each Minder had been implanted with a mandatory disulfiram-ethanol reaction device which, when in contact with alcohol, discouraged them from drinking. His first few sips tasted like nectar. But he'd not even downed a quarter of his glass before the first wave of nausea struck. He hurried back to his suite and twice vomited into the toilet whilst vowing never to break the rules again. And when he lost his grip of the glass of water he used to rinse his mouth out, it smashed against the porcelain sink.

'Shit,' he muttered, more out of habit than annoyance. He picked out the pieces, holding one up to the light. His intolerance to alcohol made him want to test another of his procedures. Charlie slowly unbuttoned his jeans, rolled them down to just above his knees, and glided across the surface of his skin with a shard. The first time he left only a faint scratch until he repeated the action with more pressure. A third time, he pressed harder until the glass was several millimetres deep. Blood oozed from the self-inflicted wound and dripped down his thigh until the denim soaked it up.

Then Charlie let go, allowing the glass to remain embedded inside him and wondering if, at any point, he would feel it. But the operation to null his pain receptors meant that physically, he felt nothing. If he was ever to be located, he could be tortured without feeling a thing and giving up his knowledge.

However, what Charlie hadn't counted on was how little he also felt emotionally. There was no hesitancy or rush of adrenaline from cutting himself, no initial panic and no remorse. For the last few years, fear, regret and anxiety had controlled him; they pulled at his strings and influenced just about everything he did. He'd often wished that he wasn't ruled by his heart. Today, it seemed, he wasn't.

He tested himself again by thinking of his friends, of the last time he'd seen them, how they had vanished from his life and how it had all been his fault. Typically, it was a guaranteed way to dampen his spirits. Only now, there was a vacancy where self-pity had once lived.

Charlie tried again, this time pushing himself further, considering what he knew about his country, its leaders, the secrets it didn't want to share and the mistruths it spread. His memory flitted between homespun lies and international cover-ups, including the real perpetrators behind a summer Olympics bombing, the explosion of an unmanned Indian spacecraft on a mission to Mars and even a Eurovision Song Contest vote fix.

He should have possessed a level of conceit because after spending years surfing conspiracy-theory websites, he was now privy to all the answers. Or perhaps he should be dismayed by the world he lived in and what the people who controlled it were capable of. But again, there was nothing. There wasn't even an urge to spill any answers to the online communities he once frequented. Instead, there was an absence.

Charlie tugged at the glass until it came free from his skin and pressed a towel against his leg to stem the bleeding. And he began to calmly wonder, if he couldn't feel physical or emotional pain, just how much of his old self remained? Who was he now?

Chapter 17

BRUNO

Name: Bruno Yorke

Previous Name: ███████ ███████

Age: 39

Previous Occupation: Stay-at-home parent

Dependents: One

Strengths: Analytical; methodical; focused

Weaknesses: Ruthless; passionate; loyal

'You are going to fuck this up,' the voice sneered.

'Please be quiet,' Bruno sighed, shaking his head. 'Give me five minutes to myself without offering an opinion.' He wrung his hands together tightly like a wet tea towel.

Bruno was surrounded by dozens of people inside the motorway service station's central seating area. He tried diverting his attention towards the buzz of the chatter reverberating throughout the open space. But the voice demanded to be heard.

'You should've told them you were struggling before you left the programme,' it continued. 'But you didn't, did you? And now, *mi parri*, you have me. You have us all.' He broke into a laugh, swiftly followed by a hacking cough.

Bruno gritted his teeth, turned slowly and fixed his gaze on an elderly West Indian man with grey dreadlocks tied loosely together, resting on his shoulders. He wasn't looking at Bruno, though. His head was cocked to one side, fixated by something on his phone. The object of Bruno's irritation laughed again, and this time, Bruno looked at the man more closely. His lips were tightly shut. He was real, but the projection of a voice was not. Once again, Bruno had attached a voice in his head to a random stranger.

Bruno turned back in his seat, pulled the brim of his baseball cap down over his face and the glasses he didn't need back up to the bridge of his nose. He wasn't sure what annoyed him the most – the derision of someone who didn't exist or the voice being correct. He *was* struggling and if he wasn't careful, he *was* going to fuck this up.

He clenched his fists, curled his toes and concentrated on suppressing the stranger's voice and all the others in the background discussing and criticising him. *Echoes* was the word Karczewski used to describe them. 'These voices are Echoes from the DNA implanted in you,' he said. 'Your brain personifies them by attaching images and voices to them even when no images and voices have been coded. They see you as their anchor. They're harmless and our case studies show that almost all of the time, they're eventually absorbed into a Minder's subconscious.' But Bruno wasn't an ordinary Minder. He wasn't like the others.

Think positive thoughts, he told himself now. *That will keep them quiet*. He recalled trips he'd taken as a boy to visit his mum's family in Wales. He loved the adventure of a long car journey as it meant hours of streaming cartoons on the screen in the back of his mother's headrest. The only interruption came from service-station stop-offs, like today's location, only he wasn't here to top up on snacks.

He dipped in and out of actual people's conversations, picking up words here and there and fragments of sentences until calm and order slowly returned to his mind. And for the duration, he kept his view locked on one man sitting five tables away.

Eventually, that person left his tray of half-eaten food where it was and Bruno followed him to the toilets. Despite the bathroom area being relatively empty, the man chose to use one of several disabled cubicles in a separate section. Bruno hovered outside, listening. There was a gentle rustling of something being opened followed by two long sniffs. It wasn't hard to infer what he was up to.

Bruno took a deep breath, removed a cloth from his pocket, wrapped it around his knuckles and just as the door unlocked, he used all his strength to shove it hard, knocking the man backwards and to the floor. Shutting the door behind him, Bruno pushed the disorientated man over while he was struggling to his feet. He slumped over the toilet pan and barely had time to stretch out his arm to protect himself when Bruno yanked it at a ninety-degree angle causing the bone to snap.

His victim opened his mouth to scream but Bruno was too fast for him. He turned him quickly, grabbed a hammer from his waistband and began hitting him in the face and head with it. He heard the man's teeth snap and slide back into his throat like bar skittles. And as he choked on them, Bruno grabbed him by his head and slammed it against a metal handrail. It took four dull thwacks before his head cracked open like a horse-chestnut case. Now unconscious and bleeding profusely, he gasped his last, bloody breath.

Bruno took a moment to regain his composure, then pulled the dead man up into a sitting position and left him slumped on the toilet seat. Finally, he took two post-circulation £1 coins and thrust them into the man's eye sockets. He pushed the eyeballs further inside until they popped like grapes and the coins fitted snugly. Then he took a step back, removed the cloth from his hand and flicked away two of the man's teeth embedded in it.

'You got him good!' came the same West Indian man's voice. ''Tis a pity he'll never know why.' Bruno turned quickly to see the dreadlocked man behind him in the cubicle. Bruno reached his arm out to touch him but he felt nothing.

'He knew,' Bruno said firmly. 'And if all these people want is money, I'll make sure it's the last thing they see.'

He took a moment for himself to absorb his actions. The first name on the kill list he spent months planning was now crossed off. And it wouldn't be long before he had set his sights on the second.

Chapter 18

SINÉAD, EDZELL, SCOTLAND

Sinéad awoke with a start. It wasn't a noise that brought her out of a deep slumber, it was the silence. She propped herself up by her elbows and took a handful of deep breaths. 'Hello?' she said, just to hear the sound of her own voice.

She couldn't remember when she had last slept so soundly. There was something to be said about the purity of the air in the Scottish countryside. It had been her eighth evening in the Angus village of Edzell and each night was a world away from the broken sleeps she had when her husband Daniel was lying by her side. Often, she'd wake up, a tightened fist filling her stomach, worrying about something she'd said or forgotten to do that would bring about his upset later that morning. Now she was no longer hamstrung by him.

Sinéad climbed out of her sleeping bag, stretched her arms high above her head and unzipped the entrance to the tent. Mile after mile of rolling green countryside lay before her under an endless blue-and-white cotton sky. A canopy of treetops sheltered her from last night's rain, and it was the pitter patter of drops falling from leaves and branches and onto canvas that had soothed her to sleep. She made out the tiled rooftops of houses and shops and the occasional winding road in the distance, weaving in and out of the village. The only reminders that a world existed outside Edzell were white wind turbines planted in diagonal lines across the hillsides and leading to other towns.

Listening carefully, she could just about detect the faint sound of flowing water. The river Esk ran towards its neighbour Brechin, some five miles away. It was under loose rocks beneath the stone Gannochy bridge where, yesterday, she had buried an emergency escape kit.

For someone who had only ever stayed in hotels, camping had been a shock to the system, but a pleasurable one at that. In fact, anything far removed from her former life was bringing her happiness. As advised by her trainers, Sinéad had spent most of her first week becoming familiar with the area. She had not visited Scotland before so it was all new and by settling in a less densely populated village instead of a large city such as Glasgow or Edinburgh, she would not need to focus too much of her attention on counter-surveillance. If she was being followed, it would soon become apparent.

Some nights, Sinéad slept in her camouflage-coloured woodland tent, yet she also maintained a room in a nearby hotel in the centre of town. Later that morning, she returned there to shower, change her clothes and tuck into breakfast.

She took in the fixtures as she ate. She liked the characterful, exposed brickwork, uneven plastered walls and oak beams of this hotel built at the turn of the last century. It was the polar opposite to her modern apartment that Daniel insisted on filling with branded furniture and fittings, each surface sparse and devoid of quirk or personality. He didn't appreciate the one-off items she bought from flea markets to restore. So eventually, she stopped.

A middle-aged couple wearing matching rose-gold wedding rings entered the restaurant. Yesterday, Sinéad accepted their invitation to join them for breakfast and learned they were visiting Scotland to celebrate their thirtieth wedding anniversary. A pang of envy touched her until she reminded herself that a relationship wasn't the only route to fulfilment.

However today, Sinéad had no time for conversation. She and the woman wished each other a good morning before she made her way back to her room to log on to the ReadWell message board. She was expected to visit weekly, but caution always got the better of her and she visited daily.

She speculated as to how many other Minders there were. Had they started off as broken as her? Had they required as much rebuilding as she had? Sinéad assumed they too were able to store and process vast amounts of data thanks to anomalies in the formation of their brains. And she wondered if they all had synaesthesia and which variation of it. As a child, schoolmates teased her when she told them music made her see colours. Now, it was something she was proud of. She was using it to protect her country.

But preventing its secrets from being revealed sometimes left her conflicted. There were dreadful, horrendous things the country had done over the centuries involving slavery, mass murder, incitement of civil war and plundering less civilised nations to line its own pockets. And when she had learned the truth of the Mumbai tsunami that killed her parents and thousands of others, it was the hardest secret of all to keep. The data she protected revealed it was one of the biggest man-made disasters in history, an underwater earthquake being the result of seabed fracking by a British-owned company. A subsequent sizeable investment in the Indian economy kept the truth under wraps. The world deserved to know what Britain had done to prevent it from happening again, but she had been sworn to secrecy. It was the price she must pay for her brand-new start.

A part of her still questioned why she had been chosen, despite Karczewski's reassurances. 'I've made so many bad decisions and put my faith in the wrong people,' she'd admitted soon into training. 'How do you know history won't repeat itself and I won't mess this up?'

'Because you have incredible determination and inner strength,' he'd replied. 'Probably more so than any of our other candidates – and our training will help you to harness it. This isn't about what poor decisions you've made in the past, it's about your courage and your focus and your ability to start from scratch. There is more to you than others have led you to believe.'

She opened a rucksack lying by her feet and checked it contained all she needed for the day. Inside was a compass, ordnance survey map, torch, energy bars and waterproofs to slip over her clothing. She kept exactly the same objects in the boot of her car, inside the tent and under Gannochy bridge. And each contained a hunting knife with a four-inch, double-edged, stainless-steel serrated blade. She had never hurt another person in her life but this version of herself wouldn't hesitate to kill to protect what she knew. No one would take her knowledge, her new life or her confidence away from her.

Chapter 19

EMILIA

Emilia's fists were clenched, both hands raised high ready to defend herself. She scanned the hospital room, but if there was an enemy present, they were invisible. It must have been another daydream.

Moments earlier, she had been imagining a faceless woman approaching her, armed with a knife. The blade slashed through the air, effortlessly slicing anyone who encroached on her path. Emilia had sensed the coolness of the blade against the warmth of her skin, then the heat of her blood as it seeped from a horizontal wound across her abdomen.

Such streams of consciousness detached from reality were becoming increasingly common. And without fail, they were so vivid, it was hard to believe they weren't real. Now, she took deep breaths as she tried to rid herself of either a memory clawing its way to the surface or her interpretation of what Ted had told her – that her colleague's psychotic state was down to Emilia piling pressure upon her. The woman had fatally attacked four of their workmates and injured Emilia. Or perhaps this build-up of anxiety was related to her forthcoming discharge that afternoon.

A week had passed since she'd collided with a car and the physical bruises were fading. But the bruises from what she had learned about the trigger for her mental breakdown were in full bloom. Meanwhile Ted had tried to prepare Emilia for her return home by FaceTiming her from their house. He had guided her through every room, partly hoping to extinguish any nerves and partly to jolt her memory. She couldn't fault his understanding.

She had not encouraged him to visit the hospital that morning, telling him she'd be engaged with a final round of brain-imaging scans and a psychological evaluation before she was released into his care. What Emilia actually wanted was a little extra time to learn about the incident that instigated her decline.

She had trawled the internet with a slew of key words until she found what she was looking for.

FAMILY OF BANKER WHO SLAYED FOUR COLLEAGES IN KNIFE RAMPAGE BLAMES 'WORK STRESS'

By Laura Mulley

A high-ranking account manager at an investment company who murdered four colleagues and injured one other has been named as Emily Shinkin.

Oxford University graduate Shinkin, 27, entered the offices of Barnett-Vincent Brothers in London's Bank area on Monday morning armed with a hunting knife, and stabbed three men and one woman to death as they arrived at their desks.

In a statement made last night, her family blamed the killings on 'a moment of madness' and claimed their daughter had been pushed to the brink by greedy bosses who had no interest in their staff's well-being.

Her father, Hugo Shinkin, said: 'We were devastated and ashamed to learn of our daughter's actions and our prayers are with the families of the victims. However, we believe the blame cannot be placed entirely at Emily's door.

'Despite reaching out many times to both her line manager and the Human Resources department regarding the extreme level of pressure she was expected to work under, Emily was repeatedly ignored. They must accept their share of responsibility for this terrible tragedy.'

I was her boss, thought Emilia. *I was the one who ignored her*. At least she hadn't been named. While most people suffering from stress didn't react in such extreme ways as Shinkin had, Emilia was nevertheless wracked by guilt for something she'd sparked but couldn't remember.

She pulled at the waistband of her jogging bottoms, enabling her to trace the faint scar across her abdomen where she had been slashed by Emily's knife. According to Ted, she was fortunate not to have been killed. He'd also informed her that in the aftermath of the murders, Emilia had been forced to take a leave of absence while an internal investigation was launched into her practices. However, her reaction to losing her colleagues was to fall into a deep depression. And later, when it became apparent she was being set up as a company scapegoat, she agreed to sign a compromise agreement and receive a substantial payout rather than try and fight her way back to her desk.

But no sum of money was high enough to compensate for her culpability. Ted recalled that over the following weeks he had grown so worried about her that he had hired a mental health specialist to visit the house and offer her treatment after her refusal to seek help of her own accord. Then soon after, Emilia simply vanished one afternoon. He had reported her to the police as a missing person and after an anxious two months, Emilia had finally resurfaced days earlier in a London hospital after being hit by a car.

Emilia fastened her bottoms again and conceded that perhaps Ted had been right in wanting to shield her from the truth. Perhaps this *was* an opportunity to start afresh rather than trying to recapture the memories of someone who had contributed to the destruction of so many lives.

Her opinion of her husband was also starting to drift. If she couldn't remember the past, it meant he was alone with their shared memories. He would rather she forgot about their lives before the accident than have her relive what destroyed her, which was completely selfless. Perhaps in time, even if her memory remained evasive, she could learn to love him all over again. She was slowly learning to feel safe in his company and that must count for something.

Loneliness was proving the hardest part of Emilia's journey. Sometimes she watched as groups of staff or visitors sat together around canteen tables sharing food and talking. She craved being part of something. From what Ted had recounted, Emilia had very few people to do that with in the months before her disappearance. She'd put her career above all else, including him.

I've been a terrible boss and a terrible wife, she reasoned. *But once I return home, I'm going to make up for it. I have a second chance to be whoever I want to be.*

Emilia suddenly decided she had spent too long cooped up inside her room. Stopping to buy a coffee from a machine downstairs, she picked a vacant seat on a bench in the empty hospital gardens.

'Do you mind if I join you?' The woman's voice startled Emilia.

Please do.,' she replied and moved along the bench. The woman put her hand in the centre of her back and lowered herself and her swollen belly slowly onto the slats.

'Lovely afternoon, isn't it? Are you a visitor or a patient?'

'Patient,' Emilia replied, pointing to her plastic ID bracelet as she pulled up the sleeves of her top.

'Same here. Pre-eclampsia. My baby isn't growing as she should.'

'I'm sorry to hear that.'

'They say it's unlikely I'll go full term; I might need a Caesarean in the next few days if my blood pressure doesn't start dropping.'

The two women chatted about their shared hospital experiences, from the bland food and uncomfortable mattresses to the antiseptic smell that clung to their clothes.

'Well, I hope things go well for you,' Emilia said. 'My husband's coming to pick me up soon so I should start packing.'

'It was nice to meet you,' the woman replied as Emilia prepared to leave. 'Can I offer you a little word of advice, Emilia? Do not trust your husband.'

'I'm sorry?' Emilia replied, sure she had misheard.

'Your husband, Ted. He is not who he says he is. You're not married. In fact, until you were admitted to hospital, you had never seen him before.'

Chapter 20

BRUNO, OUNDLE, NORTHAMPTONSHIRE

'It's just so … *white* … ain't it?' a female Echo inside Bruno's head began. 'I tell ya, it's like living inside a sugar cube, locked in an igloo and trapped in a fuckin' snow globe.'

Bruno couldn't disagree. Every wall in the rented house had been painted the same shade of white, from the kitchen to the bathroom and even the cupboard under the stairs. The owner had never lived with small, sticky-fingered children.

'Your Louie would've trashed this place,' the Echo continued. It was a new voice to him; one with a lazy, southern American drawl. 'He loved banging his stuff against the walls, didn't he?'

Bruno nodded. 'There was something about the noise of his toys colliding against brickwork, plasterboard or skirting boards that calmed him when he was agitated,' he said. 'I was forever filling holes or touching up paintwork.'

Bruno wanted to ask how she knew all this but refrained. His stored data was once again bleeding into his own memory and the two were sharing with one another. The Echo quietened, allowing Bruno more space to think about his son. Their four-month separation already felt like a lifetime. His chest tightened as he imagined how much upset he had caused the boy by removing himself from his life.

'The price you pay for Louie being taken care of is that you won't be able to see him for five years,' Karczewski had warned. 'That means no attempt to communicate with him or staff at the care home. You cannot even mention him to anyone else in your next life.'

'And if something happens to me during this process?'

'In the event of your death during or beyond it, Louie will be taken care of for the duration of his life.'

Bruno returned to that guarantee as the days moved into weeks and the longing to see Louie heightened. He was doing all of this for his son.

Bruno made his way down the two-storey townhouse's staircase. He'd picked up the keys three days earlier from a letting agent in the centre of Oundle, a market town near Peterborough which he would temporarily call home. Stringent planning laws forbade its expansion giving it an appearance of a town trapped in time. Its narrow streets, flanked by limestone Georgian properties, was picture-postcard perfect. There was a handful of pubs, bistros, boutique shops and galleries and a supermarket nearby that would serve his immediate needs. It would have been the perfect location for father and son.

The property came as furnished but Bruno had made it a priority to decorate the bedroom next to his. He pinned posters to the walls, left toys scattered about the floor and ruffled up the duvet to give it a slept-in appearance. Then he paused in the doorway and tried to imagine Louie playing in this version of the bedroom he had in their family home.

Living here made Bruno long for the house he shared with Louie and Zoe. They moved in when it was a dilapidated Grade One listed cottage, located in a much sought-after village. The scale of renovation work had required a loan on top of their mortgage. By day, Bruno was Louie's primary caregiver, a decision made when Zoe's career escalated and cemented her position as the main breadwinner.

By night, Bruno attended evening classes in carpentry, plastering, basic electrical work and plumbing. Their purse strings were often drawn tight, but they muddled along without complaint. Zoe once described it as their 'forever home' and neither could ever see themselves wanting to move. And then she wrecked it all.

'Now you know how easy it is to kill, do you think you'd have snuffed her out too?' a second Echo asked. 'I would have.'

He recognised this one from coded video interviews with Harry Crooke, a soldier who had butchered young civilians to death while stationed in Iraq in the early 2000s. Had Crooke been charged and gone to trial, he'd likely have made public four high-ranking armed forces personnel who shared his bloodlust. It had been more convenient for Special Forces to spare the army's blushes and organise his 'suicide' while on remand.

'Of course I wouldn't have killed her,' Bruno replied. 'She's the mother of my son.'

'Don't believe you, mate,' Crooke shrugged. 'I've seen you in action. You're the same as me, you like watching the light leave their eyes. And there's nothing stopping you from killing again because like me, you don't have anyone to answer to. You don't exist.'

Crooke was correct – Bruno was little more than a ghost. The only thing real about him was, ironically, the Echoes. There were hundreds of them, new voices appearing every day, all eager to be heard. They'd want to remind him of the coordinates of emergency war bunkers; locations of federal reserves or the mapping of DNA sequences to create biological warfare. They were desperate to discuss cures for diseases, subliminal messages in advertisements, illegal chemicals used in water systems and lost treasures. You name it and Bruno had an Echo with recognition of it.

But this was not how it was supposed to be. All the facts, lies and horrors he had learned about his country were supposed to be contained in one anomalous section of his brain. Instead, they were spilling with the ease of an overfilled bathtub. And managing them was a skill he had been unable to master. He likened it to a self-inflating car tyre that wouldn't stop expanding. The only way to stop it from bursting was to release the valve a few voices at a time. Once acknowledged, they grew quieter. But eventually, their numbers always swelled again.

'You only have yourself to blame; you don't deserve to know what you know,' a third Echo whispered. This time it was a young woman's voice and the cold hand that entwined with his made him jump. He turned quickly to see a bloodied face. She'd been an escort who'd been raped and mutilated by a notorious sheikh stationed in London and the murder buried deeper than the victim.

'You shouldn't be a Minder. It's your kid who solved the puzzle and who had the mental capacity to store all this data, not you,' she continued.

'There were plenty of other tests I did pass to get here,' he argued. 'It wasn't as if they handed me a new life on a plate on the basis of one experiment.'

'You cheated the programme and now it's messing with your head. And if you aren't careful, soon you're going to join the names you're targeting.'

In Bruno's mind's eye, he pictured the six faces on his kill list. And he reminded himself that he would be paying the second one a visit later that week.

Chapter 21

FLICK, ALDEBURGH, SUFFOLK

'Another sparkling water?' Grace asked. Flick nodded as they waited at the bar for the landlord's attention. 'Don't you drink anything else?'

'I'm alcohol intolerant,' Flick explained. 'My body doesn't have the right enzymes to break down the toxins in booze so I break out in unsightly red hives which is so bloody annoying.'

'Take away my wine and you might as well kill me now,' Grace replied.

It was another in a long line of Flick's half-truths. Months had passed since a warm, spicy rum and Coke had touched the back of her throat. After discovering the truth about her DNA Match Christopher, she'd come to rely on it too much to smooth out the sharp edges that wounded her. But the programme stipulated no use of alcohol, nicotine, caffeine, narcotics and most over-the-counter medications. Nothing was to enter her system that could alter the delicate equilibrium of her brain activity or that threatened to impede her clarity of thought. Abstinence from booze hadn't troubled her until tonight, when she became envious that the rest of the pub quiz team was enjoying beverage after beverage while she nursed carbonated drinks. A cigarette wouldn't have gone amiss either, but she resisted both.

It was approaching a month since Flick had arrived at Grace's coastal B&B. The two had formed a friendship, spending many breakfasts and evenings together, talking or going out for drinks or sharing meals. Grace had been born and bred in Aldeburgh so her face was familiar to many. And she became the tool Flick used to build up a social life.

Grace had recently returned to the town following her mother's death.

Flick knew how it felt to have your future rewritten by others.

'It was never my plan to run a B&B,' Grace had told Flick, 'but then neither was losing my mum when I was twenty-one. Sometimes when life gives you lemons, you need to fill your glass with more gin.' The new Flick was very much on board with that mindset. Although she filled her glass with sparkling water, not gin.

While Grace was forthcoming about who she was, Flick couldn't reciprocate. There was no mention of the restaurant she and her partners had spent seven years building into a successful business or of the family she had turned her back on. She said nothing of a man she'd never met who'd broken her heart nor the programme that had given her the opportunity to live again. And she certainly gave no clues as to what she carried inside her head.

Instead, Flick stuck to the script. She explained how she'd recently had a messy break-up from her long-term partner, and alluded to violence being a contributing factor. Karczewski explained that once people assumed domestic abuse had been involved, very few follow-up questions would be asked. With no reason to remain in her fictitious home of Stratford-upon-Avon, Flick revealed how she'd saved some money, given notice on her flat, quit her job in telesales and left to travel the country. Grace had no reason to doubt her.

That night and on Grace's insistence, Flick had accompanied her to the Fox & Hounds pub in Aldeburgh's town centre, to participate in the weekly quiz night. She cast her eye around the busy room, first looking for potential escape routes and then for anyone who might be offering her undue attention. Regarding every stranger with suspicion until they proved they could be trusted wasn't a normal way to live your life. But she and normal had been estranged for years.

Finally, after being served, they returned to Team Fish Smokers as the quizmaster read from a sheet of paper into a microphone.

'Round three, question one,' he began in a thick, east-coast accent. 'Where was Diana, Princess of Wales, buried?'

Grace's team bunched together and whispered.

'On an island in the Althorp estate where she grew up,' said one. 'I went there with my mum when I was a kid.'

Flick shook her head. 'No, it was actually …' she began, picturing the church where Diana was entombed and not the shallow island in the centre of the lake the public had been told. She cut herself short. That was information others weren't supposed to know. It was one of the many secrets she was keeping about the Royal Family, along with the much more explosive truth behind the night of Diana's death.

Her face flushed. 'Sorry, you're right,' she said. 'It was Althorp. I was mixing her up with someone else.'

She bit her bottom lip and sank back into her seat, furious with her carelessness. Then she reminded herself of Karczewski's warning that the human brain wasn't infallible, despite the tweaks he had made to hers. 'A mistake is likely to occur when you're relaxed and least likely to expect it,' he'd advised. 'You'll momentarily forget that it's something that only you know. But it's what you do in its aftermath that counts. You were chosen because of your ability to adapt, learn from your mistakes and put things right.'

For the rest of the evening, Flick remained at the table but consciously withdrew from offering suggestions despite knowing the answers to almost every question posed. It would be the last quiz she participated in. 'Can I get anyone a drink?' she asked, and with Grace's help she took a list of orders to the bar.

As she moved her credit card to the scanner to pay, a job vacancy for bar staff caught her attention.

'Are you looking for some work?' asked Mick, the portly landlord.

'I'd not really thought about it.'

'You ever worked in a pub?'

'Not since the student union bar at catering college.'

'That'll do for me. What do you think? A couple of nights a week? See how you get on?'

Flick hesitated. She didn't need to work. The funds she accessed could purchase his pub and several others in town. However, she couldn't spend her days wandering around and looking for escape routes indefinitely. 'If you're going to hide, it's best to do so in plain sight,' Karczewski had advised. 'While there are more people to assess, there are more directions to run if you're cornered.'

What could be more plain sight than one of the town's pubs? she reasoned.

'Okay,' she replied. 'Let's give it a go.'

Grace grinned. 'Looks like you're staying for a while then.'

'It does,' Flick replied. And she hoped that she wouldn't live to regret it.

Chapter 22

CHARLIE, MANCHESTER

'Good morning, One Step Farther Personal Mentoring, you're speaking to Charlie, can I take your username and the first and last lines of your address, please?'

As a woman's voice answered through his earpiece, Charlie inputted her details into the projected image of a keyboard. Inside his virtual-reality headset, a moving avatar she had chosen appeared in real-time, surrounded by her account details. Charlie skimmed through brief notes of their previous contact along with advice offered, goals reached and achievements left. Meanwhile she was viewing a synthetic version of him.

'It's nice to see you again, Steph, how can I help you today?' he asked.

'There's a promotion at work I'd like to apply for,' she began nervously. 'But I don't know if I'm the right person for it.'

'Okay, do you have the necessary qualifications or experience?'

'Yes, I stepped in for my boss for five months when she went on maternity leave.'

'So today is more about finding your confidence to apply for the role and to prepare for your interview performance?'

The avatar nodded. 'They're certainly things I can help you work on today.'

Within thirty minutes, Charlie had used his on-site training and experience from the programme to capitalise on his client's strengths, eliminate her limiting beliefs and build her morale. It was no mean feat for him, someone who no longer felt anything, let alone empathy for his clients.

Two weeks into his coaching job and Charlie had grown accustomed to spending most of his working day in a world where three-dimensional images and avatars were the norm. While this was a new and expanding sector, it had a shelf-life. Everything from the team's advice to the inflection of their tone was being recorded and studied by Artificial Intelligence's neural networks with a view to eventually replacing humans altogether.

Removing his headset, he blinked hard to adjust his sight to the daylight of the open-plan office. He estimated there were eighty or so people surrounding him, each in their booths, answering and making prearranged calls to impart their wisdom on a wide range of subjects. He made his way towards a desk across the room and tapped twice on the bridge of Milo's headset. Milo offered him a thumbs up so Charlie made his way towards the canteen. By the time he'd chosen a table and poured two mugs of tea, his colleague had joined him.

'How's your head?' Charlie began, pushing one towards him.

'Pounding like a jackhammer after last night,' Milo replied. 'Yours?'

'Same,' Charlie lied. While out with the football team he'd joined, each vodka and Coke he'd purchased had actually been without the vodka. And he'd surreptitiously poured away those bought for him when no one was looking. 'It was a good night, though, thanks for inviting me. Are you having a quiet one tonight?'

'Yeah, deffo, mate.'

THE MINDERS

On Charlie's first day of training, Milo had taken him under his wing when he spied the retro Pearl Jam T-shirt Charlie wore. He praised him for his good musical taste but Charlie didn't want to admit he'd never heard of the band and that it was one of La Maison du Court's personal shoppers who'd chosen it for him.

The two men worked within the same section and soon slipped into a routine of calling for one another during breaks and lunchtimes. Upstairs in the canteen, they'd sit and chat about football scores and old Marvel movies or take advantage of retro console gaming machines where they'd battle it out in long-forgotten games such as Grand Theft Auto and Call of Duty.

Charlie swiftly had Milo pegged as the gregarious type, and adapted his own personality to form an alliance with him. He used his new friend to replicate the social life he'd once invested so much time in back in Portsmouth. When colleagues came over to chat to Milo, he'd invariably introduce them to Charlie and within the fortnight, he'd tagged along to a birthday meal and a house party, and had joined a football team. In carving out a new life for himself, he was accomplishing all he had set out to do when he'd said goodbye to the first. At least in theory.

Because in reality, Charlie was struggling. The happiness he was supposed to be experiencing with this group just wasn't there. It wasn't their fault; they had done nothing wrong. They were a decent, friendly bunch – in fact, they were far more hospitable than his old friends had been at the end. But Charlie wasn't experiencing the closeness he'd expected. And it wasn't because they lacked a shared history. There were simply no feelings of contentment or fulfilment in anything to do with this second life, not just this group of people. There was merely an acceptance of his new circumstances.

He struggled to feel fear, regret, affection, longing, anxiety or even guilt and he wondered if his inability to fully connect with others was a temporary blip, and perhaps related to the nulling of his pain receptors. Maybe that procedure alongside the operation to implant coding into his head, plus deep-rooted therapy, analysis and hypnosis, meant that his brain was overloaded. It needed time to adjust and settle into what was expected of it.

Or perhaps it was something much simpler – his subconscious wanted to distance itself from the darkness that dominated his latter years. If it wouldn't allow him to feel, it meant he couldn't hurt.

Surely this is a positive thing? he reasoned. *I've wasted so much time smothered by guilt, that now I'm free of it, I should be elated. Shouldn't I?*

Charlie wanted to answer but he really couldn't be sure. And he couldn't muster the effort to care either.

Chapter 23

SINÉAD, EDZELL, SCOTLAND

A sheet of yellow paper was taped to the church door and the word 'Welcome' scrawled upon it in a red marker pen. Sinéad pushed it open and waited until she heard voices coming from a side room.

Week one in Edzell had been devoted to learning about the area and planning escape routes. By week two, Sinéad had checked out of the hotel, stopped camping outdoors and signed a six-month lease on a former farming cottage. There, she spent time adjusting to living alone and enjoying life's simple pleasures such as hiking through the countryside, meditation, reading and the tai chi she'd practised during training. By week three, she had met some of the village's 1,586 residents. And having built up her confidence one step at a time, now she was itching to make connections her marriage hadn't allowed.

'Volunteers required,' read the note on the Edzell church noticeboard. 'If you can help with the organising committee for the village fete, the next meeting is on Thursday, 6.45 p.m.'

The soles of Sinéad's trainers squeaked against the parquet flooring as she entered the room, all heads turning to look at the unfamiliar arrival. A group of ten or so men and women of all ages were sitting around tables pushed together in an L-shaped formation. Some had been flicking through papers and folders while others typed on tablets as they discussed how the meeting was to proceed. Sinéad's cheeks reddened as they eyed her up and down. Her hand moved as if on autopilot towards her eyelashes, before she regained control. It stopped at her chest.

'The Pilates class is tomorrow morning, hen,' an elderly man in large-framed glasses began.

'Actually, I'm hoping to volunteer for the fete if you need an extra pair of hands?' Sinéad replied. 'I saw the poster.'

'I'm sorry, please, come in and join us. What's your name?'

Sinéad introduced herself and chose an empty plastic chair as a woman she placed at around two decades older than her became the first to make an introduction. 'I'm Doon,' she replied, her handshake as warm as her smile. It immediately put Sinéad at ease. As Doon went around the table pointing to and naming each person, Sinéad quickly assessed them all, as she had been trained to do, making snap decisions on their characters based upon their mannerisms and micro-expressions. It was a good indication of who she might trust and who to be wary of.

'I'm not expecting you to remember all our names,' Doon joked, but attention to detail was another by-product of Sinéad's synaesthesia. When she learned the name of a stranger, she silently repeated it to herself in a sing-song tone and every time she saw them again, it would appear above their heads in a bright colour.

'Are you new to the village?' asked Doon.

'Yes, I am,' Sinéad replied and launched into a rehearsed speech about how she had decided to take a break from the chaos of working in London to escape about as far away as geographically possible.

'Why Edzell?' asked a man who'd been introduced to her as Anthony. His tone was friendly, but his cluster of gestures suggested something different. His foot tapped against the leg of his chair, his nose wrinkled and his cheeks raised ever so slightly when he spoke. They added up to an undercurrent of animosity towards her.

'It's a beautiful location,' she replied. 'When I drove under that stone archway at the village's entrance, there was something about it that made me want to stay here. London was fantastic, but it takes it out of you.' Sinéad didn't want to admit she'd chosen Edzell by randomly jabbing a finger inside a map of Scotland and settling on the north-east.

'We've seen a lot of people like you,' he said. 'People who've made a tidy profit down there, then turned up here with deep pockets, buying up prime property and edging locals out of the housing market. Not everybody appreciates a tourist.'

'I thought that as the owner of a restaurant you might welcome the tourist trade?' Sinéad asked. She had spotted him yesterday removing cash-and-carry bags from the boot of his car and taking them into Edzell Tavern. His licensee name was on a brass plaque above the door.

'She's got you there,' interrupted Doon. 'And if she didn't want to be a part of the community, then she wouldn't be here now, would she?'

'I'm just pulling the lass's leg,' Anthony replied. Sinéad's response was a smile as disingenuous as his.

By the end of the meeting, Sinéad had been tasked with applying to the local council for the fete's foods, drinks and entertainment licences. Doon approached her outside in the church grounds.

'I hope Anthony didn't put you off us?' she asked.

'No, I've met men like him before.' Daniel came to mind. 'They're usually compensating for something they're lacking.'

'You're probably right there. Where are you staying?'

'I didn't want to give Anthony the satisfaction of being proven right, but I'm actually in a rental property in Mulberry Avenue, and I don't think the owners are locals.'

Doon laughed. 'Yes, it's probably best you keep that quiet. Look, I'm having a few of the girls around tonight for a movie-and-wine evening. If you have nothing better to do, you're more than welcome to join us?'

'If you're sure I wouldn't be intruding, I'd love to, thank you.'

By 9 p.m., Sinéad was sitting cross-legged on Doon's lounge floor, a glass of alcohol-free white wine in her hand, and sharing a bowl of crisps with Gail, a woman around the same age as her. Gail's flawless pale skin made her dark red hair even more striking. They were the only two of the dozen women present not to be in tears at the movie.

'How have I never seen *Love Actually* before?' Sinéad asked when the closing credits appeared.

'You can only have been a wee thing when it came out,' Doon replied.

'This is why we love your classic film club ... and for the wine,' another woman added.

'It's always for the wine,' said Gail, laughing but retaining a straight face as she climbed to her feet. 'Would you like a top-up?'

'Yes, please. Let me give you a hand.' Sinéad followed her into the kitchen.

'How come you're on the non-alcoholic stuff?' asked Gail.

'Antibiotics for a gum abscess. What about you?'

'I'm breastfeeding.'

A shiver ran up Sinéad's spine, a relic of the past. Sinéad thought she heard a hint of reluctance in Gail's tone. 'Oh, how wonderful. Boy or girl?'

'Taylor, she's five months old. She's asleep upstairs. Do you have kids?'

Sinéad shook her head. 'What did you do work-wise before she was born?'

'I restored old furniture. I'd buy knackered old dressers, tables and wardrobes, etcetera from online auction sites, bring them back to life and sell them on. But babies are such a time-drain, aren't they? Since having Taylor, I have so little of it that I've got a backlog of projects in the garage.'

'Well, if you need an extra pair of hands, my dad was a French polisher and I'm a dab hand with chalk paint and sandpaper.'

A knock on the front door interrupted them. Doon answered it, then appeared in the kitchen. 'Gail,' she said and rolled her eyes. '*He's* here.'

Gail's face hardened. She gave an apologetic glance as she made her way upstairs to collect her daughter. Only then did Sinéad notice Anthony waiting in the hallway, a pushchair parked behind him. He was as surprised to see her as she was to see him. She felt the temperature between them drop.

'Nice to see you again,' he said through gritted teeth.

'Likewise.'

'Taylor hasn't been upstairs the whole night alone, has she?' he asked when mother and child appeared.

'Don't worry, we've all been checking up on her,' Doon interjected.

'I doubt she's had much sleep then if you've all been waking her up,' he muttered, and strapped her into the pushchair. 'That's a great night we have ahead of us then.'

He glared at a red-faced Gail who gave a half-wave to everyone as Anthony left first. She turned to thank Doon. 'And I'll take you up on the offer of help if you're serious?' she asked Sinéad.

'Gail?' Anthony beckoned, now at the end of the path with his daughter. 'Will you be joining us?'

She mouthed 'sorry' before closing the door.

'I wouldn't have put them together either,' Doon said diplomatically, as if reading her mind. 'But there's no accounting for taste, is there?'

Sinéad wanted to ask more but held back. Instead, she placed the wine bottle back inside the fridge. A framed photograph on the wall caught her attention. It was of Doon with a younger woman who shared the same-shaped mouth and steely blue eyes. Sinéad's heart raced – she instantly recognised her but stopped short of saying as much.

'Is this your daughter?' she asked, feigning ignorance.

'Isla,' Doon replied, her voice quietening.

Sinéad knew she should change the subject. However, she pressed on, albeit carefully. 'Does she still live in town?'

'No, she passed away eight years ago.'

'How awful. What happened?' Sinéad picked up on Doon's hesitation. 'I'm sorry, I shouldn't have asked.'

'No, it's okay. She was at university in London studying for her finals when the stress became too much and ... she took her own life.'

'Oh, Doon.'

'She took an overdose of her depression medication. She'd suffered from it for years, but her dad and I thought it was under control. It's hard losing a child in any circumstances, but when they want to go before their time ... the pain is that little bit sharper. And as a parent, it's a guilt you have to learn to live with ...' She stopped herself. 'Sorry, it's the wine talking. You don't want to hear all this.'

Sinéad shook her head sympathetically and patted Doon's arm; she offered a half-smile in return. As Doon made her way back to her other guests, Sinéad held back. She focused on the photograph of the bright, pretty young student again as two reports from the same pathologist came to mind. The first detailed how Isla had died, the second was an alternative version of events. It was that one which had been submitted to, and accepted by, the coroner as the truth.

But Sinéad knew why Isla's brutal murder had been covered up and she couldn't say a thing.

Chapter 24

EMILIA

Emilia remained in silence for much of the journey from the hospital to the house.

Ted had instigated conversation on several occasions, but more often than not, he was greeted with her reticence to communicate. He'd set his vehicle to autonomous mode and tried to encourage a tense Emilia to relax by holding her hand. It offered little reassurance. En route, he pointed out pubs and restaurants that they'd frequented before her career dominated her every waking moment.

But her mind was elsewhere. As she stared out from the passenger window, she kept her left hand out of sight and held on to the object a stranger had slipped her in the grounds of the hospital.

'Do not trust your husband,' the pregnant woman had warned, much to Emilia's confusion.

'Who ... what ... I don't understand?' Emilia asked. The woman had a nondescript appearance. Her mousey-brown hair hung in a loose ponytail, she wore little make-up and her protruding stomach backed up her claim that she was far into her pregnancy.

'It doesn't matter who I am,' she'd responded coolly. 'All you need to know is that Ted means no more to you than I do. I'm not expecting you to believe me at this moment, but you will. Use this when you're ready. We'll be waiting for you.' She pressed a glossy business card with a phone number embossed upon it into Emilia's palm.

'We? Who is "We"?'

'Take care of yourself, Emilia.' The woman patted a bewildered Emilia's shoulder like an old friend as she rose unsteadily to her feet, then shuffled back towards the hospital entrance.

Ted began to speak again. 'We're almost home. Is it ringing any bells ...? Sorry, I need to stop asking you that. It must be irritating.'

It was but Emilia didn't respond.

The car slowed as it reached a set of white wooden gates, at least two metres in height. White rendered walls hid everything from view behind them. Ted pushed a button on the dashboard screen and the gates opened, allowing them access to a cobbled driveway. The car made its way downhill until the road behind was out of sight. Ahead lay an expansive, modern house made up of three large glass-fronted cubes.

It took Emilia by surprise. Ted had prepared her for the interior's appearance when he had FaceTimed her, but he had downplayed its extensive grounds. He parked the car under a cantilever cube, and Emilia was momentarily startled by the appearance of someone opening her door.

'It's okay, Josef works for us,' Ted reassured, sensing her alarm.

'We have staff?'

'Just Josef and a few security staff.'

'Welcome home,' Josef began in a gruff European accent. His attire was casual but a bulge in his jacket pocket suggested he might be armed. It made Emilia uneasy and she wondered why Ted needed security personnel who carried weapons. She followed her husband through a set of double-aspect smoked-glass front doors, along parquet flooring framed by grey concrete walls and into a reception room. The windows offered uninterrupted views of the countryside. Ahead of her was a forest and to the right, a tennis court and a swimming pool complete with pool house.

'And this is all ours,' she muttered. It was impossible not to be taken aback by the property's splendour. However, she could not remember any of it.

'We bought it from the executors of an estate belonging to that actress Sofia Bradbury,' he said. 'You won't remember, but she was caught up in the car-hacking anarchy I told you about. After she died, her estate wanted a quick sale. We bought it cheaply, razed the original buildings and designed this replacement ourselves.'

Emilia allowed herself to be seduced by an imagined memory; of being talked through an architect's three-dimensional blueprints which then came to life with the aid of a table's projection. Then she watched as excavation machines ploughed the earth to create the space to lay the foundations.

Do not trust your husband, a voice echoed, bringing her out of her daydream. *Ted means no more to you than I do.*

A familiar chill returned to Emilia's spine. Either the stranger or Ted was lying to her. Why should she trust that woman over Ted, the man who'd dedicated so much time in trying to help her remember the past? He had not done anything to deserve her doubt. But how did that woman know who either of them was? And why would she say it if it wasn't true? Emilia reached into her pocket and brushed her fingertips against the business card again.

She followed Ted into the kitchen area. Each work surface was immaculate and clutter free, without a visible drawer handle or plug socket. The exception was a refrigerator door decorated in brightly coloured magnets. The names of countries, cities and towns were emblazoned across them, from hotels in Las Vegas to Dubai and the Seychelles. Amongst them were garish souvenirs from British towns that appeared out of place amongst the far-flung venues. It was a peculiar hint of personality in an otherwise clinically furnished house.

'They're my fault,' Ted admitted, sensing her confusion. 'It started as a joke gift when I went to Italy for work and bought you one. And then it became a tradition – everywhere I went without you, I'd buy you a magnet.'

She reached out to move one. 'Best if you don't,' Ted said quickly, his smile shifting as he put his hand out to stop her. 'Some of them are broken and will fall off if you move them.'

Emilia nodded. 'Do you mind if I explore the rest of the house alone?' she asked. 'This is a lot to absorb all at once. Just for now, I'd like to do it on my own.'

'Of course. Take your time. I'll be in the office when you're ready. It's downstairs on the ... never mind, you'll find it.'

As Emilia set off on her own journey, she examined abstract artwork hanging from vast white walls; she picked up sculptures and ornaments arranged on sideboards. She inhaled perfumes in a dressing room framed by rails of clothing, shoes and handbags. She scrolled through playlists on a speaker system and looked through brands of food inside the pantry. She took in deep breaths, allowing the concrete, mortar and wood to seep into her lungs. Finally, she leafed through wall-to-ceiling bookshelves. Amongst dozens of medical and chemistry textbooks, photobooks on architecture and art, sat a leather-bound collection of Shakespeare's plays.

Emilia hesitated as something inside her flickered to life. She saw herself inside a shop by table after table of electronic gadgets. She was choosing a tablet furthest away from the entrance, but where the doors remained in her line of sight.

She logged on to the ReadWell book message board but the image wasn't clear enough to recall what she was typing. She became aware of heavy footsteps approaching her and leaped into action. Emilia pulled her arm up at a ninety-degree angle and hit whoever it was in the face with the back of her fist. Her assailant barely gasped before she elbowed him hard in the stomach, then turned quickly and caught his leg with her foot, causing him to fall onto his back. Then she grabbed a long, sharp silver object from her back pocket, mounted him and held it above his head.

'No, please!' he choked and she hesitated. Blood poured from her young assailant's nose into his mouth, down his chin onto his white T-shirt. There, she read his name badge: 'Timothy – sales assistant'. Neither of them moved, each equally bewildered by her actions.

The recollection, if that was what it was, faded to black like the end of a movie. But before she had time to dwell on it, a vibration against her thigh alerted her to a text message on a phone Ted had given her. It was from him and simply read: I love you.

How can you love me? she thought. *You don't have the first clue who I am because neither do I.*

She glanced at the time – an hour had passed and her possessions had not brought her any closer to whom she'd been. So Emilia made her way back down a flight of stairs, passing a basement gym before reaching the only room she'd yet to set foot in – Ted's office. Two muffled voices came from behind the door. Instead of knocking, she pressed her ear against it.

'Keep your eye on her,' said Ted. 'Do not let her out of your sight. And don't let her leave the grounds alone.'

'Do you have reason to think she might run again?' came the second.

'I don't know. It depends on how much she remembers.'

'And if it all comes back to her?'

'Then if necessary, we'll have to sedate her again ...'

Emilia's stomach hollowed. *Sedate her again?* When and where had he sedated her before? Did he have something to do with where she first woke up?

As the voices grew louder, she backed away and let herself out of a door and into the garden. Nausea washed over her as she hurried across the driveway. She became distracted by the barking of two fox-red Labradors running towards her, poker-straight tails aggressively aloft. She tried but failed to remember their names.

'Hey, guys,' she said as they snarled at her. 'Did you miss me?'

But after a cursory sniff from each, they went on their way. They were as familiar with her as she was with them.

Emilia needed space and privacy to think about what she'd overheard. She remained where she was for a moment, the house behind her, mown lawns ahead. Was she trapped here? Was she being kept prisoner but hadn't even realised it?

She made her way towards the woodland until she was out of view of the main house, then continued along a flattened path curved between the pines and ash trees. Eventually she reached a different entrance from the one she'd arrived at. Approaching this new set of gates, she jumped when Josef appeared from nowhere.

'Can I help you with something?' he asked.

'Have you been following me?'

'Did you want to go somewhere?'

'I'm fine on my own, thank you.'

'I'm sure we can organise something if you need to leave the premises.'

'Why can't I just go outside if I want to?'

'Perhaps it might be a good idea if you spoke to your husband first?'

'Are you asking me or telling me?'

When he didn't reply, she knew the answer.

Emilia turned and walked slowly back towards the property, emerging from the woods and stopping at the perimeter of the lawns. Ahead was the man who claimed to be her husband, standing behind the lounge windows, watching her watching him.

Chapter 25

BRUNO, EXETER

'Please, I can give you anything you want,' the man begged.

'I doubt that,' Bruno replied, an image of Louie and him side by side in their family home coming to mind.

'Do you want the money we took from you? I can get you it. Just let me go. I'm sorry, I really am.'

Bruno found it difficult to read the man's expression under the blood covering his eyebrows, cheeks and mouth. It was impossible to tell if the apology came from the heart or from fear. As Bruno approached him, his victim contorted his naked torso, twisting it away from him so that it was less vulnerable. It was a futile effort. Bruno noted purple and red fragments of muscle tissue poking out from the deep lacerations in his back. Broken glass crunched under the soles of Bruno's boots, from the panes that he'd twice rammed the man's head through. Like his first killing in the motorway service station toilets, he had taken the second name on his list by surprise too.

'I have a family,' the man sobbed. 'I have a son.'

'So did I,' Bruno deadpanned and another image of Louie prompted his fist to fly with a life of its own, punching the man in the kidneys many times. 'You took him away from me.'

Bruno looked at the rope around his victim's neck, the other half looped around metal beams holding up the greenhouse's vaulted roof. It was the fault of parasites like this that father and son were separated.

His victim gasped for breath as Bruno recalled the last time he'd seen his boy, almost five months ago. He'd felt such joy watching Louie dancing barefoot on the artificial lawns of his care facility. Now when he thought of his son, he alternated between grief and anger. Louie no longer had either parent in his life and Bruno hated himself for that. Hot, raw tears streamed from Bruno's eyes as he hit the man again.

Bruno had visited lawyer Robert Graph's country house on a previous occasion, shortly before Bruno enrolled in the programme. His address hadn't been hard to find and then, Bruno had only wanted to reason with him; to explain how he and his colleague Jacob O'Sullivan had been lied to which resulted in Bruno losing everything. Bruno turned up unannounced on his doorstep, begging him to ask his client to reconsider. But Graph had laughed, told him he didn't care what the truth was and threatened to call the police before slamming the door in his face.

Today, he had no such opportunity. When he'd opened the door, Bruno had shoved him inside and, armed with a hammer, launched into a brutal attack. Then he'd dragged the unconscious lawyer to the greenhouse, pushed his face through glass, looped a rope he'd brought with him over the beam and hauled him up, allowing his feet to rest on a stepladder.

'This is your own fault,' Bruno began. 'You have turned me into someone I don't want to be. This is for every man, woman and child whose lives you have destroyed with no fucks given.'

He pulled back his foot and kicked hard, sending the ladder toppling to its side with a clank. The drop was not long enough for Graph's body weight to sever his spine.

Instead, the veins and arteries carrying blood to his brain slowly closed off, depriving him of oxygen and making his death a drawn-out affair. His legs flailed as his hands gripped the rope around his neck, desperately trying to release its grip. Ten minutes later, and Graph was finally dead. Before he left, Bruno firmly pushed a £1 coin deep into each of the man's eye sockets.

Birdsong emerging from the treetops caught Bruno's attention as he walked along a single-track country lane and towards the vehicle he'd parked there. He couldn't remember the last time he'd heard it. More often than not, the chattering of the Echoes blocked out all background and white noise. But today, they weren't competing to be heard. Perhaps his brain was beginning to settle into its new form. Or perhaps murder was enough to silence the dead.

Bruno recalled the first time the Echoes appeared. It was days after the implant procedure and he was still feeling groggy. Whispering had been coming from consultants outside the recovery room, but no one entered. After a time, he'd opened the door and found the corridor empty. Yet the voices persisted. Panicked, he'd told Karczewski who told him not to worry; advising that they were temporary and his augmented brain was adjusting to the new information it was storing.

But soon their numbers swelled from a handful to more than Bruno could count. It was as if he was listening to every radio station all at once and couldn't switch any of them off.

Fearing for his sanity, Bruno planned to inform one of his psychotherapists. However, outside her office and through an ajar door, he listened as she and Karczewski discussed Patient 0157, the number assigned to him. He clenched his jaw and toes tightly until his Echoes were under partial control, then listened.

'I have my concerns,' she began. 'His chemical map and thought patterns are too random. They should be settling by now. He's not responding like the others are.'

The others, Bruno reflected. How many more Minders were there?

'He has completed every level of training and passed every test, bar none,' Karczewski countered. 'The Echoes have been proven to dissipate of their own accord in past subjects. We've increased and stabilised his dopamine levels and also reduced his norepinephrine levels so that his anxiety is manageable. I see that his epinephrine levels are higher than we would like, suggesting he has anger issues, but we have yet to see them act out in a negative way, which in turn suggests he can self-regulate his temper. Why are you so concerned?'

'It's a gut feeling, Edward. He has displayed the weakest synaesthesia despite solving the initial puzzle the quickest. This programme is so much more than just a brain accepting a foreign body implanted inside it. It's about how he can live an ordinary existence and keep himself and the data safe. We cannot have a repeat of what happened last time.'

Karczewski's tone shifted. 'Adjustments have been made to ensure it won't.'

'Can we take the risk of allowing him back into the world with what he knows? Can you offer a cast-iron guarantee that he will put his duty to the country above all else?'

Her question appeared to irritate Karczewski. 'You saw the initial results – someone with his skills is not leaving the programme unless it's absolutely necessary.'

Bruno left as quietly as he arrived, deciding to keep his escalating Echoes to himself. He would rather live with them than risk being removed from the programme and having Louie's care-home funding axed.

Karczewski's colleague had been correct about his high anger levels. Since the procedure, he often felt rage bubbling under the surface ready to break through like lava from a volcano. But he trained himself to swallow it down and keep it hidden from those lab technicians monitoring the sensor pads attached to his head and body.

He waited until he was released back into the world to allow his fury to emerge and direct it towards those who deserved it like O'Sullivan and, today, Graph. And there were still four more names on his list to suffer his wrath.

Chapter 26

FLICK, ALDEBURGH, SUFFOLK

Flick sat bolt upright in bed, her skin painted in a hot, thin film of sweat. In the hazy early-morning light, she threw the sheets off her body so that they landed in a heap on the floor. She made her way to the bedroom window, unhooking the latches and lifting it open as wide as possible. She tasted the North Sea's fresh breeze on her lips as it wafted into the room and cooled her body. Slowly, her escalated pulse began to decline and return to something approaching normal.

Once again, as she'd slept, her knowledge had leaked into her unconscious, shaping her dreams. But it hadn't been just one dream, it was a succession of them, all layered one upon another, and all playing out at once. And each was made up of a different secret she was keeping safe. She wondered whether the dreams were a valve, easing the pressure inside; and if that was the case, who knows what the consequences might be if she stopped dreaming?

It was just past 5 a.m. and now, wide awake, her mind was working twenty to the dozen. It fired in all directions as if someone had lit a box of fireworks inside her head. 'It's like a temporary form of anxiety that occurs when you sleep,' Karczewski had warned the first time it happened.

'We've found that over time, it will pass. But to hasten it, take yourself out of the environment you're in and go somewhere else. As your brain takes in alternative surroundings it'll replace your dream images.'

Flick slipped on her jogging bottoms, a long-sleeved T-shirt and a pair of trainers and, hoping not to wake Grace, tiptoed across the landing and down the carpeted stairs before leaving the house. She trudged across the pebbled beach before settling on a sitting position next to a stainless-steel sculpture of a scallop shell. She drew her knees to her chest and wrapped her arms protectively around them, as if she were trying to create an impenetrable shell of her own.

She realised that her job behind the bar of the Fox & Hounds pub often took her mind away from the burden of knowledge. But she was extra cautious about the topics of conversation she involved herself in. It wasn't always easy when a sizeable proportion of the role was engaging customers in conversation. Her brain often worked at double speed, rechecking everything she wanted to convey before saying it. She was mentally exhausted by the time she finished each shift.

When she looked at her watch again, it was approaching 6.45 a.m. and she was surprised by how long she'd been there. Time moved much faster in the real world than in the solitude of her London flat where she measured it in cigarettes smoked and television programming.

As she made her way to a bakery to buy breakfast pastries for herself and Grace, she realised that Christopher hadn't crossed her mind that morning. An hour at most might have passed at home before either his or one of his victim's faces came to mind. Here, she'd slipped into a daily routine of running, yoga, bike rides, socialising and evening work, leaving no time for thinking about him. She was sure that the two months she had spent in Aldeburgh was the best decision she'd ever made.

*

A coach tour of drinkers dispersed from the bar, leaving an unfamiliar figure perched on a stool. He caught Flick's attention as he doodled in a notebook resting on his lap. She assumed from his empty glass that landlord Mick had served him earlier when she was on a toilet break.

She couldn't put her finger on what it was, but there was something a little offbeat about this man. There was nothing flashy about his fitted T-shirt, jeans, branded trainers and chunky silver bracelet, but it hadn't been absent-mindedly assembled. It was as if he were trying to blend in when by nature, he was too distinctive to be assimilated by his environment. By the faint lines framing his eyes and stretching across his forehead, Flick guessed they were of a similar age. His light brown hair was flecked with strands of grey and his darker beard was highlighted by white wisps protruding from below the centre of his bottom lip. His eyes were the bluest she had ever seen and she wondered if he'd had them coloured. But if he was that vain, he'd have likely had his wrinkles smoothed out too.

Conscious that she was now staring at him, she looked away. But each time she tried to fix her attention elsewhere, it invariably returned to him. He, however, had not looked at her once. Eventually, curiosity got the better of her and she approached him.

'Can I get you another drink?' she asked, taking his empty pint glass away and placing it inside the dishwasher. She was surprised by the timidity of her tone. He smiled as he looked up.

'I was going to have another Adnams but you've taken my glass.'

Flick's cheeks flushed.

'Would you like to join me for one?'

She declined politely but searched for a way to prolong the conversation. 'Are you from around here?'

'I live just along the beach although I've been staying in London recently.'

160

'Which part of London?'

'Usually the west, Kensington, Notting Hill, etcetera. Are you familiar with them?'

'A little,' she replied vaguely. She was a south-of-the-river girl, but she had spent many hours in Notting Hill traipsing around Christopher's neighbourhood trying to get a flavour of him. 'I went to university there,' she lied.

'What did you study?'

'Business.'

Karczewski had assured her that if anyone was to check, her name would be in the records of the London Institute for Business and Finance, along with her grades, lecturer's comments and faked photographs.

'Business? Let me guess, you went on to make your fortune in the stock market and took an early retirement.'

'I probably wouldn't be working behind a bar if I was loaded.'

'I'm Elijah,' he said and held his hand out to shake hers. She liked his name. There was something heartening, even biblical, about it.

'What are you writing?' she asked, drawn towards his notebook. It was unusual to see someone with a pen and paper instead of a tablet and stylus. He closed the cover.

'Nothing important.'

'Gone a little shy, have we, Elijah?' she teased.

'If you won't let me buy you a drink, then let me take you for dinner one night,' he asked.

His offer caught Flick off-guard. 'Oh, well, thank you – but no, thank you,' she replied.

'You're not even going to make an excuse to let me down gently?' he joked. 'No "I'm just getting over a break-up" or "I've just started seeing someone"? Just a flat-out rejection?'

Guilt pricked her. She couldn't deny an attraction to the stranger, but that's exactly what he was. He could have been anyone and without his full name or access to an electronic device to complete a background check on him, she couldn't risk it. Besides, emotional connections were strongly advised against by the programme.

'It's just a flat-out rejection, I'm afraid.'

He raised his glass to her. 'To honesty,' he said and took a swig.

Flick became distracted by a handful of new customers and moved to the other end of the bar to serve them. As they paid, she turned to take a sly glance at Elijah. Her chest deflated at the sight of his empty stool. All that remained was a scrap of paper on the bar top. She unfolded it to find a sketch; a portrait of her. It was incredibly detailed, even down to the strip of freckles across her nose that she'd assumed were invisible under make-up. Elijah had even spotted the slight indent of a teenage ear piercing in her right lobe.

An unexpected warmth rushed through her body as she folded the drawing in half and slipped it into her pocket.

Chapter 27

CHARLIE, MANCHESTER

'Mate, what have you done to your leg?' asked Milo, staring at the red, horizontal wound across Charlie's thigh.

Charlie had forgotten to cover up it with a bandage that morning and hadn't noticed it when he had changed into his football kit to play a seven-a-side match either. He turned away from Milo and faced the tiled shower wall.

'Oh, nothing,' he said casually. 'I fell off my bike and landed on barbed wire.'

'Where?'

'Somewhere along the canal path by the undeveloped section, I forget what it's called.'

'It looks pretty raw; you might want to get a tetanus shot.'

'No, it's fine, honestly.' Keen to change the subject, Charlie chose to make light of it instead. 'Are you sure this isn't just an excuse to stare at my dick?'

'Dream on, mate,' Milo chuckled. 'Dream on.'

The truth was there had been no barbed wire, only a shard from the drinking glass Charlie accidentally broke weeks earlier and kept. He had been using it to cut himself ever since. Before each incision, he stood upright in the bath with the glass in his hand to see if anticipation of the act might prompt an emotion. But nothing came. There was no trepidation, no excitement, anxiety or feeling of release from any of the lines of blood dripping down his leg and into the porcelain tub.

Yet something compelled him to repeat the action every few days. New Charlie might have disliked the old version of himself, but quietly wondered if a diluted form was lurking somewhere if only to assure him that he was still human.

'Can I borrow your shampoo?' Milo asked and Charlie passed it to him. 'I love how you have a never-ending supply of these tiny bottles,' said Milo. 'It's like you've robbed a hotel.'

Charlie still hadn't told any of his new friends that he was living at La Maison du Court. It would require too much explaining if they discovered someone earning a little over the living wage was spending his nights at the most expensive hotel in Manchester. But his conscience wasn't pricked by dishonesty. He began to question whether he still possessed one. His lies only had to continue for another week before a room became available in a flat-share with two work colleagues. Perhaps living a more ordinary existence might lead him towards normality.

Later that evening, Charlie accompanied the rest of the team to a pub adjacent to the indoor sports centre where they played their weekly matches. He'd been deliberately losing bottles of beer or pouring them away all night. And those he couldn't get away with disposing of were swiftly followed by bathroom breaks to force himself to vomit before the anti-alcohol implant did it for him and in front of everyone.

'Are you seeing anyone?' Andrew, another new friend, asked him suddenly.

'No, not at the moment.'

'What's your type? Tall, short, skinny, plus-size, boy, girl?'

'I don't really mind,' he replied. 'Well, girl, obviously.'

'It's never obviously,' Andrew continued. 'What are you Milo, pansexual? Bi? You seem to change from one month to the next.'

'Never close a door before you've opened it,' Milo winked.

'Why do you ask?' said Charlie.

'If you're in the market for a non-DNA Match date, my girlfriend's cousin is single again.' He unfolded his phone and showed Charlie her Instagram profile. She was an attractive woman with dark brown hair, prominent cheekbones and deep brown, flecked eyes framed by heavy eyebrows.

'Thanks, but I'm okay,' Charlie replied. It wasn't that he didn't find Alix attractive; he just wasn't attracted to anyone lately. Days earlier, he realised he couldn't remember the last time he'd had an erection, let alone masturbated. His sex drive had completely evaporated.

'My round, same again?' he asked the table, to a chorus of approval.

'I'll give you a hand,' said Milo and accompanied Charlie to the bar. The way Milo wrung his hands warned Charlie something was bothering him. Of the group, he was probably the closest to Milo, at least superficially.

'Good game tonight,' Milo began. 'It was ... um ... a good result.'

'What's on your mind, big man?'

'It's ... a bit ... well ... awkward.'

'Just say it.'

'That cut on your leg. I was thinking about it and it looked a bit, I don't know, too neat and too straight to have been caused by barbed wire.'

'Oh, right,' Charlie nodded. He raised his eyebrows almost confrontationally, but softened the edges with a cock of his head. 'Does it?'

Milo nodded and cleared his throat. 'It looks as if it might have been done ... you know ... well, not accidentally.

And a couple of times when we've been out, I've heard you being sick in the toilets. Even earlier tonight.'

'First you're staring at my dick in the showers and now you're following me to the toilets,' joked Charlie. 'I mean, I'm flattered but you're not my type.'

'I just wanted to say that it can help to talk.'

'About what?'

'About anything. Whatever's going on in your life that you might be having problems with. I know you're quite a private guy and I might be barking up the wrong tree—'

'You are,' Charlie interrupted.

'But I'd never forgive myself if something happened to you and I'd said sod all.'

'Milo, thank you, I appreciate it, I really do. But I'm fine. Honestly. And if there is something worrying me, then I promise I'll talk to you. Okay?'

'Okay,' Milo repeated but Charlie knew his friend remained unconvinced.

'I need a piss,' Milo said and offered Charlie a half-smile and a pat on the shoulder.

'Is that an invitation?' Charlie replied with a wink.

Situation defused, thought Charlie. Alone, he knew the old him would have been grateful to have someone show such concern. Because his former friends wouldn't have. Now he saw it as an inconvenience.

Later that night and back inside his room, Charlie was changing out of his clothes when the leg wound caught his attention again. He traced its outline with his thumb. It was slightly raised and a crimson colour. He couldn't cut into it again as it was on Milo's radar. He would have to challenge his inability to feel through a different means instead.

He recalled the profile Andrew had shown him of Alix. Based on appearances alone, she was very close to his type and once, he would have jumped at the opportunity to meet someone like her. Perhaps he had been too hasty in his dismissal.

Tomorrow, he would stop by Andrew's desk and tell him he'd changed his mind. Perhaps Alix might be the one to help him recapture what he'd lost.

Chapter 28

SINÉAD, EDZELL, SCOTLAND

Sinéad sat on a grassy bank by the side of Scotland's river Esk.

She watched as leaves and twigs floated past, some becoming trapped in mini whirlpools, others sinking or disappearing sharply from view. Last night's storm had brought silt particles from the riverbed to the surface, leaving the water a murky red colour and of indeterminate depth. Tentatively, she dipped her foot into it, grateful that her muted pain receptors enabled her to endure its icy temperature without fuss. She rolled up her jeans to just above her knees and slowly waded towards the middle. There, she removed six half-pint plastic bottles from a bag hanging over her shoulder. Each bottle contained a hand-written letter, one for each person she hadn't had the opportunity to say goodbye to before she left Bristol.

It had been one of her therapist's suggestions; a symbolic gesture and final farewell to the past. The first three letters were to her former closest friends, Imani, Cally and Leanne. Over time, Sinéad's husband Daniel had made it clear that he disapproved of the time they spent together. He resented their girlie nights without partners when Sinéad returned home smelling of alcohol and fast food. He didn't appreciate when they'd call or video-message one another. And once, when he'd scanned her emails, he exploded with anger when he read a joke she had made about their sex life. To keep the peace, Sinéad agreed to a joint email address, and deleted her own.

Her friends became such a sticking point that eventually, she chose her marriage over them. She'd been too ashamed to offer them an explanation so she avoided their phone calls and messages. It had been better to ghost them than to admit her husband was beginning to control every aspect of her life.

Last night at the dining-room table in her rented house, she recalled the carefree times they'd shared as she wrote her three letters. She thanked them for being loyal friends and admitted they'd deserved better than what she had offered.

Letter number four was to her parents whose sudden death in the Mumbai tsunami had shaped the next decade of her life. She had spent it searching for the same love they had, but in the wrong places.

The fifth letter had been to Daniel and was the most painless to write. She detailed the emotional abuse and suffering he'd caused, why she'd left him but how she no longer blamed him entirely. She was also holding herself accountable for giving him power over her and for not walking away sooner.

Sinéad wasn't ready to think about the contents of the sixth letter again. Writing it had been emotionally crippling, even with her coping mechanisms in place.

The letters hadn't included the recipients' names or addresses, nor did she sign them. She had also pierced each biodegradable bottle to allow water inside so they sank to the riverbed and the ink washed away. But on the off-chance they were found and read, all parties were unidentifiable.

One by one, Sinéad gently dropped each bottle onto the surface and watched as the current swept them away and out of sight, until only one remained in her hand. That, she gripped a little tighter than she had the others. Eventually, and with tears clinging to her eyelashes, she slipped it back inside her bag. Sinéad wasn't yet ready to completely let go of her daughter, Lilly.

The two-bedroom bungalow was empty and unfurnished when Sinéad signed the lease. Her and Daniel's apartment had been overloaded with brand new furniture and technology – the washing machine and dishwasher decided for themselves when to run their cycles and their fridge ordered its own food online. Everything she chose for her cottage was second-hand or reclaimed and Wi-Fi free. Already, it felt like the home she had always wanted.

Sometimes she would walk over to Doon's house for one of her wine-and-rom-com evenings and other nights, Doon would come over and they'd share a meal. She was like the mother figure that Sinéad had missed out on for more than a decade and a half. And she wondered if Doon's loss of her only child was partially the reason why they connected. They filled a gap in one another's lives. But their closeness made it even harder for Sinéad to keep secret what she knew about the circumstances surrounding the death of Doon's daughter's, Isla. There was so much Sinéad could reveal that would ease her friend's guilt but it went against all the rules. Sometimes she hated keeping secrets.

Sinéad's garage was as packed as her days. Inside she stored a headboard, a dining-room table, two chests of drawers and a Welsh dresser – all objects Gail had purchased from online auctions. Sinéad gave them a new lease of life with sandpapers, chalk paints, glazes, stains and varnishes. Then Gail sold them on and they split the profits. Sinéad, however, had no need for a wage so she donated her earnings to a neonatal baby unit at the Royal Infirmary of Edinburgh instead.

The two women met every other day and Gail frequently brought her daughter, Taylor, with her, something Sinéad was struggling with. Being alone with a child didn't sit comfortably with her, especially one with eyes that never stopped following her around the room. Taylor stared at Sinéad cautiously, almost mistrustfully, as if to say, *I know what you've done.*

However, something niggled Sinéad about Gail and Taylor's relationship. Both mother and daughter paid more attention to her than they did to one another. Gail went through the motions of doing all the practical things a mum was expected to do, but Sinéad sensed a disconnect. Gail didn't speak proudly of any of Taylor's developmental milestones and she barely paid her any attention when they were together. There weren't even any photographs of Taylor on her phone. Individually, they were small quibbles, but together, they were enough for Sinéad to question whether her friend was suffering from postnatal depression. Or perhaps Anthony was to blame; maybe he was undermining her confidence in her ability to parent.

'Is he a hands-on dad?' Sinéad had casually asked earlier in the week as she poured Gail a coffee. Gail's face stiffened.

'He does his best, yes.'

'It must be tough on a marriage when a baby comes into the equation.'

'It's not easy.'

'If you ever want to – you know – talk about anything, then I'm a good listener.' Gail folded her arms, a classic act of defensiveness. Sinéad did the same thing when friends asked questions about her and Daniel's relationship.

'We're good, thank you,' she replied with finality so Sinéad left the conversation where it was.

That afternoon, the garage doors were propped open while a masked Sinéad sanded the legs of a kitchen table. As the sounds of heritage musicians from her youth like Katy Perry, Rihanna and Justin Bieber played from the speakers, she paused to allow her synaesthesia to bloom. Each group of notes created primary colours that floated around the garage like helium balloons caught in the wind. The higher the pitch, the brighter the colours became. She was surrounded by reds and burned oranges when Taylor Swift played, and light blues and lilacs when Coldplay appeared. Her world was never this colourful with Daniel in it.

'Someone's enjoying themselves,' a voice came suddenly.

'Jesus!' Sinéad shouted aloud, and turned her head quickly. Gail was by the doors laughing, Taylor inside a pushchair.

'You're such a jumpy so-and-so.'

Sinéad laughed but there was no humour in it. Instead, she was quietly annoyed for letting down her guard. 'I thought we were meeting tomorrow?' she asked as she pulled down her mask.

'I have a wee favour to ask. Are you free to babysit for a couple of hours?'

Sinéad flinched. 'When?'

'Now. There's a rocking chair dating back to the 1990s that I won on eBay, but I need to collect it now from Fettercairn before the owner goes on holiday.'

'Isn't Anthony free?'

'No, he's at the restaurant.'

An awkward gap opened up between them. Gail seemed to sense Sinéad's reluctance but pursued her request. 'She's very good and she'll probably sleep most of the time she's with you.'

'I was hoping to finish this table, though, and it can't be very good for a baby being around all this dust.'

'There's no hurry, the customer isn't expecting it until the weekend.'

Sinéad's mouth became dry as she ran short of excuses. 'I ... I'm sorry, I can't,' she muttered. 'I have something inside that I need to do. I'll see you soon.'

Sinéad left the sandpaper on the floor and walked briskly back into the house, careful not to make eye contact with her baffled friend, and closed the door behind her. At the sound of the pushchair's wheels leaving the driveway, she took deep breaths and raked her hair with her fingers.

Damn it, she thought. She had handled that terribly. Sinéad reached for her bag hanging from a wall hook and retrieved a small plastic bottle. As she moulded her fingers around it, all she could think about was how Gail would never have asked Sinéad to babysit if she'd known that her friend had been responsible for the death of her own baby.

Chapter 29

EMILIA

'I need to get out of here,' muttered Emilia.

She stared from the living-room window at the rolling green hills of the countryside ahead. She caught Ted's reflection as he rose from a sofa and she flinched when he wrapped his arms around her waist. She could tell that he felt it because immediately he pulled back.

'We could go out for dinner tonight if you like?' he suggested. 'There's a wonderful Thai restaurant in town we used to visit. It might bring something back.'

'I'd like to go out by myself.' Emilia turned to face him. 'I think it might do me some good.'

'That's not something I'd feel comfortable with, not yet.'

Would you feel more comfortable if I was sedated and locked up? she wanted to ask, but stopped herself. She was still unaware of his motives or the danger she faced in confronting him. Instead, she swallowed her brewing frustration.

'I have a wardrobe full of gym clothes upstairs, so I assume I used to exercise a lot. I'd like to go for a run.'

'That's a great idea. We have a treadmill in the gym with virtual-reality headsets and belts, that mimics settings from mountain paths to the desert. I'll join you, it'll be fun.'

'No, I want to go outside.'

'Well, there's several acres of land you probably haven't explored yet. You could take the dogs with you.'

'You're not listening to me,' she sighed. 'I want to go beyond the walls, explore the area in which I apparently once had a life. I'm going stir crazy in this house.'

'It's not safe for you being out there alone. What happens if you relapse and become disorientated and can't remember where we live?'

'Then I'll find someone to ask for help. And it's unlikely to happen because I remember everything since I first woke up. Just nothing before.'

Emilia shuddered when she thought of the room where she had come back to life. She still had no inkling where or what it was or how she had come to be there. It haunted her dreams, along with the pregnant woman's warning that Ted was not her husband. Emilia had spent much of the fortnight since her hospital discharge second-guessing everything Ted had to say. She picked apart their conversations in the hunt for contradictions. And at the forefront of her mind was his reluctance to allow her to leave their property alone and what she had overheard him say downstairs.

There were other things she struggled to reconcile with too, aside from not remembering her husband or the home they'd apparently designed and built together. At least a dozen shoes from her extensive collection were a half size too small for her feet. She was sure that she could drive yet there was no indication she owned a car. Her phone and tablet had no contacts listed on either of them aside from Ted's numbers. She seemingly had no access to credit cards or a bank account. Even the dogs they'd bought as puppies appeared completely unfamiliar with her.

However, Ted had an explanation for everything. He told her she had been willing to suffer for fashion even if the shoe didn't fit; she'd lost her confidence behind the wheel after an accident so took trains to her office in London; her electronic devices were brand new and he'd cancelled her access to bank accounts when she vanished. And their dogs were loyal to whoever fed them – and for the last few months, it had only been Ted.

'All I want is to be out there on my own for a couple of hours,' Emilia pleaded. 'Don't you trust me?'

Soon after and for the first time in weeks, Emilia was almost a free woman. Dressed in a T-shirt, running bottoms and trainers, she pounded the woodland paths alone and this time as she reached the rear gates, there was no one to prevent her from leaving. But outside in the open, she hadn't run more than a couple of hundred metres along the pavement before sensing she wasn't alone. She heard the crackling of twigs and crunching of gravel underfoot from behind the other side of the wall, as a second pair of feet, perhaps more, maintained her pace.

Ted was having her followed.

Furious, Emilia darted across the road that separated two stretches of woods, running between the trees and pushing her way through the undergrowth. Her calf and thigh muscles burned after weeks of inactivity but still she ran, until she was sure she had lost whoever was on her trail. Then she bent double, her hands on her knees, fighting for breath. If Ted could lie about letting her out alone, it stood to reason he was lying about so much more. It was then that she made her decision.

She removed and unfolded a business card from her pocket that the stranger had given her in the grounds of the hospital. It contained only a telephone number. Nervously, she dialled and it rang just once before it was answered.

'Continue through the woods until you see an opening,' a woman's voice began coolly. 'Follow the bridleway until you reach the nearest village. I will be in a private dining room in the Old House at Home pub. You should be there in fifteen minutes.'

Emilia opened her mouth to respond but the line was already dead and the number was erasing itself remotely.

Chapter 30

BRUNO, OUNDLE, NORTHAMPTONSHIRE

Bruno glanced at the ReadWell message board, studying what he'd just typed.

> @Cominius: Have any of you revisited your old life simply to destroy the people who made it such a misery? Am I the only one who resents them for making me give it up for this world? Am I alone in wanting to make them pay? Or have you too taken matters into your own hands and gone back to snuff them out? Do the Echoes follow you too? Or do they see me as weak and that's why they haunt me?

His finger hovered above the 'post' button as he weighed up what the consequences might be if he posted such an incendiary message. Instead, he hit the backspace key and watched each word being erased, letter by letter.

Bruno discovered the unexpected aftermath of committing murder – an insatiable appetite for only the unhealthiest kind of food. It was as if his body wanted carbohydrates to replace those used in the exertion of killing. Greasy-spoon cafes serving meals dripping in highly saturated fats and massive calorific content were all he craved. But hefty taxes on unhealthy food establishments meant they were becoming few and far between. However, Bruno had located a speakeasy-style truckers' cafe behind a garage just outside town, with a menu containing everything that was bad for him. It was his third visit in a fortnight – and each had followed a killing.

After the lawyers came two more names on his list. They had worked under Zoe, then accused her after her death of sexual harassment. But Bruno was convinced they were opportunist liars and as a result of their unfounded accusations, they were responsible for his separation from Louie. One died from a single hammer blow to the head in his garage, the other on the doorstep to his flat with three swift thwacks.

Then in the early hours of that morning, Bruno erased the penultimate name. Jaxon Davies was the rugby player who had filmed Bruno's wife Zoe and her work colleague having sex inside an autonomous company car. After uploading it onto a pornographic website, he'd earned money each time it was viewed. And Bruno estimated from the number count and percentage of likes it had received, that Davies had made thousands from Zoe's public indiscretion.

Bruno had traced Davies's address before enrolling in the programme, as he had with lawyers O'Sullivan and Graph. He'd planned to confront him to appeal to his better nature and persuade him to take it down. Bruno hated knowing his son's mother was a tool used for sexual gratification. But before he had the opportunity to, Louie had solved a puzzle and Bruno's training had started. And once he was released back into the world, Bruno no longer cared if Davies had a better nature or not.

In the early hours of the morning, he'd hurled a rock through one of Davies's rear windows and waited in the gloom of the garden for the confused man to appear. Moments later, Bruno beat him to death using the same hammer he'd attacked the others with. And as with the others, £1 coins were left in what remained of his eye sockets.

On his return to Oundle, Bruno reflected on his transformation from devoted dad and widow to cold-blooded killer, and questioned if the potential for such behaviour had always been inside him, waiting for an excuse to reveal itself. Had its rise to the surface been a reaction to Zoe's behaviour, losing the house and then his son? Or was the procedure, the removal of pain receptors and management of the chemicals that controlled his moods, to blame, knocking everything else off kilter?

Bruno recalled how soon after his procedure, he began obsessing over the data he stored, specifically graphic accounts of hushed-up murders and contract killings. Governments, principalities and individuals justifying bloodshed for political and social purposes fascinated him. Thousands had died for lesser reasons than the names on the hit list he'd begun to compile and it helped him to justify his plans. Months later, only one name remained.

Following a hot shower and a change out of his bloody clothes, Bruno was refuelling with a full English breakfast and all the trimmings. It brought to the surface a memory of Zoe and him inside a diner on Las Vegas Boulevard. Each of their plates had contained a stack of pancakes so tall, they could barely finish a third of them.

They had hired a Jeep for their honeymoon and driven from Los Angeles to San Francisco, stopping off in Vegas, the Grand Canyon and Yosemite National Park. It was the trip of a lifetime. And in their first few years of marriage, they had continued to enjoy at least three foreign breaks a year until Louie was born.

Recent developments in prenatal testing had revealed he was likely to be on the autistic spectrum, but despite Zoe's hesitancy, they continued with the pregnancy. It wasn't until Louie's second birthday that a broader extent of his condition emerged. Flights abroad became difficult as the noise and vibrations of plane engines agitated him. Unfamiliar hotel rooms scared him and he'd repeatedly hit himself on the back of his head with his fists. Music playing from speakers scattered around pools and restaurants led to screaming fits that proved too stressful for them all.

So, Bruno and Zoe stopped going as far afield, and hired campervans instead, cramming items familiar to Louie inside them before travelling the British Isles. Bruno didn't care where they went as long as he was surrounded by his family. But sometimes, as the campervan drove itself from destination to destination, he'd catch sight of Zoe staring wistfully from the window at the passing countryside. He feared she hadn't found the happiness he had.

Later, she earned a promotion at work that saw her earnings far outweighing his, so he quit his career to be a full-time dad while she worked longer hours away from home. It bothered Bruno at the time that her absence didn't seem to trouble her. But he chose not to bring it up. Now he wondered how many other cracks in their marriage he'd papered over.

Bruno mopped up the remains of his breakfast with a slice of thick white bread and pushed his knife and fork to one side of the plate. As a waitress refilled his mug with tea, he withdrew a second phone from his pocket, an unregistered one he'd purchased that morning. He double-checked that he'd disabled locations, cookies, emails and texts before using the cafe's Wi-Fi to find the only website he planned to visit.

He allowed an Echo, a woman with a South African accent, to walk him through his implanted data on how to bypass password encryption. Once inside the website, he accessed the interior security cameras. One by one, he made use of them all to search each room until he finally tracked down who he was looking for.

Louie was sitting at a kitchen table in his residential care unit, mixing a bowl of ingredients. Just a glimpse of his son after six months of separation created an ache inside that pushed against his heart. Louie appeared perfectly content as a staff member helped him to pour the contents onto a baking tray. And without being told what to do, Louie levelled it with a wooden spoon and placed it inside an oven.

It was a bittersweet moment. Bruno wanted to be the one teaching his son new skills, not a stranger. Louie was growing up without him.

'They're doing better with him in a few months than you did in twelve years, aren't they?' a second Echo sneered. 'You weren't enough for your wife and now it appears you weren't enough for your son either.'

'Go away,' Bruno muttered, the elation at seeing Louie diminishing with the Echo's cruel tongue.

'Have you ever seen him looking so content?' it continued. 'If you didn't know better, you'd think he was normal.'

Bruno clenched his fists and concentrated hard, trying to take back control of whoever was wrestling reality away from him.

'I wonder what Louie would be like now if you'd given him up years ago? At least Zoe didn't fool herself into thinking she was any good for him.' The Echo gave a throaty laugh. 'Yep, you failed her and you failed that retard.'

Bruno rose to his feet and slammed his hands on the table so hard, his cutlery and plate jumped. 'Just fuck off and leave me alone!' he yelled. 'All of you, just fuck off!'

A speedy hush came over the rest of the cafe's patrons as all eyes rested upon him. And as he hurried out, he couldn't be sure if he was imagining them too or if they were real.

Chapter 31

FLICK, ALDEBURGH, SUFFOLK

'But I know nothing about art!' insisted Flick.

'Hold still,' Grace replied, 'and keep your eyes closed.' She took a brush from her make-up bag and began to dust Flick's eyelids with a dark, smoky colour.

'You don't *have* to know anything about art to enjoy it. It's not like they're going to quiz us at the end of the night, is it?'

'I don't even know what to wear?'

'I've already laid out on my bed some of my outfits and a few pairs of shoes for you to choose from. Okay, now you can look. What do you think?'

Flick barely recognised the woman in the reflection of Grace's mum's dressing-table mirror. Aside from lipstick and a little foundation, it had been an age since Flick had made an effort with her appearance. 'I scrub up okay, don't I?'

Some time had passed since Flick had enjoyed a close friendship with a member of the same sex. Most of her friends had been in catering and the majority were male. But with Grace, she was able to be a girl's girl again. They made their way to Grace's bedroom where she chose a white-and-yellow summery floral dress and a pair of casual shoes with a kitten heel.

'How can you travel so light?' Grace asked, commenting on Flick's near-empty wardrobe. 'I need a team of Sherpas to get me from A to B.'

'I don't like baggage.'

'Emotional or physical?'

Flick didn't reply.

'Both then,' Grace said for her. 'I know that you talk very little about the past but ...'

'I prefer to keep looking forward.'

'Okay, I can take a hint.'

Flick appreciated her concern, and was tempted to make light of her offer, but held back because it was coming from a heartfelt place.

'Who is Aldeburgh's equivalent of Andy Warhol that we're dressing up for?' she teased.

'Elijah Beckworth.'

'Elijah?' Flick repeated and turned to look at her. 'Did you say *Elijah*?'

'Yes, why?'

'I think he came to the pub last week. Dark blond hair, beard ...'

'... Twinkly blue eyes and a smile that's warm enough to melt an iceberg? That's the one.'

'And this is his show?'

'It's an exhibition. *Les Misérables* is a show.'

'Sorry, exhibition?'

'Uh-uh.'

'He drew me a picture while he was sitting at the bar.'

'You should keep that because his stuff sells for a fortune.'

Grace continued to talk but Flick wasn't listening. Instead, she concentrated on how inexplicably nervous she was growing at the idea of coming face to face with Elijah again.

Chapter 32

EMILIA

Two people awaited a cautious Emilia when she reached the private dining room at the rear of the near-empty pub. On impulse she made a mental note of all available exits before closing the door behind her. Even then, she questioned whether this was a good idea or a foolish one.

Inside, a man and woman were sitting together on one side of a wooden table. Emilia pegged him as somewhere in his forties, with a lantern-square jaw, receding hairline and dark eyes that were impossible to read. She was younger than him, with a rich brown complexion and prominent cheekbones. Her expression was part curious and part satisfied that Emilia had come.

'Take a seat,' the woman began, pointing to a chair opposite. 'You will likely have a lot of questions.'

'Who are you?'

'That doesn't matter,' she replied, batting the question away with her hand.

The casual dismissal confused Emilia. 'It does to me.'

'Move on.'

'Who am I?'

'I can't answer that.'

'The woman who gave me your number told me Ted's not my husband. Who is he?'

'I can't tell you that either.'

'Then why the hell am I here?' Emilia huffed.

'Because there are people out there who can give you those answers. But not us.'

'Who? How do I find them?'

'All in due course, Emilia.'

'I'm wasting my time.' She kicked back her chair and rose to her feet. 'If you don't know who I am, this is pointless.'

'All we can tell you is what we've pieced together. We know for certain that you and Ted aren't married, and you'd never been associated before he appeared in your hospital room.'

'He showed me our wedding photos and videos.'

'And honeymoon ones, no doubt. Along with visual records of your university graduation, pictures of you on a gap year travelling the world and breaking ground on your new home. Am I right?'

'Um ... yes ...'

'He's offered you the perfect life, hasn't he? An idyllic existence that most people would accept regardless of whether they remembered it or not. It's a tried and tested technique. Some call it brainwashing, others refer to it as coercive persuasion, mind control, thought manipulation, re-education, etcetera. It doesn't matter because they're all the same thing. With enough reinforcement and regular stimuli, in time you will believe what he wants you to believe.'

Emilia's chest tightened. 'Why should I trust you over him when you won't even tell me who you are?'

'Do you have feelings for Ted?'

Emilia went to reply but couldn't answer.

'Do you love him? Is there at least a physical attraction there? A familiarity you can't put your finger on, but that is present, nonetheless?'

'No, but that's as a result of my amnesia.'

'You don't have amnesia, Emilia.'

'Yes, I do. I've had multiple tests, I've seen specialists, it was diagnosed.'

'For the right price, even professionals can be persuaded to offer no more than a surface-level diagnosis. That includes your consultant, Dr Fazul Choudary, who mysteriously found himself free of a burdensome mortgage recently. Amnesia is not the reason that you cannot remember, it's as a result of what they have done to you.'

'*They*? Who are *they*? And what have *they* done?'

She turned to her colleague. 'Adrian?'

His voice was low and resonant, his words clipped. 'Something has happened to you that means your past has been locked away and neither you, nor we, know how to open it. But as Bianca says, there are five people who can assist you. They knew the old you. You just need to identify and locate them.'

'Where are they?'

'Four are scattered around the country, buried away under different guises, living different lives in different locations. You are living with the fifth.'

'Ted?' she asked, and frowned. 'What does he know?'

'That's for us all to discover. He has had ample opportunity to help you to date but has chosen to construct an alternate narrative. We would like to assist you in every way possible in finding the truth.'

'In return for what?'

'Our sources inform us that Ted is travelling to Europe next week. We have a business opportunity of our own that we'd like to discuss with him.'

'And if I don't agree? If I just walk away from you right now, what will happen?'

'Be our guest, there's nothing stopping you. But something's a little off about your perfect life, isn't it? None of it feels real. You are here because you don't want to remain trapped in a world of uncertainty. Without us, that's where you'll remain for the foreseeable future – or until Ted decides enough is enough and has you killed.'

Chapter 33

FLICK, ALDEBURGH, SUFFOLK

Flick had yet to take a sip from the glass of champagne she had been handed on her arrival at Aldeburgh's High Street Gallery.

She surveyed the room of a hundred or so guests and recognised some of their faces as pub regulars. But all she knew of art was from the secrets she held and was forbidden to share. She knew the whereabouts of undeclared works stolen from Jewish families by the Nazis in the Second World War and that were now under the secret charge of British aristocrats. And she recalled several old masters thought missing presumed destroyed but actually given away by the government to foreign leaders in return for favours.

But even to her uneducated eye, Elijah's work was remarkable. It featured a mixture of floor-to-ceiling oil paintings and smaller, intricate lino etchings of faces. His level of detail and understanding of his subjects captivated her. Every wrinkle, mole, pore, stray eyebrow, ear hair or unaligned tooth was on display, allowing them to be honest and unforgiving. The doodle of her that he'd left her at the bar had been merciful in comparison.

One image in particular caught her attention; it was of an elderly man with deep crevices across his furrowed brow, mottled skin and blue irises that retained their hue despite a long-departed youth. She became lost in him, imagining the stories such a weathered face must contain. But the painting suddenly stopped halfway across the left-hand side of his face.

'That's Jacob,' a voice came from behind, and goose-bumps immediately dappled her arms.

Flick turned to face Elijah. Even just a glimpse of his smile stirred the sleeping butterflies inside her stomach. She took in his smart black shirt with three buttons loosened and a hint of chest hair poking from the top. She resisted the urge to rip it open. 'Who's Jacob?' she asked casually.

'A local who lived here all his life.'

'Where is he now?'

Elijah looked up to the ceiling, down to the ground and shrugged. 'He was a funny old bugger so he could have gone either way, who knows? But he was either the nicest man you could ever meet or your worst nightmare, it depends on which way the wind was blowing. He made for an interesting subject, though.'

'What happened to him?'

'He died on his trawler. He was a lobster fisherman but one evening his boat didn't return. The coastguard found him slumped in his cabin, as dead as the water. Heart attack.'

'But what a wonderful way to go,' Flick said. 'Doing what he enjoyed the most.' She brushed away an image of a burning Christopher. He had also died doing something he loved: killing. 'Why isn't it complete?'

'I could've completed it from memory or from the photos I took at earlier sittings, but I think its incompleteness makes more of an impact. Not knowing everything makes something more interesting.'

'Are you telling her about your Uncle Jacob?' Mick, the landlord of the Fox & Hounds, interrupted. 'Funny bugger, that one.'

Flick looked to Elijah, curious as to why he'd failed to mention the relationship between artist and subject. 'Case in point,' he said without giving her the chance to speak first. 'It's always what we don't know about someone that piques our curiosity. Would you like to join me outside for some air?'

'But it's your exhibition,' said Flick.

'Which means I get to make the rules. Please excuse us, Mick.'

Grace reappeared from another room in time to wink at Flick as she followed Elijah along a corridor and into a back room, then into a courtyard garden framed by railway sleepers and flowerbeds. He held his hand out towards a nest of tables and chairs, inviting her to sit.

'Your paintings don't have price tags,' Flick began, unsure why she had chosen money as her opening gambit.

'Why, is there one that you'd like to purchase?'

'I think they probably have more zeros on them than my wage slip.'

'There aren't any prices attached because they're not for sale.'

'Then why organise an exhibition?'

'It's what I've always done and I'm a stickler for tradition. I hold an exhibition in my home town first, see which paintings people are drawn to and which ones they're not, and then make a judgement on whether they'll make my official exhibition in Birmingham in a few weeks. You should sit for me some time.'

'I already have. At the bar. Only you didn't tell me.'

'I mean properly. That was only a doodle.'

'It'll do.'

'It's a no then?'

Flick laughed. 'I'm flattered but it's a no, thank you.' Bringing undue attention to herself, even in the form of a painting, was not advisable.

'That's twice you've rejected me within a week,' Elijah pursued.

'There's a difference between saying "No, thank you" and rejection.'

'So, when you turned down my offer of dinner, it wasn't a rejection?'

Flick nodded. 'It was a no, thank you.'

Elijah gave a playful shrug. 'Unless I've read this completely incorrectly, there's a connection between us, but you're doing everything in your power to thwart it.'

Flick diverted her attention to her shoes. 'It's complicated.'

'Are you married?' he asked.

'No.'

'Are you single?'

'Yes.'

'Are you attracted to me?'

Despite herself, this was one lie Flick couldn't bring herself to tell. She tried hard not to imagine how his lips felt. 'You're very direct, aren't you?' she replied.

'I'll take that deflection to mean yes. But someone hurt you quite badly so now you struggle to trust anyone.'

Flick didn't need to reply. The look she gave him admitted as much.

'That's fine, I'm a patient man, I can wait.'

'We should go back inside.'

'Must we?'

'Yes.'

'Okay, but I will persuade you to sit for me one day.'

'Would you rather paint me or take me out for dinner?'

'We can combine the two. I'll paint you while you eat.'

'It's a no thanks to that too.'

'You're a tough cookie.'

Elijah placed his hand in the small of her back as he escorted her back to the gallery and the two went their separate ways. Grace slipped her arm around Flick's and pulled her into a quieter section, grabbing another glass of champagne from a waiter's tray as she moved. 'Tell me everything,' she began.

'There's nothing to tell.'

'You disappear outside with Elijah Beckworth for twenty minutes and return as if nothing has happened but with a smile the size of the Cheddar Gorge across your face.'

'We just talked. You know I'm not looking for a relationship.'

'And that's precisely when you're most likely to find it. Do you want to see him again?'

Flick couldn't deny that she wanted to get to know him. She told herself that it was because Karczewski had encouraged them to blend into their new surroundings which included becoming involved in relationships. But only if they were confident no emotion was involved and they could leave without notice if ordered to. She tried to kid herself there was no more to it than that.

A hangover from the past made Flick question whether she trusted Elijah. She understood the irony in expecting honesty from someone else when she was unable to offer it herself.

'Perhaps this is why you're in Aldeburgh,' Grace continued. 'Despite all that's happened to you before you arrived, this is the person you're meant to be now. And Elijah is the person you're meant to be with.'

Chapter 34

CHARLIE, MANCHESTER

'Andrew!' snapped Vicky. 'Enough! You'll have to excuse my fiancée, Charlie, he might be a great life-coach, but he could benefit from paying someone to guide him in appropriate dining conversation.'

'I've played footie with him for a few weeks now so I'm used to it,' Charlie replied and winked at his friend.

The truth was that Charlie had no idea what Vicky was apologising for. He had been dipping in and out of the conversation for much of dinner, uninterested in what either his work colleague or his wife-to-be had to say. The last thing he'd heard was Andrew recalling a client who appeared to be using his voice to satisfy more than just her mentoring needs.

'None of this matters anyway, as it'll be AI which has to deal with these freaks before long,' continued Andrew. 'The rise of machine learning means we'll be replaced within the next couple of years by robo-advisers and chat-bots in the same way bookkeepers, estate agents, couriers and car salesmen were.'

Charlie nodded his agreement and glanced at Vicky's cousin Alix. He caught her staring at him and she looked away quickly.

Soon after he'd agreed to a double date with Alix, Vicky arranged dinner for the four of them at a restaurant. Charlie was finely attuned to the body language of others and specifically micro-expressions which were often hard to fake. The way Alix held his gaze with her rich, chocolatey eyes or tilted her head as he spoke were signs of her attraction to him.

She might have ticked every box if he had still been the old Charlie. But back then, he lacked the backbone to have ever asked her out. Now, his confidence wasn't a problem, it was ambivalence. He no longer had 'a type' because he felt no attraction to anyone. However, for the purpose of the double date, he went through the motions of paying her attention, showing interest in what she had to say and asking about her life. Being involved with someone wouldn't hurt in his pursuit of the appearance of normality.

'Andrew tells me that you've just moved into a new place in Salford?' said Vicky. 'Alix has a flat only a few minutes away from you.'

'I'm renting a room in a house with a couple of lads from the IT department,' he replied. 'So far so good.'

'Have you been in Manchester long?' asked Alix.

Charlie relied upon the well-rehearsed story he and Karczewski had concocted that he'd been born to armed services parents on a military base in Aldershot, and for much of his childhood, the family had frequently moved around Europe.

'That must have been tough when you were little, leaving your friends,' Alix said, with genuine sympathy.

'It wasn't always easy,' he admitted. 'Just as I got used to one place, we were off to somewhere else. But you adapt quickly when you don't know any different.'

'Where are your family now?'

'Retired from the forces and living in Australia. They emigrated a few years back.'

'Didn't you want to go with them?'

He pointed to his pale arms. 'With my skin tone? I'd be burned to a crisp within an hour.'

'Alix, tell Charlie about your job,' encouraged Vicky. Her inflection suggested Charlie might be impressed.

'I work in a nursery,' she said, almost shyly. 'It's not that exciting.'

'She's great with kids,' added Vicky. 'You should see her; she has a natural way about her. Very maternal.'

'Babe, chill,' Andrew muttered and Vicky side-eyed him.

'I'm just pointing out that my friend is a very nurturing woman.' She turned quickly to Charlie. 'What about you, Charlie? Do you want kids?'

'Not tonight, no,' he joked.

'But eventually?'

Again, he returned to the script. 'If I met the right person, then yes, it's something we'd discuss.'

'Have you done the Match Your DNA test?' Vicky continued. Alix's eyes bored into him.

'No, I haven't,' he lied. 'I prefer to let things develop organically, rather than chemically. But it's completely up to the individual, isn't it? How about you, Alix? Have you taken it?'

'Yes,' she admitted, 'But my Match is an eighty-eight-year-old great-grandfather in Central Pakistan.'

When Andrew let out a laugh, Vicky nudged his ribs with her elbow.

'It's okay,' Alix continued. 'I can see the funny side of it too; the one person I'm supposedly biologically made for is pushing ninety. We have one another's contact details but neither of us got in touch.'

'You never know, Alix, he could be a millionaire at death's door looking to leave all his money to a beautiful young bride,' teased Andrew.

'I'll take my chances elsewhere.' She briefly glanced at Charlie. 'I'll leave it to fate to decide who I should be with.'

When Vicky cleared her throat pointedly, Alix corrected herself. 'Okay, fate *and* Miss Matchmaker over there.'

The evening and the conversation flowed and Charlie was aware he should have been sitting on cloud nine. But even when they gave each other a peck on the cheek goodbye and arranged to meet at the weekend – this time just the two of them – he didn't leave with the expectation this was the start of something new and exciting.

Back in his house-share bedroom, Charlie lay on his back on his bed, his hand in his underwear, touching himself as he imagined peeling off Alix's clothes and slowly working his mouth around her body until, finally, they made love. He became aroused but try as he might, he couldn't climax. His erection was a biological reaction to physical stimulation and nothing else. Had he not touched it, his penis would have remained motionless. Alix didn't arouse him because no one did. And he was neither annoyed nor disappointed by it. Only curious as to how far he would need to push himself to feel *anything* again.

Chapter 35

SINÉAD, EDZELL, SCOTLAND

'I owe you an apology,' began Sinéad.

Hovering awkwardly on Gail's doorstep, Sinéad looked towards the small posy of wild flowers she'd picked that morning on a woodland walk. Now, it felt like a childish gesture.

A week had passed since the friends had last met. Twice, Gail had appeared at Sinéad's house and on both occasions, Sinéad had hidden behind the kitchen door and ignored the bell. Eventually she recognised that she was allowing history to repeat itself. She was isolating herself and treating Gail in the same way she had handled her friends after marrying Daniel. She'd even ignored a visit from Doon in case they too had been discussing her.

'Can I come in and explain, just for a few minutes?' Sinéad asked. Gail hesitated, before stepping to one side. Sinéad followed her into the kitchen where they'd chatted over mug after mug of flavoured tisane teas. Gail offered Sinéad her usual seat at the island and filled a mosaic-patterned teapot from the boiling-water tap. Gail laid the flowers on the draining board.

'Last week …when you asked me to look after Taylor …' Sinéad began. 'I wanted to, I really did, but I just couldn't.'

'Why not?'

Sinéad considered modifying her backstory but this was *her* story. This wasn't a secret she was keeping for national safety. Her brain was too crammed with the lies of others to make up more of her own. It was time for honesty.

'Before I came here, I was married,' she began, her line of sight now directed beyond Gail and into the garden. 'We weren't a good combination and it was only after I escaped him that I fully appreciated just how toxic our relationship was. But a couple of years after we married, I fell pregnant. By then, I'd already suffered several miscarriages and when you've been through something like that more than once, you automatically assume the worst. Only this time, the worst didn't happen.'

Sinéad paused and felt the warmth of her friend's hand rest on her arm. She heard Taylor's light breathing quietly coming through a baby monitor. Sinéad's throat tightened.

'Lilly was born at six-forty-seven a.m. in hospital on a Monday morning after twenty-eight hours of labour. She was our – she was *my* – little miracle. A wee thing at four and a half pounds, she was just perfect. Then five weeks to the day after coming into the world, she left it.' The words snagged as she said them.

'I'm so sorry,' said Gail. She pushed back in her chair and stood behind Sinéad, wrapping both arms tightly around her shoulders. Sinéad recalled that in the immediate aftermath of Lilly's death, no one had offered that same comfort. Not Daniel, not the paramedics, nor the police.

However, the sound of the front door opening brought a premature halt to their conversation. The women fell silent until Anthony appeared in the kitchen. Catching sight of his wife's guest, his face dropped. Its recovery wasn't fast enough to fool Sinéad. She had seen it many times before in Daniel's expression. She was not welcome and she doubted if any of Gail's friends ever were.

'I didn't know you were expecting guests,' he began.

'She wasn't, I was just passing by and thought I'd drop in,' Sinéad replied.

'Is ... everything all right?' he directed towards his wife.

'Can you give us a few minutes, please?' asked Gail.

'Why?'

'We're in the middle of something.'

Anthony's posture straightened, as if assuming he was the topic of conversation. Gail continued the deadlock before offering Sinéad an apologetic glance and leading her husband out of the kitchen and into the lounge where their daughter was sleeping. The door closed, but Sinéad couldn't help but hear their conversation through the baby monitor.

'I'm not allowed in my own bloody house because she's here?' Anthony hissed.

'We were discussing something personal ...'

'And so were we this morning until you decided that we weren't any more and walked out. What could she have to say that's more important than us trying to sort out *our* problems?'

'Please, not now, Anthony.' Gail sounded weary, as if this was a frequently traversed argument.

'What have you told her about us?' Anthony pressed.

'Nothing.'

'I don't want you talking about our issues with a complete stranger.'

'I'm perfectly capable of making my own decisions without needing your approval first,' Gail countered.

'So my opinion doesn't count? But when does it in this bloody house?'

Gail muttered something Sinéad couldn't quite hear before, without warning, there came the unmistakable sound of a slap. Sinéad's eyes opened wide.

Anthony had just hit his wife.

Sinéad's immediate reaction was to burst into that room and put her combat training to good use, breaking the hand

Anthony had used to hurt her friend with. But Karczewski's words repeated in her head. 'Don't put yourself in situations you don't need to be involved in,' he'd warned. 'The more you risk your own safety, the more you risk the programme.'

While Daniel had fallen short of physical abuse, he'd made up for it by slowly chipping away at her morale until it had been completely eroded. Could she really stand idly by and watch another woman suffer at the hands of a bully?

The programme comes first, she reminded herself. *You have to walk away.*

Reluctantly, Sinéad had little choice but to listen to her gut. She quietly opened the back door and made her way across the garden, taking a shortcut over the fence and through the field of towering wind turbines, growing angrier and angrier at her inertia.

Arriving back at the cottage, Sinéad turned on the radio to quieten her shame, jabbing at buttons until she found a classic pop station. She turned the volume up as high as the dial allowed. The colourful notes that usually surrounded them were notably diminished. She hadn't seen so many dull greys, blacks and browns floating around a room in a long time.

She also fretted about baby Taylor living in a house where domestic violence was the norm. That made her thoughts return to Lilly. She still recalled with clarity every pore in her daughter's beautiful face.

She hadn't been the easiest of newborns. The first week had passed without issue; she fed little and often, slept on and off for around eighteen hours a day and only cried when her belly craved warm milk. But by the middle of week two, the routine Sinéad was beginning to take for granted began to fray. Lilly cried with alarming regularity, for hours at a time and for no apparent reason. Nothing pacified her; not cuddles, food, dark rooms, park walks, fresh nappies or the vibrations of Sinéad's moving car. Convinced she was sick, twice Sinéad insisted their GP examine her daughter but he found nothing medically wrong.

By the third week of little to no sleep, an exhausted Sinéad begged a reticent Daniel for help. Instead of offering much-needed support, he questioned why she wasn't able to understand her baby's needs when other mothers could. He also reminded her that because she was breastfeeding, there was little he could do to assist. Finally, he convinced her that mother and daughter might settle more easily if they slept in the nursery.

It was Daniel who had found his daughter's lifeless body that New Year's morning. Lilly was still in the crook of her mother's arm, face up and with Sinéad's nipple in her mouth. Sinéad awoke to the sound of Daniel yelling and grabbing the baby from where she had fallen asleep in the armchair feeding her.

Unable to comprehend what had happened, Sinéad begged paramedics to bring her daughter back to life as they carried out chest compressions on her tiny frame. But it was too late. A fast-tracked coroner's report revealed that Lilly had likely choked to death on her exhausted mother's milk.

'I don't care what the inquest rules: we'll tell everyone it was Sudden Infant Death Syndrome,' Daniel said. 'We don't need anyone knowing you killed her.'

His words cut deeply. He insisted that Sinéad register the birth and death alone, suggesting it might help her to accept her culpability. But Sinéad was already well aware of what she had done. And following the funeral – a private ceremony with just the two of them in attendance – he point-blank refused to talk about his daughter again.

But the accidental death of a child, especially at the hands of a parent, became all-consuming. There were no support groups for women like her, no online forums she could join to talk about her guilt. She trawled the internet instead, bookmarking news stories about family members who had mistakenly killed their children in other ways. It was a scab she couldn't stop picking at. Over and over she read about grandparents running over their grandchildren in vehicles, accidental drownings in baths and pools, medication overdoses and babies forgotten about and left inside cars during heatwaves. She was no better than any of them.

Her compulsion to pick at her eyelashes began in the aftermath of Lilly's death. Each time she assumed she could feel no more pain, she would pluck at them to remind herself there was *always* more pain to be felt if she dug hard enough. What started deliberately soon became a habit, and she would stare at her reflection every morning and evening, scanning for regrowth. The deeper the root, the more the sting, and the more satisfaction she felt. She was not alone, she discovered; many people were compelled to do it often in response to stressful situations. The NHS's website even gave her condition a name – trichotillomania.

The grief following Lilly's death eased over time but the guilt did not. Daniel's unwillingness to try and ease her burden resulted in her continuing her preoccupation until eventually, her eyelashes gave up and stopped growing back. He told her many times that without them, she resembled a reptile that was ready to cry at any given moment. Part of it wasn't far from the truth, because her eyes were constantly weeping as she no longer had a barrier from dust, grit or pollen when she blinked.

Sinéad begged Daniel to sell their apartment but he refused; his compromise being that while they were out for the day, he'd arranged for a removals company to take away Lilly's cot, changing table, wardrobe, Moses basket, clothes and soft toys. No keepsakes remained.

For months, Sinéad scoured local charity shops hoping but failing to find anything that had once been touched by her baby. Even now, miles away from home in Edzell, she struggled to pass a charity shop without taking a quick glance through the window at the baby clothes hanging up on the rail.

Chapter 36

EMILIA

The recorded voice memo came from a withheld number and appeared soon after midnight. Emilia turned down the volume of her phone and pressed it against her ear, just to be sure Ted couldn't hear anything from his suite next door.

The caller's accent was male and British but he possessed no regional accent. She was sure that it was synthetic. Such computer-generated voices were near-perfect in their diction, but were let down by their intonation. Emilia, however, could spot the devil in the detail, even if she didn't know how she had acquired such a skill.

'Nine p.m. tonight at the Paquis Lighthouse,' was all the voice said. She went online for directions.

It had taken all Emilia's powers of persuasion before Ted allowed her to join him on his forthcoming business trip. He'd claimed prolonged travel might have a negative effect on her health so soon after her car accident, so she had sought written approval and a Fit to Fly certificate from an independent medical consultant to prove him wrong. It meant Ted had little excuse but to book her a ticket.

By breakfast, their commercial flight from London's Luton Airport to Switzerland's Genève Aéroport had landed. And once Emilia and Ted had bypassed the usual customs channels and been escorted by airport security staff to an awaiting autonomous vehicle, they were en route to their Lake Geneva hotel. Ted's attention was diverted towards the contents of his tablet and the programme of meetings as Emilia nervously prepared her part of the plan.

'Don't you get fed up of being watched all the time?' she asked, turning to look at the car behind containing his security personnel.

'Sometimes,' he replied. 'But it's part and parcel of my job.'

'Which is what exactly? Because every time I ask you what you do, you fob me off with partial answers.'

'That's unfair. Biochemical engineering is a sensitive subject in this day and age, especially in the direction the world is moving right now. Information is no longer safe and can easily fall into the wrong hands.'

'Don't you trust me?'

'Of course I do, but governments need to be assured that what I know is protected.'

'You work for our government?'

'I go where the work takes me. And if that means being shadowed by the two giants behind us, then it's a small price to pay.'

It must be something to do with biochemistry that Bianca and Adrian want from him, Emilia thought. Despite her having asked them again, they had refused to elaborate on who they represented or their end goal. *Are they spies? Or perhaps Ted is one? Is that such an unlikely possibility? Do Bianca and Adrian want to meet him on neutral territory to attempt to turn him?* Once again, she questioned what she was getting herself involved with by luring him to the lighthouse before reminding herself that she owed him no loyalty. He'd lied to her. She had no choice.

'Am I going to see you at all today?' she asked. 'How long will you be in meetings?'

'Probably late into the evening.'

'How about we meet for dinner?'

'I doubt I'll have the time.'

'Surely you're allowed a break, even if it's so that we can get some fresh air. Come on, it'll be good for you; it'll clear your head.'

'I'll try,' he replied, but his answer was noncommittal.

'It's just that it looks like such a beautiful city from here,' she continued. 'It feels like it might be the start of ... I don't know ... something new.'

'What do you mean?' he asked, his eyes finally meeting hers.

She smiled coyly. It was the first time she had indicated any interest in him in that way. 'Let's see where the night takes us, shall we?' She looked to the dashboard and noted they were two minutes from their destination of the Grand Hotel Kempinski Geneva. 'Pull over here,' she said. 'Let's walk the rest of the way.'

Visibly buoyed by his wife's turnaround, Ted obliged. And flanked by his team, Emilia entwined her arm with his, continuing the charade that something was altering inside her. The touch of his skin against hers sent an unforeseen warmth cascading throughout her veins. It felt ... familiar.

She took her mind off it by staring at the view ahead. The bay was framed by buildings no more than six storeys high. To their left was the vast expanse of the silvery green Lake Geneva itself, and in the distance, the snow-capped Alps. Under different circumstances, there might be something romantic about it.

Emilia located the Paquis Lighthouse at the end of a concrete runway. It was unmanned and resembled a scaled-down replica of a real beacon. But if all went according to plan, it was where she would lead Ted tonight and where Bianca and Adrian would assist her in learning the truth about who she was and what he'd been hiding.

After their arrival and check-in at the hotel, Emilia didn't see her husband for the rest of the day so she passed the time window shopping around the old town. And when that failed to take her mind off events to come, she returned to her hotel where she stared from the window in the direction of the lake, the uncertainty of the night ahead playing louder than the television behind her.

Chapter 37

FLICK, ALDEBURGH, SUFFOLK

'Somebody has mail,' said Grace in a sing-song voice. She dropped an ivory-coloured envelope into Flick's lap.

'Who, me?' she asked and leaned forward in her chair on the B&B's balcony.

'No, Queen Catherine. Who do you think?'

Flick hesitated before opening it, immediately wary. 'It's been hand-delivered,' Grace added, returning with a rack of toast and two mugs of tea.

Flick's name was handwritten across the front in gold lettering. She cautiously tore open the seal. Inside was a postcard; on one side was a photograph of the incomplete portrait of Elijah's uncle. On the other, it read:

Come to the house on Wednesday and give me a hand. Wear something old x

An address was included below the signature. A spark fired inside her.

'Is that from who I think it's from?' asked Grace. Flick handed her the invitation and Grace cocked her head as she read it. She placed a hand over her heart. 'I have such high hopes for you two.'

'You know I'm not looking for a relationship.'

'But you're both so right for one another! I know some-thing shitty happened with your ex, but Elijah could be your Prince Charming.'

Flick rolled her eyes. 'My life isn't a bloody Disney movie,' she said but Grace wasn't listening.

'Ooh, perhaps he might be your DNA Match! You just need to get his saliva by asking him to lick something ...' She finished the sentence with a cheeky wink.

But the mention of DNA gave Flick the chills. 'No, he's not,' she said firmly.

'Don't you believe in it?'

'I know who my Match is and he wasn't who I hoped he'd be.'

'Oh, I'm sorry. I assumed once you found them, that was it? You were set for life.'

'Not always.'

Grace's stare remained locked on to Flick, as if expecting more of an explanation. But for Flick, the conversation was over. She'd already revealed more than she had intended.

Chapter 38

EMILIA

Emilia glanced at her watch: she was ten minutes ahead of schedule. *Soon,* she thought, *soon I'll know who I am.* But her excitement was tempered by a growing unease.

It was a warm, balmy evening as she left the hotel's entrance, crossed the road and made her way towards the chalky-white lighthouse. To one side were small, moored boats, masts hoisted but sails down, and their hulls covered with brightly coloured tarpaulins. To the other side, a bevy of swans were feeding together, all but one of them paired. She stared at the solitary one, a kinship forming.

Emilia had already sent Ted a text message and a map to confirm the time and location of where they could meet during his break from meetings. He responded with a simple 'Yes.'

> Live dangerously and give your security team the slip.

> I don't think I can.

> Do it for me. Let's be a normal couple for a few minutes. You won't be disappointed.

> Okay. I love you. ❤

Even now, you're still playing a part, she thought. And for a moment, she allowed herself to imagine he was genuine.

Alone on the jetty, Emilia made her way to one of five green benches and took a seat. She focused her attention on the Jet d'Eau, a gush of water bursting from the lake's surface 140 metres high into the air. A gentle breeze caused the spray to slant slightly and spread a cool, fine mist against her flushed forehead and cheeks.

It wasn't long before she heard the sound of soft-soled footwear on concrete and Ted took a seat beside her. She was almost sick with nerves as he kissed her on both cheeks.

'I'm sorry I'm late,' he began. 'I haven't got long. I've really missed you.'

Had she not known any better, she might have been taken in by his sincerity.

'Where's your security?'

'I gave them the slip,' he replied with a wink. 'I told them I was going back to the suite to take a shower, then slipped away through the fire exit. You're a bad influence.'

'Who am I, Ted?' she asked suddenly. 'Because I know you've been lying to me.'

He paled. 'Where is this coming from? Has something happened? Are you feeling all right?'

Emilia spotted a female figure from the corner of her eye. It wasn't Bianca, but a young mum walking hand in hand with a toddler. *Where is she?* she thought. The plan had been for Emilia to lure Ted there alone before Bianca and Adrian appeared and questioned him. Regardless, she pressed on.

'I know that I don't have amnesia. And I know that you're not who you say you are.'

'I've told you everything I know,' he replied, perplexed.

'Have you, Ted? Really?'

'Yes, of course I have!'

'Why did you lie to me about us being married?'

Ted hesitated just a moment too long for Emilia to believe any rebuttal.

As he opened his mouth, a glint of light caught her attention. She turned to see a long, metallic instrument slicing through the air before it plunged deep into Ted's skull.

He slumped to his side on the bench and then rolled to the ground. A horrified Emilia screamed and pushed herself away but lost her footing, also falling to the ground. She scrambled backwards on all fours until her shoulders were pressed against the railings.

'Ted!' she gasped and stared open-mouthed at the young mum who was now slipping the murder weapon back into her coat pocket. Emilia recognised it from a memory. She had brandished one herself in her recurring dream when she attacked a staff member in an electronics shop. But Emilia had not used it like this woman had. Then, as casually as the stranger had arrived, she walked away, still with the toddler in tow.

Emilia focused on Ted's body. The wound was only a few millimetres in width, but in depth, the tool used to skewer his brain had gone deep. A cascade of blood seeped from the hole, trickled down the side of his head and gradually pooled around it like a crimson halo. Ted's mouth frothed with foamy bubbles before his dark brown irises rolled back into their sockets leaving empty, shiny white ovals in their place.

This was her fault. She might not have used the murder weapon, but she had lured him away from his security team. *He's dead, he's dead, he's dead ...* she repeated to herself. *What the hell have I done?*

Chapter 39

FLICK, ALDEBURGH, SUFFOLK

The modernity of Elijah's beachfront property contrasted with that of its traditional neighbours.

From the shoreline, Flick surveyed the large oblong building clad in black corrugated iron. There were only a handful of new properties built on the former car park and within spitting distance of town. And his was unlike any of the others. A waist-high wire fence separated the green lawn from a sandy path and pebble beach. Even from this distance, Flick could see straight through the two-storey glass front aspect and out to the other side. If she lived here it would take hiding in plain sight to a new level.

She approached the front door, still uncertain as to why she had agreed to his invitation. Again, she tried to pick apart Elijah's motives and find a reason to put herself off him. She recalled a feature she had read in an online magazine in which it was explained how society places single people into four categories. She reluctantly identified as one of the four Ts.

A study by anthropology students at the University of Brighton reveals that those who have not been Matched are either Tourists, TBCs, Turn-Downs or Tough Luckers.

Tourists – Enjoy dating a wide number of partners before they register their details with Match Your DNA.

The TBCs (aka To Be Continued) – Registered with Match Your DNA and are sexually active with others but have yet to find a Match.

Turn-Downs – Those who identify as preferring to find love the traditional way and without biological assistance or remaining in untested relationships.

Tough Luckers – Someone who's already been Matched but is unable to be with their pairing for a multitude of reasons, such as illness, geographical distance, insurmountable age gap and unwillingness to experience an alternate religion or sexuality to their own. Often the most frequently maligned category and belittled for being unable to make love work.

Flick was a Tough Lucker – it didn't matter that Christopher was a serial killer or now dead. She was forever tainted in the eyes of the majority. But which one was Elijah? Was he only showing an interest in her until his Match came along? Her instinct suggested he was a Turn Down. By knocking on his door, she could be about to make her already complicated life that little bit more problematic.

'Will your indecision take much longer?' Elijah's teasing voice appeared through an intercom.

Flick's heart skipped. 'You've been watching me?' she replied, her face reddening.

'Only for about ten minutes.' She hadn't realised she'd been there for that long.

The door buzzed and hesitantly, she took a deep breath and entered, walking slowly along a corridor until she found Elijah. He was standing at the top of a clear Perspex staircase, dressed in a stained T-shirt, shorts and an old pair of cream-coloured Converse trainers. His hands and wrists were caked in powder.

'Come up and join me,' he invited.

'You're expecting me to go upstairs with someone I barely know?' she asked. 'Really?'

'If I was trying to seduce you, I'd have at least washed my hands first. As I wrote on the postcard, I need your help.'

Only after pausing again to take in her surroundings for potential threats did Flick follow him to an open doorway. Rap music played in a room so wide, it took up much of the first floor. Incomplete canvases were propped up against the walls and shutters blocked out direct sunlight from a pitched-glass roof.

'I'm trying something new,' Elijah began and passed Flick a pair of Perspex goggles. She slipped them on and he handed her a chisel, beckoning her to follow him towards a slab of marble on a table in the centre of the room. It was the shape of a head, but its features had been drawn on with chalk. 'Now, hold the pointed chisel in that spot while I find the mallet,' he continued, moving her hands and the tool in the direction of the crown. Flick's pulse raced at his touch.

On his return, he remained behind her and she instinctively gripped the chisel tighter, in case she had to use it as a weapon. Her body tensed as he gently tapped at it with the mallet. Shards of marble fired in all directions like shrapnel. Flick felt the warmth of his skin against her neck and cheek. She was sure he was doing it deliberately, but she didn't care.

'What are you making?' she asked, trying to distract herself from her arousal.

'What are *we* making?' he corrected her. 'It's a sculpture.'

'I might not know much about art but I know what a sculpture is. Who is it of?'

Elijah adjusted her chisel again and she felt the firmness of his chest as it pressed against her back.

'It's of everyone so it's going to be made by everyone. It'll be made up of different parts of faces of people I know.'

Flick was momentarily disappointed that others would be contributing. 'But you're the first,' he continued, his lips brushing against her ear.

'And what's the thinking behind it?'

'It's about our community and how we're all made up of the people we surround ourselves with. None of us is an island, no matter how much water there is between us. Even you.'

'Me?'

'You.'

'I don't understand what you mean.'

'Yes, you do. I get you.'

'You "get me"?' she repeated, irked by his implication. 'You hardly know me.'

'I know enough to think we're alike. We give out just enough of ourselves to make everyone around us feel like we're their best friends, but hold enough back to stop from committing completely.'

'You make a lot of assumptions, Elijah.'

'But I don't hear you telling me I'm wrong.'

Flick was prepared to explain how she didn't need anyone; how she was perfectly fine on her own. But she didn't. Instead, she leaned into him and placed her lips on his. As they kissed, an energy rushed through her that she hadn't felt in an age. And moments later, she was pressing Elijah's naked body against the cool of the marble sculpture – an image of the town that made him, and that was chipping away at her too.

Chapter 40

EMILIA

Emilia screamed for help but there was no one in sight apart from the killer. The bitter tang of death cut through Lake Geneva's salty air. It was a harsh, metallic aroma that once caught on the back of the tongue, stubbornly remained, like freshly set amalgam fillings. Each new breath became a battle to hold back waves of nausea, but such high levels of anxiety couldn't be suppressed for long. It found an alternative release through trembling limbs and beads of sweat. She had been set up. Ted had been murdered and it was all her fault.

Then without warning, four figures – two male and two female – hurried forward and passed the woman and child who were now walking in the opposite direction. The casual attire of labelled baseball caps, T-shirts and jeans were at odds with their purposeful pace and deadpan expressions. And against the backdrop of the gentle waves lapping at the lake's shore, the clean-up operation began.

One spoke in German into an earpiece and looked across the bay. A white speedboat, indistinguishable from others using the water for pleasure, appeared silently and pulled up close to the lighthouse at the end of the jetty where his colleagues waited in silence. Two more people exited it, jumping into the lake and landing knee deep: another remained at the wheel.

With the speed and precision of a Formula One pit stop, they lifted the body onto the boarding deck, boarded it again, reversed the boat and took off as quickly and as unassumingly as when they had arrived. Moments later, it was heading towards the white-capped Swiss Alps; the only trace that it had ever been there were the wide ripples left in its wake.

With a sharp turn of her head Emilia caught the remaining two figures pouring bottles of something across the ground to dissolve the blood into nothing. Another reconnected wires attached to a lamppost-mounted security camera.

Suddenly two pairs of hands tightly gripped her upper arms, hurrying her away from the murder scene and back towards the main road. Ahead, two four-by-four vehicles were parked by the side of the road, their windows as dark as their bodywork.

They're going to kill me next, she thought.

It was enough to send a sudden jolt of adrenaline coursing through her body, bringing with it a fight-or-flight instinct. Drawing deep from a long-forgotten existence, her arms were the first to shake free before landing a punch square in the throat of the shorter of the two captors. As he gasped for air, both hands were wrapped around his neck and his head drawn downward, where a knee collided with his stomach. Preparing for the second assailant's attack, the hunted was now the hunter. She dropped to the ground as the man lurched forward and thrust out a leg until her heel connected with his kneecap. It was swiftly followed by an agonising crack and a scream.

After scrambling back to her feet, Emilia ran at breakneck speed towards the two cars, now only about a hundred metres ahead. Another rapid decision had to be made –

which direction to go in? Right would take her out of town but give more options for an escape further afield; left meant heading towards the centre of town where there was a higher density of people and more witnesses. There was also a better chance of locating a bolthole in which to lie low while figuring out what to do next. But the decision was snatched away when the doors of both vehicles opened.

Six new opponents stood their ground, each brandishing firearms. The odds of surviving this were infinitesimally small. She came to an abrupt, breathless halt. Whatever was coming next would be completely out of her control.

'Get inside, Emilia,' came a voice. An interior light illuminated the vehicle, revealing Bianca's presence.

'You're going to kill me, aren't you?' Emilia panted.

'If your death had been part of the plan, we wouldn't be having this conversation. You'd be lying dead in the grounds of the hospital.'

Emilia turned to look again at her aggressors and had little choice but to comply. Inside, Bianca took a metallic hipflask from inside the armrest and offered it to Emilia as the car sped away.

'It has a light synthetic mood enhancer inside that'll help to relax you. You're in shock.'

'I don't need to be sedated.'

'Every vital sign your smart watch is recording tells me differently. You have an elevated heart rate, high blood pressure, you're sweating and your breathing is rapid.'

'What do you expect?' Emilia tore the watch from her wrist and threw it into the footwell. 'Why did you kill Ted? He was going to tell me who I was.'

'Hell was more likely to have frozen over before Edward Karczewski ever admitted that he knew your truths.'

Emilia faltered – she had never referred to him by his full name before, only the shortened form of Ted. But when Bianca said it, it sounded familiar, as if she had heard it in its entirety many times before.

'And by erasing him,' Bianca continued, 'we are sending a message to the others – that we are coming for every last one of them. Those who know your true identity are buried deeply, Emilia, and Ted's death will flush them out. Our deal still stands. We want to help you find the four who remain in the hope that one of them gives you the truth. Somewhere inside you, you know how to find and expose them.'

'How when I don't even know who the hell I am?' she asked, exasperated.

'We are confident that you will find a way.'

'And why would I want to? How do you expect me to live with myself knowing that I'd be luring them to their deaths too? Because that's what going to happen, isn't it? You're going to murder them too. Why?'

'They call these four people the Minders and they're protecting something that doesn't belong to them.'

'What is it?'

'Information of a sensitive nature that is of no use to you, or us even, but which the world will be a better place without.'

'According to who?'

'According to those of us who know what's best for this country.'

'You're not working for our or any other government, are you?'

The corners of Bianca's lips rose. 'No, Emilia, we most definitely are not.'

Emilia took a sharp intake of breath as the penny dropped. 'I know who you are! I read about you while I was in hospital. You're terrorists! You're the Hacking Collective!'

'As I have explained before, who we are is of no conse-quence to you. You help us to find the four and you are free to try and get the truth from them about who you are. And once you are finished, then it becomes our turn. As long as they give us what we want, they'll be allowed to live.'

'I don't want any part of this.'

Bianca shrugged. 'As I told you when we first met at the pub, you are free to leave at any time.'

'Just like that?'

'Just like that.' Emilia searched for the door-release button. 'I'm sorry it hasn't worked out,' Bianca added. 'I wish you the best of luck out there. It is a pity, though. Watch.'

Bianca's eyes moved to the windscreen, and Emilia's followed. With the flick of a button, it became a television screen with the words 'live feed' appearing in the top-left corner. Footage was being broadcast of a steep slope and a grassy playing field in the distance.

'Zoom in and split screen,' Bianca ordered and the camera focused on a group of young people dressed in brightly coloured football strips and two girls in particular. Their appearances were identical – they had same straw-berry-blonde hair scraped back into ponytails and the same determined expressions. Their only differences were their coloured boots.

'Your daughters,' Bianca said without warning. 'Cassie and Harper. And the man on the touchline with the dog by his feet, that's your husband, Justin.'

Emilia gasped, her attention flitting between a slim, red-headed man and the girls. She was scared to blink in case they vanished as quickly as they had appeared.

'The scar across your belly that Ted told you was from being slashed by an employee?' continued Bianca. 'That event happened but had nothing to do with you. You didn't even work for a bank. Your wound is actually a Caesarean scar.'

Her mind raced and she desperately wanted to remember anything about them, but instead, she drew a blank. However, she was convinced they were related because somewhere deep inside, Emilia *knew* she was watching family. The maternal force was too intense on sight alone for this to be a lie. She was a mother and a wife.

'Take aim,' Bianca added and three red, circular dots appeared, one on each of Emilia's family's heads. 'Snipers,' Bianca continued. 'One word from me and all three will die here and now, right in front of you. What's it to be? Will you be leaving or staying in the car?'

Chapter 41

BRUNO, OUNDLE, NORTHAMPTONSHIRE

She moved from room to room, completely unaware of Bruno's presence.

From inside his parked car adjacent to her house, he watched carefully as she went about her business. Her property was palatial compared to his former bedsit. It was an immaculate detached Victorian building, renovated and stretching across three floors. The latest model of a top-of-the-range autonomous car was parked on her drive. His hackles rose as he calculated the value of her material possessions. *I bet inside you're as empty as me*, he thought.

Karen Watson was the sixth and final name on his list. And by the end of the night, she would be dead.

It was the second time Bruno had been in her presence that day and earlier, he had been even closer to her than he was now. He'd volunteered to take a dog for a walk from a nearby homeless pet shelter knowing from previous reconnaissance missions exactly where to find Watson. She was a creature of habit and took her golden retriever for a countryside walk every other day, choosing to sit on the same bench by the river Nene.

'Go and be a dog,' Bruno whispered into Oscar's ear and dropped the lead. Once Oscar clocked the other pet, he made a beeline for it. The retriever rose to its feet and the excitable pair began running circles around one another, their leads entwining.

Bruno fumbled with his jacket pocket and felt the shape of the hammer inside it. He hoped the dog was not aggressive as he would rather not kill that too.

'I am so sorry,' said Bruno as he approached Watson. He hoped that distracting her with Oscar would make it easier to strike quickly. However, a couple walking arm in arm slowly towards them put paid to that plan. For the moment, he would have to wait.

'Luna, come here!' Watson ordered but her pet wasn't listening. Soon, neither dog could move as their leads were wrapped around one another's.

'I'm a bit new to this,' Bruno continued, playing for time and feigning embarrassment as he began unravelling Oscar. 'He belongs to a dogs' shelter and I've volunteered to walk him.'

He caught a longer glimpse of her, his first close-up. She was a handful of years older than him, he knew that already, but she appeared younger. Her frame was slight and her smile kind. He hadn't appreciated how striking she was each time he'd followed her from a distance. He blinked his attraction away.

'That's a lovely thing to do,' Watson replied, her dog finally free. 'Luna's six but she still thinks she's a puppy.'

Bruno suddenly became lost for words. Watson wasn't like the others on his list. It wasn't because she was the only woman, it was because she was ... *different* ... and he couldn't put his finger on why. 'She's a beautiful girl,' was the best he could manage.

He reciprocated the 'hello's the passing couple gave. If he killed Watson now, they could identify him. And when a line of schoolchildren and their teachers appeared, he knew his moment had passed.

'We'd best be heading home,' Watson said and offered him a smile that he returned before she disappeared from view.

I know where that is, Bruno thought. Which brought him to where he was sitting now.

'Hey.'

The Echo startled Bruno. He turned quickly, taken aback to find a young boy with a missing jaw in the back seat of his vehicle. Warren Hobbs had been the victim of a sadistic eighteenth-century British aristocrat, another secret hidden from the world. 'What's wrong?'

'Why?' Bruno replied, disguising his unease.

'Because you aren't yourself,' said the boy.

'That woman in the house. She's done something to you.' While he looked like a child, he spoke as an adult.

'Of course she has. I don't kill indiscriminately.'

'That ain't what I mean. I know you. We all know you because we're a part of you. Every one of us. She's stirred something up inside you.'

The fine hairs on the back of Bruno's neck stood to attention. 'How long are you all staying for?'

A second Echo took both of them by surprise; this time from the passenger seat. They turned sharply to see a woman dressed in a 1940s-style smart grey suit and heels. Bruno recognised her as Ingrid Barford, an Oscar-winning British actress who passed secret intelligence to the government about Russian operatives she had relationships with. 'We are here for as long as you want us to be, darling. Who knows? That's up to you to decide.' She shrugged her shoulders and smiled sweetly, then began applying a red lipstick.

'But I don't want any of you here.'

'You can keep telling yourself that, but you're fooling yourself, kiddo. You'd miss us if we left.' She winked and turned to stare at the house.

Bruno couldn't allow his unwanted guests to distract him any further. The only person who mattered was Watson.

'You should do it now,' Hobbs continued, his tone excitable. 'Get it over with and make her suffer.'

Bruno didn't respond. It would make perfect sense for him to exact his revenge upon her now, because until it happened, he'd remain a man caught between two lives. However, that two-minute conversation they shared had humanised her, something he hadn't expected. And it was in danger of holding him back.

As darkness enveloped the town, Bruno was struck by the urge to check in on Louie again. Days had passed since he'd last accessed the cameras that kept his son safe. And whilst it was strictly against Karczewski's rules, it paled compared to his other crimes since his release. He removed one of several unregistered, unused mobile phones from a bag by Barford's feet and followed the same routine as before.

The sight of Louie asleep in his bed was both comforting and agonising. In night-vision mode, he could just about make out the Tyrannosaurus rex toy that Zoe had bought him on a trip to London's Natural History Museum. He had started taking it to bed with him soon after her death.

Leaving Louie without saying goodbye was the hardest thing Bruno had ever done. And it was all because of vultures like Watson; people who were too preoccupied with greed and how much they could steal from others.

How can she live this life of luxury while Louie and I are kept apart? he thought. *To hell with the plan. She's going to pay for what she's done now.* His rage travelled from nought to sixty in a heartbeat.

Bruno pulled at the lid of the armrest and removed the hammer inside it. But as he took hold of the door handle, an outdoor light illuminated Watson's porch, swiftly followed by half a dozen others stretching the length of the driveway. The front door opened and she appeared, along with an inkling of attraction. *No*, he told himself. *No*.

'Hurry up and get this done,' Hobbs encouraged, the remaining top half of his jaw smiling. 'It'll only take one well-placed whack and the whore will hit the ground like a bag of spanners. By the time anyone finds her, she'll have bled out.'

But as the car door opened, a minivan appeared in the road, driving towards them. It parked outside her house and Bruno slackened his grip on the weapon and lowered himself in his seat, despite the darkened windows. Watson made her way to the road outside, just metres away from him.

The driver exited and greeted her. A moment later, a motorised wheelchair moved down a ramp and Watson threw her arms around its occupant, a young girl, and kissed her cheek. The girl followed Watson into the house before the doors shut and the outside lights turned off. As the van pulled away, a logo stencilled along the side revealed that it belonged to the All Bodies activity holidays company.

'Who is she? Barford asked, a dozen Echoes repeating the question. Of all Bruno had learned about Watson, there were no indications she was a parent.

'I don't know,' he replied.

'She probably hasn't locked the front door yet,' Barford continued. 'It wouldn't take much for a big strong boy like you to break it open and do what needs to be done. How about it, kiddo? How about we get this over with now so that we can all move on?'

Bruno didn't reply. He would need to learn more about Watson's relationship with the girl before her fate was sealed.

Chapter 42

SINÉAD, EDZELL, SCOTLAND

Sinéad braked sharply when she recognised Gail's car. There weren't many flame-red Land Rovers in Edzell.

Sinéad was returning from neighbouring Forfar with copies of licences for food, beverages and entertainment for the forthcoming village fete when she spotted the vehicle. There had been no communication between them since she had overheard Anthony slap Gail. And Sinéad's inaction had played on her conscience every day since.

The bells of Edzell church tolled as Sinéad pulled into the car park. She thought back to those friends who had tried to intervene in her relationship with Daniel. She had responded to them with indignation so why should Gail be any different? Regardless, she couldn't sit back and allow another Daniel to break someone else's spirit.

She made her way across the grass and towards the children's play area, where she found Gail sitting on a bench, her baby in the pushchair facing away from her. Once again, there was no interaction between mother and daughter. Gail hadn't heard her approach and appeared lost in thought, staring at a climbing frame ahead. Nervous, Sinéad fought the urge to find comfort by tugging at her eyelashes. 'Hello, stranger,' she began. 'How are you?' She'd half-expected Gail to be surprised by her appearance, but if she was, she gave nothing away.

'I'm good, thank you,' Gail replied coolly.

'Are you really?'

'Why wouldn't I be?'

'Only it seems like you've been avoiding me.' When Gail didn't reply, Sinéad knew she would need to tread extra carefully. 'You have nothing to be embarrassed about.'

'It wasn't how it sounded.'

'I know that it was.'

'Well, I'm sorry you had to be there to hear it. It's never happened before.'

'You have nothing to be sorry for. Gail, I've been exactly where you are now. It was only after I left my husband when I truly understood how emotionally abusive he was ...'

Gail shook her head. 'You've got it wrong. Anthony isn't like that. I'm the problem, not him. He's a good man, a good father ...'

'No matter how subtly he plays it, I've heard the condescending way he speaks to you. He makes it sound like whatever's going on between you is all your fault. I know how he operates because it's what Daniel did to me—'

'Please, stop,' Gail interrupted. 'Just because your marriage failed doesn't mean I'll allow mine to do the same.'

There was an animosity in Gail's words that Sinéad hadn't heard before. She glanced at Gail's hands. Her nails were bitten down to the quick and the skin around them was mottled. Still, Sinéad pressed on.

'You can't change someone who doesn't want to change. Think of Taylor. Do you want her to be raised by a bully?' Gail's cheeks reddened. 'Please take it from somebody who knows. A friend once told me there was a life to be had away from my husband, and I found it. You need to find yours away from Anthony or he will grind you down to nothing.'

THE MINDERS

As Gail nodded slowly, Sinéad felt a wave of relief washing over her. Perhaps she had succeeded where so many of her former friends had failed. Maybe Gail needed someone like Sinéad to spell it out to her.

Gail raked her hand through her curls and turned to face Sinéad as she stood up and released the brake from the pushchair. 'I will tell you this one time only. Keep your fucking nose out of my business and stay away from me.'

Chapter 43

FLICK, ALDEBURGH, SUFFOLK

As pre-dusk fell, Flick couldn't wipe the grin from her face as she made her way home from Elijah's. She thought back to the programme and how she had voluntarily agreed to a contraceptive implant that made it impossible to fall pregnant. It was also supposed to diminish her sexual desires. However, the latter had failed at the first hurdle. For much of the afternoon and early evening, her urges had spilled out across Elijah's studio floor along with her clothes.

She was relieved the B&B was empty on her return as she wasn't ready for Grace's interrogation. Flick chose to sit outside on the patio, the final moments of the sun's rays warming her smiling lips as music played on the radio. The feeling of not having a care in the world lasted for approximately two minutes before her calm was shattered by the news headlines.

'A top-ranking government adviser has been killed in a boating accident,' the newsreader began. 'Edward Karczewski's body was discovered washed up on the shore of Switzerland's Petit Lac by locals in the early hours of this morning. Mr Karczewski, known to friends as Ted, was reported missing after fishermen found his speedboat empty and drifting. Investigators are not treating his death as suspicious.'

Flick froze; the only part of her to move was the frantic pounding of her heart. She hurried to the radio but failed to find any other news channels that repeated the story. Conflicted, she grabbed Grace's tablet from the work surface. Use of devices was strictly against the rules but the exceptional circumstances justified her trawling the internet for more details. Moving as quickly as possible to leave a minimal online presence, she located a website featuring video footage of Karczewski's body being zipped up inside in a black body bag and carried into a waiting ambulance.

She continued her search until she stumbled across amateur footage taken from an alternative angle, a close-up of his face and head. It was definitely her handler. But it was his crown that caught her attention. The ultra-high-definition footage made it possible to zoom in closer to a parting of his wet hair. It revealed a solitary wound to his skull.

Flick desperately wanted to give its positioning the benefit of the doubt. Perhaps it was an injury resulting from Karczewski's body hitting rocks before washing up ashore. But it was too much of a coincidence for the man who ran the programme to have died of an injury in exactly the same position where the Minders' data had been implanted.

She was convinced it was a message. If Karczewski could be compromised, then so could she.

Chapter 44

CHARLIE, MANCHESTER

'The taxi's here,' shouted Milo from the front door of his house.

Behind him, his friends slipped on their coats and made their way towards the waiting vehicle.

'Vicky's messaged to say they'll meet us in town for a quick one before they go home,' said Andrew, holding his phone to his ear and recounting a voice note to Charlie. 'Apparently Alix is "very much looking forward to seeing you again". How many dates will this be?'

'I'm not counting,' Charlie replied. But he was. It would be the third time they had seen one another alone since their double date with Andrew and Vicky. Their first date had been at the Manchester Art Gallery, taking in an installation inspired by world religions. It fascinated Alix, but Charlie, less so.

'Do you believe in God?' she had asked him and he shook his head. 'Are you atheist or agnostic?'

'I'm not sure I know what the difference is,' he replied.

'Atheism is about what you don't believe and being an agnostic is about what you don't know.'

'Then neither,' he replied, a little too quickly. But inside his head he knew a truth about deities, religions and belief systems and couldn't share it with anyone.

'What do you believe in then?' Alix pursued.

Charlie thought on his feet. 'I believe in the inherent good in people, I believe in hoping that things will get better for our fractured world, I believe you don't need a shared piece of DNA to fall in love with someone ... and of course, I believe in Father Christmas.' He put the conversation to bed with a kiss.

Their second date had been drinks at a pub outside town and the third, a home-cooked dinner at Alix's house. He had not left until the following morning.

'Tell her I'm looking forward to it too,' Charlie replied to Andrew. He wished that he had been but the reality was that he was completely indifferent.

'You could tell her yourself if you bought a bloody phone that didn't need winding up to work.'

'I'm anti-technology ...'

'Yet you counsel clients through a virtual-reality headset and an avatar.'

As Charlie approached the car door, he took in the driverless cab.

'Ready for a big sesh?' Milo asked and patted both hands on his friend's shoulders. But Charlie hesitated.

'I thought we'd booked one with a driver?' he asked.

'It's all they had and it was cheaper.'

'I'd have paid the difference.'

'Come on, lads!' yelled a voice from inside the car.

Milo continued to walk but Charlie had stopped. 'Everything all right?' Milo asked.

'Yeah, fine. Look, I'll meet you boys in town.'

'Don't be daft, get in.'

'No, I fancy some air. I'll see you at the pub.'

'Nobody needs air before a pub crawl.'

'They do tonight,' he said. 'Besides, I don't trust them.'

'What, the lads?'

'No, driverless cars.'

'Here we go again with your Neo-Luddite nonsense,' Milo teased. 'You know they're safe now, don't you?'

'And so are lifts but you have an irrational hatred of them. You always take the stairs.'

'Don't change the subject. Cars can't be hacked again if that's what you're worried about?'

But Charlie knew different. He held back from revealing that there were at least two more root access vulnerability points that hackers could exploit. The government was aware of the flaws but not even its highest-ranking programmers had found a way to seal them shut and maintain a successful operating network. 'It's just a prefer-ence,' he added.

Milo turned and approached him. 'Mate, seriously, what's the problem?'

'Nothing's the problem.'

'You can tell me. My offer stands, I'm here if you ever need someone to talk to.'

'Honestly, it's all good. Go, or you'll make everyone late.'

Charlie waved as the cab exited the street, leaving him alone. Milo was the most perceptive of them all but following his suggestion that Charlie might be self-harming, Charlie wanted to place a little distance between them. However, working together and sharing the same friends made it difficult. Sometimes in the office or when they were all out together, Charlie sensed Milo's eyes drilling into him as if trying to gain insight into who he'd been before arriving in Manchester. But for what purpose? Was he being a friend or was Milo attracted to him? Milo didn't label his sexuality and his body language and micro-expressions suggested it might go either way.

As Charlie began his thirty-minute walk into the city centre, memories of his former friends inside an autono-mous taxi dominated his thoughts. More than three years had passed and he could still remember every moment about that day. It had been the first time in months Charlie had gathered them all together and he'd booked a driverless people carrier to take them to a Portsmouth football match, playing away at neighbouring Southampton.

Anxious for the day to run smoothly, he'd started drinking early to calm himself. But his nerves made way for irritation once the others arrived at his house. They were less interested in reacquainting themselves with him and more concerned with their mobile devices and a terrorist attack being broadcast across social media. It took the lure of tequila shots and the arrival of the taxi to prise them from their screens as he shepherded them into the vehicle. Finally, as they laughed and joked, his anxiety evaporated and it didn't matter that they'd forgotten it was his birthday; they were together again, just like old times.

It was on the outskirts of Southampton when Charlie felt queasy. Broken air conditioning, the heat from seven men's bodies in a confined space combined with the alcohol he'd consumed meant that seconds after Charlie pressed a button to open the window, he pushed his head out and vomited. And once he'd started, he couldn't stop. The others playfully cheered his misfortune as Stelfox ordered the car to pull over and Charlie sprinted along the grass verge next to the dual carriageway and allowed himself to be sick again.

He was wiping his mouth with the back of his hand when he heard the sound of the minivan's hydraulics closing the car door. 'Very funny,' he moaned and approached the taxi. 'Lads,' he shouted as it began pulling away. His walk became a jog and he chased it along the slip road to the amusement of those inside. Stelfox shrugged his shoulders as if to say that while he wasn't responsible, it was funny nonetheless.

Tonight, as the bright lights of Manchester's city centre grew ever closer, Charlie felt almost detached from his memory of what happened next. He wondered how many of his old friends had been distracted by him not to notice the articulated lorry travelling along the wrong side of the road before it ploughed into them.

The force of the collision sent plastics, polymers and metal flying in all directions and he'd dived to the ground and covered his head to avoid being hit. It was as if someone had transported him on to the set of a Hollywood film. It was hard to differentiate between either vehicle, mangled and melded together like a macabre sculpture.

Charlie ran towards the debris as another car lost control and hit the central reservation. In the distance more vehicles careered down banks or collided with one another.

But nothing could have prepared him for the view inside the wreckage of the people carrier. At first, he could only make out blood and limbs ripped from torsos. There was Bailey's tattooed arm severed from its shoulder and Mark's face, missing from the mouth down. Stelfox was still breathing but unconscious and separated from both legs.

'Hang on,' Charlie pleaded. 'Please, just hang on.'

Hands trembling, he pulled his phone from his pocket and dialled 999 but to his disbelief, the line was engaged. Many times more he hit redial until he understood that nobody was coming to help. That was the moment his legs gave way and he dropped to his knees. He waited for almost four hours until a fire engine and ambulances finally reached that road.

Over the following months, it didn't matter how many appointments Charlie kept with his counsellor, how much positive enforcement she imparted or the dose of medication he used to numb his post-traumatic stress disorder. The only voice he believed was that of Stelfox's widow, Julia. She spotted him when she turned to watch her husband's coffin being carried along the aisle of the crematorium.

'This is your fault!' she yelled across the hushed room. 'You couldn't accept they'd outgrown you. You had to keep pushing and pushing to see them. They were only going out because they pitied you. It should be you inside that box, not him, not any of them.'

Before the programme, Charlie kept their memories alive by saving their voicemail messages and booking their usual table at the pub to watch England's games. But Julia's hatred became his truth. Her words haunted him as much as the blood-soaked bodies inside the taxi did.

And it wasn't until he underwent the procedure to implant the country's secrets inside him that he discovered how right she was. Many of the autonomous vehicles that collided had been selected by the Hacking Collective based upon who had been involved in their promotion. Charlie's involvement hadn't been hiring the vehicle but his freelance graphic design work in which he'd helped to deliver a government advertising campaign to promote the benefits of autonomous cars.

However, a covert inquiry had suppressed that information from the public, ruling that it would benefit no one if they learned of the inadvertent role they might have played in the deaths of so many.

Charlie returned to the present and estimated that the pub where he was to meet his new friends was now five minutes away. He wasn't ready for their company just yet. Instead, he took a detour along the Rochdale canal towpath and paused to settle on a bench and make the most of the quiet before the noisy night ahead. He spotted at least a dozen illuminated cranes dotted about the skyline, each standing above buildings in various stages of completion. Advertisements made up many of the moving images across the sides of offices, but it was a television inside a canal boat moored in front of him that grabbed his attention.

The screen was filled with an image of Edward Karczewski. Charlie hesitated as if he was imagining it.

Then he moved towards the window and peered through it to take a closer look at the caption underneath: *Government adviser dead in boating accident*. He didn't need to hear what the newscaster was saying to know that his life was about to shift gear once again.

Chapter 45

SINÉAD, EDZELL, SCOTLAND

'I've done something really stupid,' Sinéad began as Doon opened her front door. It was mid-morning but Sinéad didn't question why Doon was still wearing her pyjamas.

'Come in,' she invited, her expression impassive. The two made their way into the lounge where Sinéad attended Doon's weekly wine-and-rom-com-movie nights. 'What's happened?'

Sinéad paced the room, trying to put her thoughts in order before she explained the domestic violence she had heard at Gail's house and how her friend had reacted when offered help.

'Perhaps give her space for a few days and then approach her again?' Doon suggested. 'Apologise for pushing her into a corner but assure her that if and when she is ready to talk to you, you will be there to listen.'

'But I've been where she is now,' Sinéad protested. 'I know that sometimes all it takes is one sentence from a friend to make you completely re-evaluate your life.'

'As you say, *sometimes* that's all it takes, but not always,' said Doon, her tone clipped. 'It might have been like that for you, hen, but it's not the same for everyone. You were ready to listen, but Gail isn't there yet.'

Sinéad sighed and glanced around the room, only now noticing the curtains were still closed. 'Is everything okay?' she asked and took in Doon's appearance more closely. Her cheeks were drawn and her eyes were pinkish red as if she and sleep were estranged. 'Have you been poorly?'

Doon hesitated before clearing her throat. 'Today's the anniversary of my daughter's death,' she began. 'I always struggle at this time of the year.'

'Oh, Doon, I'm so sorry,' Sinéad replied. 'I can't imagine how difficult it must be.'

'The hardest part is knowing how much pain Isla must have been in before she took her own life. Her dad and I had seen her a couple of weeks earlier and we should have picked up that something was wrong. I'm her mother, it's my job to notice.'

Sinéad felt something tug inside her head, like the pulling of a loose stitch. Her memory flicked through its Rolodex until it settled on Isla's case file. What she knew about Isla's death was forcing her two worlds to collide, and she didn't know if it was making her anxious or providing her with a unique opportunity to bring comfort to someone she was close to. 'You have nothing to feel guilty for,' she said.

Doon swallowed hard. 'You couldn't possibly know how it feels when the child you love believes death is a better option than the life you've given her. I tell you, it hurts like nothing else, Sinéad. I should have been there for her.'

Sinéad opened her mouth, then thought better of it and closed it again.

'It's my fault that she died because I didn't pick up on the signals that she needed me,' Doon continued. 'I have to live with that and sometimes, like today, I wonder how much longer I can keep going for.'

Doon sat on the sofa and buried her head in her hands as Sinéad put her arm around her shoulder while Doon sobbed. Sinéad recalled the photographs of the plush hotel

suite in which Isla had died. She saw with clarity the pale-
ness of the girl's semi-naked body, her post-mortem
bruising and the dried blood around her mouth. 'You can't
keep feeling responsible for what may or may not have
happened,' said Sinéad.

'There's no may or may not about it,' Doon cried. 'If I
could turn back the clock I know I could've saved her life.'

In that moment, Sinéad's stitch came loose and she knew
what she must do. To hell with the programme this one
time. Telling Doon the truth couldn't do any harm to it.
Her stomach cartwheeled at the prospect. She held Doon
gently by the forearms and stared her directly in the eye.
'There's something I need to tell you,' she began. 'It's about
Isla. I know things, Doon. I can't tell you how I know them,
but you have to take my word for it that I'm privy to sensitive information.'

Doon sat upright. 'What do you know?'

Sinéad took a deep breath; there was no going back now.
'Isla didn't commit suicide. She was killed.'

Doon immediately withdrew herself from Sinéad's grip.
'No, she wasn't; I was at the inquest. I know what happened.'

'Your daughter died in room forty-six of the
Loughborough hotel in Russell Square on July the sixth,
eight years ago, is that right?'

'Yes, how do you know that?'

'That part is a matter of public record. But what isn't is
that the friends she was with were part-time professional
girls, Doon. They were escorts, university students paying
for their education by keeping wealthy foreign men company.'

'You mean they were prostitutes?' Doon asked, her head
tilted and brow creased.

'Isla was hired to entertain a wealthy Saudi Arabian
sheikh, one who regularly gave MI6 important intelligence
but who was known by them for his violence towards
women. He was responsible for Isla's death.'

'No,' Doon replied, adamantly. 'No. I don't believe you.'

'I'm sorry, I really am. It was covered up by our intelligence services because the sheikh was worth more to them as a free man than he was extradited or behind bars.'

Doon shook her head and became increasingly agitated. 'Why would you say such a thing?'

'Because it's the truth. And as your friend, I cannot allow you to spend the rest of your life believing Isla's death was your fault when it wasn't suicide that killed her.'

The slap across Sinéad's face was so swift and unexpected that she hadn't seen it coming.

'You're a liar!' yelled Doon. 'How dare you tell me Isla was a prostitute! My daughter wasn't a whore! You're sick! You're a sick woman!'

'But I was only trying to help you understand ...'

'Who the hell do you think you are?' she continued, now close to hysterical. 'You come into our village trying to be one of us, pretending you want to be our friend but all you've done is stir up trouble for Gail and me. You're cruel and you're heartless and you're not wanted here. Get out of my house.'

Sinéad hurried to her feet. She badly wanted to defend herself. However, the fire in Doon's eyes made her realise she had completely misjudged the situation. There was nothing she could say that would make it any better. Being informed that Isla had actually been murdered, her death hushed up and that her killer was unlikely to face justice would be even harder for Doon to process than her own culpability. Because with the former, there would never be closure. It was easier for her to blame herself.

'I'm sorry,' Sinéad muttered, before leaving the sobbing woman alone. Her attempt at trying to help someone by imparting her secrets had failed abysmally. Not everyone craved the truth. For some, ignorance was a far better option.

Chapter 46

EMILIA

The house Ted told Emilia they'd designed and built together was empty when she returned to it.

There were no cars parked on the driveway, no lights were shining from inside and there was no one to greet her. An apprehensive Emilia unlocked the front door, tentatively stepping inside. Her footsteps were quiet as she made her way along the corridor to the main living area. She listened closely for signs of company, but she appeared to be alone.

Earlier that morning, Adrian and Bianca had accompanied her on the recently launched Eurostar from Switzerland to France and then to London. And at King's Cross St Pancras station, a waiting car drove them out of the city and to the house. It came to a halt a few hundred metres away from the gates to Ted's property.

By reaching the house as the sun had yet to rise, Emilia hoped to avoid Ted's staff. It gave her a small window of opportunity to search the property for evidence as to where in the country Ted had hidden the four people who knew the truth about Emilia.

'He was the only one who was aware of their locations,' Bianca had explained in the car. 'That information was too important to have died with him. You need to find it. And

245

you'd better hurry up because his body has washed up ashore.'

The memory of his swift but savage murder flashed again before Emilia's eyes. Despite his lies, he had not deserved to die, especially at the hands of terrorists. She briefly contemplated telling the police all that she knew, but what *did* she know? What evidence had she that they existed or who they – and now her – were working for? It sounded like the ramblings of a madwoman with a missing memory. They could just as easily be a figment of her imagination.

She also reflected on the version of herself that had emerged during the clash with the assailants who'd escorted her to Bianca's car. Where and how had she learned those combat skills?

'We know they have safe houses and we know where they are located,' Bianca added. 'You just need to get those people there.'

Emilia's first port of call was Ted's office. Like much of the house, its decoration was minimal. The sole colour came from a wall containing racks of vinyl albums. She picked up the only photograph on display, a framed image Ted hadn't shown her of the two of them together at an altar. She was dressed in a simple white gown, him in a shirt and tie, and they faced one another as a woman officiated at their 'wedding'. It was quite convincing.

She directed her attention to his smoked-glass desk. There was no computer or tablet visible or drawers underneath to search. She skimmed through the first of two notepads placed upon it but it was empty. The second used a bookmark but the page it opened at was blank. Then she noticed that the bookmark was actually a swipe card containing the name Edward Karczewski and his photograph. On the bottom-right-hand side of the card was a symbol for the Houses of Parliament, a black-and-white outline. *So much for biochemical engineering*, she thought.

Who was he really? Adrian and Bianca were playing with fire by murdering a government official. And she was guilty by association.

There were no filing cabinets in the room, no cupboards and nowhere to store paperwork. As a last resort, she flicked through some of his album sleeves hoping they might be camouflage for something that could help her. But they were empty, even of records.

A search of Ted's bedroom proved equally fruitless. She rifled through every pocket of his jackets and trousers, then through three briefcases and two chests of drawers. She scoured each room until she reached the floor-to-ceiling bookshelves that ran the entire length of a wall. Finally, she found herself in the kitchen surrounded by the contents of cupboards she'd emptied across the floor. As she feared, nothing gave away who these four strangers were or where they were located.

Emilia peered through the windows, relieved that there was still no sign of anyone else in the house. Her head ached so she took two painkillers from a packet, opened the fridge door and removed a bottle of water. As she closed it, she caught sight of the decorative magnets Ted had explained to her. They were a peculiar thing for him to collect and put on display in a house preoccupied with minimalism. A plastic Mickey Mouse from DisneyCity India, a colourful koala bear from Australia and Leaning Tower of Pisa from Italy demonstrated he was well travelled. The British regional magnets were even less apt. There were a handful of these and she wondered why he went to the trouble of buying them from counties that were so close. A memory of one of the first conversations they had in the hospital room came to mind. 'As corny as it sounds,' Ted had said, 'it was as if we were drawn together like magnets.'

When she had tried to move one of them before, Ted stopped her, claiming it was fragile. Now, it felt perfectly stable as she picked it up to examine it. It was of a church and when she touched a plastic bell in the tower, it played a synthesised version of the hymn 'In the Secret of His Presence'.

Like a bolt of lightning, it struck her. As each note was released, she pictured four faces she had seen on the CCTV footage on the monitor in the room where she first awoke. They had been sitting alone at tables in different rooms. Two men and two women, their faces were still as clear to her as day. Then without forethought, she began grabbing and separating the British magnets from the international ones. All four included their place names – Manchester, Edzell, Oundle and Aldeburgh. Intuitively, she realised they were the locations that Bianca was so desperate to learn of. But she didn't know who was living where.

Another magnet was more familiar than the rest – she had seen it earlier today. It was the side profile of a marble bust of William Shakespeare, she recalled. She returned to the bookshelves where she found a section containing leather-bound editions of each of his plays. Every spine contained a profile image of the writer's head and shoulders and all but one was facing to the left.

The Two Noble Kinsmen was the exception and she recalled it immediately. In a part-memory in which she'd attacked a man in an electronics shop, she had typed this play's title into the ReadWell website's discussion boards.

Quickly searching for it on her phone, she discovered only a handful of mentions of it on ReadWell but no posts in the last few years. What was its relevance? A description referring to it as Shakespeare's final play helped something else to slot into place. The play was a reference to something coming to an end, she was sure of it. Perhaps like the end of a mission? *That's it*, she thought. *This is how they communicate with one another*.

Suffused by excitement and anticipation, Emilia created a new post, typing it several times because her trembling fingers kept making errors. Eventually she pressed the 'return' button.

The Two Noble Kinsmen.

She held the phone to her chest but the delight in her achievement was short-lived when she heard voices elsewhere in the house. Quietly, Emilia made her way downstairs to a set of bifold doors which offered her access to a patio. From there, she ran towards the woodland where she knew she could reach the rear gate and let herself out.

She turned her head to catch several figures in pursuit. She couldn't be sure how many there were but she wasn't going to wait to find out. Faster she raced until the divide between them was too far for them to catch up, yet the further apart they became, the louder their voices were. It didn't make sense. She couldn't make out what they were saying but their unintelligible chatter terrified her more than being able to understand them. Their mutterings rang in her ears until she was forced to throw her hands over them to block them out.

As she made it out of the gate, along the road and back towards Bianca's car, she caught just one of their words.

Traitor.

Chapter 47

BRUNO, OUNDLE, NORTHAMPTONSHIRE

Bruno leaned against a set of railings outside the reception area of the sandstone building, waiting for the automated sliding doors to open.

Twenty minutes had passed since he'd followed Karen Watson and the girl in the wheelchair from their home to here. He'd waited until they had entered before he left his car. A hammer, his murder weapon of choice for all the names on his list, remained inside the glovebox. There was something about using that weapon that appealed more than a knife or a firearm. It was more personal, more destructive, it took more energy to swing it and land blow after blow than simply plunging a blade into someone's flesh. It was messier but he was careful – he chose his moments when there were no witnesses, no CCTV cameras and he left no trace of himself.

Bruno's pulse elevated ever so slightly when Watson returned to view, now alone, and making her way along the corridor and towards the exit. He removed his phone from his pocket and as he approached her, he pretended to be distracted by something he was reading. He made sure to collide with her, dropping the device to the floor.

'I'm sorry,' he began, bending over to pick it up.

'I haven't seen one of those for a few years,' she replied, looking at the clamshell-shaped device.

He raised his eyebrows. 'Oh, hi, it's you,' he said, and added a smile for good measure.

'Hello there,' she replied. From her expression and polite response, there was recognition but she was struggling to place him.

'Last time it was my dog crashing into yours by the river and now it's me.'

'Oh, of course,' she said, the penny having dropped. 'For a moment I thought you were another parent.'

Another, he repeated to himself, *Like she is. So that child is definitely her daughter.*

The warmth radiating from her smile drew Bruno towards her. He liked how she spoke softly and precisely.

'Well, I might also be the parent of a pupil here soon,' he continued. 'My son is moving to join me in Oundle so I'm checking out the local schools. Do you have a child who goes here?'

'Yes, Nora, my daughter.'

Bruno looked to the sign above. 'Oundle Academy', it read. 'How long has she been here for?'

'She started when we moved here about a year ago and she adores it. I looked at a few mainstream schools but opted to go private instead as it offered her more opportunities.'

'I've been to visit two in Peterborough and one in Stamford but it's difficult to know if you're making the right decision, isn't it? They tell you everything you want to hear but you're never sure if it's just because they want your business.'

'I can definitely recommend the Academy.'

'Perhaps you could tell me a bit more about it some time?'

Bruno interpreted Watson's hesitancy as her trying to decide if she was being asked out or if he genuinely wanted advice. She hedged her bets.

'What are you doing now? I need to take the dog for a walk if you'd like to join us?'

'If you're sure you don't mind?' He couldn't have engineered this any better.

Watson opened the tailgate of her car and her dog Luna jumped out and sniffed Bruno's ankles. Watson led the way as they strolled around the village, the expansive grounds of neighbouring Oundle school and a churchyard, while discussing the extracurricular activities the Academy offered to children who needed a little more physical or educational assistance. Eventually, they gravitated to a cafe in the high street. It wasn't until they were seated that he pretended not to know her name and they made their formal introductions.

'Where's your son at the moment?" she asked, sipping from a coffee mug.

'I didn't want to disrupt him more than necessary so Louie's been staying with his grandparents in Bath until I get the schooling situation sorted out. Although he's on an All Bodies residential course this week in Scotland.' Even Bruno was surprised at how casually the lies tripped from his tongue.

'You used his name,' whispered an Echo. 'You used Louie's name.' *Fuck,* he thought, he had. Watson was prising open something inside him. It had been months since he'd been able to talk about his son with someone who actually existed and had not evolved from data.

'Oh, Nora was there earlier this week,' Watson replied. 'Don't you think it's a brilliant organisation? It's all she can talk about.'

'Why does she go to the Academy, if you don't mind me asking?'

'She has fibrodysplasia ossificans progressiva. It's a progressive genetic disorder that only affects about one in two million people. In laymen's terms, it's turning her body into stone. Her soft tissue like her muscles, tendons and ligaments become solid and bone-like over time.'

'And is there a cure?'

'No. And if she has surgery to remove the bone, her body produces even more of it. But mentally, she's as sharp as a pin, quite advanced for her eleven years. If her condition is managed properly, she could live to around forty years, but that can radically reduce as she's prone to infections ...'

Karen's sentence trailed off and Bruno noticed her gaze leave his and travel beyond the window and to the street outside. He rejected the urge to reach out and hold her hand.

'Does Nora have brothers and sisters with the same condition?' he asked.

'It's just us and no.' She offered nothing about her marital status. But Bruno was already aware of what she wasn't telling him. He knew all about her husband.

'My wife died, so it's just myself and Louie,' he replied.

An alarm sounded on her watch, interrupting them. 'Oh, goodness, is that the time?' she said. 'I'm sorry, I have a dentist's appointment at midday.' She opened her purse to remove her payment card but Bruno dismissed her with his hand.

'No, please, it's on me,' he replied. 'Thanks for your advice about the Academy.'

'I can't let you do that.'

'You can get the coffees next time.' For a moment, they held each other's gaze and his stomach began a series of backflips. Watson appeared hesitant to say something before eventually plucking up the courage.

'If you're at a loose end on Wednesday afternoon, I promised Nora a picnic at that spot where you first bumped into us,' she continued. 'You're welcome to join us. About four p.m.?'

'I'd like that,' he replied. And despite himself, he realised he genuinely would. 'I'll see you on Wednesday then,' he replied.

Watson leaned in to shake his hand but Bruno misinterpreted it and moved to kiss her cheek. She turned her head to reciprocate but pecked him on the lips by mistake. Each was as flustered as the other before Watson led Luna out of the door. He watched as they made their way along the road.

'Look at you, you bloody idiot.' He turned his head and saw Roger McAllister, the late CEO of a pharmaceuticals company which had made extensive advancements in the field of precision cancer medicine. His team of scientists successfully sequenced the genomes of tumours, making them more treatable with drugs they had also developed. However, he had ensured the findings remained publicly undisclosed as he earned more profits from long-term cancer treatments than short-term cures. And by law, the government couldn't force him to share his findings. 'Wipe that grin off your face,' McAllister continued. 'Why isn't she dead yet? You've had plenty of opportunities, you fucking pussy.'

Bruno hesitated. The Echoes had been contradictory of late. Some supported his plan for Watson, others fought against it. But getting to know her was diluting the contempt he felt towards what she'd done. He could no longer, in good faith, kill her as he'd planned. Instead, he was coming up with an alternative. But he needed a little time to work out the technicalities for it to succeed. 'I have something in mind which will take a little longer,' he began.

McAllister's frosty breath glazed Bruno's face. 'You are here for one reason and one reason only. Grow a fucking backbone and get on with it.'

An image of Nora in her wheelchair came to mind and McAllister knew what he was thinking. 'You didn't give a second thought to the families of the two lawyers you beat to death, did you?' he continued. 'What about that rugby player? Did he have kids?'

'I don't know.'

'Because you didn't bother to find out, you just wanted them all dead. But now you're losing your edge. Just because she has a child as defective as yours doesn't mean she gets special treatment. Do you hear me?' McAllister didn't wait for a response before he vanished.

On his return home, Bruno made his way upstairs into the room he had replicated to resemble Louie's former bedroom and curled up on the bed. He tried to imagine Louie's scent on the sheets and pictured his son sleeping under his arm. Bruno could just about make out the fluorescent decorative stars he'd stuck to the ceiling. Soon night would fall and they'd make themselves visible. 'Shall we make a wish on them?' he often asked Louie, but Bruno's wish was always the same – to hear his son's voice, even if it was only once.

He took his phone from his pocket and logged on to the ReadWell message board, the first time that week. He typed in *The Two Noble Kinsmen* and pressed search. He hadn't counted on the results yielding a result, and especially not this one.

Chapter 48

FLICK, ALDEBURGH, SUFFOLK

> The Two Noble Kinsmen.

> The Two Noble Kinsmen.

> The Two Noble Kinsmen.

The title of the play had haunted Flick for three days since it had been posted online. Its appearance warned of an imminent threat to the Minders' safety.

Protocol dictated that as soon as they read the message, each was expected to leave their current location and make their way to a safe house in Northamptonshire. An identical message would be left for a maximum of seven consecutive days. That was to allow enough time to see it, leave confirmation of their impending return and make their subsequent arrangements. No further information would be offered as to the reason until their arrival.

Following Karczewski's murder, Flick had anticipated the recall message. But not knowing how advanced the other Minders' preparations were – or even how many of them existed – was frustrating.

With Grace away for the night visiting a university friend, Flick didn't want to be alone in the B&B so she'd asked to stay at Elijah's house. For much of the evening, she catnapped as he slept soundly next to her. Her dreams came thick and fast until eventually, she gave up on a restful night and relocated to his lounge. She wrapped herself in a tartan throw and sat cross-legged on the sofa. As the sun rose over the North Sea, she understood why Elijah had installed floor-to-ceiling windows when he'd designed his home. It was as if she were immersing herself in a moving piece of art, the cascading colours outside making her believe that she was part of a painting. It was a brief but welcome distraction from her reality.

And the reality was that Flick was conflicted. She knew reparation for the opportunity to start afresh was to put her country's security before her own needs. But turning her back on the second life that had saved her from her first was agonising. And time was running out.

Think, she told herself, *think. There must be another way.* For the second time that week, she disobeyed the programme's regulations and engaged the use of technology. She asked the house's OS to switch on Elijah's wall-mounted television screen and search for more news about Karczewski's death. To her surprise, there was nothing – no updates and no follow-up stories. Delving deeper, there was no longer any trace of his death or evidence that he had ever existed. Even the Twitter account that posted footage of his body's retrieval was deactivated. She slumped back into the sofa, puzzled.

Flick picked up her phone and read the recall message yet again. Only this time, something caught her eye. It was a minute detail that she'd missed. She drew the device closer to her eye to see if tiredness was affecting her vision. It wasn't.

There was an extra keystroke between the words 'Two' and 'Nobel' in the first message. The rest had just one.

Flick specifically recalled Karczewski explaining how such a communication would be sent via a secure computer algorithm and each message would be absolutely identical. So, was this extra space a computer glitch? It seemed unlikely. *Am I clutching at straws?* she asked herself. If she wasn't, the Minders' only means of communication had been compromised by a third party.

A panicked Flick logged off and pushed the gadget to one side, then glared at it. Five minutes passed before she picked it up again and logged in. The extra space was still there. The algorithm did not make mistakes. There was something wrong about this. With her heart racing, she began to type her first ever message.

@Ariel: Won't be finishing The Two Noble Kinsmen. Need a little extra space so I've decided to start Julius Caesar instead.

The sorry tale of Caesar and the trap that led to his murder was a warning to the others that not everything about the recall was as it seemed. She hoped to God that she wasn't mistaken and putting their lives at risk for the sake of a simple error.

When she heard Elijah's footsteps coming down the stairs, Flick placed her phone under a cushion and changed the screen from the internet to a music video station. He leaned over the back of the sofa and kissed the crown of her head.

'What's that?' he asked, tracing with his fingers where he'd kissed her. 'It feels like a tiny lump.'

That's where I underwent a procedure to store everything the government doesn't want you to know, she wanted to say. *And now someone is trying to lure me out of hiding to get it.*

'A war wound from being the only girl with four broth—' she replied instead, suddenly stopping short. *Damn it*, she thought and wanted to punch the cushions.

'You have four brothers?' he asked. 'Whenever I broach the subject of your family you never want to talk about them.'

Flick had to shut the subject down quickly but she was no longer thinking clearly. The best she could offer was a shrug. 'It's a conversation for another day.'

Inside, she quietly feared there might not be many days left for her in Aldeburgh.

Chapter 49

CHARLIE, MANCHESTER

Charlie wasn't aware a courier had dropped the plain white box onto his desk until he removed his virtual-reality headset. It was the only time he had requested post to be delivered to the office, so he was aware of its contents. He knocked it to the floor and pushed it under the desk with his foot when Milo approached. His parcel was not Milo's concern.

'Are you coming for lunch?' asked Milo and Charlie declined.

'I have some stuff I need to sort out,' he replied vaguely.

'Okay, tomorrow then? We should try that new Mexican restaurant in the Trafford Centre.'

'Sure.'

It had been days since they'd last shared food together and Charlie wondered if Milo was aware that he was being kept at arm's length. It wouldn't matter if he had because it was likely Charlie would be leaving Manchester in the next couple of days and on his way to a safe house.

He fumbled for the box and found it next to the emergency backpack he kept hidden under the desk. Since the recall message, he had left one in his cubicle, a second in the hotel suite and another under bushes by a disused section of a canal towpath. A fourth was stored in a locker in the People's History Museum. Each contained basic necessities that would assist in making his escape from Manchester easier. However, he had held back from confirming his return following the notice until other Minders had posted confirmation that they too were leaving. There was too much to give up here until it was absolutely necessary.

Moments later and in the privacy of a toilet cubicle, Charlie unpacked the Match Your DNA testing kit from the box, removed the mouth swab, moved it around his tongue and cheeks, placed it inside a test tube and stuck a new adhesive label to the front. Later, he would slip it into the post-room to arrive at its destination by the next morning.

Before leaving the bathroom, he logged into the ReadWell message board to check if the fourth of seven recall notices had gone live. Instead, he spied a new one from someone posting under the name of Ariel.

The stubble on Charlie's chin bristled as he rubbed at it, puzzled. Any reference to Julius Caesar meant a Minder suspected a trap. But suspecting one and there actually being one were two very different things. And they were the contrast between Charlie leaving or remaining where he was and suffering the consequences. By now, he should be concerned. Yet he felt nothing.

He slipped outside, careful to avoid Milo's eagle eye, and chose a small cafe in a side street to eat lunch alone. As he waited for his order, he took his mind off Ariel's warning by considering what the results of the DNA test might be. His last account was deleted when he entered the programme but yesterday, he'd arrived at work hours before everyone else and used an empty computer terminal to access a virtual private network. There, he created an encrypted and untraceable third-party email address, followed by a brand-new account. It was where the results would be sent.

It was Alix who had reignited his interest in finding if he'd been Matched. The more time they spent together, the more he realised how perfect she would be for him if his circumstances were different. If *he* were different. She was everything he could want – warm, witty, attractive, intelligent, a good conversationalist, maternal and driven. Yet she was not enough. Perhaps the only person who could make him feel again had registered with Match Your DNA in his absence. Maybe they were waiting for him and soon he could experience that euphoric rush of love so many boasted of.

It struck him that if he were being recalled and Alix and his new circle of friends were to vanish from his life overnight, he'd be unlikely to miss them. He would simply move on and make new friends, and remain just as emotionally detached from them too.

He logged back on to ReadWell and reread Ariel's message a handful of times. What was she trying to tell him? 'Need a little extra space,' he said aloud, and on the fourth time of reading it, he noticed she had left two keystrokes between 'extra' and 'space'. Charlie returned to the original recall message, then the second and third and spotted the second space between the words 'Two' and 'Nobel' in the first. Computer-generated messages did not make errors like that.

Slowly, he nodded his head as he understood Ariel was trying to warn them. A complete stranger he was unlikely to meet might have just saved his life.

Sleep did not come easily to Charlie that night. But at some point, he must have drifted off because he was awoken in the morning by Alix's voice coming up the stairs. 'Which drawer do you keep the tea towels in?' she asked.

'I'm not sure,' he yawned.

'You've been living here for three weeks, haven't you dried any dishes yet? If we ever share a place together, that'll be the first thing to change.'

Alix was red-faced when she returned to the bedroom moments later carrying mugs of tea. 'Not that I mean we *are* going to move in together,' she continued. 'Just in case you think I'm one of those women who after a few weeks of dating is already picking her wedding dress and the colour of the nursery.'

Charlie pulled back the duvet and she climbed into bed again. 'I'm not worried,' he replied. And he wasn't. Because whatever he had with Alix was not going to last. He no longer had the capacity for love and eventually, she would see that. But for the moment, his performance as a keen boyfriend was perfectly convincing.

He had ruled out any plans to leave Manchester for now, but it was never far from his mind that somebody out there had tried to lure the Minders to the safe house. For what purpose, he did not know. But it wasn't likely to be a positive one.

He and Alix had barely spent a night apart in their time as a couple. She was smitten with him. He didn't find her company unpleasant, but like everything else, it was neither offensive nor non-offensive. She had made no complaints about his performance in the bedroom; his lack of sex drive was easily remedied by over-the-counter medication. And ejaculation came as a result of physical stimulation, not emotional. But even his orgasms didn't bring about their typical rush of pleasure.

Alix's phone pinged with a news alert. 'Look at this,' she began and showed him the screen. 'It says Sweden is bracing itself to be held to ransom by the Hacking Collective. Dad was telling me we should withdraw all our bank savings because Britain will be next.'

'The Hackers can try but they won't succeed,' Charlie replied flippantly.

'Why not?'

Because everything they want to keep secret is hidden inside your boyfriend's brain, he thought. 'The government will have planned ahead for it, won't they? We won't be blackmailed.'

'I hope so. The hackers inflicted so much damage with those driverless cars. One of the teachers at work lost control of her Mini and it drove into a traffic light. She got whiplash.'

Try being hit by a lorry and losing your legs, then bleeding to death like my friends did, he wanted to reply, but held his tongue.

He waited until Alix was in the shower before he returned to ReadWell. There were no updates from Ariel or any of the others, so he added his own.

@Bassanio: Julius Caesar sounds like a good read. Thanks for the tip.

Charlie was going to remain where he was. But as with everything that was supposed to scare him, he had no fear of the future. Instead, he pledged to push himself as far as possible in the pursuit of understanding who he was now.

Chapter 50

SINÉAD, NORTHAMPTONSHIRE

'Northampton – five miles,' read the electronic road sign ahead.

Sinéad checked her speedometer – she was still below the limit. She had been showing caution for the last 438 miles by using only B-roads because motorways and super-highways contained too many speed cameras and number-plate-recognition systems. This way, she hoped to avoid the police and reach her safe-house destination as quickly as possible following the Kinsmen recall message. But it also meant her journey from Scotland to the Midlands had taken over fifteen hours. Only when the tiredness became all too consuming had she come to a halt in the dark corner of a supermarket car park and slept just long enough to recharge her batteries.

When she awoke, she thought of Doon and how she must be feeling today. Sinéad realised she had been caught in the moment when she had told her about Doon's daughter's murder. She had thought the truth would set Doon free, but it hadn't. It had released her from one prison, only to lock her up in a second.

Sinéad reflected on how she had felt on learning through implanted data that her parents' death in the Mumbai tsunami was as a result of fracking, covered up by the

British government. Greed and industry had killed them, not an underwater earthquake. There would be no prosecutions, and fracking continued in the same region. The information left her furious but powerless because under the terms of the programme, there was nothing she could do about what she knew. Now Sinéad understood that she had put Doon in the same position she had been in. It had been a terrible error in judgement and part of her was relieved there was a recall. Perhaps she wasn't cut out for this second life. But it was going to get a lot tougher before it got better.

She pulled at an eyelash as she drove and its needle-sharp sting as the root came to the surface brought her a moment of relief. When it faded, she repeated the action, as she had done frequently over the last few hours. Each eyelash was carefully placed on her thigh to form a semi-circle.

Sinéad glanced in the rear-view mirror at her sleeping passenger and took a deep breath. She knew that she was in trouble. But there was no doubt in her mind that she had done the right thing in kidnapping baby Taylor.

SINÉAD, EDZELL, SCOTLAND

Yesterday, a shocked Sinéad had been coming to terms with the prospect of her new life reaching a premature end. The recall message had taken her by surprise, but she hadn't questioned it. And she knew that she must leave as soon as possible. But there were two stops she wanted to make before leaving Edzell behind.

The first had been a symbolic gesture. She had travelled on foot to the same part of the river Esk where she had previously cast five bottled letters downstream. She was finally ready to allow the sixth letter to set sail, and it was the most important one. Sinéad had written it to her daughter Lilly. It was a heartfelt apology for failing to be the mother her child had deserved. It had taken an age to complete, each word hurting like a punch to the stomach as she recalled every minute of the night she found her baby dead. Teary eyed, she knelt upon the grassy bank before letting go of the bottle, along with her guilt. She would never forget the precious weeks spent enraptured by her much wanted child. But it was time to forgive herself for what she had done.

She heard a splash as she stood up and realised her phone had fallen from her pocket and into the water. She quickly grabbed it, dried it on her sleeve and turned it on. Nothing happened. 'Damn it,' she snapped. It meant she couldn't check the boards to see how many other Minders were readying themselves to leave.

Sinéad parked on the roadside, adjacent to the last house in the village, for her second stop. Gail's red car was the only vehicle on the driveway, suggesting Anthony wasn't there. The house was located a distance away from its neighbours on the only road in and out of Edzell; Sinéad wondered if it was coincidence that they were too far from their neighbours to hear the domestic violence under its roof.

Sinéad remained in her vehicle as she rehearsed how to approach Gail. After the Doon debacle, she paused to consider whether it might be wiser to climb back into her car and leave. But she owed it to her friend to try to make her see that she was better off without Anthony. Sinéad had the finances at her disposal to help Gail to relocate and live a life without oppression. She gathered herself and left the car.

Baby Taylor's shrill cries caught her attention as she approached the front door. Sinéad peered through the lounge window and spotted the infant strapped in her car seat and placed precariously on a narrow coffee table. She watched and waited and the time taken between the cries and her mother's appearance was so long that Sinéad questioned whether Taylor was actually alone in the house. The child's face was red and crumpled as a long-buried urge inside Sinéad began pulling at her, an overwhelming need to pacify the baby, to comfort her, to feel her head resting on her collar bone and her warm milky breath connecting with her neck.

Eventually Gail appeared and Sinéad backed away from the window. As she turned her head, however, there was a second scream, a long and persistent one, but this time coming from an adult. Her attention returned to the lounge where Gail was hunched over her daughter, back arched, shoulders forward and mouth wide open, bellowing at the terrified tot.

Sinéad craned her neck, convinced her eyes were deceiving her. They weren't. Instead of comforting Taylor, Gail was taunting her, pushing her face ever closer to the infant and screaming in time with her. Then she raised both her hands and slammed her fists hard against the sides of the car seat, heightening the baby's agitation. 'Shut the fuck up!' she yelled. 'Just shut the fuck up!' Not surprisingly, the frightened baby cried louder until, to Sinéad's horror, Gail slapped the child's face. Then she stormed out of the room, slamming the door shut behind her. Moments later, music blasted from a room upstairs.

Sinéad released a breath she hadn't realised she'd been holding. How had she gotten her friend so wrong? Either Gail was well skilled at hiding her true self or Sinéad had only seen what she'd wanted to see. She had long suspected postnatal depression might be the cause of the disconnect between mother and child, but PND did not make mothers violent and neglectful. Then she recalled the conversation in which Gail defended her husband and blamed herself for the problems in their marriage. Sinéad had been all too willing to cast Anthony as the villain, not his wife. What if Gail had been the one to slap him, not the other way around?

But there was someone she needed to prioritise above the mess of that couple's relationship. Taylor. And there was no way on earth that Sinéad was going to leave a vulnerable baby inside that house a second longer.

She would not let two children down in her lifetime.

Without considering the consequences, heart pounding in her throat, Sinéad made her way along the side of the building, unlatched the gate and quietly opened the kitchen door. Upstairs, the music boomed, she assumed to drown out Taylor's continuing wails. Inside the lounge she gently picked up the baby in her car seat, and caught the odour of a full nappy Gail had failed to change. Then Sinéad hurried into the kitchen, grabbed a bag of nappies from the kitchen side and raced back to her car, where she buckled Taylor into the back seat and began to drive.

She was breathless for the entire journey south through the village until she passed under the Dalhousie Arch, marking her departure from Edzell. Only when she reached the English and Scottish border three hours later did she begin to breathe properly again.

There had been many stops on their journey to change nappies and purchase wet wipes and auto-heated formula. Years had passed since Sinéad last nursed a baby and as she held Taylor in the crook of her arm and fed her with fluttering hands, black-and-white memories of Lilly returned in waves. They began with the moments after discovering she had died; her greyness and how cold her head felt as she'd stroked her wisps of hair and begged her to come back to life.

But now as Taylor drank, the colour returned to Sinéad's recollections. She remembered Lilly's red rosebud lips, the twitch of her pink button nose as she suckled, the blondness of her eyelashes and the gentle, random leg kicks and flicks of her wrists. Instead of recalling the baby she lost, she thought of the one she had cherished.

SINÉAD, NORTHAMPTONSHIRE

'I don't think it's much further,' Sinéad told Taylor as her car came to a halt at a set of red traffic lights.

They were leaving Northampton town centre and growing ever closer to their destination when Sinéad tried to predict what might happen once she reached the safe house. How would Karczewski and the other Minders react when she appeared with a five-month-old baby? Her reasoning wouldn't matter; it was completely against protocol. But as long as Taylor was away from Gail and Anthony, that was all that mattered. She could only hope Karczewski would accept that she'd had little choice.

Minutes later, Sinéad's car climbed a steep hill until she reached the rear of Great Houghton village. She located a private road stretching down a slope and towards a stack of farm buildings. She pulled up alongside a gate and pressed a buzzer. A green light flashed but no voice came. Instead, an illuminated screen invited her to scan both irises and input a fifteen-digit code she'd memorised. Only then did the gate open and allow her to approach the farm.

Sinéad parked in front of a cattle shed next to a shiny off-road vehicle, at odds with the mud surrounding them. She gave the farmhouse the once-over but the reflective glass windows and solid metal doors made it impossible to glimpse inside. 'I promise you that you're safe now,' she assured Taylor with a confidence she didn't really possess.

The front door automatically opened and she and Taylor cautiously ventured inside. A gentle breeze took her by surprise, nipping at her eyes and forcing her to keep blinking. The door closing triggered lights to illuminate a suburban home, not the hi-tech space she'd imagined was hidden behind its traditional facade.

'Hello?' She spoke but there was no response. She made her way through the dimly lit living room and into a dining area. Shrink-wrapped plastic covered the furniture, sofas and walls. In the next room was a kitchen, leading into a pantry and an old-fashioned larder. They too were all covered in thick dustproof sheeting.

'We must be the first ones here,' she muttered aloud and tried to open a window to release the musty smell. It wouldn't budge and she didn't know the code on the digital lock attached to it. When Taylor began to whimper, Sinéad glanced to her watch and assumed it must be feeding time. She placed the car seat on a kitchen table, rubbed her eyes and turned the tap on to wash her hands, only nothing came out of it. She opened the fridge door to see if there was any bottled water but it was empty and unplugged.

'Why would there be nothing waiting for us when they recalled—'

But Sinéad wasn't afforded the opportunity to finish. Instead, she felt someone behind her grab her hair, yank her head backwards and jab something sharp into her neck. The room started spinning as she fell to the floor.

Chapter 51

EMILIA

The woman's head twitched as the effects of the anaesthetic began to wear off. A line of saliva stretched from the corner of her mouth and ran down her chin as she groaned.

The injected dose had knocked her unconscious for an hour; enough time for Emilia to arrive, accompanied by Bianca, Adrian and an assembly of faces she hadn't been introduced to. It had also given them time to bind their victim to a chair with plastic restraints. Clear transdermal medical patches were affixed to her wrists, neck, fingertips and chest to monitor her vital signs.

Outside in the farmyard, Bianca and Adrian's team waited by their cars. Inside, it was now just Emilia and, according to her National Identity Card, Sinéad Kelly, although Adrian had warned it was likely a false name. Her real self would have long been buried.

So far, Sinéad was the only one of the four to have accepted Emilia's recall message as genuine. She had been located on the approach to one of the few safe houses that Bianca's surveillance team had identified and monitored with drones and field operatives. She had kept to herself that she knew the faces and the locations of the other three. Something was warning her not to show her hand just yet.

Emilia took advantage of their time alone to study Sinéad's appearance. The only unusual thing about her was the small clumps of missing eyelashes which left her eyes naked. The rest of her appearance was so unassuming and ordinary that Emilia questioned what Sinéad had done or what she was privy to, to warrant such drastic attention. Emilia had also asked the same question of herself many times. Who had she been for terrorists to need her help? And was it a life she really wanted to return to when this was all over?

Neither Adrian nor Bianca offered an explanation as to why they wanted to find Sinéad or the three missing others. She just hoped that, for Sinéad's sake, she told them everything.

Suddenly, Sinéad's eyelids fluttered, then opened wide, startled. Emilia pressed the earpiece and microphone she'd been given deeper into her ear canal. Sinéad tried to move, to no avail.

'Where's the baby?' she asked.

'She's outside with the others. She's safe.'

'I want to see her.'

'I'm sorry but you can't, not yet.'

The two women regarded one another until Emilia noticed a flicker of recognition cross Sinéad's face.

'You know me, don't you?' Emilia asked, eyes narrowing. Sinéad didn't answer. 'I'm familiar to you, I can tell.' Again, she remained silent. 'Look, I really need your help, Sinéad. I need you to tell me who I am and what you know about me.' Sinéad's face remained deadpan. 'I'm sorry that you're in this position but I had no choice.'

Sinéad focused directly on her captor. 'We all have choices. You've chosen to be a traitor.'

It was the second time Emilia had heard the word used as a weapon against her. First, from the figures chasing her through the grounds of Ted's estate, and now from Sinéad.

'A traitor? To whom?'

273

'To yourself and your country.'

Emilia took a step back. 'I have no choice,' she said. 'I know they are bad, bad people because I've seen first-hand what they're capable of. So, please, for your own sake, just comply. I don't want to see anyone else get hurt.' But Sinéad simply looked away. Emilia knelt in front of her so their lines of vision were level. 'Something happened to me that means I don't have any memories from earlier than three weeks ago. I was told that you and three others can tell me who I am. And if you do that, I'm sure I can talk the others into letting you go. Have we met before?'

'No,' Sinéad replied.

'But you know who I am?'

'Yes. And I know what you did.'

Emilia's stomach pitched. Sinéad's ominous tone made her almost reticent to ask. 'And what did I do?'

When Sinéad shook her head, Emilia explained all that she'd learned since waking up, including the threat to her family if she didn't assist. Sinéad's response was unreadable.

'Whose baby did you bring with you?' Emilia continued. 'I'm told she's not yours. If I can prove to you that she's safe, will you talk to me?'

Sinéad's eyes reached Emilia's and she gave a slight, almost imperceptible nod. 'Okay, wait here,' Emilia continued. Then closing the front door behind her, she made her way to the empty cattle shed where Adrian was waiting. Three more dark vehicles had joined them.

'Where's the baby?' Emilia asked.

'Being checked over by a medic,' Adrian replied.

'I told Sinéad she could see her if she talked to me.'

'I heard and I can't let that happen.'

'Why not?'

'Your approach isn't working. She's not going to break. Look at her stats.' Adrian pointed to a screen displaying Sinéad's stress and anxiety levels. Each was much lower than average, and diminishing with every heartbeat. It was as if she was shutting herself down, preparing for an inevitable outcome.

'You didn't see the way she looked at me when I told her she could see the girl. It might make all the difference.'

'You're wasting your time. This is a dead end.'

'I've only been in there for a few minutes. You can't expect me to give up just like that. This is my life we're talking about.'

'Emilia,' Adrian said firmly. 'We have had to make a call on this and we've decided to end it now.'

'You said I could have as long as it takes.'

'In this business, decisions are fluid.'

'Please, just hold back for a bit longer.'

She left Adrian and found the baby being examined in the vehicle Emilia had arrived in. She lifted the girl and pressed her against her chest as she marched back to the farmhouse. Pushing the door open, she approached Sinéad from behind, the baby starting to become restless, her arms and legs flapping.

'Look, Sinéad, she's safe and well like I said,' Emilia began. 'But I can't guarantee how long that'll be the case for you. I'm begging you, please tell me what you know about …'

Emilia's voice faded into nothing when she spotted a trail of blood across the wooden floorboards. It led to Bianca, who was standing just outside the shadows, a spectral figure with sharp, discerning eyes. She clutched a Stanley knife in one hand and a slender silver object in the other.

Chapter 52

BRUNO, OUNDLE, NORTHAMPTONSHIRE

Bruno was unwilling to admit why his apprehension was escalating as he made his way along the countryside path to meet Karen Watson and her daughter. But deep down he knew that it wasn't only the prospect of revenge that was drawing him towards her like a magnet.

The recall notice had placed a deadline on his mission. He reminded himself that today was Thursday and he now only had until the weekend to find a way into her home or revert to the original plan. And he honestly didn't know if he could kill her like he had the others.

There was one enormous benefit to an early recall – if his mission was coming to a premature end then according to his contract, he and his son would be reunited four and a half years earlier than planned. And they would be financially set for life.

Bruno scanned his surroundings as he approached the picnic spot on the banks of the river Nene, close to the bench where he had engineered their first meeting. Surrounded by lush green meadows and woodland copses, his grip tightened on his supermarket shopping bag and the lead attached to Oscar, the homeless pet he was volunteering to walk. He hoped the dog might reaffirm to Watson that he was a decent, caring man. And quietly, he wondered if somewhere inside him that man remained. Because much time had passed since they'd last been acquainted.

As they rounded a corner, Bruno spotted her, kneeling on a picnic blanket and removing the lids from Tupperware boxes. He paused for a moment to take her in; a forgotten memory returning of Zoe once doing the same thing.

'Remember what Watson has done to you,' a faceless Echo began, swiftly followed by a chorus of approval from others. 'Don't lose sight of the fact that she deserves everything that's coming to her.' Bruno waited until the Echoes faded and he was ready to approach her.

'Hi ...' he began, then promptly became tongue-tied. He ended the sentence with an awkward smile.

'Hello there,' Watson replied, rising to her feet. 'I'm glad you could make it.' This time, their mutual pecks on each other's cheeks landed successfully.

'I didn't know what to bring, so I kind of brought everything,' Bruno admitted, lifting the shopping bag to show her.

She pointed to the tartan picnic blanket behind her and bags from the same supermarket he had shopped at. 'Great minds think alike.'

Bruno acknowledged the young girl sitting in a wheelchair whose smile was as broad and genuine as her mother's. On her lap was an illustrated guide to river birds, and by her side, their dog Luna was lying on the grass until she spotted Oscar. As her lead strained, Bruno unhooked Oscar and the two dogs began eagerly sniffing around one another like old friends.

Bruno reached to shake Nora's hand, but her flexibility was limited. So he lengthened his arm to fill the gap as they introduced themselves. It was difficult not to take in her appearance as he asked about her book. She reminded him of a delicate porcelain figurine, albeit one with a Mediterranean skin tone and olive-green eyes. She was the complete opposite of her mother. Nora's torso favoured the left side, her neck the right. Her limbs were awkward and short and had he not known she was eleven, he couldn't have attached an age to her. Her electric wheelchair had all-terrain wheels and was operated by a remote control strapped to the palm of her hand.

'It wouldn't take much to push her into the river, would it?' The Echo with a German accent was as sudden as he was sinister. An elderly man with sunken cheeks, a white beard and clad in an old-fashioned surgical apron and mask appeared behind Nora. Bruno recognised Claude Zimmerman as a pioneer in paediatrics who'd escaped Nazi Germany and relocated to England. It was only years later that British investigators discovered he had actually been an active Party member and had experimented upon Jewish children. However, his past was quietly overlooked in exchange for the positive discoveries as a result of his barbaric procedures. Bruno shuddered as Zimmerman placed his hands upon Nora's wheelchair.

'Just a little shove and she'll be lying on the riverbed choking on the reeds.'

You're not real, you're not real, Bruno repeated to himself. But Zimmerman wasn't inclined to leave. 'You know what I'm saying is true,' Zimmerman continued. 'If you really want to punish the mother for her sins, then punish the child.'

'Are you okay?' asked Nora, turning to see what was capturing his attention. He returned to her and Zimmerman vanished.

'Just a bit of hay fever, I thought I was going to sneeze,' Bruno said. 'Are you as hungry as I am?'

She nodded and they made their way back to the blanket where Bruno unpacked his contribution of fresh vegetables, packets of cold meats, salads, dips and rustic breads. As they ate and talked, he kept to the subjects of school, Nora's recent residential adventure and life in the town. Bruno hadn't appreciated just how much he missed normal conversation and there were moments when he began to forget himself.

'Can I take the dogs for a walk?' Nora asked.

'Is your GPS on?' Watson replied and Nora pushed the soft skin on the underside of her wrist until a small, pale green light illuminated. 'Okay, well, don't go too close to the water. Your chair can do many things but floating isn't one of them.'

Bruno watched as she set off with the two dogs on leads, then became alarmed when as she turned a corner, Zimmerman reappeared. From behind a tree, he waved at Bruno, and followed her.

You're not real, you're not real.

'Have you made a decision on which school you're sending Louie to yet?' Watson asked.

She remembered his name. It had been an age since he'd heard anyone else use it. And he found himself wanting to talk about his son. He explained Louie's limitations and his abilities, the objects that made him smile, how he communicated without words and what Louie had taught Bruno about himself. Twice he paused as his throat tightened.

He hated himself for it but he was drawn to Watson. Bruno even allowed himself a moment to consider what kind of stepmother she might make if their circumstances had been different.

'I'd like to send him to the Oundle Academy but I think it might be out of our price range,' he continued.

'It is expensive,' Watson nodded, and dipped a celery stick into a hummus pot. 'I couldn't have afforded it had ...' Her voice trailed off. She was self-editing. But Bruno already knew how the sentence should end. It reminded him that he wasn't here to make life easier for her by changing the subject, so he waited for her to finish. '... had my husband Mark not died,' she added.

'I'm sorry. What happened to him?' he asked.

'It was the day that driverless cars were hacked. The vehicle Mark was a Passenger inside crashed into the side of a bridge. Only he wasn't alone, he was with another woman.'

Bruno's heart thrummed at her admission and images repeated of Zoe and Watson's husband having sex in the car they later died inside. He thought he might relish Watson's pain; instead, there was no satisfaction to be gained by opening the old wound. Still, he pressed on.

'Did you know about them?' he asked.

Watson shook her head. 'No. We'd grown apart but then all couples go through highs and lows, don't they? I assumed we'd get back on track eventually. I should have tried sooner.'

'I assume that Nora doesn't know the full story? I guess it's not the kind of thing your daughter needs to hear.'

'No, she doesn't. And she's not actually my biological daughter. She's Mark's daughter from his first marriage. Nora's mum died soon after she was born, then Mark and I met when she was two. I never formally adopted her but after Mark's death, there was no question that she wasn't going to remain with me. I would do anything to protect her and safeguard her future.'

Bruno contained his surprise; it was why he hadn't found a record of Watson having a daughter when he'd first investigated her.

A gruff laugh caught him unawares. 'Would you like me to locate a violinist?' Zimmerman's Echo muttered in his ear. 'I'm sure I can find one who'll play "Cry Me A River" while Nora drowns in it.'

Bruno was relieved when Nora appeared unharmed with the dogs. But for the rest of their afternoon together, her parentage weighed heavy upon his shoulders. The fallout of his alternative plan for Watson would hurt her daughter equally, if not more.

'Mummy, can Bruno and Oscar come for dinner at the weekend?' Nora asked. Bruno tried to hide his delight – it was a way into her home and just want he needed.

Watson blushed. 'I'm sure Bruno has better things to do.' She looked to him as if hoping he hadn't.

'Actually, no, I don't,' he replied, his smile rare but genuine.

Later, they set a time and as they packed up the remains of their picnic and walked slowly towards their cars, he imagined Louie was with them and holding his hand. He watched Watson help her daughter, and then Luna, into the car before holding his key to his own start button.

But first, he reached for his phone to check again for ReadWell messages; he was puzzled by a small red flashing circle in the top-right corner of his screen. The phone was not supposed to accept any form of incoming communication.

The frosty breath of several Echoes in the car's rear seats grew colder and they shuffled closer, all curious to discover what the icon meant. Hesitantly, Bruno clicked on it and a video began to play.

A woman stared at the camera, her mouth gagged as someone carved the name 'Sinéad' into her forehead with a blade. And as the blood seeped down her cheeks, a silver instrument was raised two, perhaps three, centimetres from Sinéad's skull, then a button released, and almost too fast for the eye to register, something inside it penetrated the crown of Sinéad's skull. Sinéad's eyes opened as wide as possible, and never shut again. Bruno replayed the message twice more to assure himself this was genuine and that he had not started a descent into madness.

He hurriedly logged on to message board and discovered Ariel's message. It didn't take him long to decipher that it was a warning that the original recall message was fake. It had been a trap and now someone had murdered a Minder. And in doing so, they had also killed off his chance to be reunited early with Louie. Bruno slumped in his seat, deflated.

It took no time at all before his disappointment manifested itself into anger and all he could picture were the faces of the six people who had separated father from son. He detested every last one of them. They had all deserved to die. And so did Watson.

He glared at her car through his windscreen; it had still not pulled away. She was a sitting duck. He reached for the hammer in the glovebox and withdrew it, threw open the door and climbed out. *Fuck the new plan, this is going to end now*, he thought. And with his grip firmly around the handle, he rushed towards her.

Chapter 53

FLICK, ALDEBURGH, SUFFOLK

Within an hour of witnessing a recording of Sinéad's murder, Flick fled Aldeburgh.

Earlier that day, her shift behind the bar had been a welcome distraction from the fake recall notice. If she was incorrect and it had been genuine, it was the first day of a life lived on borrowed time. Her only comfort was that she wasn't alone. Following the warning message, Minders using the Shakespearean character names Bassanio and Cominius indicated they too would not be returning.

Suddenly it struck her that if the notice was real, then her funding should now be cut off. She poured herself a mineral water and tapped her credit card to pay for it – it was accepted. Now more than ever she was convinced the withdrawal request was a hoax. But who had infiltrated their clandestine world?

'I'm taking my break,' she told landlord Mick and made her way to an empty table in the corner of the room. Flick gazed out of the window and towards the dark clouds over the sea and the rain lashing at the patio umbrellas. The weather was mirroring her own unrest, or perhaps, she feared, it was a warning of something worse to come.

As if on cue, her phone vibrated. The screen displayed a red circle, something that hadn't appeared before.

Hesitantly, Flick scanned the pub to ensure privacy and pressed play. And her stomach churned as seconds later, she witnessed the first Minder captured, mutilated and murdered.

With no time to think twice, Flick slipped out of the pub, returned to the B&B to pick up her emergency rucksack and breathed in the post-storm air as she hurried through the rear garden and towards a gate leading into a ginnel. But Grace caught her pre-flight. She eyed Flick up and down, and then looked at the backpack hanging from her shoulder.

'Are you leaving?' she asked and Flick nodded. 'But I thought you were happy here?'

'I am, I was,' Flick replied. 'But it's time to move on.'

'Why?'

'It … just is.'

'You're a terrible liar.' *If only you knew*, Flick thought. 'Come back inside and maybe I can help.'

'I can't, I'm sorry.'

'Is it Elijah? Has he done something to hurt you?'

'It's nothing like that.' Flick threw her arms around Grace. 'I've transferred cash into your account to pay for my room up until the end of the summer so you won't be out of pocket,' she said with a trembling voice. 'Please look after yourself.' Then she turned her back on her friend, allowing the gate to close behind her.

Flick tossed her backpack across the rear seats of a driverless robo-taxi service she had ordered and which was waiting for her several streets away. And as it pulled away, she wept for the life she was leaving behind. There was always going to be a risk she might have to turn her back on it at a moment's notice. But when that moment arrived it hurt like hell. She thought of Elijah and their fledgling relationship. She would never get the opportunity to explain why she was leaving; her only hope was that Grace could persuade him he was blameless and to convey the pain she'd witnessed in Flick as she left.

Flashbacks of her pre-programme existence flooded her memory, of how she turned her back on the career and people she had loved because of who her DNA was linked to. Three years of misery had followed, of self-induced solitude and clinical depression. The thought of returning to that person and that life suddenly sparked something inside her.

'No,' she said. 'Not again.' She couldn't allow herself to be swallowed up and spat out by the actions of others again. History was not going to repeat itself.

Grace was sitting in the garden of the B&B when Flick opened the door. Her friend's eyes were glistening. 'Have you forgotten something?' she asked and Flick shook her head. 'Does that mean you're staying?'

'Yes,' Flick replied and as she dropped her backpack to the floor, Grace offered her a tight hug before leading her into the kitchen.

'What happened?' Grace asked for the second time that afternoon, and poured Flick a mug of tea from a pot.

'I can't tell you,' said Flick. 'And please don't ask me for details because I don't want to lie to you.'

'Has it got something to do with why you left London?' Flick nodded.

'Are you in danger?'

'Yes, I think I might be. And I'm scared that if I stay, I might put you and Elijah at risk.'

'I can look after myself,' Grace said dismissively. But neither she nor Flick knew who they were up against.

'If I'm to stay, I need you to tell me if anyone turns up here asking about me.'

'Like who?'

'That's the problem. I genuinely don't know.'

Grace nodded. 'I'll ask others for help too.'

'They'll want to know why.'

'Then I'll tell them you have a psycho ex-boyfriend or something. You're liked around here, you know. People in this town look out for their own.'

With just those few reassuring words, Flick knew she had made the right decision to return. Whatever threat she faced, she stood a better chance of fighting back by being in a community than by standing alone.

Chapter 54

EMILIA

'Pull over,' demanded Emilia.

'I'm sorry?' Bianca replied, her view fixed on a tablet as the autonomous car continued moving forwards.

'Pull the car over *now*.'

'That won't be happening.'

'I swear to God if you don't, I'm going to break every window in here.'

'Good luck with that. They're bulletproof.'

Emilia's rage reached boiling point. She had been trapped inside the car for thirty minutes and all she could think about was Sinéad's mutilated body. She had to get out of that vehicle as a matter of urgency.

Bianca sighed and signalled to Adrian to touch the dashboard screen. The car slowed, eventually pulling into a lorry park. Emilia pushed at a button to release the door lock but it wouldn't budge until Bianca pressed the override switch. It was another reminder of the control they had over her.

Outside, Emilia placed both hands, palms forward, against the side of a rig and lowered her head, taking in deep breaths.

'Emilia,' began Bianca, now standing behind her. 'If there had been any other way—'

Emilia didn't think before she acted. She turned around at speed, raised her right fist and caught Bianca clean in her nose. Her other fist collided with what should have been Bianca's ribcage, but came against something solid that she assumed to be body armour. It gave Bianca an advantage so she punched Emilia in the stomach, landing two more kidney blows before she collapsed to the floor. Emilia was down but she wasn't out. She kicked her leg and caught Bianca in the ankle, causing her to cry out loud. Then she pulled it back to repeat the action on the other ankle when she felt a pair of hands under her arms dragging her away across the asphalt. 'Enough,' snapped Adrian.

'What the hell do you think you're doing, you dumb bitch!' shouted Bianca. It was the first time Emilia had seen her ruffled.

'You didn't need to kill Sinéad!' Emilia yelled.

Bianca pinched at her nostrils to stop the flow of blood. 'She wasn't going to tell you a thing no matter how much you begged her. We were wasting time.'

'Or you were scared that if she told me everything, I wouldn't help you find the other three.'

'Oh, I know you'll help us find the others if you want to see your goddamn family again.'

'How do I know they're even mine?' Emilia argued. 'You could have deepfaked them.'

'You knew they were your family the moment you saw them,' Bianca hit back. 'You might not remember them but something buried inside you felt the wrench. I saw it in your eyes.'

'And to carve Sinead's name into her forehead? Why?'

'As a clear warning to the others that we are coming for them.'

'But it'll have the opposite effect. They'll bury themselves deeper.'

'Or by shaking the hive, we'll see what flies out.'

'I saw the wound in the top of her head. Your people did the same to Ted – why?'

'You just need to do as you're told and stop asking questions.'

'Why do you call them Minders? What are they taking care of?'

'Did you not just hear what I said? Stop asking questions or so help me God …'

Only when Emilia calmed did Adrian release his grip. She clambered to her feet and wiped her moistening eyes. A male voice took her by surprise.

'Everything all right?' a bearded man asked through the wound-down window of his truck. He stared only at her as Adrian and Bianca fell silent.

'Yes, I'm fine,' Emilia said but he didn't seem convinced. 'Thank you, though,' she added before his vehicle pulled away.

She turned to Bianca. 'I can't do this; I can't be responsible for anyone else's death. I'm not a killer like you.'

'You don't have the first clue who you are,' she snapped. Adrian placed his hand on her arm as if advising her to stop. She ignored him. 'But I promise you this. The next time you get slap happy, I will shut your family down once and for all and I'll make you watch.'

Emilia needed time on her own to process what had happened. And she planned to keep quiet with what she knew about the surviving Minders until she was sure how to use it to her advantage and not theirs.

'Bianca,' said Adrian suddenly, his finger held to his ear as if listening to something. Both women turned to see his irises darting in all directions as images appeared in his smart lens. 'Based on the description Emilia gave us of the park she found herself in where the tunnel ended, field ops scoured the area and detected a handful of Victorian storm drains. Only one of them led under the streets and stopped at a specific building. We sent a team but it's vacant.

So they used cameras attached to neighbouring buildings to identify everyone who had entered and left in the last nine to twelve months, cross-referred them to their National Identity Cards and then searched for those who'd gone off-grid. There were only four who had stopped using their bank accounts, store cards, who cancelled utility bills, no longer shopped online, had not visited a doctor, dentist, stopped paying National Insurance and so on. Sinéad was one of them. We have photos of the three others.'

Damn it, thought Emilia. But at least they didn't know where to find them. Not yet, anyway. And the sinister smirk that crept across Bianca's bloody mouth indicated what would happen to the others when they were discovered.

Chapter 55

CHARLIE, MANCHESTER

The wind's bitter sting felt as if it were penetrating Charlie's skin and biting his bones. He tasted it with his tongue as it parted his chattering lips and ruffled his hair. Yet its chill wasn't harsh enough to make him uncomfortable.

Instead, he removed his jacket, jumper, T-shirt, trainers and underwear until he was completely naked, standing on the roof of Manchester's tallest hotel. His body shivered, but his disconnect from fear and pain remained. He had to push forward.

Charlie peered over the edge. From fifty-two storeys high, Manchester's streets resembled a child's play mat, painted in bright colours and littered with toy cars. Just below him, a window-cleaning gantry caught his attention. He carefully climbed inside as its metal frame swayed and clanked against the side of the building with each new gust of wind. Then he lifted himself up until he was standing on its narrow edge, one hand holding the chains that precariously moved the contraption up and down, his toes curled around the metal rim. All that separated Charlie from death was one violent blast. He closed his eyes and imagined himself falling, then taking off into the night sky and being carried away to the horizon.

Charlie had retained his room at the La Maison du Court despite moving into a flat-share; it did no harm to retain his bolthole should the need arise for somewhere to escape. It was all the more important now that someone had killed a Minder. In the office toilets that afternoon, he had opened the message sent to his phone and watched as Sinéad was butchered. However, it didn't prompt him to question his own safety. Instead, as he replayed the footage, he became fixated by Sinéad's stoic expression. How might he feel in the moment he knew he was going to die?

Her murder was the reason Charlie had found himself hovering outside the service lift of the hotel, waiting for a member of staff to enter before he followed them inside. Once they departed at their floor, Charlie continued until he reached the roof, tiptoeing past masts and aerial towers until he reached the edge. Alongside driverless cars, death and loneliness, heights had been the phobia that scared the old Charlie the most. Standing on a rooftop's ledge was different to pressing his head against the window of his suit. It would be the biggest test of how much of his former self remained.

He waited patiently for a shot of adrenaline to course through his veins or for panic to rise from the pit of his stomach. But neither developed. And not even the wind's icy tendrils could penetrate him. Charlie would have to accept that this was how it was going to be from here on in – he was a man who feared nothing because he felt nothing.

'Mate, what are you doing?' A voice came from behind, carried by the breeze. Charlie turned his head as a figure approached.

'Milo?'

'Whatever it is that's troubling you, there must be a better way to deal with it than this.' He was wheezing.

'Why are you breathless?'

'I just walked up fifty-two flights of stairs. You know my issues with lifts.'

'What are you doing up here?'

Milo held up his hand; there was something between his fingers. 'You left a hotel-room swipe card at my house yesterday. I swung by to drop it off at the reception desk when I saw you take the staff elevator to the roof.'

'I work part-time here,' said Charlie calmly.

'No, you don't.'

'Why do you say that?

'I went into your room before I came up here. Your stuff is in there. I recognised your trainers. How can you afford to stay in a place like this?'

'I'm standing naked on a hotel roof and that's the question you ask?'

'Because I don't know what else to do,' he shrugged. 'I'd like to be your friend but you keep us all at arm's length.'

'Us? Who else knows about the room? Who've you told?'

'Nobody, honestly, you can check my phone if you don't believe me. So, what's going on? Why are you up here?'

Charlie cocked his head. Milo was somebody he could talk to. He was kind, giving, thoughtful and non-judgemental. Perhaps he might help, even if he couldn't know the complete story. 'Have you ever just stopped … *feeling*?' he asked.

'What do you mean?'

'Has your head ever become so overloaded with details, with experiences, with bad shit, that it just won't take any more, so it just kind of … shuts down?'

'I guess we all have bad days.'

'I'm not talking a bad day, a bad week or even a bad month. I'm talking about a bad all the time and the only way you survive is to close yourself off.'

'I guess that's part of life, isn't it? You just find a way to get on with it.'

Charlie let out a laugh with no humour attached. 'With respect, you have no idea what life is about, Milo. And you have no idea of what it's like to be one of the only people who does.'

'Why don't you put your clothes on and we can go downstairs and talk about it?'

'If I did talk about it, I'd probably have to kill you afterwards.'

'Okay,' smiled Milo. 'I'll take that risk. Let's start by stepping back onto the roof.'

'Why, do you think I'm going to throw myself off it?'

'Honestly? Yes. Why else would you be up here?'

'To remind myself who I was before I gave it all away.'

'Who you were? Who took it away from you?'

'I was a sad, miserable man, Milo, living a lonely existence, unloved, unlovable, a nobody. But despite all those flaws, at least I wasn't dead inside. At least I felt something. Now, I feel no more emotion than the artificial intelligence that's going to take our jobs.'

'Why would you want to go back to being miserable?'

'Because at least I knew who I was then. Now I have no idea. And the worst thing is that I can't muster up the enthusiasm to even care.'

A sudden gust of wind shook the gantry; Charlie held on with both hands. But as he approached the gap between gantry and roof, he came close to losing his footing. Milo hurried towards him, reached for the chain and pulled it, steadying the rocking device. It allowed Charlie to step back safely onto the roof.

'Thank you,' he said. And without forethought, Charlie moved his face towards Milo's, tilting his head until his lips touched those of his friend's. Their complete attention was locked onto one another as Charlie kissed him. It was Charlie's first same-sex kiss; not born from desire but desperation to spark something inside him by trying anything new. Milo didn't protest or withdraw, but he didn't participate either. Charlie was the first to disengage.

'Look, mate, I'm not denying there's ... *something* ... between us,' said Milo. 'But all I want to be is your friend today. Is that all right?'

Charlie nodded. 'Understood. Can I have my room key, please?'

Milo removed it from his pocket and passed it to him. With one hand, Charlie took it and for a second, hesitated, as if weighing up the pros and cons of what was to come next. Then with the other hand, he used all his strength to shove his unsuspecting friend as hard as he could, and watched him fall over the edge, fifty-two storeys down to the road below.

Chapter 56

BRUNO, OUNDLE, NORTHAMPTONSHIRE

Bruno paused to turn his head when he reached the porch.

The Echoes were trailing him from his house to Watson's but were far from subtle in their endeavours; he'd heard whispers and faint footsteps the entire journey. He could just about make out a gathering in a neighbouring garden. And he chuckled at the absurdity of being stalked by his own imagination.

He clutched a bottle of Italian white wine he'd purchased at an off-licence, pressed the doorbell and heard it chime from inside. He recalled the moment days earlier when he lost all control and, armed with a hammer, his intention was to attack Karen Watson in her car. She was two metres away from death when he overheard mother and daughter singing along to show tunes on the stereo. What he would have given for that to have been him with Louie.

He took a figurative and literal step back as his rational side took control. Killing Watson would only offer him temporary satisfaction. And even his ever-diminishing sense of decency drew the line at murdering a parent in front of their child. Bruno was going to return to Plan B and tonight he would take everything away from Watson that she had stolen from him.

A camera whirred as it changed position and pointed towards him. 'Hold on,' she asked via the intercom.

Through the frosted panes of glass her shadow grew before the door opened. 'Hello,' she said, flustered. She wore no make-up; her hair was scraped back into a tight ponytail and her clothes were crumpled. Her naturalness gave him butterflies.

'Is everything all right?' Bruno asked. 'Dinner is tonight, isn't it?'

'Yes, but not for another couple of hours.'

'Oh God, I'm so sorry. When Nora said come for five o'clock, I thought it was a bit early. I must have misheard.'

'Yes, it was seven,' Watson said apologetically, even though it hadn't been her mistake. 'Nora is still at Saturday school; I'm picking her up in a few minutes.'

'Okay, look, no worries, I'll just walk home and come back later.'

'Didn't you drive?'

'No, it's such a beautiful afternoon that I thought I'd come on foot. It only took half an hour. I'll go and have a pint at the Ship and come back for seven.'

'No, no, I can't let you do that. Besides, your wine will get warm.' Watson stood to one side and beckoned him in. Closing the door behind him, he followed her into a large, open-plan kitchen. Bifold doors stretched the length of a flat, landscaped garden. It was every bit as beautiful inside as it was from the outside.

'I'll have to leave you on your own while I get Nora, though.'

'Is there anything I can do to help out with dinner?'

'No, it's all prepared. The lounge is to the right, make yourself at home or help yourself to a drink from the fridge.'

Bruno watched Watson hang her apron on the wall. 'Once I steal everything, I'll be gone by the time you return.'

'Okay, well, I keep the gold bullion in the cellar and the diamonds are in the safe behind the Picasso. I'll be back in about half an hour.'

Bruno made his way into the lounge as the front door closed and he absorbed his surroundings. Despite its size, its decoration was warm and cosy and reminded him of his former family home; the home he had been forced to leave because of people like Watson. Shelves creaked under the weight of her books, two large plump sofas surrounded an open fire, and a huge television screen was attached to the wall. It wasn't hard to imagine Louie and him living happily there.

He peered from behind the window shutters, waiting until Watson's car reversed off the driveway. He'd deliberately arrived early knowing Nora was schooled on Saturday afternoons and counted on Watson's inherent trust to leave him alone there. She saw the good in people, but she had misread him.

Bruno moved swiftly from room to room searching for a tablet or computer. Eventually he found a tablet, a paper-thin device stuck to the fridge. Then using techniques and hacks he had learned from his implanted data, he bypassed Watson's iris and biometric scans to access the gadget and its apps. First, he located her online banking accounts, as easy to break into as the device. There were three in her name, one for savings, one for bills and one in her daughter's name. He totted up the funds at her disposal – there was close to £2 million.

This was his money that she had stolen.

It was Watson and lawyers including O'Sullivan and Graph – Bruno's first two victims – who ensured he would not receive a payout following Zoe's death. Zoe's employer had, however, paid large sums in compensation to the two men who accused her of sexual harassment after her death to keep it from being made public. As one of the top five firms in the country for its commitment to staff welfare, it was desperate to protect its reputation.

Breaking the morality code by having an affair with Zoe meant that Watson's husband's dependents wouldn't receive a payout either. She had jumped on the bandwagon of Zoe's other two accusers and claimed Mark had also been coerced into having sexual relations with Zoe; that he had told her on several occasions he feared for his job if he didn't give her something. Bruno didn't understand why the company had not refuted this. They had all witnessed the footage of the two having sex and it was obvious that he was a more-than-willing partner. Yet they still readily accepted Watson's word that it was harassment and paid her to keep quiet too.

To recoup their losses, they sued Zoe's estate and won, picking at what remained of Bruno's life like a wake of vultures stripping a carcass bare. He was plunged into bankruptcy.

Today, Watson was clueless that the man she had left inside her house was about to strip her of her ill-gotten gains and transfer her savings into one of his old accounts. Later that evening, the money would be buried in new foreign accounts scattered around the globe that Watson was unlikely to ever find. Soon she would learn how it feels to be broke and helpless.

Chapter 57

FLICK, ALDEBURGH, SUFFOLK

Flick sat bolt upright in bed, the room spinning like a disorientating fairground ride. She gripped the bunched-up bedsheets, waiting for the image of a bloody Sinéad to pass.

A sudden feeling of nausea meant she had taken to Elijah's bed late that afternoon. She had slept for an hour or so before the dreams began in earnest and she'd woken herself up in a panic. She pressed the back of her head against the headboard until the bedroom came to a standstill.

There were still so many questions hanging mid-air following Sinéad's murder. Who had killed her? Why did the killer want the remaining Minders to know he'd located one of them? Had he hoped her death might panic them into making mistakes? Had Sinéad made errors that Flick could learn from? And why had Karczewski's death been removed from online news sites?

Taking her phone from under the pillow, Flick was unsteady on her feet as she made her way to the bathroom. She closed the door softly so that Elijah couldn't hear her from his studio and sank to the floor to vomit as quietly as she could. She dabbed a damp flannel against her burning forehead but when it failed to cool her down, she stripped off her T-shirt and knickers and sat in the shower under a jet of lukewarm water.

THE MINDERS

The days and nights after Sinéad's death were spent trying to continue as if everything was perfectly normal in her abnormal world. If she wasn't spending time with Grace or working behind the bar at the pub, then she was at Elijah's house. Her daily runs and unaccompanied time watching the sun rise from the beach were a thing of the past. Her new routine might have been keeping her captive but it was also keeping her safe.

Turning off the shower, Flick patted herself dry with a towel and made her way downstairs into the kitchen, grabbing a cranberry juice from the fridge.

While the dizziness had dulled, the nausea remained, and soon, she was rushing to the kitchen sink to be sick again. She rinsed her mouth with water when an awareness hit her with the force of a lightning bolt.

'Oh, no,' she gasped. 'Oh Christ, no.'

Chapter 58

BRUNO, OUNDLE, NORTHAMPTONSHIRE

Bruno estimated he had approximately twenty minutes left until Karen Watson returned home. But as he was about to press the transfer button that would drain her of her finances, a photo-album icon on her home screen labelled 'Family' caught his attention. Curious, he skimmed through its contents. Amongst the photographs was a video clip of a very young Nora in her first motorised wheelchair. Her body was more flexible back then and she giggled as she spun in circles, and he could hear out-of-shot warnings coming from her parents advising her to be careful.

Another clip was more recent and featured Watson guiding her daughter around their new home, explaining the extensive renovation work being carried out to ensure it was wheelchair friendly. A camera lingered on Watson for a moment. She was clearly emotional as she regarded Nora and their dog Luna exploring the garden together. Bruno recognised pride when he saw it. He too would take time out of his day to watch his son doing nothing in particular. It made him miss Louie with an intensity that for a moment threatened to swallow him.

A photograph of Watson's husband caught him unawares. Bruno purposely avoided images of the man Zoe had slept and died with; he'd only seen overhead video footage of the two having sex. Mark was not as Bruno had imagined – not a devilishly handsome Mr Darcy type, swooping in and sweeping unhappily married women off their feet. Instead, he was quite short in stature, of average looks and with a slight stomach paunch.

'You're having second thoughts, aren't you?' The ensemble of Echoes had made their way from Watson's neighbour's garden into her kitchen. A young man stepped forward, dressed in a blue Royal Navy uniform. Both sleeves and a trouser leg were scorched by fire and the skin on his arms was either blackened or burned raw. 'There's no shame in admitting this feels wrong.'

Bruno shook his head, but he was conflicted. 'If I don't do it, then what's been the purpose of all of this?'

'Have the people you killed brought you any closer to getting your wife or son back?'

'No.'

'The satisfaction you found from their murders – how long did it last?'

'Not long.'

'What will you achieve by taking away everything Watson and Nora have?'

'I'll get justice for Louie.'

'Destroying this family won't give you that. Two people made a very stupid mistake, and you, Louie, Watson and Nora have all been made to pay the price. Zoe hurt you in ways she could never have anticipated. But what you're doing is purposeful. You need to let go of that life and build a new one.'

'How, when I can't have the two people I want to do it with me?'

He returned to the home screen and scanned other folders, opening one titled 'Legal'. It contained Watson's historic correspondence with her lawyers. Their team of private investigators had discovered emails and text conversations between Zoe and Mark, messages that Bruno had never seen.

Now, as he read them, he saw no 'I love you's or promises to leave their respective partners. They had not bonded over a carnal desire for one another, but over their children's disabilities. They discussed how inept they felt about their capacity to parent compared to their partners' skills. Zoe admitted to feeling shut out of Louie and Bruno's 'boy's club' and Mark believed he was a spare part in his own home. This was certainly not a man being coerced into sex; this was proof of a relationship.

He looked at the date stamped on the folder – Watson had evidence of this while she was making her claim for sexual harassment damages. Yet still she proceeded with them knowing full well it was a lie. It had been accepted and she'd received a payout which led to Bruno's financial ruin. However, now he'd got to know Watson, he could see she had done it with the best of intentions, to provide financial stability for her vulnerable daughter. Might he not have done the same for Louie if their roles had been reversed?

The destruction of Bruno's family had been collateral damage that Watson had unwittingly caused. And now it was as if someone had turned off a smoke machine, enabling him to see clearly again. The contempt he also felt towards Zoe and Mark was dissipating and being replaced by pity. He was still alive, he was still a parent. They weren't either.

And just like that, he made a decision. He shut down his and Watson's bank account pages, cancelling the planned transfer. Then he wiped his eyes, unashamed that the Echoes were witnessing his tears.

He needed to leave. Watson would be back in ten minutes, according to the clock. He wouldn't be here when she returned. But before he slipped away, he would make use of her Wi-Fi and access Louie through the care facility's security cameras. He watched his son being guided to his bedroom by a member of staff. And this time around, instead of his chest tightening each time another person interacted with Louie, he was grateful that his sacrifices meant Louie was getting the best help.

As Louie climbed into bed, the carer reached over and took Louie's favourite toy from his arms, the green Tyrannosaurus rex his mother had bought him. And without warning, the carer hurled it across the room. *That's an odd game*, Bruno thought.

A puzzled Bruno straightened and frowned as he watched Louie leave the bed to fetch it. However, the staff member pushed him back onto the mattress by his shoulder.

'Get off him,' Bruno growled as his son was separated from the one object that comforted him the most. Twice more, he reached for his toy and twice more, he was refused it. And when Louie's face scrunched and his mouth opened to scream, the carer slapped the boy hard across the head three times before leaving the room.

Bruno remained motionless – was his damaged mind now completely augmenting reality? He looked to the Echoes; they were as gobsmacked as him. He tried to rewind the footage but the option wasn't available.

'No, Bruno,' came the burned sailor's voice. But Bruno wasn't listening. 'No,' he repeated, more firmly. 'Don't do it, you have to move forward. You can't go back. You have to protect us.'

'You're imagining it,' said another voice, the boy with the missing jaw. 'He's perfectly safe.'

But the rage inside Bruno was rising again. He rose to his feet when a figure by the door caught his attention. From a distance, he assumed it to be another Echo, at least until she spoke.

'Why are you looking through Mummy's files?' Nora asked, her brow furrowed.

Chapter 59

EMILIA

Emilia pinched her eyes with her thumb and her forefinger, then squeezed two drops from a bottle she'd purchased at a pharmacy to clear the blurriness. Frequent use of her tablet was taking its toll on her vision.

Her vehicle had pulled into the car park hours earlier than her appointed time. It hadn't taken her long to reach the Luton roadside eatery, positioned adjacent to a busy dual carriageway. She parked a distance from the other vehicles, positioning herself next to a row of hedges and with a clear view of the building ahead. Through the cafe windows she counted twenty or so families and couples tucking into all-day breakfasts and early dinners.

Adrian's invitation had come out of the blue. He had sent the location of the cafe to her satnav, advising her that by attending, 'You will have a better understanding of who you are and why you must set your conscience to one side in your search for the truth.'

As she awaited their arrival, she continued busying herself by sifting through hundreds and hundreds of digital pages of notes, photographs and data about each of the Minders exhumed by Bianca and Adrian's team. She'd naively assumed that once online data had been deleted, it would never be seen again. 'Nothing disappears for ever,' Bianca had said casually, as if she should already know this. 'The word "erased" is extinct. Everything is "filed" for use at a later date.'

Such harvested data included the shops the three favoured, their holiday destination preferences, medical histories and their family backgrounds. Each piece of information assisted Emilia in building up a profile of the elusive three and where they might be hiding in the areas she had identified. She didn't know who was where, and she had no plans as yet to tell Adrian or Bianca she knew they were in Aldeburgh, Manchester and Oundle.

She had skimmed their current social media profiles and if she hadn't known better, she would have believed each one was somewhere different in the world, luxuriating on vast, sandy beaches, hiking across South American backpacking trails, fruit picking on Australian farms or chasing Pacific waves with a surfboard. Everything was backed up by deepfake video images.

Emilia left her vehicle when Adrian and Bianca pulled up alongside her. Bianca thrust a dark-blonde hairpiece and black-framed glasses into her chest. 'Put these on,' she ordered and Emilia reluctantly did as she was told. Moments later, Emilia barely noticed when the waitress asked her for her order. She was too busy staring at her daughters Cassy and Harper, accompanied by her husband Justin, who were approaching the cafe's entrance. She was about to jump to her feet when she felt the firm grip of Adrian's hand squeezing her wrist and pulling her back down again.

'Face me and don't take your eyes off mine until I tell you differently,' he prompted. Emilia hesitated and his grasp became tighter. 'Say or do anything that identifies you and I'll execute all three of them right here.' He moved his jacket to one side so that she could see the gun in his holster.

Now from the corner of her eye, Emilia could just about see her family entering the cafe and choosing a table directly behind hers. Her pulse raced as she cocked her head and heard her excited girls choosing from the menu.

'Waffles and syrup with strawberry milkshake,' said one.

'Me too, but I want a raspberry milkshake,' added the other.

Emilia was scared that if she moved even a centimetre, she might lose track of their conversation. Instead, she remained perfectly still as she eavesdropped. Her children and husband chatted about school, homework and a cinema trip he'd promised them. They only quietened when their food arrived.

Emilia, Adrian and Bianca ignored the waitress who came to take their order. As she walked away muttering under her breath, Emilia tried to remember how it had felt to have two lives growing inside her. And for the briefest of moments, it was as if she could still feel them wiggling, alongside the rhythmic vibrations of their heartbeats against her chest. Was it the product of her imagination or her memory?

'How did you know they'd be here?' Emilia whispered.

'He brings them here the same night every week after school. They like it because it reminds them of you. When they were younger, you'd bring them here after football practice. Justin told friends he thought it might help if he didn't break too many routines after they lost you.'

'Do they think I'm dead?'

'You can either keep asking questions or you can keep listening. And make sure your face remains pointed towards me or ...' He finished his sentence by making the shape of a gun with his fingers and pointing them at his head.

Emilia hung on to her family's every word. But to hear them thriving without her was heartbreaking. Later, pushing their empty plates to one side, they made their way to their car to carry on with their lives for yet another day without a mother or a wife.

As soon as the doors closed behind them, several red, circular dots of light appeared on their backs as they had done the first time she'd seen them via video link. 'No!' Emilia gasped. 'I'm begging you, please don't kill them.'

'One word, Emilia, one word is all it will take. I don't want to, but I will if you keep withholding information from us. You can have them back; you can be the one taking them out for milkshakes and waffles again very soon. You only have three more people to find before you'll get every-thing you want. Now where are they located?'

How they knew that she was privy to such information was beyond her. Emilia had no choice but to reveal what the fridge magnets at Ted's house had helped her to recall, and give away her only bargaining chip. The red dots vanished as quickly as they appeared.

Adrian and Bianca were the next to exit, leaving her trembling and alone. Being in such close proximity to her family had provided her with a snapshot of how it might be for her one day. But Emilia wanted it now.

And in that moment, all her frustration, resentment and longing superseded every other emotion. She balled her fists and curled her feet, squeezing them so tightly she feared her fingers and toes might snap. Every muscle in her body was rigid and pulsed as she tried to hold herself back from hurling anything moveable across the restaurant. She didn't care who the objects might hit, as long as they connected with someone who then felt the same pain she was suffering.

But instead of lashing out, Emilia internalised each nega-tive feeling. If she were to get through this, she would need to be as strong and ruthless as Bianca. She would have to push her conscience to one side like members of the Hacking Collective did in the pursuit of their goals. And if she didn't get what she wanted from the remaining Minders, they must suffer the consequences. Because her family was her priority, not the well-being of the Minders.

Chapter 60

BRUNO, OUNDLE, NORTHAMPTONSHIRE

Bruno glared at Nora, expecting her mother to follow her into the lounge at any moment. The child was older than her years and regarded him with the suspicious eyes of an adult.

'Where's your mum?' he asked. 'I thought she was picking you up from school?'

'The minibus brought me home. Why are you looking through her things?'

'I'm not.'

'Yes, you are.'

'Why do you say that?'

'My phone is broken so this morning I borrowed Mummy's spare for emergencies.' She pointed at the screen. 'It says on here someone on another device is looking at her bank accounts. And you are holding her tablet.'

'My phone's broken too so I was checking my email.'

Her face screwed up. 'You're telling fibs. You were looking at her money and photographs of Daddy.'

Bruno struggled to muster up a believable excuse. 'She asked me to sort something out for her,' he said vaguely. Nora's wheelchair moved backwards ever so slightly as she continued staring at him, as if she was waiting for a better explanation. He tried a different tack. 'How was school? What do you do there on a Saturday?'

Nora refused to answer. The Echo of Nazi Zimmerman parted the crowd of his counterparts still gathered inside the house. 'Tell her to mind her own fucking business,' he ordered. 'Explain what happens to little girls who don't.'

'I'm going to call Mummy,' said Nora and ordered her phone's OS to dial Karen's number. Bruno hurried towards her and snatched it from her hand. When he saw a frightened Nora's bottom lip quiver he tried to kneel and talk to her at her level. But before he could say anything, the chair spun around and sped towards the front door. Bruno had no choice but to run after her and using all his weight, he shoved the chair hard so it careered into the wall. But he hadn't appreciated how lightweight its frame was and it toppled over, sending Nora sprawling to the ground. He heard the unmistakable sound of a bone snapping.

'Oh, Jesus,' he gasped and went to pick her up. She was as light as a feather and as she looked at him, he felt something warm spread across his arm. The terrified child was wetting herself. A second later, she passed out.

Bruno remained in the hallway, the sound of Zimmerman's laughter ringing in his ears. Panicked, he moved towards the front door but had second thoughts and hurried back to the kitchen. Then he grabbed her mobile, ready to dial the emergency services.

'Do that and you're fucked,' Zimmerman continued. 'The police will be on your trail the second she wakes up. Buy yourself time. Lock her in the summerhouse in the garden. By the time Watson finds her, you'll be out of the village and you could be heading anywhere.'

'I heard something break, I've injured her.'

'And what about your own kid? What state will he be in if you're behind bars?'

For once, Zimmerman was correct. With no other choice, Bruno laid the unconscious child on a sofa inside the summerhouse with a blanket covering her body.

THE MINDERS

'Your mum will be home soon,' Bruno said gently. 'I promise you'll be okay. I'm so, so sorry.' And after dumping her wheelchair next to her, he found the key in the lock, secured it, and ran.

The last time he had experienced such guilt, he had been leaving Louie at the residential unit, but at least he'd had his son's best interests at heart. Today it felt much, much worse.

Chapter 61

CHARLIE, MANCHESTER

The days following Milo's death were a performance. Charlie mustered up his finest acting skills to impersonate a friend consumed by grief.

He dutifully attended Milo's funeral service at the Manchester Reform Synagogue, then his burial, and planned to participate in a tribute football match the following week. Their mutual friends spent more time together than usual, supporting one another, sharing memories or blaming themselves for not spotting the signs that Milo was struggling.

None were aware that Charlie had a room in the hotel from which Milo had fallen or that he had been questioned by police as to whether he had heard or seen anything that night. The hotel prided itself on the privacy of its guests, many of whom were celebrities staying on Charlie's floor and the two above it, so there were no security cameras.

The disinterested detective hadn't asked if Charlie had known the deceased and he hadn't volunteered the information. Charlie's impression was that the investigation was routine as there was no reason to suspect foul play.

'He was the most level-headed of all of us,' a tearful Andrew had told Charlie. 'It just doesn't make sense why he'd do that. He had everything to live for.'

'You can never *really* know a person,' Charlie responded. 'No matter how much you think you do. We all hold something back.'

Less than thirty minutes after killing Milo, Charlie climbed inside a hot bath. He replayed Milo's split second of confusion as he was pushed to his death. It was a spontaneous act that had even taken his killer by surprise. If Charlie were capable of the emotion, he might even have been envious of his pal's weightless descent through the sky like a swooping bird.

The murder was cruel and undeserved and a waste of a life. But for Charlie it had served an important purpose. Its failure to bring him grief, or regret, or to even prick his conscience meant that he knew for certain he was never going to be the same man as he had been. It was something he had to accept.

He had heard on the grapevine that Milo's father was in the process of setting up a mental health charity in his son's name to encourage young men to freely discuss their emotional well-being. Charlie vowed to make a generous but anonymous donation because it seemed like something the old Charlie might have done. More and more frequently, he was relying on that version of himself to be the moral compass for his replacement.

When he wasn't with the others, Charlie spent his time either at work coaching clients or with Alix. She'd lavished attention on him since Milo's death, and he wondered if she was trying to be supportive or if she was concerned that he too might be harbouring dark thoughts he didn't want to share. He was, but not ones he could tell anyone.

Milo's death didn't monopolise Charlie's thoughts, though. It was the deaths of Karczewski and the Minder

Sinéad that preoccupied him. He had taken to purchasing more second-hand tablets to use once only in public areas, and piggyback other people's hotspots and Wi-Fi. Then he'd dispose of the devices, leaving the faintest possible online footprint.

He visited alternate locations multiple times daily to log back into his conspiracy theory message board and check for theories about Karczewski. There were scores of suggestions as to why his handler's death had vanished from newsfeeds but none he gave credence to.

Today, he was rereading them in Alix's flat, using her neighbour's unsecured connection. Before he logged out for the evening, he glanced at other subject headings.

> #Manmade Pandemics
> I have evidence they've all been bio-engineered to monitor us – why won't the authorities listen?
>
> #The truth behind Stonehenge
> An extinct race of giants called the Nephilim created it
>
> #The Illuminati are real – here's proof
> It was created to bring chaos to an orderly world
>
> #Hacking Collective is Government Sanctioned
> A state-developed scheme for ethnic cleansing
>
> #Match Your DNA is bullshit
> It's a modern-day cult to keep us under control

They would kill to know what I know, Charlie thought. And for a moment, his fingers hovered above the keyboard as he was tempted to give them the truth about everything from protected government paedophiles and patented viruses to UFO sightings and Deep State civil servants who were really in control of the country.

The sound of Alix returning from work broke his concentration. He folded up the tablet she didn't know he owned and slipped it under the sofa cushion.

'Let's go away for the weekend,' she began, taking a seat next to him. 'Mum won a competition to spend a weekend in a country hotel that she can't make now. I think we need a change of scenery after everything that's happened.'

Charlie was immediately reluctant. New locations needed scrupulous research first to ensure their safety. 'I'm not sure if I'm great company at the moment,' he replied. 'Wouldn't you prefer to go with one of your friends?'

'No, I want to go with you. And it'll do you some good to get away for a couple of days. I know Milo's death hit you hard. I can see it whenever anyone talks about him – you look so guilty.'

'Guilty?' he repeated.

'Yes, but you have nothing to feel bad about. It wasn't your fault or anyone else's that he took his own life. So let's just get away and enjoy some me-and-you time.'

Charlie nodded, vowing to work on his 'guilty' appearance. 'Okay then, if it's what you want.'

Alix folded her arms. 'Well, don't sound so enthusiastic about it,' she huffed.

'I am, really.'

'You know, sometimes I can't fathom you out. You say and do all the right things but it's as if inside, you've read a guidebook on how to be a boyfriend and are going through the motions.'

It's exactly what I'm doing, he thought.

'I get that you've had a tough time of it of late,' she continued. 'But sometimes I'm not sure if you want us to be together.'

'I do, honestly. Just because I'm not great at expressing my emotions doesn't mean I'm not fond of you.'

'*Fond?*' she repeated. '*Fond?* You are *fond* of a friend, you are *fond* of a dog, you're not *fond* of your girlfriend. You might as well have described me as *nice*.'

'You know what I mean. I am more than just fond of you. But it's going to take a little bit more time for me to get to where you are now.'

Charlie wrapped his arms around her shoulders and leaned in to kiss her cheek. 'Be patient with me,' he added. 'I promise I'm worth it.'

But quietly, he knew that he wasn't. And he had no interest either way whether she believed him.

Chapter 62

BRUNO, EXETER

The Echoes were conspicuous by their absence, after being ever-present for months; Bruno had grown accustomed to them. Today, they had all but vanished without warning. Their silence should have helped Bruno to concentrate, but instead, it added to his unease.

He had spent much of the last fortnight inside a budget hotel room in Exeter, located opposite Louie's care home. He was constantly glued to the facility's live feed on burner phones to see if the attack he thought he'd witnessed by a member of staff had actually happened. It had yet to be repeated and hand on heart, Bruno couldn't be sure that he hadn't imagined it like he imagined the Echoes. For now, he decided to allow his son to remain in the facility but under his watchful eye. There had yet to be any sign of Louie's attacker on duty again, making Bruno further question his own perception of reality.

He was prepared to remove his son at a moment's notice. But assuming he was now wanted by the police for assaulting Nora, he couldn't just march into the reception and demand his son be brought to him. On a previous reconnaissance mission, Bruno identified an emergency exit with a glass window in close proximity to Louie's bedroom. If he was attacked again, with a few carefully placed whacks

Bruno should be able to smash the glass with his trusty hammer, open the door and lead Louie back to the car in less than a minute. By the time the police were alerted, father and son would be on the road. Bruno still hadn't figured out where to, but at least they'd be together.

'I can't let you take him with you,' an Echo began, cutting through the silence inside the car. It startled Bruno because it belonged to someone he knew. Bruno turned to find Karczewski in the rear, dressed in a dark suit, a pair of horn-rimmed glasses in his hand and his legs crossed at the knee.

'You?' Bruno asked in genuine surprise. Karczewski nodded. 'How long have you been here?'

'On and off since you left Oundle.'

'But you weren't implanted in my brain like the others. Am I imagining you?' Karczewski nodded again. 'Are you the voice my conscience is using?'

'Yes. Consider me your moment of clarity,' Karczewski continued. 'Unless you leave, you are putting everything at risk. The programme, your knowledge, the country's security and not just your own life, but your son's too. You saw what they did to Sinéad. Could you watch Louie being tortured to get what they want from you?'

'No parent could.'

'What information would you give up to make that stop? What would you trade for Louie's life?' When Bruno couldn't answer, Karczewski closed his eyes. 'And that's what concerns me. I went out on a limb for you, Bruno. I guaranteed your doubters that you were capable of starting afresh and leaving the past, and your son, behind. But it was hardly any time at all before you began your killing spree and now, you're spying on your son.'

'I shouldn't have been on the programme. It was Louie who solved the puzzle, not me.'

'Nevertheless, the data is inside you. Your level of synaesthesia was borderline which in all likelihood is the reason for the prominence of your Echoes. However, you displayed aptitude in your determination, loyalty and self-preservation amongst many other things. And you can salvage this situation by leaving your hotel room, climbing into your car and pressing the ignition button.'

'And leave my son behind to be hurt again?'

'You cannot trust yourself to know what really happened. You still have time to do what is best for him and for your country, and leave.'

Bruno was and had become many things. But above all else, he was a parent. 'No,' he said quietly. 'Not until I know Louie is safe.'

Karczewski slipped on his glasses and shrugged. 'I hope you change your mind – for everyone's sake,' he added and then disappeared.

As more hours passed, the Echoes began to reappear, one by one. Some were more vocal, begging him to flee, while others hurled insults at him. The one thing they all had in common was that they wanted to survive. And without Bruno, they couldn't.

By mid-afternoon, Bruno's stomach began rumbling. Still focusing on his phone's screen, he opened the door to his hotel room to walk two streets to the nearest supermarket. He glanced at the outside through a corridor window when he spotted Louie's attacker disembarking from a bus. As he paused to rummage through his bag, Bruno sprang into action. He sprinted through the hotel and the reception doors, across a car park and then into a road until he was metres away from his mark.

The assailant was much taller and broader in the flesh than he appeared on CCTV, but Bruno wasn't intimidated. The first blow from his hammer hit the man on the back of the neck. He used such force that his victim dropped to his knees.

Next, Bruno used the weapon with short sharp thwacks against his ribs and the man rolled to his side. Then Bruno pushed him onto his back and mounted him, grabbing either side of his head and slamming it against a concrete kerb.

'Stop, please stop,' the man begged breathlessly. He tried shielding his face with his arm as Bruno raised the hammer over his head.

'I saw what you did to him,' Bruno hissed, flecks of spit landing on the man's face.

'I didn't do anything!'

'Then why do I recognise you?'

'I'm a temp, I've never worked here before. I promise.'

'You're a liar! I saw you hitting my son. I watched you through the cameras. He's just a little boy.'

'I don't even know who Louie is.'

'Then how do you know his name?'

The man realised his error and covered his face again as Bruno hit him twice more. Bruno heard a shuffling of feet behind him as his imaginary audience approached. Any last-ditch attempt to beg for mercy would go unheeded.

'No, wait,' the man cried.

'Wait for what? What could you possibly say to stop me from killing you?'

'I was paid to do it!'

Bruno hesitated. 'Paid by who?'

The man's eyes flicked to Bruno's right, as if looking in the direction of the Echoes. But as Bruno turned his head, there was just one person behind him, and that wasn't a hallucination.

'By her,' the man said.

Chapter 63

EMILIA

Bruno and Emilia sat opposite one another, each staring the other in the eye, neither wanting to be the first to show weakness and look away.

His arms and legs were restrained by metal cuffs as he sat in the back of the vehicle Bianca had assigned Emilia. He had put them on himself while Emilia pointed a loaded gun at him that she had swiped from a car at the safe house following Sinéad's murder.

Emilia knew time was of the essence and that she had only minutes to interrogate him before Bianca and Adrian arrived. After that, Bruno's fate beyond her car was likely sealed.

'Do you know me?' she began as the doors closed. Her tone was more assured than when she had first confronted Sinéad. Bruno eyed her up and down.

'I know a lot of people,' he replied.

'I think I'm familiar to you. I need your help. I need you to tell me who I am.'

He ignored her question. 'I'm not going to survive this, am I?' he asked. 'You're not going to let me see my boy again.'

'I have no choice, Bruno.'

He rolled his eyes. 'I've been using that as an excuse for my behaviour for a while ... blaming other people for doing things I thought they'd pushed me to do. But the truth is, you and I are here because of what we've done, not them. If you're going to kill me, you should own it. Because what you're about to do to me is all on you.'

An increasingly embittered Emilia ran her hands through her hair and rubbed at her eyes. 'I don't have time for your self-help sermon. I really need you to tell me what you know about me.'

'Or what? I'm a dead man?' He let out a sharp laugh. 'I think that ship has already sailed, hasn't it?'

The clock was ticking. Bianca and Adrian had given her ten minutes to get the truth from him before they took matters into their own hands and for a purpose that had yet to be explained to her. Her only bargaining tool was Bruno's son Louie. Once Bruno had been identified, background research discovered his Achilles heel – a boy with autism who resided in a care facility in Exeter. Emilia immediately made plans to use Louie to flush him out.

'Out of interest, how did you find me?' he asked.

'By identifying faces caught on CCTV entering a building in London – where you were trained, I assume – and who then went off grid. When we found your son, I put myself in your shoes and thought it was unlikely you'd be able to leave him alone completely. The least intrusive way was to use internal cameras which is when we found the network's data flow had been compromised, by you, I presume. Getting you back here was easy.'

'And how do you feel about hurting a child with special needs to do that?'

Now it was Emilia's turn not to answer the question. 'I have no memory whatsoever of who I am,' she replied instead. 'All I know is that I have a husband and two daughters who I'm trying to get back to, in the same way you've come back for Louie. You hold the key to helping me find myself.'

'I will if you let me see my son first.'

Emilia sighed. 'I don't have the time or the power to make that happen.'

'Then I'm going to do your children a huge favour by telling you nothing and keeping them safe from you.'

Emilia's voice cracked. 'You can't do that. It's not fair.'

'Was it fair when you killed the other Minder?'

'I haven't killed anyone – that was Bianca and her people in the Hacking Collective.'

Bruno shook his head and laughed. 'I'll hand it to you, you're a great actress!'

'What do you mean?'

But Bruno was too preoccupied by laughing to respond.

'Stop it,' she said, tears of frustration forming.

The sight of her wiping them away appeared to amuse him further and his laughter grew louder.

'I said, stop it!' she repeated, this time banging her fists against the car seat to emphasise her demand. 'Stop laughing at me!' But by now Bruno's laughter was escalating, louder and louder until the noise grew deafening. It wasn't the only sound to reverberate: it was gradually accompanied by whispers enveloping the exterior of the vehicle. But Emilia couldn't identify a single sputtered word.

Through the windscreen she spotted a small group of people huddled in a garden further along the road. She counted four of them and her body tensed. 'Leave me alone!' she screamed at them. 'Leave me the hell alone!'

She threw her hands over her ears to make the cacophony stop, but it failed to suppress them for long. The piercing whispers and Bruno's laughter culminated in an explosion of sound that was now coming from the inside too and made her head ready to burst.

And then it happened. A new Emilia came to life without warning, conscience or forethought.

Chapter 64

BRUNO, EXETER

Bruno caught sight of his reflection in the metal object swiping down upon him, and heard the crunch as it penetrated his skull.

His attacker cocked her head and yanked it out as quickly as it had landed. Her brow furrowed as if trying to read his thoughts. It was only as she turned that he noticed another person in the car with them, a figure sitting in the front passenger seat.

Louie.

Bruno tried to reach out his hand to touch him, only nothing moved but the very tips of his fingers.

'I'm sorry,' he whispered. 'I'm sorry your mum and I didn't do better for you.'

'It's okay, Dad,' Louie smiled. 'You don't need to look after me any more. I'll be all right.'

In their twelve years together, Louie had been virtually mute, not even speaking in Bruno's dreams. Now, in his dying throes, Bruno was hallucinating that his son had found his voice. It was the only voice he had ever wanted to hear and the comfort it offered was immeasurable.

From the window he caught a glimpse of Echoes gathering beyond the vehicle he was dying inside. They arrived one at a time and then in twos, before groups began appearing. Eventually, the car park was packed with the faces of people he'd conversed with and others he'd only learned about. Some showed him concern, others were tearful and some angry. Each held the hand of another.

Bruno sensed his assailant watching him, before she placed her lips to his ear. 'You see them, don't you?' she asked.

Bruno wanted to nod, but the wound was too deep for even basic motor functions. He was no longer capable of even a perfunctory motion. 'What do they want?' she continued but he couldn't respond.

Instead, Louie, the Echoes, and the rest of the world living and imagined faded away into darkness at exactly the same moment. Bruno was aware of what was to happen after he breathed his last. He had made his peace with all he'd done wrong. And he was sure that he wasn't as frightened of the unknown as the woman was who had just killed him.

Chapter 65

FLICK, ALDEBURGH, SUFFOLK

Flick let the plastic stick fall into the sink. Then she unboxed another and followed the same action before placing it face down next to the first three. As she waited a further minute to pass, she sat on the lid of the closed toilet seat and ran her palms across her face.

How is this even possible? she asked herself. *How the hell am I pregnant?*

Karczewski's programme did not expect its Minders to refrain from sexual activity during their five-year tenure, but implanted contraception for both sexes was mandatory. Anything that left a Minder vulnerable to decisions based on emotion rather than self-preservation was restricted. And top of the list was falling pregnant.

Her five-yearly STI jabs which ensured her immunity from all known infections were up to date, and she assumed the implant making her temporarily sterile was working because she hadn't had a period in seven months. She had assumed there was no need for her and Elijah to use contraception. She flipped the fourth test over and its results mirrored the others. She was definitely pregnant.

Flick hurried outside and threw all the tests in the B&B's incinerator bin, melting them within seconds. If she'd ever needed a cigarette or a friend to confide in, it was now, but she couldn't have either. This was going to be another segment of her life that she couldn't reveal. Grace was already bursting with enthusiasm when it came to Flick and Elijah's relationship, keen to know if Flick saw a long-term future for them. Flick's answers were vague, not because she didn't want to commit, but because she couldn't see beyond the rest of the day let alone the rest of her life. Someone had killed Sinéad and Karczewski and that overshadowed any plans she could make. And she knew Grace would urge her to keep the baby. But Flick had already made her decision.

Back in the kitchen, Flick slathered two slices of toast with Marmite and took a seat at the table. Elijah weighed heavy on her mind. Morally, it was right he should know she was pregnant but she could never tell him. She loved what they had together, but while she continued to hold back so much of herself from him, theirs could never be a genuine relationship. He deserved better.

She caught herself rubbing her stomach and promptly dropped her hands down by her side. She wasn't going to allow herself to start showing empathy to a cluster of cells she hadn't asked for.

Motherhood wasn't something Flick had given much thought to in her teens, twenties or even now. While her friends were moving around the country – and some across the world – to be with their DNA Matches, Flick had made her restaurant her priority. She assumed that children would follow once she met her Match but being linked with a dead serial killer put paid to that. She had long since comes to terms with it never happening for her.

The longer Flick allowed her pregnancy to continue, the more it would slow her down, make her less perceptive and put the programme at risk. The data and intel she was privy to was more important than the man she had feelings for and the baby she didn't want.

Remaining so hyper-vigilant every waking minute since the killings was already taking its toll. So, for much of the day, she tried losing herself in her mindfulness techniques, of self-hypnosis and of just sitting on the beach and becoming lost in the now. But nothing worked; she was still every bit as anxious as when she had seen the results of the first pregnancy test. Perhaps leaving Aldeburgh, even if only for a weekend, might help to clear her mind?

When Grace appeared, she had an idea.

Chapter 66

EMILIA

A beam of light passing through the car's passenger window brought the stain to Emilia's attention. Only when she pulled the wristwatch closer to her face did she realise it was Bruno's blood. She removed a tissue from the glovebox, dampened it with bottled water and wiped it away.

Next, she examined her fingernails: there were traces of his blood under them too. She wet her fingertips and began scraping the underside of the free edges with a paperclip. Deeper and deeper she probed as she replayed Bruno's final moments. After plunging the metal instrument into his skull, she became aware that his line of vision had fixed upon someone in the distance. Emilia turned and realised they were looking at the same people. It came as such a relief that he too had seen the four figures that had been following her for all these weeks that she wanted to cry. She hadn't been imagining them.

'You see them, don't you?' she had asked and he had given an almost imperceptible nod. 'What do they want?' she continued but Bruno had already journeyed too far into the other side to answer.

Killing him was born out of fury at his laughter and refusal to tell her what she wanted to know. She likened her response to that of a demon from her past shaping itself in the present and taking control of her nature.

What kind of person was I back then if I can kill so easily now? she asked herself. But now was not the time to dwell on her actions in the past or present. 'You must set your conscience to one side in your search for the truth,' Adrian had advised her and that's precisely what she was doing.

Bianca had been the first to open the car door and witness the aftermath of Emilia's attack. 'Well, look who just woke up,' Bianca exclaimed, her arms folded and her mouth beaming. 'You're a fast learner.'

She beckoned two field operatives who moved quickly and efficiently, bundling Bruno's body into a waiting van. As the side doors opened, Emilia caught a glimpse of a second body inside, that of the staff member she'd paid to attack Louie.

Something warm and wet returned Emilia to the present. She had dug too deeply when cleaning her fingernails and now her own blood was merging with Bruno's. She used a tightly pressed tissue to stem it and felt the pressure building inside her once more.

She set the car's windows to privacy mode so that nobody could see what she was doing inside. Then she opened her mouth wide and screamed as loudly as her lungs would permit. Her body bent double as she struggled to squeeze every inch of air from them. And once empty, she repeated the action.

Her throat and lungs burned like she was swallowing scalding water but she wasn't ready to stop. Even though the pain was close to unbearable it still wasn't enough to eject the demon from inside her.

Chapter 67

FLICK, LEICESTERSHIRE

Grace's car stopped on the horseshoe-shaped driveway of a country house and luxury spa in Leicestershire. A concierge with an androgynous appearance, slicked-back hair and clad in a smart white uniform, removed their luggage, loaded it onto a cart and programmed it to go to their rooms. Behind them, Grace's vehicle drove itself away to park and left them to take in their surroundings.

Flick hadn't realised just how plush the retreat was going to be when she'd asked Grace's OS to book a spa in the countryside for a weekend getaway. 'Wow, just wow,' muttered her friend as the double doors to the entrance opened into a towering grey neolith foyer. Neither could hide their surprise at the grandeur.

Once they had unpacked their luggage in the linked double suite, they put on their slippers and white cotton robes and booked their treatments for the next two days. They passed a group of guests practising tai chi on immaculately cut lawns as they took a leisurely walk around the grounds. Others made use of tennis courts, a giant holographic chessboard or the eighteen-hole golf course.

'I don't think I ever want to leave here,' said Grace, drinking it all in. 'I don't mean to pry but how can you afford to treat both of us on a bar staff's wages?'

'I have access to funds,' Flick said coyly.

'A lot of funds?'

'I'm comfortable.'

'So why work at the pub? And why are you staying in a chintzy little B&B if you can afford to stay at the Ritz?'

'Aldeburgh doesn't have a Ritz.'

'You know what I mean.'

'I'm more comfortable being around my kind of people.' Flick chose her words carefully. 'And before I arrived there, I'd shut myself away from the world for a very long time. This is a fresh start for me. Now, enough with the questions. I have a hot yoga class to find.'

'Are you sure it's safe to do it in your condition?' Grace asked.

Flick caught herself just before saying she'd already asked the receptionist privately if it was safe for pregnant women. 'My condition?' she repeated.

'You know, being super rich?' Grace chuckled. 'You wouldn't want the gold coins in your yoga pants to melt in the heat.'

'Oh, you're hilarious.' Flick feigned a smile as she walked away.

Later and alone, Flick caught herself with the palms of her hands resting against her stomach again. Only now, waiting outside the yoga studio for the class before hers to finish, she allowed them to remain.

As she scanned passing guests, she fixed upon a man sitting opposite her reading a magazine. She was sure they hadn't met, but there was something vaguely familiar about him. A therapist appeared from behind a closed door and called his name.

It was only as the object of her attention followed the therapist that Flick noticed a mobile phone had fallen from the pocket of his robe and onto the sofa. 'Excuse me,' she said, leaning over to pick it up.

A sudden rush of oxygen filled her lungs as she drew a sharp intake of breath. She turned her head to face him, removed her phone from her pocket and held them side by side. The unbranded, silver clamshell devices were identical in every way. They weren't the only people in the world to own that model, but he was betrayed by his expression. As soon as he saw the phones side by side, he drew his lower lip between his teeth and his eyes bored into hers. Both knew in that moment they had just come face to face with another Minder.

'Follow me, please,' the therapist continued, and led him to a treatment room.

'Thank you,' he muttered as Flick passed him his phone. And as he left, his head turned to face hers, their eyes still inextricably locked on to one another's.

Chapter 68

CHARLIE, LEICESTERSHIRE

The woman with the identical telephone to Charlie's did not appear surprised to see him when she opened the door of her suite. They greeted one another with a nod and didn't speak until Charlie was inside. She gave the corridor the once-over before closing the door behind him and locking it.

Her room was located on the second floor and in the middle of the hotel. She was surrounded by other guests in rooms adjacent, above and below hers. Charlie had chosen his and Alix's room based on the same criteria when they checked in. Less isolation meant less exposure.

After his initial reluctance to spend a weekend away with Alix, Charlie was glad he'd relented. Now as he and his Minder counterpart took up positions on opposite sides of the suite, he swept the room for signs of danger. There was something awkward about where she chose to stand. He remained close to the door, but she had decided against the French windows, a spot he'd have picked if it was his room. Instead, she hovered by a minibar. But once he spotted the ice bucket and pick within her easy grasp, it made sense. He gripped a little tighter against the shaft of the knife hidden in his pocket.

'Where's your friend?' he began.

'In her room, having an early night.'

'Do you mean you've slipped her something to knock her out?' He raised a knowing eyebrow and she looked at her feet. 'I'm not clutching at straws then?' he continued. 'You're like me.'

She nodded. 'So how do you want to go about this?' she asked. 'Do I tell you my name?'

'No, I don't think so ... we'll have to wing it as the protocol of coming face to face with another Minder wasn't part of my training.'

'Same here. Let's keep personal details to a minimum and that way, after tonight, we can trust one another. Who's your handler?'

'Karczewski. You?'

She nodded. 'Do you know he's dead?'

'Yes. And I assume you saw what happened to Sinéad?'

The woman nodded again. 'I feel awful about that. I wish I'd spotted that use of an extra space in the recall message earlier, then perhaps she might still be alive.'

'You saved my life. Maybe she made another mistake we don't know about. It's easy to do. We have all this stuff in our heads but we're still human. Look at how I dropped my phone. That was stupid.'

'I almost let one of my secrets slip at a pub quiz night,' she said sheepishly.

'Which one?'

'Princess Diana.'

'The tunnel or the other driver?'

'Neither – the burial spot.'

'Ah,' Charlie nodded. 'I almost told my girlfriend why I was neither agnostic nor an atheist.'

'Oh my God,' she said with a short laugh.

'Which one?'

It was a joke that only they understood. She moved towards a fridge and beckoned him to take a seat on the sofa. Charlie loosened the grip on his knife as she sat opposite him, pouring two glasses of red fruit juice from a jug. He waited until she drank from hers before doing the same.

'It's days like this when I miss a real drink,' he said.

'I'd kill for a Marlboro Light. Have you tried alcohol since the implant?'

'Yes, but it never ends well. Can I ask … have you changed a lot from the person you were before all this?'

She considered the question. 'Yes, I don't think you can go through this process without everything shifting inside you. I've realised that everything I know will always keep me at arm's length from the rest of the world. But it doesn't mean that I have to shut myself off. I can still have a life, of sorts.'

'A life that's based on bullshit.'

She appeared surprised by his candour.

'Sorry,' he said. 'That was unfair.'

'No, you're right, I suppose, yes, it is based on lies. But it's still a better and more truthful life than the one I had before. Now I have a purpose, I have passion, I have a sense of self. I'm … *happy*. For the most part. Or at least I was.'

It wasn't the answer Charlie had hoped for. He wanted her to admit that she was like him and found it impossible to feel anything, no matter what the provocation. But she was quite the opposite.

Time passed as they discussed some of the sensitive information they carried inside them and what had shocked and appalled them the most. They spoke about the programme itself, the treatment they had undergone, the training and the side effects. Charlie thought he recognised a flicker of disappointment in her when he admitted he didn't suffer night terrors or multi-layered dreams as she did. But he held back from detailing his diminished empathy or the lengths he'd gone to kick-start his emotions, such as killing Milo.

'I used to be a bit of a conspiracy theorist before this all began,' Charlie added.

'You must be living the dream with all that you know now.'

'You'd think, wouldn't you? It doesn't feel like the dream, though, does it?'

'No. Have you given any thought as to what we're supposed to do now that our only contact within the programme is dead and there's no safe house we can trust?'

'There must be a backup plan in place,' she said. 'Karczewski will have had deputies or people higher than him pulling his strings who are aware of us. I think our only choice is to sit it out.'

'I don't know whether I can do that for another four and a half years without knowing what's going on.'

'Five years is the maximum amount of time it takes for the bead that contains all this data to dissolve into our systems, right? And it will take all the classified information that we know with it. So even if we are stuck in limbo for that long, there is an end date. But I don't think it will come to that. Karczewski told me many times that this was a temporary measure until they built an impenetrable fortress around their servers and bunkers. Once that's done, we'll have our freedom back again and we'll be sipping rum on a beach in Barbados for the rest of our lives.'

A noise coming from her friend next door interrupted them. They paused until they heard her toilet flush.

'What does she know about you?' Charlie whispered.

'The same as everyone else – that I don't like to talk about my past.'

'Is there anyone else you've gotten close to?' Charlie picked up on her guilty expression. 'I'm the only person you don't have to lie to,' he added.

'I have a boyfriend and that's brought with it an unexpected complication … I'm pregnant.'

'Shit! Didn't they put you into temporary sterilisation?'

'Yes, but either my body rejected it or something went wrong.'

'You know you're supposed to get rid of it, don't you?'

'It's not an "it",' she said sharply.

'Sorry, I didn't mean to cause offence.'

'No, I shouldn't have snapped. I'm just a little confused right now.'

'Are you going to keep it? I mean, the baby?'

She shook her head. 'What about you? Is it serious between you and the woman I spotted you with earlier?'

'No.'

'Does she know that?'

The question caught him off-guard. 'No, I suppose not.'

'In the end we're going to hurt everyone around us, aren't we?'

The question was rhetorical so they sipped from their drinks.

'So now that we know about one another, where do we go from here?' Charlie asked.

'I know there's usually safety in numbers but I don't think that's the case with us.'

'Well, maybe when our five years are up, we'll meet properly.'

'Yes,' she said. 'You can buy me that rum in Barbados.'

Charlie made his way to the door, then stopped when their phones vibrated in unison. They looked to one another, knowing immediately what it meant. She approached him as he clicked on the red circle in the corner of the screen.

The footage appeared to have been shot inside a vehicle. Two people were present – a man who was restrained and a woman who could only be seen from behind. He appeared to be laughing and she was holding her hands over her ears until she suddenly burst into life. With her face still hidden, she plunged something long and sharp into his head and a thin jet of blood sprayed out like the first oil from a newly tapped well. Moments later, when he was still moving, she carved the name 'Bruno' into his forehead with the same sharp device. The camera focused on the name before the screen went black.

Charlie felt his fellow Minder's hand gripping his arm as her eyes snapped to meet his. She was horrified by what she was watching, but he was not. He had to pretend.

'You should leave,' she said and moved to open the door. Charlie followed her but before he left, she grabbed hold of him.

'Stay safe,' she whispered in his ear, and hugged him tightly, only letting go when she spotted someone standing behind him.

Chapter 69

CHARLIE, LEICESTERSHIRE

Alix cleared clothes from a chest of drawers and a wardrobe rail, tossing them into her suitcase.

'Please don't be like this,' Charlie said but even he recognised the apathy in his tone.

'Who is she?' Alix asked.

'It's not important.'

'I saw you in the spa together and then you spend an hour in her bedroom and you tell me it's "not important"?'

'It wasn't that long, was it?'

'I should know because I was standing in the corridor outside waiting for my boyfriend to come out!'

'She's a friend of a friend.'

'Do you think I'm an idiot?'

Charlie didn't think that of Alix, but he did want her to stop shouting. He required space to process the implications of Bruno's murder along with all he and the other Minder had discussed and shared.

'She's your DNA Match, isn't she?' Alix continued. 'You actually arranged to meet her here, you two-timing bastard.'

'My Match? Where did that come from? I don't have a Match.'

'This begs to differ.' She reached inside her bag and brandished a tablet. 'The man who claims to be someone "who doesn't trust technology";' the man who doesn't even have an email address or proper mobile phone actually hides a tablet under his sofa. The same man who reckons he's a Turn Downer and would "rather rely on instinct than chemistry to find a partner" receives an email confirming he's taken a test *and* been Matched.'

'I have a Match?' he repeated.

'You don't deny it then?' yelled Alix and hurled the device at him with such ferocity that had he not batted it away with his arm, it would have hit him square in the jaw. 'Good luck to you both, you're welcome to one another. You could have had a bloody brilliant life with me but you've blown it. I deserve better than an emotionally bank-rupt arsehole like you.'

Alix shut her suitcase and wheeled it to the door.

'Let me pack my stuff and we can talk about this on the way home,' Charlie said, but he didn't mean it. All he wanted was to read what the email had to say.

'Are you stupid enough to think I'm going to drive you home? The moment this door closes, you'll never see me again.'

He didn't say goodbye because before the door even had time to slam shut, Charlie was already picking up the device from the floor to read the email. 'Match found,' the subject heading read.

He took a deep breath as for the first time since becoming a Minder, something inside him began to stir.

Chapter 70

FLICK, IPSWICH

Flick held a stylus between her fingers and a digital clipboard on her lap, and stared blankly at the wall ahead. She had gone as far as filling in her name before she stopped.

She glanced at the other women inside the private clinic's waiting room. Some, like her, were alone, others were accompanied by friends, partners or parents. Nobody made eye contact with one another. But all were there for one purpose – to end their pregnancies. Flick guaranteed nobody had the same reason as her for terminating a child.

It was the first time she had been alone since viewing Bruno's murder. An image of his bloody face and name carved into his forehead lingered in her memory. She'd also been struck by his apparent lack of fear; there were no tears, no recriminations and no last words, only an acceptance of his fate and even laughter before his killer snuffed him out.

For the best part of the month that followed, Flick used this second Minder's murder as an excuse to shy away from confronting the problem growing inside her. Until this morning. When she awoke in the B&B, she knew that at ten weeks pregnant, she was more than halfway to the recently reduced legal abortion limit of eighteen weeks. Borrowing Grace's car, she found herself at a clinic in nearby

Ipswich, ready to eliminate the complication she was carrying.

Earlier in the week and in a moment of vulnerability, she'd visited Aldeburgh's library to read a pregnancy guidebook. She learned that the cluster of cells inside her had morphed to the size of a strawberry. There were paddles where its limbs would eventually develop and even though it couldn't hear anything, she'd found herself frequently talking to it. It was then that Flick realised she was developing an affection towards it. She had to get rid of it before she no longer had the choice.

She pointed the stylus in the direction of the box asking for a brief medical history summary. She was unsure whether to fabricate it in case it was ever traced back to her, or to be truthful. The Minder she'd met at the spa was the first person in so long she had been able to be honest with. She hadn't realised how much she had missed it.

But in the end, it didn't matter. Because try as she might, she could not bring herself to write another word. Her hands trembled as she deleted the file before handing the clipboard back to the receptionist.

She left the building – still as two people, not one.

Chapter 71

FLICK, ALDEBURGH, SUFFOLK

Rap music blasted from each of the speakers placed throughout Elijah's home. Although not to her more pop-orientated taste, Flick didn't mind as his favoured genre helped him to concentrate as he worked. And while he was upstairs putting the finishing touches to the marble sculpture for his forthcoming exhibition, Flick filled her time rearranging his kitchen cupboards and throwing away anything approaching its use-by date.

Quite why, she didn't know, as the twice-weekly cleaning service Elijah employed had only visited yesterday. But earlier, she had also cleaned out his fridge and washed all his cushion covers. She stopped suddenly. 'Am I nesting?' she said aloud and, for the first time, she didn't automatically consider pregnancy a negative thing. She dismissed the question: it was far too early for that instinct to have surfaced.

Carrying a child had stirred up many an emotion in her, including thinking about the family she'd cast aside in London and how excited they'd be for her if they knew. She wondered what they thought as they scrolled through her Facebook photographs which suggested she was living a carefree life backpacking around the world. Her only regret was not saying goodbye.

Flick's dilemma over Elijah and the baby weighed heavy on her mind. She wouldn't be able to hide her pregnancy from him for long. Even so soon, her stomach was beginning to harden and in a few weeks, it would start to protrude. He had a right to know that he was to become a father, but what else should he know about the woman expecting his baby?

The music stopped and moments later, Elijah descended the staircase. 'I'm driving over to Snape to pick up some canvases,' he said and gave her a peck on the cheek.

'What, now?' she asked, her face paling at the prospect of being left alone. The murder of Karczewski and two Minders left her constantly on edge.

'I'll be a couple of hours at the most.'

'I can come with you if you like?'

Elijah's eyebrows knitted. 'I know I keep asking this, but are you sure you're okay?'

'Yes, why?'

'It's as if you've been struggling to relax lately. I see you when we're curled up on the sofa together and you're twitching your legs or biting the insides of your cheeks. Most people return from spa breaks refreshed but you've been like a cat on hot bricks for weeks.'

His canny observations caught her off-guard. 'No, I'm fine,' Flick replied.

'Has this got something to do with the exhibition tomorrow? You said large crowds make you uncomfortable. I won't be offended if you've changed your mind and don't want to come.'

'No, I do want to, it's your big night. Just as long as you don't expect me to appear in front of the cameras, I'll be all right.'

'Okay. We'll only have to stay a couple of hours in Birmingham and then we can head back to the hotel and make a weekend of it.'

'And before that, you won't let me see what else you've been working on up at your studio in the old church?'

'Nope, but I can't wait for your reaction.'

Elijah winked and closed the door behind him. His car had yet to exit the drive when Flick manually locked all the doors to the house, closed the windows and turned on the outside perimeter alarm. Only then could she try and relax. She lay across the sofa, her knees raised close to her chest, staring out towards the sea. *This would be a good place to raise you,* she told her baby. *If we spent the rest of our lives here, I wouldn't complain.*

A woman Flick didn't recognise caught her attention outside. She was hovering a little too long on the sandy path separating Elijah's house from the pebbled beach. And she was giving the house more than just a casual glance. She wore a blue T-shirt, mirrored sunglasses and jeans, and her dark hair was tied back in a ponytail. She was holding her phone up towards the property, as if recording it. Flick sat upright. 'House, privacy glass,' she ordered and the windows switched from opaque to mirrored.

She continued to stare at the stranger, who was now holding the phone to her ear and pointing her finger towards the property. And Flick became unnerved when she was joined by a man, overdressed for the balmy climate in dark trousers, a shirt and a jacket. Flick frowned as he patted his jacket pocket as if checking something was still there.

Their undue interest in the house didn't sit comfortably with her and her body tensed. Her intuition suggested she should leave quickly. Scrambling to her feet, she slipped on her trainers, grabbed her phone and a vegetable knife from the kitchen side, hiding it under the waistband of her jeans.

She exited through the front, only to stop at the sight of two large all-terrain vehicles with blacked-out windows parked on the grass verge directly opposite the house. She was sure they hadn't been there earlier. The window of one was ever so slightly ajar, as if someone was watching her from behind it.

Flick was surrounded.

Chapter 72

CHARLIE, MANCHESTER

Charlie traced the scar on his thigh through the surface of his jeans.

It was raised and ridge-like, despite him not reopening the self-inflicted wound for weeks. He pushed his finger a little deeper until it flattened, and then deeper still to make an indentation. He felt nothing physically, but emotionally, something inside had definitely started to deviate. The action was making him squeamish.

It wasn't the only thing that had altered. He was feeling apprehension and a joy he had not experienced in as long as he could remember. His Match Your DNA notification was reshaping everything. That single email was lighting the embers of the Charlie of old, but without the crippling anxiety. And tomorrow, he would be coming face to face with the person he'd waited his entire adult life to meet.

He removed a crisp white shirt from its packaging and slipped it on. He attached a pair of platinum cufflinks and zipped up his black leather Chelsea boots. Then he studied his reflection in the mirror, confident in his choice of ensemble.

Charlie had not dwelled on what he had lost the night a furious Alix stormed out of his life. Instead, he clicked the email link informing him of his Match, paid his fee and almost immediately, Rosemary Wallace's details arrived. She was a twenty-nine-year-old nurse in County Louth, Ireland. He waited until he had returned to Manchester before he made the first approach via a new burner phone and email address. The conversation flowed without effort. Rosemary enjoyed travel, was fascinated by conspiracy theories and felt her Matched friends had outgrown her. It was as if she was reading from his script. Naturally he was suspicious.

He cross-referenced all she had to say with social media profiles and the web, electoral register and the School of Nursing and Midwifery in Dublin searching for untruths, exaggerations or signs this was a trap. Only when he was convinced that she was genuine did he allow himself to accept that he might have found his Match.

After several days and dozens and dozens of emails, Charlie had been the first to pose the question about meeting in person. But with her on a poorly paid nurse's salary and him unable to leave the country, he offered to book and pay for her flight if she was willing to travel to meet him. She accepted.

Charlie removed his clothes and hung them up neatly inside his wardrobe where they would remain until his date. He reflected upon the last week and how he had chosen to lie low at La Maison du Court, turning his back on anything involving the life he'd forged for himself in Manchester. The friends, the job, the house-share and the woman who'd loved him were cast aside like an outfit that was no longer in fashion. He must close those chapters for good to get the future he'd always wanted.

Only occasionally did he give thought to his pals and wondered if they missed having him in their lives, especially so soon after losing Milo. Had he been around long enough to have made an impact? Unlike his childhood friends, he sensed this group actually cared about him, even if he'd been unable to reciprocate. He briefly considered contacting Andrew to assure him of his safety but changed his mind.

He'd not sought out Alix to apologise for his behaviour, which brought with it another emotion he hadn't felt in some time – guilt. However, it would be too complicated to explain why she had caught him leaving another woman's bedroom at the spa without having to lie further about who he really was. It was more convenient to allow her to believe he'd cheated on her and make a clean break. Perhaps one day he'd find a way to say sorry.

Charlie slipped on a pair of tracksuit bottoms and a hoodie and made his way to the door. He owed it to the programme to remain vigilant, so this would be the third time he visited the pub in Chinatown where he planned to meet Rosemary. He'd already viewed it from outside, and today, he was going to choose and reserve a table where they could sit and not be recognised by anyone passing the window. He'd also locate escape routes and hide a weapon in one of the toilet cisterns.

He desperately wanted to believe that his Match was genuine, but Bruno's murder was still fresh in his mind. He and Sinéad had clearly made mistakes that had led to their deaths. Charlie was not going to do the same. He had a reason to live.

Chapter 73

FLICK, ALDEBURGH, SUFFOLK

Flick's skin grew tight as she hurried back inside Elijah's house, locked the door again and ran through her options. She couldn't call him for help and risk him being hurt in the event of an ambush, and if she called the police, there would be an official record of their visit and Flick didn't want to be documented. But if she were to remain where she was, she'd be a sitting duck. There was no choice but to strike first.

As she opened the bifold doors, she formulated her plan of attack. First, she'd take out the man with a punch to the throat or a kick to the groin and then a knife to his thigh, and if she was lucky and caught his femoral artery, he'd bleed out while she overpowered his accomplice. A stab to her neck could be messy but might give Flick enough time to escape before reinforcements arrived. Then she could run to Aldeburgh's caravan park, pick up the disused railway track at the rear and double-back on herself. Halfway to Thorpeness, she'd locate the camouflage tent and sleeping bag she'd left hidden under a hedgerow weeks earlier. Finally, she'd escape the town through its surrounding fields.

'Why are you staring at this house?' she snapped as she approached the couple. 'This is private property.'

The man responded by moving his hand inside his pocket as his accomplice drew closer. *This is it*, thought Flick. She pulled her arm back and hit him just where she'd planned, square in the throat. He clasped it, and as he moved backwards to avoid a second attack, lost his footing on the sand and fell to the ground. Without thinking, Flick pulled the knife from her waistband and held it above his head as the woman screamed.

'Please don't,' the man gasped.

'He's lost control of the drone,' his accomplice begged.

Right then she spotted the object he had retrieved from his pocket. His phone lay next to him – the screen contained an image of a drone with remote-control directions.

'Why is it flying over my house?' Flick yelled. 'Who's paying you?'

'No one, it's for his YouTube channel, it's about luxury homes,' the woman said.

'You don't have permission.'

'I asked the man who left a few minutes ago if it was okay,' the man added. 'He said I could, as long as I didn't give out his address.'

Flick stepped two paces back and looked up. Wedged against the chimney stack was a drone. The couple posed no threat to her – she had made a terrible error in judgement.

Aware of the fracas, a crowd was gathering so she turned on her heel and hurried back to the house. Once inside and securing it behind her, she threw the knife to the floor and ran up the stairs. Flick was feeling irrational and vulnerable and wanted to hide under the bedcovers like a child until Elijah returned. Then she could admit everything – who she was, what she knew, about their baby and how she was a danger to herself, to others and their child. Elijah was the only one who could help her.

Flick stopped in her tracks when she reached his studio: inside, there was an open door she hadn't seen before disguised by panelled walls. Curiosity got the better of her and she entered, running her fingers across the wall until she found a light switch.

The slate floor of the side room was covered in scuffs and paint marks, and canvases fresh and old were propped against the walls. She looked through them. There were two early illustrations of what became the incomplete painting of Elijah's grandfather, plus other alternative versions of work she recognised from the exhibition she'd attended in town.

Further inside were more unfinished paintings, but this collection was only made up of portraits of women. There was a familiarity about them, but she couldn't pinpoint why. Some of them were bloodied, others depicted faces contorted by fear. They were unsettling. It was only when she reached the final one and recognised the nose piercing on the young subject that her jaw dropped.

It was Kelly, the waitress she'd employed at her old restaurant, and who her DNA Match Christopher had murdered.

Flick clasped her hand over her mouth as she hurried back to the partial sketches of the other women, and only now, she recognised each one of them. They were all Christopher's victims. Elijah was the anonymous artist she'd seen on TV in her flat months earlier who had caused a national furore with his controversial exhibition, capitalising on Christopher's sickening violence.

Flick had replaced one monster with another.

** CONFIDENTIAL **

TOP SECRET: UK EYES ONLY, CLASSIFIED 'A'

THIS DOCUMENT IS THE PROPERTY OF HIS MAJESTY'S GOVERNMENT

MINUTES OF JOINT CYBER-ESPIONAGE / INTELLIGENCE COMMITTEE ASSESSMENT MEETING 11.6

'EMERGENCY MEETING RE: THE ALTERNATIVE APPROACH TO STORAGE OF CLASSIFIED DOCUMENTS'

** Please note this is an account of the minutes taken from the above meeting. Portions of text and certain participants have been redacted to prevent threats to security. **

LOCATION:
███████████, ██████████

MEMBERS PRESENT:
Dr Sadie Mann, Director of Psychiatric Evaluations
Dr Sandra White, Deputy Head of Neuroscience
██████ ████████ ████████, Ministry of Defence (MoD), Porton Down
██████ ████████, MI5
William Harris, HM Government's Minister for Central Intelligence

THE MINDERS

NON-MEMBERS PRESENT:
Prime Minister Diane Cline
QC Barry Hunt, personal lawyer for Prime Minister Diane Cline

---

BARRY HUNT, QC: As your lawyer and friend, Diane, I would like to take this opportunity to suggest it may not be to your advantage to be privy to any details that might follow. Perhaps you'll reconsider my advice and leave?

PRIME MINISTER: It's been eight weeks since Karczewski's body washed up on the shores of Lake Geneva, and now a second person we believe to have been enrolled in this programme has also turned up dead. What happens if whoever is doing this gets to the others before we can reach them?

███████ ████████████████, MoD: Protocols are in place …

PRIME MINISTER: I don't mean to be rude ███████████, but to hell with your protocols. This is *my* country we are talking about and *my* fitness to lead it. If it becomes public knowledge that I've sanctioned taking our secrets offline and put them in the brains of four human guinea pigs, there will be pitchforks and flaming torches trying to burn me out of Downing Street.

BARRY HUNT, QC: If you leave this meeting now, the worst-case scenario is that we can use the defence of plausible deniability and claim you were only involved after the fact.

PRIME MINISTER: Barry, the barn door is wide open and the horses have well and truly bolted. ██████████ ███████████ ███████████, I need to know what happens to this sensitive data if these remaining Minders aren't located and brought back to safety.

█████ █████ █████, MoD: There is a chance some aspect of this information will be lost for ever.

PRIME MINISTER: How much is 'some aspect of it'?

█████ █████ █████, MoD: Worst case scenario – eighty per cent. Best case – around forty per cent.

PRIME MINISTER: Let me get this clear in my head – there are no backups, no hard copies saved anywhere else and no more DNA sitting in a bloody petri dish waiting to be implanted into somebody else?

DR SANDRA WHITE: Not in our laboratories, no.

WILLIAM HARRIS: A part of me can't help wondering if this might be a blessing in disguise. It's a brand-new world we are living in and these are difficult times. Would it really do us that much damage if the worst parts of our history were erased?

█████ █████ █████, MoD: I think it would, yes.

PRIME MINISTER: Which is why when I first learned this plan was being developed behind my back I said it was a ridiculous, dangerous idea. I cannot convey to you all how furious I am for allowing myself to be talked into it. So how are we going to get the remaining Minders back?

WILLIAM HARRIS: The message boards formerly used to communicate recalls are compromised so it's unsafe to return to them. And Karczewski took his files detailing the participants with him to the grave. However, on the retrieval of his body and repatriation home, his killers weren't aware that he too was a carrier of data.

THE MINDERS

PRIME MINISTER: I've read the autopsy report and there was no mention of this.

WILLIAM HARRIS: Parts of it were redacted. Whoever murdered him had no reason to believe he stored information inside him, so the wound to his head was designed to send a message to us and the Minders. He actually stored the names and photographic images of all the Minders in a chip embedded in his calf muscle.

PRIME MINISTER: How do we replace them?

WILLIAM HARRIS: There is an approach we would like to suggest, but it is a radical one and an adapted version of what we were to do if any of the Minders went rogue. But it will require misdirecting the whole of the British public.

Chapter 74

FLICK, ALDEBURGH, SUFFOLK

Flick lay on her bed in a room cloaked in silence.

The window usually remained slightly ajar on the nights she spent at the B&B, enough for her to fall asleep against the distant backdrop of waves lapping against the shore. Tonight, it was firmly shut tight. Her make-believe life was over.

Not only was someone trying to kill her but she was pregnant by a man with a questionable moral compass. How could she have gotten him so horribly wrong?

Flick's reaction to Elijah's exploitation of Christopher's murder victims mirrored the aftermath of her discovery of him as her DNA Match – she retreated behind closed doors. This time, she locked herself inside the B&B to buy herself some thinking time.

'I have a stomach bug,' she'd warned Grace. 'If it's contagious I'd best keep away from you and the other guests.'

By choosing not to confront Elijah about his paintings earlier that day, she had denied him the opportunity to explain. But whatever his justification was for them, it would make no difference because she had already made up her mind. Someone who benefited financially from murder victims was not someone she wanted to raise a child with. Elijah wasn't the man she had built him up to be, and perhaps she must shoulder some of the blame for that. Her expectations had been too high. Very soon, she would be out of his life and searching for a new location to do it alone.

Her fabricated illness coincided with Elijah's last-minute additions to his exhibition. He'd been working long hours at his home and at the nearby disused church he leased. It gave her time and space to make plans.

Unable to sleep, Flick made her way into the darkness of Grace's garden and placed all her belongings, aside from one outfit hanging in her wardrobe, into the incinerator. With the press of a button, it was engulfed by flames. She looked up and into the distance and spotted the neon crucifix attached to the church steeple. It was illuminated which meant Elijah was still there, working through the night.

Back in her room, she spied the pencil portrait he had drawn of her on the evening they'd first met at the pub. She screwed it up and dropped it on the chest of drawers.

She checked the time – it was 2.30 a.m. Around eighteen hours remained before she was to leave everything behind and her next adventure could begin.

Chapter 75

CHARLIE, MANCHESTER

Charlie glanced around the bar of the Chinatown pub as he anxiously awaited the arrival of his DNA Match.

The time was approaching 2 p.m. and from his table at the rear of the room, he counted a dozen or so customers using it as a remote office, working on laptops and sipping from reusable coffee cups. Although he foresaw no obvious threats to his safety, it didn't help him to relax.

Rosemary would be arriving soon and he welcomed the return of the butterflies to his stomach, something he hadn't felt in months. And the anticipation of coming face to face with her was making him a little light-headed. He fought back the urge to break into laughter.

Charlie took another sip from his glass of cola, partly to lubricate his dry throat and partly for something to do with his fidgeting fingers. He caught his reflection in a mirrored wall tile. He was smartly dressed, but not too smart: he hadn't wanted to appear as if he'd made too much effort when it was precisely what he had done. It was hard to get the balance right when you're about to meet the woman who'll change your life for ever.

He tried to imagine how it might feel the moment they saw one another, and whether they'd feel a rush of euphoria simultaneously or apart. Would it hit him immediately, or would it take a few hours? It was different for every couple, he'd heard. Charlie hoped he'd feel it straight away; he'd waited long enough.

He checked the flight times on the mobile phone he shouldn't possess; Rosemary's plane should have landed an hour ago at Alan Turing International Airport. Then he checked the app he'd used to book her a robo-taxi to the pub and saw that it was on its way. She should be arriving within the next few minutes. As Charlie drained his glass, the sound of a bell pinging came from every phone and laptop in the room. His was a burner with no traceable number so it couldn't receive news alerts. He wondered what had happened.

He raised his hand to catch the waitress's attention and order another drink. But she was hunched over her phone and engrossed in a conversation with a waiter. Suddenly he felt their attention move towards him at exactly the same time, their faces wearing identical expressions – suspicion. They moved towards the barman who mirrored the same response. Something felt very, very wrong.

Chapter 76

FLICK, BIRMINGHAM

The journey to the launch of Elijah's exhibition had been a quiet one for Flick. In the rear of the helicopter, Elijah had spent much of it discussing the night ahead with his agent Jenna or wearing a virtual-reality headset to 'walk' around the gallery and communicate to the curator and art technicians which works needed moving last minute and to where.

Flick spoke very little for the hour-long flight, staring from the window at the decline of green spaces below and the encroachment of concrete jungles.

Elijah's hand pressed softly upon hers. 'I think I owe you an apology,' he began.

'For what?'

'For being a useless boyfriend, especially as you've been poorly. I've just got to get through tonight, then everything will return to normal. Thank you for your patience; I can't wait to see what you think.'

He leaned towards her, cupped her chin and kissed her. Flick couldn't deny she would miss his touch. But having discovered how he had profited from Christopher's murders with his anonymous artwork, she could no longer trust him. And to leave him meant leaving Aldeburgh. She had considered departing yesterday with the aid of survival equipment left hidden around the town. But she was in no danger so it made more sense to remain where she was, then hitch a helicopter ride to the country's third-biggest city the next day. It was so central she could travel just about anywhere from there.

Later, as the car that picked them up from the heliport pulled up outside the city centre's Mary Russell Gallery, Flick was feeling uneasy about the night to come. She was the last to exit the vehicle as a photographer approached. 'You go,' she told Elijah, shying away from the lens. 'I'll follow you inside in a few minutes.'

Elijah's smile wilted. 'I was hoping you might change your mind and walk in with me. Can't you make an exception to your "no pictures" rule?'

'I'll be in soon enough.'

He nodded and kissed her forehead. Then Flick waited until Elijah was inside before she made her way up the concrete steps and flashed the doorman her invitation. Once inside the packed room, the scale of Elijah's work took her breath away. Against a backdrop of double-aspect white walls and ceiling-mounted access lights, his portraits had a much greater impact than they had hanging from the walls of Aldeburgh's more compact gallery. Some of his work she recognised from there or from his home studio while others were unfamiliar.

An unexpected pride at his achievement simmered within her. And when she saw the completed marble head she had helped him to carve, she recognised her own eyes amongst its facial components. She couldn't be sure if it was the emotional impact of his work or the pregnancy hormones that was causing her eyes to brim.

She dabbed at them with a napkin taken from a waiter's tray as a hush fell over the gallery. Guests were ushered into the main exhibition hall, where to a round of applause, Jenna introduced Elijah and handed him a microphone. A closed curtain covered something behind them. Flick eased further and further back into the shadows as guests began recording him on mobile phones and smart glasses.

Elijah cleared his throat. 'The people closest to me will know that I prefer to let my work do the talking, so I'll keep this brief.' He scanned the audience as if searching for Flick. 'What you are about to see is the culmination of much hard work and the assistance of many, many people. But first and foremost, I'd like to thank a certain someone – she knows who she is – for inspiring my first journey into art and multi-media. She has put up with my long absences without complaint, my secrecy over this project and despite her dislike of city life, she's here tonight to witness something inspired by her. This body of work is dedicated to you.'

Before she had time to react, Elijah moved to one side and the curtain fell, revealing a metre-tall, three-dimensional holographic image of a person. Flick held her hands to her mouth when she recognised that she was looking at herself.

Quickly, the moving graphic grew in height and at the same time, another version of herself appeared behind it. And soon after, a third. By now, the first Flick was at least two metres tall and began walking through the audience to rapturous applause as the second followed it. Meanwhile, yet more Flicks generated behind them.

'What have you done?' she gasped aloud.

From her position at the rear, Flick was the last person each figure walked through before one by one, they vanished into the wall and then regenerated elsewhere in the room. Horrified, she moved to one side as the procession manoeuvred in different directions throughout but it was impossible to avoid herself. It was a completely immersive experience for guests as they reached out to try and touch 'her' or burst her like a bubble. They took video footage, photographs and selfies.

It was beyond Flick's worst nightmare; her anonymity was in tatters. Her stare met Elijah's as he approached her, grinning proudly, expecting her approval in return.

'Make them stop!' she yelled above the rumble of the crowd.

'What's wrong?' he asked.

'All these versions of me, stop them now!'

'But they're the climax of my show,' he protested.

'You had no right to involve me without my say-so! I'm begging you, Elijah, stop them right now!'

He looked at her, a mixture of confusion and disappointment, and turned to signal to whoever was controlling the computer program to bring it to a premature halt. As soon as the last hologram had vanished, he turned to Flick but she was already hurrying towards the exit.

Chapter 77

CHARLIE, MANCHESTER

Charlie glanced nervously at the app for the taxi he'd ordered Rosemary. She was now only five minutes away. Then he looked back towards the staff behind the bar of the pub. Their attention was still fixed on him but he had no idea why. It made him uncomfortable.

He hesitated, torn between what he wanted to do and what he should do as a Minder. When images of Bruno and Sinéad's bodies came to mind it forced him into making a decision. *I need to get out of here*, he thought.

Charlie grabbed his jacket from the back of the chair and, trying to appear as casual as possible, made his way to the door without turning around. It was only when he heard someone shouting 'Hey!' followed by the sound of pounding feet that he was certain he was in trouble.

Outside, he broke into a run. Weaving through traffic, he crossed Mosley Street and made his way towards Booth Street. It wasn't a direct route, but it would take him towards the Arndale Centre, a once popular but now neglected shopping area. It was still enough of a draw for him to find safety in numbers as he worked out what the hell was happening. *Perhaps you over-reacted, perhaps the staff weren't looking at you?* he asked himself. But Charlie was trained to read people and the staff had been staring at him for a reason.

He turned to look behind him; relieved to see that he'd lost whoever had been trailing him from the bar. He slowed his pace and removed his phone from his pocket, logging back on to the taxi app. Rosemary's cab was about to pull up outside the pub. His heart wrenched as he thought about her waiting alone for him inside. Perhaps he could return and try and catch her attention through the window from the other side of the street? Then he remembered he'd reserved their table specifically because it wasn't in view from the outside.

Instead, he began typing her an email on his burner phone, explaining that he'd been delayed and asking her to wait for him. It might buy him time to find an alternative location for them to meet. In his haste, he wasn't watching where he was going and collided with someone. It knocked Charlie's device out of his hands and to the floor, shattering the screen. He picked it up, frantically jabbing at buttons but it was inoperable.

He turned to the man who had broken it and who was now walking away with two others. 'Fucking idiot!' said Charlie. 'Look what you've done.'

The man stopped and also turned. 'You walked into me, sunshine,' he replied, then cocked his head and turned to his friend. 'Hey, it's him, isn't it?' He pointed to something behind Charlie.

'Yeah, for real!' one of the man's friends said. 'It's the terrorist.'

Charlie followed their gaze, and saw a giant moving billboard attached to a building and broadcasting rolling news. His face was plastered across it, along with a caption.

WANTED: Charlie Nicholls – Key member of terrorist cell planning atrocities throughout Britain.

Government reward for live capture:
£500,000. If located, contact
police immediately.

'Oh, Jesus,' Charlie gasped, just as three men's hands restrained him. Charlie immediately fought back, twisting and squirming his way from their hold. They were no match for his combat skills. He had been taught to fight quick and dirty and it took just a few carefully placed punches, kicks and headbutts before he was once again running hell for leather through Manchester's streets.

He pushed his way through the public as he continued towards Arndale, sending some sprawling to the ground as others cursed at him. Now it appeared that every moving billboard in the city was filled with larger-than-life images of his face and the bounty attached to his capture. He understood why, back in the pub, everyone's electronic devices had sounded at once. It was a nationwide alert for him.

'Stop that fella!' shouted a voice from behind. He turned to see that the three men he'd attacked were now giving chase. 'He's the terrorist!'

Charlie's pulse pounded in his ears as he ran from street to street, alternating between busy and quieter roads he knew off by heart. It was too risky to continue to Arndale so he made his way to a deserted warehouse overlooking Piccadilly Gardens that he knew was only frequented by drug users and alcoholics.

He pushed his way through a graffiti-stained door until he was inside, and settled in a quiet, darkened corner, fighting to get his breath back. Between his own gasps, he heard the drunken arguments of some and the snores of others sleeping it off. He could make out very little through tiny gaps in the wooden planks of the boarded-up windows. With no phone display, Charlie asked his OS to compose an email but it didn't answer him.

However, Charlie's phone pinged, which meant he'd received an email, and Rosemary was the only one with his address. He punched the planks in frustration until his knuckles grazed.

His thoughts turned to the billboards. Who was trying to expose him? If it was the government, its methods went against protocol. Karczewski had warned him that if he failed to spot or ignored seven recall messages, he would be treated as an enemy of the state but it would be dealt with privately. It didn't make sense. The recall was a hoax and these billboards were offering a reward for his capture alive.

Before he had the opportunity to give it more thought, his phone began ringing. Charlie held it in his palm, unable to read the number. He had no choice but to press the accept button on the side of the device.

'Charlie,' a female voice began. He didn't reply. 'Remain where you are and we will be with you in two minutes.'

'Who are you?'

'My name is Dr Sadie Mann, Director of Psychiatric Evaluations. I worked with Karczewski.'

'Why have you left me so exposed?' he seethed. 'My fucking face is everywhere.'

'It was the only way to bring you into the open. We are sending someone to pick you up.'

'Why the hell should I believe you? Two of the other Minders have been murdered, haven't they?'

'We are aware of that. We need to bring you back in and this was the only way. You are currently at a disused building in Parker Street, correct?'

'How do you know that?'

'Look out for a dark grey Mercedes.'

Charlie's mind raced. He was adept at escaping but not when the whole country was searching for him. How long could he continue alone?

'Charlie,' the voice continued. 'Are you still there?'

'Yes, I am,' he replied.

'Wait where you are.'

'Not a chance,' he said and hurled his phone at the wall. Then he grabbed a dirty discarded coat from the floor, opened the warehouse door and ran for his life.

Chapter 78

FLICK, BIRMINGHAM

Flick scanned Birmingham's skyline until she located the silver dome of the Bullring Shopping Centre.

Once she reached it, she would head to the locker where a basic wardrobe of practical clothing she'd secretly ordered online yesterday from Grace's account should have been delivered. A five-minute walk would take her to New Street station where she could catch a train south to Gloucester, then a coach to Bristol. Another train would carry her to Trowbridge where she planned to buy a car and make her way to the coastal county of Cornwall. A popular part of the country for holidaymakers and surfers, there was an abundance of holiday accommodation that would enable her to lie low until she decided on her next course of action.

'Flick, hey, wait up!' Elijah's voice came from behind, catching her off-guard. She continued walking without turning around. 'What's wrong?'

She wasn't ready to hear anything he had to say. She had informed him many times that she valued her privacy but he had broken her trust in the most public way possible. He had also put her life, and their baby's, in danger.

'Please,' he shouted again. 'Just stop.' Flick knew he wasn't going to give up until he'd been heard.

'What the hell did you think you were doing?' she began as she turned. Her lips were pursed, steam almost rising from her head. 'Who gave you the right to turn me into a piece of art?'

'I thought you'd like it. Everyone in the gallery is blown away by it.'

'I'm not everyone! If you had any idea who I am you'd know this is the last thing I'd want. Go back to your party and leave me alone.'

As Flick turned, Elijah's hand reached out and brushed her arm. Before she had time to process her actions, she had him pinned up against a bus shelter, one arm pressed against his throat and the other drawn back, ready to strike him. She let go just as quickly, ashamed and flustered.

'Who the hell are you?' he asked, his disbelieving eyes glaring into hers.

And for the briefest of moments, Flick desperately wanted to answer. But for the safety of all three of them, she held back.

'You've ruined everything,' she snapped. 'Why couldn't you have used someone else's face? Grace, or one of the countless other women who'd be desperate to sit for you?'

'Because they don't possess your depth. This installation represents all the versions of you, the ones I witness every day and the ones you hide.'

'Elijah, you shouldn't have left me so vulnerable.'

'Then tell me who you are and stop keeping secrets from me.'

Flick let out a sharp laugh. 'Secrets? Let's talk about secrets, shall we? Tell me how much money you earned off the back of the London murder victims?' Elijah's mouth opened but no words followed. 'I know that you're the artist responsible. I saw the early paintings hidden in your storeroom. You must have known what you did was wrong because you didn't put your name to them. You didn't even exhibit in Aldeburgh – isn't that where all your work debuts? You exploited those poor women for financial gain. Haven't their families been through enough without you piling on the misery?'

Elijah's face reddened as he shook his head. 'The point was to separate the victims from the crime. And I didn't put my name to it because this was about those women, not some celebrity artist who decided to paint them.'

'Why not paint them as they were before they were killed? Not afterwards, all tortured and bloody.'

'I'm aware it was a polarising subject matter but art is supposed to be provocative. And for the record, I didn't earn a penny from it. The profits raised more than half a million pounds for a woman's refuge charity in Sussex. My mum and I spent a year living in a shelter when I was a kid, trying to escape my violent dad. It made me feel like I was giving something back.'

Now it was Flick's turn to lose her footing. She hesitated, but was unwilling to back down. 'I just think there are better ways to make your point without glorifying what he did. We're over, Elijah.'

'So, what, that's it? You're going to use this as an excuse to walk away from us, just like that? It feels like you're looking for a reason and this is a convenient one.'

'You don't know what you're talking about.'

'It's yet another thing you're keeping from me.'

'What does that mean?'

'It means that when it comes down to it, I don't know the first thing about you, do I? Your family, your background, who you were before you arrived in Aldeburgh? Who are you, Flick? What don't you want me to know?'

It was as Flick turned away that she caught sight of it. A digital screen covering the length of a bus displayed her photograph with the words 'Wanted' and 'Terrorist'. She froze, desperately trying to make sense of it. Whoever had killed the others had found a way to expose her.

She turned quickly to Elijah in the hope that he hadn't spotted it. But as the bus pulled away, there were two more behind it with exactly the same display, and they grabbed his attention. As a puzzled expression took over his face, Flick became consumed by the need to tell him everything, have him hold her in his arms and hear that she was safe with him. Just as quickly, she reminded herself she was not that person any more. She was a self-contained unit trained to look after herself.

'Jesus,' he gasped, but before he could say anything else, Flick took a deep breath, dropped to her knees and turned to face a group of men crossing the road. Her sudden scream was piercing.

'Help me, please, help me!' she yelled and pretended to be crawling away. She shouted for help again, partially obscuring her face with her hand in case they too might recognise her. Instead, the concerned strangers sprang into action and rushed in her direction, one helping her to her feet as she counted five others rounding up and circling a perplexed Elijah. 'He was trying to abduct me,' she sobbed. 'Get him away from me.'

Willing to take her word over his without question, they hurled abuse and punches at Elijah while the woman he loved ran away from him and towards another new beginning.

Chapter 79

CHARLIE, MANCHESTER

Charlie had some fast decisions to make.

The giant digital billboards containing his image that were illuminating so many city-centre buildings had forced him to abandon his plans to hide in plain sight. Instead, he would concentrate on making his way to a locker inside the People's History Museum. There, he could pick up a backpack he'd left on a previous trip that contained basic weapons, body armour, a camouflage tent, another burner mobile phone and maps. Repurchasing such essential items would involve visits to different shops and leave him remaining exposed for longer.

From the museum, he would sprint to Alexandra Park. The former Victorian landscaped greenery was now hidden under a patchwork quilt of canvas tents housing immigrants who'd flocked to the UK before it shut its borders a year earlier. Even slum dwellers in sections of India's poverty-stricken Calcutta had a better quality of life than those consigned to this quarter. But Charlie reckoned that once under the cover of his own tent, he might remain safe until nightfall at least.

He pulled up the collar of the discarded coat he'd grabbed from the warehouse so it covered his chin and mouth, but gagged at the odour of stale sweat and urine which had seeped into its threads. As he half walked, half jogged, it wasn't just his own safety that preoccupied him. He agonised over poor Rosemary. The one saving grace of this whole sorry mess was that he hadn't emailed her his photograph so she wouldn't know who her Match really was. She would think she'd been stood up but not by Britain's most wanted man. It might have been the lesser of two evils but it didn't stop him from feeling as if someone had reached into his chest and was squeezing his heart.

Charlie kept his head down until he reached Shudehill, a road behind the Arndale. From here and at his current pace, he estimated he could be at the museum within five minutes. Without thinking, he made the mistake of looking directly at a passing mum with a child in a pushchair. Only a few footsteps later, he heard her shriek: 'That's the terrorist! That's him!'

Without turning, Charlie began to sprint, weaving his way in and out of people and streets, crossing roads and forcing cars into emergency stops. But the more he ran, the more attention he was drawing to himself and he heard footsteps and loud voices chasing him. If he could maintain his pace through another handful of streets, he could hide in a less redeveloped area somewhere by the river Irwell until the pack lost his scent.

But without warning, a side tackle lifted him off his feet and into the air. As he landed Charlie heard and felt the crack that shattered his collarbone and wrist. The side of his head made a dull thud as he hit the concrete. He felt no physical pain, but it disorientated him. He looked up as the first of many punches began to rain down upon his face and body. And soon, the grey sky above him blackened as the growing crowd blocked out the clouds.

'Don't kill him, there's a reward of half a million,' someone argued.

'Don't fucking care,' yelled another voice. 'Terrorist scum don't deserve to live.'

The breaking of his nose was swiftly followed by short, sharp kicks to his head before his dental implants dislodged and hit the back of his throat. And once fists collided with his eyes, it became almost impossible to see. He struggled to breathe with each kick to the stomach and ribs yet despite all this, Charlie was able to think with clarity. He was sure that he was about to die.

This is karma for what I did to my friends and to Milo, he thought. *It's everything I deserve for wanting something more. I'm sorry, Rosemary. I'm going to die like I've lived: hurting everyone I care for.*

Charlie's left arm felt as if it was about to be wrenched from its socket and his ankle dislocated as those who wanted a share of the reward battled against those who wanted him dead. Some grabbed at him, pulling him back and forth until he felt he might split in two.

The sudden loud blast of a car horn was followed by the screeching of tyres and the yelling of panicked voices. Charlie just about caught the darkness lifting until only one shadow remained.

'Get away from him,' a voice ordered, then Charlie flinched at the unmistakable sound of gunfire and panicked footsteps running away. 'Get up!' it continued but he didn't register that the command was directed at him until he felt his arm being yanked. 'We don't have much time.' Before he knew it, another bullet was fired, followed by more yelling. Suddenly he was being dragged along the street, then propped up and pushed face first upon the seat of a vehicle. He used the little strength he had left in his legs until he was completely inside and heard the doors shut.

'I told you I didn't want your help,' he gasped but his protests were ignored.

'Drive us to the M62,' his rescuer continued. 'Override speed limits.'

As the autonomous vehicle pulled away from the murderous mob, Charlie heard the banging and clattering of hurled objects bouncing off the bodywork.

'I said I didn't need your help!' Charlie repeated. His missing front teeth gave him a lisp. He tried to sit upright. 'What happened? Why was I exposed? You could have got me killed.'

'Open your eyes.'

'Do they look as if they're going to open?' Charlie snapped. 'They're fucked like the rest of me.'

A rustling sound and the opening of a packet was followed by two cool compresses settling on his lids. Charlie blinked slowly until the face of the person who had saved his life came into focus. Their expression was impassive, as if waiting for his reaction before they said anything else.

'It's you!' he said. 'I thought you were dead?'

Chapter 80

EMILIA

Emilia processed Charlie's reaction to her and tried to keep her response unemotional.

'You recognise me?' she challenged. A bloodied Charlie squinted at her through slits for eyelids. 'Who told you I was dead?'

'It's in the data up here.' He tapped the crown of his head. 'So how and why are you bringing me back to them?'

Her body itched with anticipation. She desperately wanted to keep him believing that she knew what he was referring to. It might have been shock or adrenaline but Charlie's thought processes were moving quickly, flip-flopping from one conversation to the next.

'It was the burner phone that gave me away, wasn't it?' he continued. 'You picked up on that crowd's concentration of a mobile tower usage, used an IMSI Catcher to get everyone's numbers and messages and through a process of elimination, you isolated mine.'

She nodded.

'I bloody knew it. Then you sent a drone to see exactly where I was.'

Again, Emilia agreed. 'Before we go any further, Charlie, I need you to tell me who you think I am and why you believed me to be dead,' she said.

Charlie appeared aggrieved by the request. 'Are you kidding? If it wasn't for you people exposing me, I wouldn't be in this clusterfuck.'

'It's just a precaution. I can get you to safety once you tell me what I need to know.'

Beneath both fresh and drying blood, Emilia thought she saw Charlie's face pale, as if something was slowly awakening. 'What make of car is this?'

'Um, an Audi, I think.'

He looked out of the window to the bonnet. 'A grey Audi,' he said. 'Because the people who called my phone said they were sending a Mercedes for me.'

Emilia swallowed hard. Someone had located him before her. It meant they probably weren't far behind them.

'You're not working with the government, are you?' he continued.

As Charlie scrambled to pull himself upright, Emilia only just dodged his foot when he aimed it at her ribs.

'Charlie, no,' she said firmly but as she moved to restrain him, he found a second wind. 'No, listen to me.'

His fists flayed but in his battered and bruised state, his coordination was off-kilter and they were easy to dodge.

'I didn't expose you,' Emilia replied, fending off his poor aim. 'But I can help you. Tell me what I need to know and then I will help you to safety.'

This time, Emilia wasn't fast enough to avoid a left hook that caught her clean in the cheek, pushing her head into the window. Charlie drew from a hidden strength to launch himself at her, his fists punching any part of her body he could connect with. But he was no match for Emilia's agility and strength. She caught him clean in the remains of his broken nose before grabbing the gun from the waistband of her jeans and pointing it at his head. Finally, he gave up. And now their only fight was to regain their breath.

The screen of her phone illuminated – only Bianca and Adrian had her number. She hadn't told them where she was going but with a tracking device on the gadget and inside the car, it wouldn't be long before they too descended, along with the government, and one of the rival parties whisked Charlie away before she got her answers.

'We can help each other,' panted Emilia. 'I don't remember who I was back then but you do. They'll already be tracking us but I can get you to safety.'

Charlie hesitated, his eyes rapidly working his way around her face, searching for gestures that she was lying. But she was telling the truth. If she got what she wanted, she would let him live.

'Why did you kill the other Minders?' he asked.

'I swear to you I didn't.'

Emilia could almost taste how close she was. All Charlie needed was an extra little encouragement.

'You're a liar. I saw what you did.'

'We are in the same boat,' she pleaded. 'We're as desperate as one another. Something happened to me which means I don't know anything before a few weeks ago. Tell me who I am and what you know about me and I'll drive you back to the pub where you were supposed to be meeting Rosema—' She stopped abruptly. Charlie glared at her.

'How do you know about Rosemary?' he asked slowly. 'Or that we were meeting at a pub?'

Emilia wasn't quick enough to think on her feet and for Charlie, the penny had already dropped. 'She doesn't exist, does she? *You* are Rosemary.' His body seemed to fold in on itself.

Emilia recalled how Charlie had proved tricky to expose in a city of 3.5 million people. Then out of the blue, something struck Emilia. 'Charlie is a twenty-five-year-old single man with no known girlfriends or boyfriends,' she'd told Adrian. 'I wager that like most people who've grown up in the shadow of Match Your DNA, he has an account.'

Moments later and Adrian's team had an answer. 'There are two accounts using different names but both with iden- tical DNA. And both are unmatched.'

'What are the odds?' Bianca asked.

'Nine in seventy trillion. Even twins don't have identical DNA.'

After identifying Charlie, they used algorithms to sift through his tens of thousands of pages of internet history to learn his likes and dislikes and gain an insight into his personality. Then they created an entire life and social media history for the fictitious Rosemary, a character named after a very old Lenny Kravitz song that Charlie had favourited on his streaming playlists. And within days of them sending Charlie notification of his 'Match', he'd responded.

His conversation had been initially cautious, and Emilia hadn't pushed him. But soon they were messaging regularly and he had paid for her flight from Ireland to Manchester. But the government's unexpected release of his image that morning had taken Emilia and the Hacking Collective by surprise. Instead of being picked up by the team and escorted from the pub as planned, he had fled on foot and they'd had to track him.

Now, as their eyes remained fixed on one another's, Emilia could see how crushed he was. 'I'm sorry,' she said eventually and a small part of her meant it.

'I believe that you don't know who you are,' Charlie replied. 'And I'll give you your answers. Not because I want to help you or believe that you'll get me to safety, but because the truth is going to hurt you just as much as you've just hurt me.'

Suddenly, what sounded like two shots rang out.

Emilia yelped but before she had time to identify the noise, it was followed by two more mini explosions. Whatever the cause, it was derailing their vehicle. Swerving across the road, the car hit a central reservation before flipping over onto its roof and throwing its occupants around like ragdolls. Finally, it landed back on its axles and scraped to a halt.

A shooting pain ran through a disorientated Emilia's spine as she pushed herself up from the rear footwells and looked out of the back windscreen to assess the damage. Behind the stinger used to burst the tyres, a crowd was approaching her car. She couldn't let them come for Charlie, not when she was so close to the truth.

She scrambled around the car until she found her weapon on the front passenger seat, lifting it to fire a shot through the back window. She protected her face with her hand as it rained glass shards. And it had the desired effect as the mob scattered. Emilia had bought them time.

'They're backing away,' she told Charlie, quickly scanning their outdoor surroundings to see where they could escape to. 'I don't know how long I can keep them back so we need to get the hell out of here. Can you open the door?'

When Charlie didn't respond, she turned her head. 'Charlie, I need you to focus. Can you open the door?'

Only now did she notice that he was slumped across the driver's seat, unconscious. 'Damn it,' she muttered and went to turn his head so she could pat his face and waken him. It was then that she saw his eyes were wide open and his neck angled in an unnatural position. It was clearly broken. Charlie was dead.

'No!' she yelled. Even knowing it was a futile manoeuvre, she couldn't give up without a fight; she tried to locate his pulse, then pushed him across both seats and gave him chest compressions. But it was too late. This gang of greedy faces had robbed him of his life and her of an explanation.

The anger she felt towards Bruno when he laughed at her was nothing compared to the rage against Charlie erupting inside her now. Emilia raised her balled fists above her head before beating his lifeless chest and arms with every ounce of her strength. Saliva frothed in the corners of her mouth as the frustration consumed her. Then from the glovebox and without knowing why, she grabbed the metallic silver device she'd killed Bruno with and skewered the exact same spot on Charlie's scalp. But it wasn't enough to quell her fury. There were others who needed punishing too.

It took two kicks before the crumpled door released and she could exit. The crowd continued making its approach toward the car, determined to get its pound of flesh and a cut of the reward money. Emilia saw every face before her as someone who had prevented her from being reunited with her family. And without forethought, she marched towards them, removed her weapon and began firing at will. Even when they screamed and turned on their heels, she continued to shoot until the bullets ran out, and she watched their bodies drop to the ground as fast as each spent cartridge.

PART THREE

TEN WEEKS LATER

Chapter 81

FLICK, CORNWALL

Rainwater pooled on the metal bench and seeped into Flick's jeans, dampening the backs of her thighs and her bottom. She tugged at her waterproof jacket until there was enough fabric to sit on, but it exposed her forehead to the drizzle.

The weather had been poor since her arrival in Cornwall weeks earlier, but she had grown accustomed to it. She opened a pre-packed sandwich purchased in a tearoom she'd passed at the beginning of her six-mile hike. There were slim pickings on the shelf and the two thin layers of brown bread housing a sliver of ham and a thin slice of processed cheese was the best it had to offer. 'Sorry,' she said to her baby bump, apologetic that today, she'd yet to digest anything with nutritional value. As she nibbled it, she took in the rolling landscapes of Cornwall's Tidna Valley that surrounded her.

She ran her fingers through her shorn black-dyed hair. She was still becoming accustomed to it, along with her coloured contact lenses and glasses. The several pounds of baby weight she'd put on helped to fill out her face and stomach and made her look less like the terrorist the whole country was still on high alert for. Her new alter ego 'Martine' had, fortunately, yet to be recognised.

Flick took out the news story she had printed at a library weeks earlier. She had read it so often that the paper print was creased and smudged.

TERRORIST FOUND BUTCHERED

By Louise Beech

Police have confirmed body parts discovered in a car in Manchester belong to terrorist Charlie Nicholls.

A post-mortem could not confirm how Britain's most wanted man was killed due to 'significant sections of his body being missing'.

A source told the Online Post: 'It appears he was torn apart by a mob that forced his car off the road, in the hope that they might get a share of the £500,000 government reward for his capture.

'Both feet, his torso and a hand have been passed to the police but his head, legs, an arm and fingers have yet to be located.'

Nine people also died in gunfire that afternoon, in a shootout police believe to be between rival bounty hunters.

No matter how many times Flick read it, it didn't lessen the impact of his manner of death. And once again she shed a tear in memory of the only Minder she had ever met.

Flick had made her most recent home a rented caravan in a park on the outskirts of Bude. She'd been careful to choose one located away from the other static homes and fitted her own electronic locks to the windows and doors along with an alarm system. Each of the four rooms and even the bathroom contained a hunting knife with a serrated blade that was within easy reach. She had also scoped the surrounding area for exits, parking her car in a nearby street that could be approached from five different directions. She had done all she could to protect herself, her secrets and her baby.

Taking a swig from a bottle of fruit juice, she slipped her hands inside her jacket pockets and rubbed her stomach. Not so long ago, she'd have berated herself for showing her baby affection. Now it was second nature and she hoped it offered him or her as much comfort as it did its mother. At more than four months pregnant, her belly now displayed a definite paunch and it appeared to be growing as the library textbooks suggested it would by now. But a transient lifestyle and a complete mistrust towards all things official and traceable meant she had yet to book hospital scans or register with a midwife.

The swell of the waves crashed against the cliff's rocks below. They were more aggressive than Aldeburgh's waters and she missed the latter's calming rhythms. She tried not to dwell upon those she'd left behind, or the hurt she had caused to Elijah. But solitude gave her plenty of thinking time and made it difficult not to linger on anything else. Distance had given her clarity; what she had done to Elijah was unforgivable and she prayed his injuries weren't serious. But at the time, she felt she had little choice. He paid the price for her panic. She wondered what he thought of her now and whether he hated her as much as she hated herself. Grace wasn't far from her mind either. In a short space of time, they'd become close.

Flick decided that despite what had happened to Charlie, she was safer out in the open than if she turned herself in to a government which had slapped a reward on her head. She would remain in the field for as long as possible, or at least another few months until the child was born. She did not trust the baby's safety with authorities.

As much as she appreciated Cornwall's solitude and privacy, Flick longed to return to Aldeburgh. She accepted that it had been a manufactured, false reality, but her feelings towards the place and its people were honest. She was merely going through the motions in Cornwall, filling her days with long walks whilst avoiding anywhere densely populated, and her nights with books she'd always wanted to read. But it was little better than when she hid herself away in her London flat.

She tugged her hood so that it covered her forehead, and continued to explore a wet and grassy Morwenstow. But when the drizzle turned to rain, she went back to her car. She hovered at the edge of the car park first, scoping the other vehicles until assured it was safe to return to her own. She ran her fingertips along the undercarriage, wheel arches and sills to check for tracking devices. Then she confirmed the memory-card slot in the satnav was still empty before the engine sparked to life.

Suddenly, she felt it – the phone in her pocket was vibrating. Each of the three times it had done this before, it had contained footage of a Minder's murder. Charlie was the last video to have been sent, although he appeared dead before the silver device that killed the others plunged into his skull. And no name had been carved into his forehead.

She could only assume that after a ten-week gap, it was alerting her to the death of another Minder. How many of them were left? Flick's heart raced as she turned off the engine and removed the device. Just as she feared, the red circle disclosed that it was another video clip. She gripped the phone, opened its case and pressed play without allowing herself to think.

This time it was different. The camerawork was shaky, indicating that the killer was on the move. It was hard to tell where they were as the lens was pointed towards a cobbled pathway before eventually coming to a halt at a porch. Flick's heart sank when it focused on a front door that she immediately recognised. It was Grace's house.

She watched helplessly as a hand reached out to ring a bell. A moment later, it opened. Grace was standing there, unaware she was being filmed. 'Hi,' she began. 'Can I help you?'

The voice that replied was an unfamiliar woman's. 'Hi there, do you have any rooms available, please?'

'Say no, say no, say no,' Flick whispered.

'Yes, we do,' Grace replied as Flick held her breath. Grace opened the door with a friendly 'Follow me,' and the woman entered. 'We have three different types,' continued Grace, with her back to the guest. Two of them come with en-suites and the other—'

Grace wasn't given the opportunity to finish. Flick watched helplessly as a weapon fired hundreds of volts of electricity into Grace's neck, before her friend crumpled to the floor.

Chapter 82

EMILIA

Grace's breaths were short and shallow as she lay sprawled across the floor. The current that had soared through her body moments ago had left her completely incapacitated. Her eyes were open but she was barely blinking.

The distance between the Emilia who awoke frightened and unaware of who she was and the woman right now were too far apart to be measured. It didn't matter what Bruno had believed, she *hadn't* been given a choice, she *had* been pushed into this. It was the actions of others that had conspired to turn her into a merciless hunter. Grace was more collateral damage in her search for the truth.

According to the magnets stuck to Karczewski's fridge and by a process of elimination, Flick's last known location had been narrowed down to the small coastal town. By publicly identifying her, the government had ensured every amateur detective and his dog had converged on Aldeburgh. The pub where she'd worked, the church hall where she exercised, her artist ex-boyfriend and the bed and breakfast she'd made her home had all been deluged with visitors, each hoping to be the one to bring Flick out of hiding. But she was still very much a free woman.

Emilia's initial search of the town and its people ten weeks earlier proved fruitless. But Emilia was convinced that wherever her target was residing now, Flick wouldn't be able to stay there for ever. She'd maintained a job and made friends in Aldeburgh; she had put down roots there so it was likely she'd left hurriedly and reluctantly. Perhaps there was a way she could be persuaded to return?

Fortunately, the public's fervour to find Flick had curtailed since the government had rescinded its reward following the aftermath of Charlie's death. As a result, Emilia approached Bianca and Adrian, urging them to deploy another team to sweep through the town again and hunt for leads that might have evaded them first time around. Bianca had been reluctant to allow Emilia any involvement after the shootings. She was 'mentally unstable' and 'a danger to herself and everyone around her', apparently. By the time she eventually convinced them, the town was less saturated.

Eventually, however, they appeared to take Emilia's word for it that she'd had little choice but to react so drastically. She was unarmed and escorted to Aldeburgh under the direct supervision of experienced field operatives Gardiner and Lago.

Their arrival coincided with the town's annual three-day carnival weekend. It attracted thousands of extra tourists which offered plenty of camouflage. Earlier, dozens of members of a samba band dressed in reds, whites and blues danced with drums hanging from their necks as they followed brightly decorated floats weaving around the town. As the music played, Emilia took a position from the top of the high street and slipped on her smart glasses, setting them to binocular mode. She then used facial-recognition software to scan the faces of the crowds lining the roads as far as the eye could see. There was no sign of Flick.

Later, the three separated to ask in shops and cafes about their mark. But all were regarded with suspicion and the fed-up town closed ranks; they gleaned nothing they didn't already know. It was only later when Emilia viewed footage of interviews from the other two's body cams that the young woman who ran the B&B caught her attention. She was clearly accustomed to – and annoyed by – strangers enquiring as to whereabouts of Britain's most wanted woman. But Emilia intuitively read something else in her micro-expression – disappointment. She suspected they had been more than landlady and tenant; they had been friends. And even weeks after her sudden departure, this Grace girl was still struggling to come to terms with who Flick had really been. It was how Emilia was going to lure her out of hiding.

As the afternoon's celebrations made way for evening, Emilia found herself standing over Grace's trembling body, watching the helpless electrocuted woman's arms jerk. Gradually Grace's fingers spread out and her wrists turned as if preparing to crawl away. It was a futile gesture. The heel of Emilia's boot crushed Grace's fingers.

'I don't think so,' Emilia said quietly. 'This is only beginning.'

Chapter 83

FLICK, ALDEBURGH, SUFFOLK

The smart glasses were shaking in Flick's hands as she slipped them on. Her irises directed the zoom function to scan the property, fifty metres ahead. The curtains behind each of the three windows were closed and the lights turned off. The front door, however, was slightly ajar.

She switched to thermal-imaging mode in the hope it might pinpoint how many people were inside. But the glasses, all the motorway service station had to offer, were inexpensive. A faint yellow dot appeared upstairs in the house, suggesting someone was inside.

Flick desperately wanted to run across the road, burst through the doors of the B&B and discover exactly what Grace's attacker had done to her. But she was certain this was a set-up designed to ensnare her. So she took shelter from the weather under the porch of an empty property instead of reacting with a knee-jerk response.

The cloak of dusk she'd arrived under had made way for nightfall, the sky illuminated by a rainbow of colours projected by the bright lights of a nearby fun fair, merry-go-round rides and stalls. She'd forgotten it was the final day of the carnival and the vast number of participants made remaining unnoticed more challenging. The rain that had soaked her that morning in Cornwall followed her cross-country but hadn't put off hundreds of people parading along the nearby high street, carrying illuminated Chinese lanterns on sticks and making their way to the beach to end the celebrations with a firework display later that night.

Flick arched her back and pushed her fingers into her lower spine where a painless throbbing had appeared. She was unsure if it was the pregnancy or the long drive knotting her muscles. She'd had plenty of time during the seven-hour journey to Aldeburgh to decide how to respond to Grace's plight. Her conscience wouldn't allow her to do nothing, but more importantly, she made the decision to no longer run from the person who wanted her dead. It would be an impossible feat to keep looking over her shoulder for the next four and a half years and at the same time, provide a safe, secure environment for her baby.

The enemy had succeeded in what they'd set out to do. They had lured Flick out of hiding and back into the open. But if they wanted to kill her, she wasn't going to make it easy for them.

Her glasses targeted the B&B one last time before Flick removed a hunting knife from her pocket and slipped it inside the right sleeve of her coat. She practised snapping her wrists back to judge how quickly it could slip out.

She made her way towards the end of the garden and to the road outside Grace's house. Flick ran her fingers up and down the gateposts searching for sensors that might warn Grace's captor of her arrival, but they were clear. There were no laser alarms surrounding the length of the path either.

Arriving at the front door, she assumed it was nerves making her stomach flutter until she realised it was the baby turning inside her. She rubbed it, almost apologetically, and hoped her stress levels weren't being felt by her child. Not for the first time that day she questioned whether she was doing the right thing. But this was uncharted territory – there was no right or wrong, only survival of the fittest.

Flick wedged the front door open with a rock as she slowly stepped inside the entrance hall, moving towards the lounge. Her glasses revealed the room to be empty. So were the communal dining room, kitchen, utility room and bathroom. Upstairs, it was the same for each guest bedroom with the exception of the one she had once rented. As she approached it, thermal-imaging sensors made the yellow dot expand. If it was Grace, she was radiating heat and that meant she was alive.

Flick swallowed the sour taste of bile as it rose up into her throat. The cool tip of the hunting knife grazed her wrist as she turned the door handle and slowly opened it. The first thing to strike her was the intense heat. Only it wasn't coming from a body, but judging by the circular shape of it, from an electric heater next to one. Then she spotted a figure lying on the bed.

'Grace?' she whispered, her voice no louder than a whisper. 'Grace, please wake up.' Flick drew closer and fumbled until she could place two fingers on the side of the person's neck, searching for a pulse. She withdrew her hand when she felt something wet. She frantically located the bedside light, illuminating Grace's body. Her throat had been slashed.

Flick cast her gaze across her friend; her skin was a greyish white; her lifeless eyes stared up at the ceiling. Blood had oozed from her throat and seeped into her T-shirt and bedsheets. The heater had been used to fool the thermal-imaging camera and had already dried the blood brown. Grace's hands and feet had been bound, but she hadn't been gagged. Flick shuddered at what level of pain her terrified friend must have suffered in her final moments.

A tidal wave of emotions threatened to consume her. She sank to her knees, grabbing Grace's hand as she apologised over and over again. This time, the bile rose too high to swallow and she only just made it to the sink to vomit.

As she palmed Grace's eyelids shut, she spotted something poking from the corner of her mouth. She carefully parted Grace's lips and removed a scrap of balled-up paper. As she uncurled it, she recognised it as the line drawing of Flick that Elijah had sketched the night they met.

It struck in an instant. Flick had spent so much time worrying about Grace that she hadn't given a thought to who else the killer might use to reach her.

Elijah.

With rain lashing against her cheeks, Flick ran through the back streets and alleyways before reaching the road behind the beachfront. She kept her hood pulled over her head, to protect her from the elements and to avoid being spotted by lantern-bearing carnival-goers heading to the beach.

She couldn't think clearly enough to prepare herself for what she might find inside Elijah's house. And on her arrival, the privacy glass had already been on, giving nothing away about the activities inside. Unlike Grace's B&B, she didn't scope the building before entering. Instead, she keyed in the digits to the security code and his front door opened with a click. Then she clasped the handle of her hunting knife, ready to strike at a moment's notice.

Flickering lights greeted her as she entered the corridor, illuminating the Perspex staircase. The bass-heavy rap music that Elijah favoured as he worked blasted throughout the house, offering her a shred of hope that the killer had not yet reached him. Slipping on her smart glasses again, Flick made her way along the corridor until she reached the unlit, open-plan kitchen and lounge. There was no sign of Elijah even with the thermal-imaging lens.

She felt another twinge in her back but didn't have time to pay it attention. Instead, she made her way upstairs until she reached the closed door of his studio. *Please be alive*, she thought and pulled at the handle to open it.

Suddenly, a figure inside rushed towards her. Instinctively, she ducked, then swung her knife out in front of her, slicing the air with the blade. However, the figure vanished as quickly as it had appeared.

A disorientated Flick turned, trying to locate the person, only for another to appear on the other side of the room. They too flew towards her, then vanished as she tried to strike them. It was only when a third came at her that she saw who the enemy was – herself. They were the three-dimensional moving holograms of her, the ones Elijah had created for his exhibition. Flick scowled at the soulless, empty, ghost-like apparitions and wondered how far removed from her they actually were.

Without warning, they changed direction and began marching towards a frosted-glass window. There, they paused in height order, from the tallest at the front to the real Flick at the back, like a row of Russian dolls. It was as if they were staring at something.

'OS – turn off music and clear glass,' Flick yelled. The room fell silent, enabling her to see outside. It was then that she spotted the building in the distance. There was a yellow cross illuminated on the steeple and a dim light coming from inside. It was the former church that Elijah used as his second studio. That's where the killer was hiding him; that's where Flick would find them both. And that's where she, Elijah, their baby and the secrets that she held might die.

Chapter 84

EMILIA

Emilia splashed water against her face until her skin cooled. She gave a short, sharp sniff under each arm, aware of her sour body odour. There had been no time that day to change her clothing or to freshen up. She slipped off her top, washed her armpits with liquid soap and water, then warmed the damp patches of material under the hand drier.

She glanced upwards as she made her way from the vestry's bathroom back into the echoing stone church nave. The ceiling was so high that in the dim lighting, she couldn't make out the detail painted upon it. She took in parts of the stained-glass windows that she could see which depicted the firing of arrows into a saint. She too knew how it felt to suffer at the hands of others.

It won't be long now, she thought. Once she got what she needed from Flick, she would find out who she was, be free of the Hacking Collective and reunited with her husband and daughters.

Her earpiece beeped and she took a deep breath. She had already rehearsed what was to come next.

'Delta Team, an update, please,' Bianca's voice began. Emilia looked over to Gardiner and Lago. All three remained silent.

'Gardiner, what's your status update, please?' she repeated.

She still didn't get her answer. 'Lago, your location?' This time there was a pause before Bianca spoke again. 'Where the hell is everyone?'

Emilia cleared her throat. 'The agents you assigned to babysit me are otherwise engaged,' she said calmly, looking to both men again, smiling. Their expressions remained unmoved.

'What's that supposed to mean? Where are they?'

'They're here with me.'

'Then tell them to answer me.'

When Emilia failed to oblige, Bianca hesitated again, as if she was trying to read between the lines. She chose her words carefully. 'What have you done, Emilia?'

Emilia moved her head back in the direction of Gardiner and Lago. She had swiped Gardiner's weapon and used it on both of them. Gardiner was lifeless and slumped over a pew, blood no longer trickling from a bullet wound through his temple. Lago lay face down on the concrete flagstones and displayed an exit wound just above his ear.

'They served their purpose and now I'm going to finish this alone,' said Emilia.

'Get their GPS locations ...' she heard Bianca ordering someone. 'She's out of control. I warned you this would happen ...'

'You're wasting your time,' Emilia continued, looking at the broken tracking devices next to the bodies.

'Emilia, I need you to tell me where you are. We need to bring you in immediately. You cannot compromise this mission by going rogue, not when we've come so close to our goal.'

'I need to see this through to the end and on my terms so that I can be with my family again. I only have one chance left and she'll be here any minute.'

'Emilia,' Bianca continued and for the first time, Emilia sensed panic in her inflection. 'We can help you. But first you must tell me where you are so that we can come and get you.'

Emilia removed her earpiece, let it fall to the floor and crushed it underfoot. Then she took Gardiner's gun from where it rested on the ledge and put a bullet through her phone.

She turned to look at where she had convinced the operatives to leave Elijah after they'd beaten him and dragged him from his home and into the back of their van. His arms were outstretched horizontally and his wrists and legs bound to a wooden crucifix. Another rope had been used to tie his neck to it and he was gagged with a cloth.

'It won't be much longer now,' she said. 'Soon we'll all know who we are really supposed to be.'

Chapter 85

FLICK, ALDBURGH, SUFFOLK

Flick leaned against a granite headstone and bent double, clutching her stomach and gasping for breath. Raindrops dripped from leaves on the oak tree standing tall above her, onto her cheeks and down her neck.

The sprint from Elijah's house to the deconsecrated church of St Paul took less than ten minutes. Fear and adrenaline drove her onward alongside a desperate hope that Elijah wasn't another victim caught in the crossfire between her and the woman who wanted her dead. But pregnancy and the stress of the last twenty-four hours were physically weakening her along with a gripping feeling in her side that was spreading from her back to her stomach.

The illuminated neon cross attached to the church's steeple shone like a lantern in a lighthouse, propelling and repelling her in equal measure. It warned of danger ahead yet beckoned her towards it.

She could just about see its dimly lit interior through the stained-glass windows. Squeezing the knife handle now firmly in her grip, she slipped on her glasses and approached the church's large wooden doors. Flick tugged the metal rings until she was inside a pitch-black porch. In night-vision mode, her glasses helped her to find the handles to the next set of doors, and then … nothing. The battery ran out. She cursed them and discarded them to the floor.

It was the first time Flick had been inside Elijah's second workspace. Unsecured wooden pews were scattered about and used as leaning posts to prop up full-sized canvases. Paint-splattered boards protected parts of the original flooring and large sheets of cloth were nailed to walls and covered some windows. A bank of at least a dozen computer screens was lined up against a wall where she assumed Elijah and his team had perfected Flick's holograms. The altar at the far end was only just visible; behind it, a crucifix.

A noise from that area caught her attention. The sound was human and a mix of a howl and a groan. Chills spread across the surface of her skin as she took a few cautious paces closer to it. Then, without warning, the effigy of Jesus on the cross came to life. She quickly retreated until, through the dim light, she realised there was someone attached to it.

'Elijah!' she cried out. But as she hurried towards him, the unmistakable sound of a safety catch being removed from a weapon stopped her in her tracks.

'Ordinary people probably wouldn't know what this sound was, but you and I aren't ordinary, are we?' a woman's voice began.

She recognised it as belonging to the woman who had electrocuted and murdered Grace. The grip jabbed Flick sharply. She didn't reply or turn around to see who was holding her at gunpoint. When Elijah groaned again, weapon or no weapon, it was all Flick could do to stop herself from trying to free him. 'Are you okay?' she directed towards him instead.

Emilia let out a humourless laugh. 'Does he look okay? He's strapped to a cross and slowly choking to death.'

As Flick turned to face her assailant, she held the hunting knife behind her and out of sight. At the same time, the town's annual fireworks display burst into life with a crack of thunder and bright, purple lights, illuminating the woman's appearance. A bar across a window cast a shadow over her eyes, giving them a hollow appearance. But she recognised her nonetheless.

'I thought you ...' began Flick.

'... were dead,' said Emilia. 'Yes, I get that a lot. Drop your weapon.'

'I don't have one.'

A much louder bang rang through the air and at first Flick thought it was another firework exploding. It was only when Elijah let out a muffled yell that she realised it was a gunshot. The woman had just fired a bullet into him.

'If you want to play a game of rock, scissors, paper, knife and gun, then I think I might have the upper hand,' she continued. 'Drop it.'

'Please, let him go,' Flick begged as the knife hit the flagstones. More fireworks exploded, casting the room in yellow and white streaks. 'This is between you and me, Elijah has nothing to do with it.'

'Look at him up there on that cross. I've turned him into art like he did to you with those holograms. Perhaps I could sell this to the Tate Modern and make my fortune? Have you ever been? I might have, but I can't be sure.'

Flick's stitch was growing ever more debilitating, and she fought hard not to bend over double. She didn't want to let Emilia have any more of the upper hand than she already had. But still she felt no pain. 'What do you want from us?' she asked.

'Not "us", only you. And you know the answer to that.'

Her captor looked ready to respond when something appeared to distract her. She turned her head sharply and moved the barrel of her weapon so that it pointed over Flick's shoulder.

It meant that besides Elijah, there was someone else in the room with them.

Chapter 86

EMILIA

'Hello, Emilia.'

The greeting appeared from behind Flick, a disembodied voice hidden in the twilight of the church. 'I think it's time we talked.'

Its familiarity was immediate but made no sense. Only when the figure moved and a firework's white light caught his eyes and lips did every wisp of air leave her lungs.

'Ted,' she began, and swallowed hard. He offered her a brittle smile. 'You're … you're alive?'

'Looks can be deceiving.'

'But I was there when they killed you!'

As he took another step closer to her, she steadied one trembling hand with the other but kept her gun pointed at the ghost.

'I'm not here to hurt you,' he assured and she believed him. His tone was as calm and persuasive as it had been when he'd reassured her that he'd look after her following her discharge from hospital.

'I don't understand,' she continued. 'I saw them stab you and take your body away. How are you here?'

'Because you saw what you wanted to see,' he replied. 'As you are doing now.'

Emilia looked at Flick for her reaction. But Flick continued to glare at her captor, looking equally rattled.

'What do you mean I see what I want to see?' Emilia asked.

'You're correct when you said you watched me die. I'm now what you used to refer to as "an Echo". Perhaps not so much constructed by your data, but more accurately someone from your past who is bleeding through to your present.'

Emilia struggled to make sense of what he was saying. 'You *are* dead?'

'Alas, very much so.'

She let out a breath she hadn't realised she was holding and shut her eyes tightly. When she opened them again, he was still there. Dead or alive, there was no question it was definitely Ted.

'It wasn't what I wanted, I promise you,' she replied, as if urgently needing to clear her conscience. 'But you'd lied to me about everything, about who you were, our marriage, my career and all I wanted was the truth. In return for bringing you to the lighthouse, they told me they'd get it out of you. But they didn't tell me they were going to kill you. I didn't want to work for the Hacking Collective but they left me no choice.'

'You're not working for them.'

Emilia's eyebrows drew together. 'I'm ashamed to admit that I have been.'

Ted shook his head. 'I admit that I wasn't completely honest with you because I believed that for your sake, it was better for me not to be. But you are also guilty of lying to yourself. You're not working for the Collective and the night I died, there was nobody else on that jetty in Geneva but you and me.'

'What? No, you're mistaken,' she exclaimed. Ted's attention remained fixed on her. 'Do you not remember seeing the young woman with a child … a little boy … she came up behind us and before I realised what she was about to do, she stabbed you, and then others arrived in cars and a boat to take your body away.'

'You're rewriting your memories with an alternate version of reality that's more acceptable to you. The people you think killed me are your projections. They weren't there. They're Echoes. *You* killed me.'

Emilia shook her head. She remembered it as clear as day: the assassin, the clean-up operation, Bianca and Adrian afterwards … that was how the series of events unfolded.

Wasn't it?

Now a doubt was creeping in as she ran through the sequence of events again, the memory beginning to modify itself. This time, her recollection featured no killer, no boat and no strangers attempting to force her along the jetty. Suddenly all she saw was a long, sharp silver spike in her hand that she now recalled was a medical device called a Shroder, followed by an unsuspecting Ted glancing into the distance. Taking the opportunity to strike, she calmly embedded it with force into his skull. Then she rolled him into the water before running back towards the road and passing a woman with a pushchair.

'No,' Emilia said adamantly. 'That didn't happen. You're doing something to me. You're alive and you are screwing with my head. I didn't kill you.' She moved her aim towards Flick. 'Tell him.'

'Tell who?' Flick asked.

'The man I'm talking to! Tell Ted that I didn't kill him.'

'But he's dead.'

'No, he's fucking not!' she yelled. 'Look at him, for God's sake, he's standing right behind you! Who else do you think I've been having a conversation with?'

Flick turned to look behind her and then back at Emilia. 'I'm sorry, but I don't see anyone but you.'

An angry Emilia's aim alternated between Ted and Flick, her finger gradually putting pressure on the trigger. Suddenly something struck her. 'Do you know who Ted is?' she asked. Flick nodded her affirmation. 'How?'

'Because if you mean Edward Karczewski, then he trained me. He trained all of us. He trained *you*.'

'To do what?'

'You used to be one of us, a Minder, and he was head of the programme.'

'And a Minder is what exactly? And what programme?'

'It's a coded name for someone with exceptional perception. We were specially selected, trained and medically manipulated to store the country's most sensitive data inside our brains. And it remains inside us for up to five years or until the government has time to finish its plan to safeguard the UK from the threat of hackers. But taking on the role means turning our backs on anyone we know and love for that period of time.'

'That sounds utterly ridiculous.'

Karczewski laughed. 'As ridiculous as you having a conversation with a dead man? Or of not remembering that you killed him?'

'If I am like her then why can't I remember any of that data?'

'Because your implant and data were removed in a procedure a year ago. Your training and skills remained; however, there was a complication that left you in a catatonic-hybrid state. The procedure damaged your brain.'

Emilia recalled the video footage she'd watched of herself twelve hours before she first awoke. She had been horrified to see herself being walked and fed by staff, as if she were a zombie.

'The operation caused scarring and significant damage,' Karczewski continued. 'In the months that followed, you showed no response to external stimuli, no psychomotor activity and no interaction with your environment. Then one day and without warning, your brain, well, simply restarted. It was as if you'd come back to life – and then you disappeared.'

Emilia shifted from one foot to another. 'You made me like this – that's the truth you didn't want me to know.'

'The truth is much more complicated than that. Your name is actually Dr Megan Jane Porter, although you prefer to go by MJ. Emilia is the codename you use to communicate with other Minders on message board. It's a name taken from Shakespeare's *The Two Noble Kinsmen*. And *you* are responsible for this version of yourself because *you* were the neuroscientist who created the procedure to implant DNA data into human brains.'

Emilia let out a snort. 'Me? Do you expect me to believe that?' But her face crinkled as an image slowly returned; a painting or graphic swirling with shapes, numbers, musical notes and words. 'I ... I ... I was a volunteer. That's right, I solved a puzzle ... yes, I remember it ... it was a puzzle only a certain number of people could figure out.'

'You didn't solve it – you designed it. The puzzle and the programme were devised by you.'

'This is bullshit. Bullshit! You're a liar. I am not imagining you, you are here, right in front of me, no matter what Flick says.'

'Then shoot me. If you're not fabricating me, you'll kill me.'

Without hesitation, Emilia pulled the trigger. A panicked Flick dived for cover under a pew as the first shot rang out, but Karczewski remained where he was. Twice more she fired and twice more he remained uninjured and upright.

Emilia took a step back, her mouth open and her hands trembling.

'Do you believe me now?' he asked.

'Yes,' she whispered. Thoughts raced around her head like hens in a coop breached by a fox. She couldn't trust anything about herself any more. 'Who am I, Ted?' she asked.

'You're one of the country's foremost neuroscientists and we worked together for the government in biochemical counter-espionage. It was your synaesthesia that gave you the idea to devise this DNA-storage project. But you admitted to me that your initial test results were flawed – memory bleeding and Echoes were serious side effects that had the potential to derail the programme. However, you believed they were temporary and would vanish once each brain settled. You manipulated the results of your clinical trials to get the answers you wanted and insisted on becoming a Minder yourself to prove your concept.'

'What side effects was I covering up?'

'Those related to episodes of schizophrenia, hallucinations, psychopathy, paranoia ... in your absence, we came up with solutions for the second selection of candidates. At least, with some of them.'

Emilia frowned. 'Second selection? Are the Minders I found not the first?'

Karczewski shook his head. 'No, they're not. Four of the first five were killed out in the field.'

'What happened to them?'

'*You* happened. With no monitoring or the safety net of the lab to keep you grounded, the Echoes convinced you the other Minders were enemies of the state and selling their secrets to the Hacking Collective. Back then, all five of you were able to communicate with one another, so you used their trust to get them to reveal where they were located. And one by one, you executed them with a Shroder, the implement that pinpoints exactly where the implants are and destroys them.'

Emilia's eyes remained locked on Karczewski's, searching for signs of deception. There were none. She directed her attention towards where Flick had been standing. 'Get up before I start shooting again.'

Flick's head slowly appeared, followed by her body, until she was facing Emilia.

'Is what he's saying true?'

'I … I don't know what he said …'

'He said I killed the first handful of Minders. Is it true?'

'It's what it says in the data implant.'

Karczewski continued. 'After their murders and for reasons you never explained, you appeared suddenly at the laboratory and told us what you'd done. I kept you hidden there, hoping the reversal procedure you developed would be successful and I'd get the old MJ back. But some of your procedures were flawed, leaving you temporarily catatonic. Then you awoke, created another false reality and escaped, and this time you believed you were being manipulated by Bianca and Adrian to track down the new Minders. But Bianca and Adrian don't exist.'

'Of course they do … this all started with them. They're trying to find me now.'

'They were pseudonyms used by two of the first Minders, again based on Shakespearean characters, alongside Gardiner and Lago. The existence of that team is all in your imagination.'

'Liar!' she said defiantly. 'They were all working for the Hacking Collective. I shot Gardiner and Lago before Flick arrived. Look.' Her head turned to where she'd left their bodies but the area was empty. 'Where are they? What have you done with them?'

'Bianca, Adrian, Lago and Gardiner are the figures that you think have been chasing you. Your first four kills were actually the Echoes who haunt you. Everyone you think has been helping or hindering you only exists inside your own imagination … the pregnant woman in the hospital grounds who warned you about me, my killer … you are, and have only ever been, working alone.'

414

'No! I'm not mad!' Emilia shouted. 'Tell him,' she directed at Flick. But Flick looked like a rabbit caught in headlights, unsure of which direction to turn.

'Think back to each scenario you have been involved in,' continued Karczewski. 'Was there any interaction between Bianca and Adrian and a third party not affiliated to your mission? A shop assistant, a police officer, a member of the public? Are there any witnesses who can prove you haven't been alone in all of your excursions?'

Emilia frantically recalled every situation she had been in with Adrian and Bianca but aside from their own field ops, they had never spoken to or been acknowledged by anyone other than her. He was correct: she had been alone in the hospital grounds; the jetty in Geneva; the Eurostar she travelled in; the lorry car park where she thought she had attacked Bianca. The truck driver had only asked her if she was all right because she was alone. The waitress at the cafe where she'd seen her family had muttered something under her breath when Emilia had ignored her because she was the only one present.

'My children!' she said suddenly. 'I've seen my real family,' she blurted out. 'Justin and the girls, I saw them at their school, then I sat behind them in a cafe. I've watched videos and seen photographs of us together. I felt a physical connection between us. Something inside me longed to be with my family again.'

'You weren't longing for *them*,' Karczewski said, his tone unexpectedly softening. 'You were longing for what they have. You and I tried to start a family naturally and then through IVF but after five years, we had no success. Your yearning to become a mother has manifested itself with imagined feelings for two children you've never met. And their father, well, he's an ex-boyfriend of yours from university. He has since married and they are his daughters. You once showed them to me on his Facebook profile.'

'I have a Caesarean scar ...' She lifted up her top to expose her stomach, but no scar existed. Ted waited quietly and patiently as Emilia processed his revelations.

'But everything I've done, the people I've killed, it was so that I could be with them again,' she said. 'If they don't exist, it means it's all been for nothing.'

'I'm sorry, MJ, I truly am.'

'And you and I ...'

'Everything I told you about how we met and our marriage is true. It's why, after the first killings, I didn't want to tell those in charge that you'd returned. They would have kept you off the books and locked you in a secure unit without trying to treat you. I couldn't let that happen so I told them your life had been terminated until I could work out how to help you.'

'If we were that much in love, why did I want to be a Minder? Because Flick said that means being separated for five years. Why did I want to be away from you for that long? Why didn't you fight for me?'

'Being unable to have a family changed your perspective on marriage. You became distant, you pushed me away and threw yourself into this project. When you told me you wanted to be one of the five, I begged you to change your mind. But you'd already undergone the procedure without telling me; the DNA was already inside your head. After you were hit by the car, I naively thought this could be our second chance. But along with your brain's reconstruction came the Echoes' regeneration.'

It was almost too much information for Emilia to absorb. Her head was spinning with flashbacks of the life Karczewski described along with her behaviour. Now she wished she had taken his advice all those months ago and used her amnesia to start her life afresh.

'What about the baby?' she said urgently. 'The girl Sinéad brought with her to the safe house?'

'You left her in the village pub's toilets before you drove away.'

'Is she okay? Is she safe?'

'How could I know that? I only know what you know.'

'The story about my colleague who killed four people we worked with – that was an actual event but it had nothing to do with me, did it?'

'No, I planted a seed of doubt in case the truth of what you did to the first four Minders ever bled through. If that happened I hoped your memory would cross wires and attribute what you did with another event so you wouldn't realise your involvement.'

A deflated Emilia paced back and forth in silence, contemplating what the revelations meant. 'What will happen to me now?' she asked eventually. 'What should I do?'

'It's up to you.' Karczewski moved towards her and placed his hands on her shoulders. 'MJ, what you need to remember is that what your brain has done is nothing short of miraculous. Following a significant trauma, it's come back to life. This has potentially huge implications for neuroscience. You could put right your wrongs by helping the team that once worked for you.'

'You said they'd lock me away and leave me to rot.'

'That was before your brain repaired itself. Now you're an anomaly.'

'I'm a laboratory rat.'

'You're a case study.'

'I'm a killer.' Emilia let out a long, exhausted puff of air. Her arms were sapped of energy and fell to the sides of her body, but still she held on to her weapon. Twice she had lived this life and all she had to show for it was a trail of bodies and a head full of voices. She had the answers she craved, but they were the wrong ones.

A groan caught her attention and she glanced towards the crucifix; she realised that she alone must have found the strength to tie Elijah Beckworth to it. She looked again to Flick and noticed her face was grimacing and her hand was resting on the middle of her stomach, as if protecting something valuable. The penny dropped and a sour smile edged at her lips.

'MJ,' Karczewski continued. 'Just put the gun down on the floor and walk away. It's the only thing you need to do.'

'And if I return to the facility, what if it happens again? What if I kill more innocent people?'

'But you won't.'

'You can't *know* that because you're not real. You are one part of my brain that's communicating with the other. Now that I know who I was and what I've become, how can I take the risk of ever being her again? I do believe that you wanted the best for me, but by hiding me, you allowed the monster inside me to return. You allowed it to kill again, only this time, you were a victim too. And I'm truly sorry for that. But I think this is the end of the road for me. If I lost myself again, I don't know that I could ever come back.'

In one swift manoeuvre, Emilia placed the gun's muzzle to the slight lump at the crown of her head, pointed it in a downward motion and pulled the trigger.

She was dead before she hit the ground.

Chapter 87

FLICK, ALDEBURGH, SUFFOLK

'No!' yelled Flick, and from her position behind the pew, her body recoiled at the sound of gunfire and the split second of muzzle flash. Then Emilia fell from view.

Flick clasped her stomach tighter, as if to shield her unborn baby from the horrors of its mother's world. Then she waited, half expecting Dr Porter, or MJ, or Emilia or whoever she'd thought she was, to rise from the dead and come for her next. But nothing happened. She moved slowly towards her and only when she saw a pool of blood around MJ's head and shoulders, did she know for certain that she was dead.

The gripping feeling in Flick's back and stomach was becoming more persistent but though it still didn't hurt, it was affecting her ability to remain on her feet.

The thunderous sound of Aldeburgh's fireworks display reached its climax, with a crescendo rainbow of colours turning night into day. Only when it stopped and she heard Elijah gasping for breath did she remember what had brought her to that old church. She hurried to her feet and ran to him, yanking the gag from his mouth.

'Elijah,' she said, the word breathy and brimming with desperation. She placed her ear next to his mouth – shallow, near-silent breaths could just about be heard. She sensed he didn't have long left. Flick returned to the aisle where she'd dropped the knife and used it to hack at the ropes binding his legs, wrists and neck to the crucifix. He fell towards her as she tried to support his weight, the two of them tumbling to the floor in a heap of limbs.

'Elijah,' she repeated, her voice now reduced to a tremble. 'Please talk to me?'

There was still no response. She carried out a fingertip search of his body until she located the bloody bullet wound in his thigh. If it had penetrated the femoral artery, he would already be bleeding to death unless she was quick. She unhooked his belt and tied it tightly around his thigh as a temporary tourniquet. All she wanted was to look after him, to make up for the anguish she had caused.

'Please, hang on,' she continued and patted his pockets, searching for a phone. He wasn't carrying one.

She scanned the gloom of the church for a landline but didn't know where to begin. However, she recalled Aldeburgh's only remaining public telephone box from one of her many walks as she committed the town to memory. It was only two streets away. Flick ran as fast as her legs could carry her, clutching her stomach and stumbling as she hurried through the lashing rain. And after dialling the emergency services and anonymously warning the operator of an injured man and dead woman in the church of St Paul, she hung up and returned to the building.

Flick hesitated as she gripped the large metal rings to open the doors. She knew that as much as she wanted it, she couldn't be with Elijah when the ambulance and police arrived. There was too much explaining to be done. If, as she hoped, this was all over, the best thing she could do for everyone was to disappear back into the night as quietly as she had come. She made her way to the far corner of the churchyard, using a full-height gravestone to hide behind.

'Come on, come on, come on,' she muttered impatiently, wringing her hands as she awaited the ambulance. If there had been any doubt before, now she understood why Karczewski had warned against forming emotional attachments. All who came into contact with her were dead or injured. She desperately wanted to be with Elijah in that church, comforting him and telling him how much she loved him. But happy-ever-afters were not written for people like Flick.

She thought about Dr Porter. Their paths had not crossed and by the time Flick was enrolled into the programme, she was just a name in a file, stored inside her head. The deaths of the first four Minders had been hushed up, lessons had been learned, techniques tweaked and alterations made so that her actions could never be replicated. The data suggested that Dr Porter had been killed, but now it was clear she hadn't been. The world was so full of lies that even the data she stored in her brain couldn't be trusted.

Despite the cruelty inflicted by Dr Porter on the other Minders and Grace, there was a side of Flick that pitied her. She had witnessed the confusion and turmoil in her face as she debated and argued with a person who was not present. Flick listened helplessly as she had quarrelled with herself, her subconscious and repressed memories doing battle with her present to reveal the truth. If it meant Dr Porter had been acting alone, then there was no longer a threat to Flick's safety.

Finally, a first responder's vehicle arrived, blue and red lights flashing, followed moments later by an ambulance, then two marked police vehicles. Another sudden gripping feeling in her stomach caused her to fall to her knees. And when she slipped her hand inside her underwear and saw her fingertips were red, she feared the worst. It was all she could do to stop herself from asking for help to treat her miscarriage. Instead, she waited until Elijah was carried out on a gurney flanked by paramedics, an oxygen mask covering his nose and mouth. Only then did she quietly disappear in the car she'd arrived in hours earlier.

Once again, Flick was back on the road, potentially the last Minder standing from both programmes.

THREE YEARS LATER

** CONFIDENTIAL **
TOP SECRET: UK EYES ONLY, CLASSIFIED 'A'
THIS DOCUMENT IS THE PROPERTY OF HIS MAJESTY'S GOVERNMENT

MINUTES OF JOINT CYBER-ESPIONAGE / INTELLIGENCE COMMITTEE ASSESSMENT MEETING 11.7

'THE ALTERNATIVE APPROACH TO STORAGE OF CLASSIFIED DOCUMENTS'

** Please note this is an account of the minutes taken from the above meeting. Portions of text and certain participants have been redacted to prevent threats to security. **

LOCATION:
██████████████, ██████████

MEMBERS PRESENT:
Finn Braxton, Operations Director
Dr Sadie Mann, Director of Psychiatric Evaluations
Dr Pascal Foley, Deputy Head of Neuroscience
████████ █████████ █████████, Ministry of Defence (MoD), Porton Down
█████████ █████████, MI5
William Harris, HM Government's Minister for Central Intelligence

NON-MEMBERS PRESENT:
Prime Minister Diane Cline

_____

PRIME MINISTER: I'd like to keep this brief. What's the status of the programme?

FINN BRAXTON: The five most recently appointed Minders from Cycle Three are a year into the programme with no reported complications or side effects.

PRIME MINISTER: And we are still tracking them?

FINN BRAXTON: Yes, Prime Minister. Communication remains minimal through social media channels but the transdermal patches they wear and the bioresorbable health sensor implants keep us up to date with their physical and mental statuses.

███████ ███████ ███████, MoD: And as former special forces personnel, these candidates continue to remain discreetly armed at all times. But there have been no occasions to date when the necessity has arisen to draw their weapons.

PRIME MINISTER: By my calculations, thirteen months remain until they and the last remaining Minder from Cycle Two will find their beads dissolving. Is that correct?

FINN BRAXTON: Yes. But our programmers are four months ahead of schedule. In all likelihood, we will be the most unhackable country on earth by March next year. At that point, Cycle Two and Three Minders will be recalled and their data retrieved.

PRIME MINISTER: Tell me about the retrieval process. We cannot risk a repeat of what happened to your predecessor Dr Porter when she was subjected to it.

DR PASCAL FOLEY: Her methods have now been redeveloped and perfected, seemingly with no negative reactions.

PRIME MINISTER: Good. One last thing – when Miss Kennedy has been recalled and her data retrieved, I'd like to meet her. ▇▇▇▇, can you ensure that is arranged as soon as possible.

▇▇▇▇ ▇▇▇▇ ▇▇▇▇, MoD: Is that a good idea, ma'am?

PRIME MINISTER: She has sacrificed more for this country than anyone else in recent times. Her will to survive despite all the odds we have put her through is remarkable.

WILLIAM HARRIS: She will be financially recompensed when this is over.

PRIME MINISTER: Money cannot buy five lost years and erase threats to her life. The very least I owe her is a handshake and a personal thank-you. Has there been any contact with her?

WILLIAM HARRIS: We know roughly her whereabouts but there has been no direct contact, no.

PRIME MINISTER: She has no idea of how appreciative we are? I will do my best to rectify that sooner rather than later.

EPILOGUE

FLICK

The mid-April heatwave was approaching 32 degrees, according to the digital temperature gauge attached to the top of the lifeguard tower.

As Flick slathered her face and arms in factor 50 UPF, she welcomed the light breeze coming in from the sea. A beach marker revealed that half a metre of land had been lost to the water in the space of two years. Global heating was shrinking and eroding many unfortunate coastal towns, including Aldeburgh. The construction of an unsightly three-metre-high sea wall further up the coast was a temporary solution. Flick wondered how much of the town she loved might be left fifty years from now.

The more time she spent alone – three and a half years, to date – the more time she considered the future and how hers might have played out had her decision been different and she'd been allowed to be a mother.

She swigged water from a bottle and replaced it in her backpack along with the sun cream. Touching a button on the arm of her sunglasses, she zoomed in on two figures ahead. They were jumping in and out of the shoreline waves with an excitable black Labrador by their sides. Butterflies circled her stomach every time as she watched

Elijah and their son Leo playing together. They brought out the child in one another.

Leo had been her miracle baby. The back and stomach stitches she'd experienced the night of Emilia's suicide and Elijah's near-death had been debilitating. Soon after leaving the town, she had been forced to park in a supermarket car park and lock herself in the disabled toilets, bleeding and anticipating the loss of her baby. But to her surprise, it petered out. Flick ventured into the shop, bought panty liners and a burner mobile phone and Googled the symptoms. She discovered that she was likely having a Threatened Miscarriage, which involved bleeding even though her cervix remained closed. It didn't mean she had miscarried. And she had sobbed for an hour the next morning when she felt the baby move inside her.

Now, her heart swelled as she watched Elijah hugging his son. Even to a stranger's eye, their closeness was undeniable and she felt a twinge of envy prick at her. Elijah had been the only parental figure in the boy's life. Days after giving birth under a false name in a Cheshire hospital, Flick had walked out of the maternity ward entrance alone, having given her son a tear-stained kiss goodbye and leaving a note pinned to his Babygro alerting the neonatal team to his father's name, address and telephone number.

Abandoning the one thing she loved most in the world left her heart in a million pieces. But she knew that it was in Leo's best interests to live a stable life and that was something Flick had been unable to offer him.

The only physical reminder of her son was a navy-blue sleepsuit with white velvet stars upon the chest. She'd dressed him in it that first night, then replaced it before she left. Weeks later, when she was crippled by longing and could barely eat or move, there were moments when she became convinced she could smell traces of her baby lingering on the arms she held him in and the lips she kissed him with. Sometimes she imagined him still inside her, turning from side to side, kicking, hiccupping or making her stomach flutter. Without Leo, she was a lost soul.

Her baby aside, Flick's life following Emilia's suicide had been uneventful. Seven months after the government exposed Flick and launched its hunt for her, she read that she had apparently been captured and killed. Quite why she didn't know. But even though she was no longer a target in fear of being identified, she had still spent the rest of her time travelling the length and breadth of the country, rarely remaining in one area for more than a couple of months. There was nothing to suggest that she was being pursued but it was hard to shake the feeling that it wasn't beyond the realms of possibility. She made acquaintances but not friends and certainly no one came as close to her as Grace. Life as the only remaining Minder was a self-imposed one of isolation.

Many times, she'd visited the ReadWell boards, on the off-chance that other government staff aware of the programme had left her a message informing her of what was expected next. Or perhaps new Minders had been appointed and deployed and were now communicating with one another using the same means as she had used. However, there was never anything to be found. But last night, some-thing had happened that had changed everything.

She had turned on the television in her motel room and chosen a rolling news channel. It was the news ticker that caught her attention.

CREDIBLE HACKING THREAT TO UK – PM ADDRESSES PARLIAMENT.

Since she became a Minder, many more countries had been under cyberattack from the Hacking Collective, and most recently Luxembourg and Belarus had fallen. Finland, Spain and Australia were also close to breaking point.

Flick turned up the volume as the newsreader spoke. '*This afternoon during Question Time, Prime Minister Diane Cline assured her own party and the opposition that the United Kingdom was "uniquely prepared" for any attack. She said that security measures were in place and that Britain was still on target to become the world's first unhackable country. However, despite repeated calls for evidence, she refused to offer any.*'

The screen cut to footage recorded earlier that day of the PM leaning against the podium in the House of Commons to address her own party and the opposition. 'When the freedom of our country is under its biggest threat since World War Two, it would be foolish of me to risk our safety by explaining how such measures will work. I implore you to have faith. I have gratitude to, and complete confidence in, those brave people behind the scenes who have sacrificed their lives as they once knew them, their careers, relationships and their families, to keep us safe from the Hacking Collective and every other unseen enemy that wants to bring us to our knees. You have not been forgotten about.'

As studio pundits debated back and forth what the Prime Minister meant, Flick was convinced that it was a coded message directed at her. And it was as if a weight had been lifted from Flick's shoulders. It meant the programme hadn't died with Karczewski and there were people out there who knew she existed. While the Collective remained active and new security measures were still being developed, she was needed. She hadn't been separated from her baby for nothing.

A year remained until she completed her term and the data would either be removed or would dissolve, taking her knowledge with it. She must remain in isolation until then, protecting herself and serving her country.

Since giving birth to Leo, Flick had returned to Aldeburgh every four months or so, each time sporting an alternative appearance – new hairpieces, baseball caps, contoured make-up altering the appearance of her bone structure, glasses or coloured contact lenses. And after leaving fresh flowers each visit by Grace's graveside, she either sat inside her car behind blackened windows or hovered on the beach, watching Elijah's house from a distance, waiting to spy on the child and the life she was missing out on.

Sometimes she was fortunate to catch glimpses of them, and at other times, she had waited days and eventually given up, assuming they had gone away with Elijah's work. Today was one of the more successful days; she had been afforded the opportunity to watch them for about an hour as they walked the dog and then threw a ball at one another.

You did the right thing, she told herself. *They're safe and they're happy.*

Flick turned her back as they began walking in her direction and towards the house. She planned to wait until they were inside before she left town again.

Their dog brushed past her legs and it was all she could do to stop herself from bending over and stroking him, as if touching its fur might allow her access into their world. Next, she became aware of Leo's small feet hurrying along the pebbles and towards the dog.

'Rupert,' he squealed, 'it's home time.' Flick waited until he'd passed her before she glanced over her shoulder to watch him from behind. Her heart quivered at their proximity, just as it had the first night they lay next to one another in the hospital ward. It was just as difficult now as it had been then to tear her gaze away from him.

Suddenly, she felt another presence approaching her, Elijah's feet much heavier as they pounded across the stones. Shivers spread across her body when for a second at most, Elijah's little finger entwined around hers as he walked.

'One more year to go,' he whispered as he passed her. She felt his warm breath on her cheek and she closed her eyes.

'One more year,' she repeated and wanted to cry and laugh at the same time.

A previous guise on her second covert visit to town hadn't prevented Elijah from recognising her. He had studied her face in such detail for his exhibition that no disguise could fool him, even from metres away. Then, she had broken the rules and told him everything.

Now, without turning to look at one another, Flick waited until Elijah and Leo were far enough away before leaving them again to continue their life without her. At least, for the time being.

ACKNOWLEDGEMENTS

The Minders is my seventh novel and probably the most challenging book I've written to date. Our son was born two months prematurely during the writing of the first draft, weighing, at his lowest point, just 2lb 7oz. He was hospitalised for the first month of his life as all our efforts went into caring for him and helping him to thrive. And that meant a delay in this book's completion. I couldn't have finished it without the help, support and (at times) tough love of my husband John Russell and our awesome little boy. My biggest thank-yous of all, however, go to Beccy Bousfield and the Neonatal Unit team at the Calderdale Royal Hospital in Halifax. Without you, we might not have a determined little lad who makes us laugh every day and is already eating us out of house and home.

It's the end of an era for my wonderful editor Gillian Green and me, now that she has moved on to pastures new. It's been a blast working with her so closely on *The Passengers* and now this. I'd also like to offer my gratitude to my new team at Cornerstone, especially Ben Brusey and Sam Bradbury.

Thanks to those who helped with the creation of this book, including the brilliant neuroscientist Dr Cindy Schroeder PhD, Kath Middleton, David Kerrigan and Karen Kemerson. Gratitude to my early readers, Rosemary 'Mother' Wallace (thanks for letting me borrow your name),

Carole Watson and Mark Fearn. As always, thank you to my fellow writers Louise Beech, Darren O'Sullivan and Claire Allan for your ongoing support and for keeping me constantly amused.

As is often the case, I am indebted to book clubs around the world, both online and in person, who invest time in reading my stuff. Thanks to Tracy Fenton from THE Book Club, Wendy Clarke and the Fiction Café Book Club, the Rick O'Shea Book Club and Lost in a Good Book. Thanks to the countless blogs, instagrammers and podcasters who have supported me over the years – you are unsung heroes.

Thanks also go to my mum Pamela for your constant support, and my friends Rhian and Richard Molloy. I hope this book continues to offer you more piffle for your pound.